NIGHT AMBULANCE

NIGHT
AMBULANCE

NICHOLAS RUDDOCK

BREAKWATER
P.O. Box 2188, St. John's, NL, Canada, A1C 6E6
WWW.BREAKWATERBOOKS.COM

LIBRARY AND ARCHIVES CANADA CATALOGUING IN PUBLICATION
Ruddock, Nicholas, author
Night ambulance / Nicholas Ruddock.
ISBN 978-1-55081-635-8 (paperback)
I. Title.
PS8635.U34N54 2016   C813'.6   C2016-900767-7
Copyright © 2016 Nicholas Ruddock

We acknowledge the support of the Canada Council for the Arts, which last year invested $153 million to bring the arts to Canadians throughout the country. We acknowledge the financial support of the Government of Canada and the Government of Newfoundland and Labrador through the Department of Tourism, Culture and Recreation for our publishing activities.
PRINTED AND BOUND IN CANADA.

Breakwater Books is committed to choosing papers and materials for our books that help to protect our environment. To this end, this book is printed on a paper that is certified by the Forest Stewardship Council®.

To Cheryl

IT was almost midnight when she went under the wharf with the boy from Grand Falls. Dusk had slipped behind the hills a long time ago.

He offered her his hand and said to her, a question mark in his voice, "Come on down?"

But she didn't need his hand.

"I'm okay, I've been on these rocks a thousand times."

"At night?"

"No, not at night, just daytime, but still."

There was no one else around. She hesitated.

"It's this way, Rowena, come on down."

He disappeared into the pitch dark and, in retrospect, perhaps it was the question mark in his voice that made it seem reasonable because she followed him, balancing on her sneakers, first one foot, then the other. She stepped after him through the gash the hurricane had made, where the trawler had broken everything to bits.

She slipped through the same opening, where he had gone, into the same pitch-black irregularity. He was no longer visible. The yellow light from above, which had been flickering with moths—the light which had lent familiarity to her while they were up top—no longer had a chance of getting down to them; it was blocked by the wharf, it angled away and glistened on the slippery shore-rocks, sea-green by day and black by night, running out towards deeper water, towards the Reach. She could hear waves from out there, the almost-silent lapping of them.

"I don't know," she said, "where are you?"

"Right here."

He was only a few inches away. She put out her hand and his arm was there. She pulled her hand back.

"Low tide," she said, "otherwise we couldn't be here."

"Tide? I don't care about tides."

She supposed he cared nothing about tides because Grand Falls was inland, there was no ocean there, no tides, but she cared a lot, she always had, so she said, quickly, "The moon runs the tides, it pulls on the oceans by gravitational force."

At that he laughed.

"Rowena, give me a break, you can't even see the moon tonight, it's behind the clouds."

She put out her hand again, the other way. It touched wood, cold and wet.

"You don't need to see the moon," she said, "to know it's there."

There was a wavery-watery echo to both their voices.

"This is enough for me now," she said.

"Hang on, let me show you what we've been doing."

He was the youngest one of the crew from Grand Falls. They'd been there in Bell Harbour now for more than a week, repairing the damage from the storm, the tail of the hurricane which had whipped through. The work had to be done, they were told. They'd set up a pile-driver on the wharf and half-blocked the roadway with fifty or sixty new logs, neatly stacked, already peeled and stained with creosote, and all day long the pile-driver slammed away, driving those new logs down into the rocks and stones, into the sea bottom that looked so solid but apparently wasn't.

Now, finally, Rowena could see shadows. There was light after all, light from nothing, light shading where there was nothing but black before. The boy was still beside her.

"Tide's rising," she said, "so we need to get back."

But the truth was, for someone who knew, the tide wasn't rising. It was ebb tide and the sea-level would stay like that for an hour or more, and he wasn't listening to her anyway because he said to her, "You know this is one lousy wharf, half the wood's rotten, the other half's worse and the boss says the whole structure's like an egg carton, ready to collapse, whoever built it should be ashamed of themselves."

Then he stopped talking and she could hear the slow dripping of water from the high beams, from what must have been condensation up there, or the last rain.

"Look at this, Rowena, for God's sake, this is one of the main supporting beams yet it's rotten on the outside, and on the inside it's waterlogged."

"I'm going home now," she said.

She knew his name but she didn't want to use it.

"We need to cut this one out completely, the boss said yesterday, otherwise the whole structure's a deck of cards. See this? It's punky."

He reached the blunt shadow of his arm up and away from her and she heard a piece of wood snap.

"I hardly touched it, feel it yourself, Rowena, here."

He put his hand on her wrist and guided her to what he said was the waterlogged beam, to the slickness of it. All she could see was a massive gray shadow now running at forty-five degrees away from her.

"Watch your footing," he said.

"Okay, I feel it, it's a rotten log."

"Watch out for barnacles, they're sharp."

"I know that."

He wasn't touching her then so she turned on her own and the splintered gash in the wharf was only ten feet away and she took a step in that direction but quickly his hands were on her waist from behind, and she felt herself picked up in the air and turned around.

"You're light as a feather, you are," he said.

"Put me down."

Now his face was level with hers.

"Not yet, not quite yet," he said, and he was holding her up in the air with ease.

The boy from Grand Falls seemed to have the strength of a thousand men and she no strength at all.

"Let's do this, Rowena."

He let her slide down through his hands and arms until her feet hit the rocks, the water, and she slipped sideways but he kept her from falling and lifted her and walked her back three feet, four feet, as though they were stuck together, and he too slipped once but they didn't fall. He pinned her, not roughly, but she was pinned like a specimen up against one of the big uprights, round and soft, cold and wet, and the cold seeped through her shirt within seconds, a sodden pressure between her shoulder blades.

"Okay?" he said.

What was he asking her?

There was nothing for her to say. In the daytime he had red hair but now she could only see the dark orb of his head and the dark cave closed round her, all the world she had.

He whispered, "Christ, Rowena, you are some pretty even in the dark."

One of her legs, the right, was angled off a bit to the side and his knee was jammed into her. Then he let her go. He stood back. He unbuckled his belt, the *clink*. He pulled at her shirt and some of the buttons popped.

"Stop," she said.

His hands were like living ice on her breasts and now she had lost her hearing as well as all enterprise.

He proceeded to unzip her jeans and she did nothing, said

nothing, the immoveable post at her back, her voice stolen, arms fallen to her sides.

His hand went down between her legs, cold on cold, inside or outside her underpants, at first she couldn't tell. Time passed and must have passed some more. Then water was dripping down her neck again and he was pulling away from her.

"I never thought you'd do that, Rowena, never."

She bent down awkwardly, the post still there, turning to one side and pulling her pants up, her jeans. They'd been down as far as her ankles and she was shaking and the use of her hands was still not hers. The zipper, trembling, five tries before she got the snap to close.

"Never in a million years," he said.

He too was fiddling with his waist, with his belt, and his buckle went *snick*, a confident closing sound.

She was soaked through, soaked everywhere, the back of her shirt stuck now between her shoulder blades, her sneakers, her left foot for sure under water so she lifted it up and put it down again, trying to find purchase on a rock. But it slid back in. More water dripped from the beams and now she could hear it again, the dripping, and closer to her she could hear his breathing, a soft tuneless whistling.

"You okay?" he asked.

She pulled the front of her shirt back together, covering her chest.

"Jesus damn," he said.

She couldn't walk out like that, with her shirt wide open. She found one button, two, she managed it.

"Let's go," he said, "this way."

He touched her again, nudging her back the way they came.

"Go on, Rowena, you go first."

She sluiced her way along, slipping, grabbing something, a two-by-four slippery as grease.

"Fucking wharf," she heard him say, and he laughed at his own wit and then she was at the opening and out. She stepped up the tumbled shoreline to the roadway. He was right behind her and took her by the arm and said, "Over there," and they stood together in the shadow of the shed.

Bell Harbour it said over the door in worn red letters in paint on wood, barely legible.

"This town, I don't know, I think you need a new sign."

She looked at his face in the weak light. A bat dipped behind him, after the moths.

"Anyway," he said, "I've got to go."

He kissed her on the cheek. Kissed her on the cheek as she stood there stunned, and then, because he was billeted on the other side of the harbour, he walked around the fresh pile of logs, to the left, and that was it. After he made the turn by the Legion she couldn't see him anymore. Not that she was looking, she was staring straight out over the end of the wharf, out to the night sea, to Chapel Island.

She could say she fell, that the meadow was wet, she slipped, her feet flew out from under her and down she went. Or a culvert gave way. They could be like bear traps, those things, after dark. Her father's plaid shirt—it was hers for a year now—she could fix the buttons given half an hour. It wasn't as bad as she thought, none of the material had been torn. She did it up as best she could, and tucked it in. Her house, one of seven in a line of houses that ran, one after the other, up along the shore to the right—no lights on in any of them that she could see—hers was the last one, its usual silhouette up against the high forest, a white pale against the irregular darkness. She shivered, but the little bit of wind had died down. Mist obscured the stars. No moon.

No moon, no tide.

She walked around the pile of logs. She couldn't see Iron Skull, the mass of it, on nights like this you never could, but she felt it there across the Reach, the wall face plummeting straight to the sea, looming. Small waves shuffled up against the near shoreline, thirty feet below. She walked, feeling the squish of her sneakers, the road inclining upwards. Mosquitoes, one or two, a tiny whine, a warning in her ear. One landed on her neck and she rolled it over dead with her fingertips, sensation returning. Then she was home and the creak of the gate, the creak of the back door, the dog in the kitchen *whoof* by the stove, the creak of the stairs, the room where her father and her mother slept, door closed. Her brothers, nothing would ever wake them.

In the bathroom, she turned on the light and undressed, and there was blood on her underpants and dark spots too on the inside of her jeans and all of it wet enough for her to have to say that she didn't just slip and fall on the grass, she actually went halfway into the creek. Above Cluetts, you know the place. And what were you doing there? Walking. She sat on the toilet. She was sore down below and wiping herself, more blood. She stood up and looked in the mirror over the sink and her face, the right side, looked red, abraded. She flushed the toilet. Then she heard a door open and her mother's footsteps coming down the hall, her mother knocking on the bathroom door.

"Row, everything okay?"

She'd hooked the door shut, locked it, but she covered herself with a towel and said, "Sure, everything's fine, I'm just brushing my teeth."

Which she did, and her hair, tangled and wet, fell over her forehead as she did so, and her mother went back to bed.

"Night-night then, Row," she said.

The footsteps retreated, the coast was clear. She wrapped her underpants, her socks and the plaid shirt inside the jeans, rolled them into a tight package, turned off the light, unhooked the door and slipped down the hall, a wraith in the white towel. In her own room, she pushed the jeans into the back of the closet, dropped the towel, put on her pyjamas and, in bed, her feet were cold against the sheets for half an hour, and the cracks in the ceiling were the same as ever. Tomorrow was a Saturday, no school.

She fell asleep but in the morning was the first one up. She let the dog out, put on the kettle, and then everybody else was there—"Good morning, hi, hi, good morning"—the usual maelstrom, races on the stairs. She fried herself an egg, cracked eight more for the rest of them.

"One fried egg, that's all?" her mother said to her.

"I'm not that hungry."

"Where were you last night?"

"We hung out by the wharf."

"We fell asleep early," her mother said.

Rowena looked out the window from the kitchen table. The sun was now burning through the mist and with it came a north-east wind slapping up the Reach, cooler, fresher. She touched the windowpane. Whitecaps, a loosening of the weather.

"I think maybe I'll go swimming today," she said.

"We'll come, we'll come," her brothers said.

"Don't forget soccer," said her father, "the boys can't go with you, Row."

Upstairs, she took her bundle of derelict clothes, still sodden, heavy, and slipped them into a brown grocery bag. In a woolen sweater and her back-up jeans she left the house, again through the creaking of the gate, and she set out, turned left and walked away from town, away from the wharf and headed for the barasway, where the river ran down from Iron Skull, from the high barrens, from the ponds in behind, down to the sea. There the stream formed a pond of salt and fresh water, a brackish tidal mix behind a sea-thrown barricade of stones. No one was ever there mornings. She knew she'd be alone, she'd have it to herself, even all day long. The chill in the air pretty much guaranteed it.

The walk from her house took half an hour, the petering-out of the gravel road, then the dump, the gulls and the ravens picking through it, then the foot-beaten path through long grass.

The damp from last night's clothes was seeping through the grocery bag, under her arm. A pinkish stain came through, so twice she turned it over, rotated it away and under so she couldn't see it or feel it. There was a gray wisp, a cloud on the tip of Iron Skull, flattening it.

At the barasway at last, no one there, she turned up towards the forest and walked beside the river to Big Falls, only a hundred yards uphill. There was a separate pool there within the clatter of the tumbling water, the trees a windbreak. She put her parcel down on the loose stones and looked back down to the ocean, and then in a trice she took everything off, all her morning clothes. Naked, she shivered under the sky and dove into deep water. She surfaced and swam back to shore and climbed up, scrambled up the loose shifting rocks of the incline. She took a bar of soap from her bag, lathered herself with it from neck to toes and dove in again. In and out, washing, soaping, and then she treaded water, water the colour of iron or tea, and though it wasn't warm, it wasn't nearly as cold as the ocean would have been, nor was she as exposed, and she washed her hair like that, submerged to the shoulders, pushing her feet rhythmically off the gray rock that formed the slanted side walls.

The eagle she knew from Farmer's Cove flew over.

"Hey," she wanted to say, but she waved her hand instead, knowing she couldn't be heard over the tumble of the river, the falls, the waves beating on the shore below.

The bird heard her anyway, tilted its head in her direction and "Row," the bird said.

She ducked her head under so it didn't matter if she was crying. She came up, the bird was gone.

She pulled herself out of the water. Her feet caused a small avalanche of stones. Now the sun, the late morning heat tumbled down on her from the spruce forest, down into the stream to the ocean, into the torn kelp seaside. Now and then, around her, spontaneously, another rattle of stones fell prey to gravity. Iron Skull was close to her, hard up against the blue heavens and the gray wig of cloud had blown away. To the northwest, she could see the smaller bump of Devil's Knob and really, this could be paradise but paradise was free of all concern, so this could not be paradise for her.

She re-dressed, dumped her sodden grocery bag out and set to work. It was laundry time. With the same soap, scrubbing against the rocks, dipping and wringing, it looked like it all came clean. Drying was the easy part—she just laid out the shirt, the underpants, the jeans beside each other, slanted sunward, and the shirt and the underpants were dry in half an hour. Same with the grocery bag. The jeans took longer. She sat there, her arms around her knees, mesmerized by the waterfall, the river going by. The sun continued to beat down and she felt a tingling on the back of her neck. When the jeans were dry, she stood up, then bent down to repackage the laundry and went home.

"Row? You missed lunch, there's a ham sandwich in the fridge," her mother said.

She could hear the pile-driver still hammering away, just like it was doing yesterday, almost non-stop, when she'd walked down out of curiosity, nothing more. It had been hard to hear then over the chainsaws. Sawdust flew in the air, sawdust fell over the side and fell between the new boards, sawdust clotted on the water and drifted under the wharf.

"Keep away from there, honey," one of the men had said to her, "that's creosote, you can burn your skin on that."

She was standing a few feet from the pile of logs. Despite the warning, she bent over and touched one of them anyway and her fingertip came away black as ink. She rolled it on her left inner arm and made a fingerprint there. It was true, the creosote tingled on her skin. She shaded her eyes as another man swung a sledgehammer, hitting down on large six-inch spikes, driving them down into new lumber, but then he half-missed one and it helicoptered up in the air, glinted like silver and zipped down into the sea.

"Shit," he said.

He teed up another, slammed it home, hitting it even harder.

"Take that, you…" he started to say but then he saw Rowena and he apologized.

"Oh, sorry, I didn't see you there."

"It's okay," she said.

She stepped off the wharf and clambered down on rocks to the water. Two men with hard hats and hammers and flashlights were sloshing around inside the hurricane gash, looking up. She crouched by the water's edge and rubbed the black fingerprint on her arm, trying to get it off, but it smeared. She'd need turpentine for it.

Above her, another curse and another nail flew over her head and this time it bounced off the rocks.

The two men under the wharf came out from underneath together, stamping water off their boots, and she heard one of them say that it would probably be the end of the month before they'd be out of there. The other one, who was much younger, took his hat off.

"Hi," he said to Rowena.

Then he turned to the older man.

"How'd this happen?"

"Tail end of a hurricane. Trawler tied up on that side, one of the ropes broke, she got hammered in here, sledgehammered. Pounded for five or six hours and something had to give and this was it."

"So we still have a ways to go?"

"Yes," the older man said, "we'll be here a while yet."

The older man lit a cigarette and picked his way back up the rocks to the roadway.

"Hi," the young man said to Rowena again, passing by her.

And she said, "Hi" back, and for some reason she stooped, picked up a small stone and threw it out to sea.

"Nice arm," he'd said.

JACK MAHER, twenty-three, newly minted just three months ago as a police constable in St. John's, lived in one of the clapboard houses on Garrison Hill even before he qualified as a policeman. He'd been there now for over a year, first with two friends from high school who shared the rent but then those two moved on, their circumstances having changed—one for the better, one for the worse—so he was living alone now, paying all the bills for the fifth house from the top of the street, a street which fell perpendicularly off the face of the city below the Basilica. There were ten or twelve houses there, together in a row on one side only, the west side, staggering down the hill, holding onto each other because of the steep incline, rooftops and chimney tops jagging down in synchrony with the front stoops, most of the houses painted the brightest of the primary colours, one after the other.

Things were going well for him. He could afford the place on his own. It was June, summer was around the corner and here he was coming off three straight nights, unlocking and pushing open his front door, which stuck somewhere up high but gave way to a quick shoulder push, as it always did, and he went straight through to the kitchen, put the bag of groceries on the table and called her on the phone.

He said to her, "Tryphena?"

Such is happiness, he was suffused with it.

And she said, "Yes, it's me all right, how are you, Sheriff?"

Now and then she called him *Sheriff*, as though he saddled up and rode a horse instead of driving a cruiser when he went to work.

"I'm good, and I actually talked to the Chief himself last night for the first time, down by the cells."

"The cells? What were you doing down there?"

"I collared someone."

She laughed.

"Collared, you mean literally collared?"

And he said, yes, he had literally collared the guy, grabbed him by the neck of his coat at three in the morning.

He told her how he was out Topsail Road, just turning around in a parking lot, the one by the lumber dealer, and lo and behold his headlights, with nothing on their mind but making the turn, flashed across the chain-link fence that surrounded the property. And what did he see? Someone had cut a hole through that fence. He got out, he turned off both the motor and the headlights, and with his big flashlight—the one nearly as long as his arm, the one that doubled as a cudgel—he walked over to the vandalized wire. He flicked the beam over the gravel, over the torn scraps of paper and plastic bags thrown up there by the wind. He ducked through the sharp-cut edges and went on to circumnavigate the building but there was nothing wrong, just a ladder up against the wall at the back. Curious, that. He shook it gently, the ladder went up to the roof and beyond. He looked through the next low window and inside there was a flashlight a lot like his moving around.

"That's scary, Jack that's scary," she said, interrupting him.

"Not really, statistically there's nothing to be scared about, these robbers don't carry weapons."

So he waited in the shadows underneath the ladder and he was right because, five minutes later, the ladder started to shake and quiver and down came a guy with a bag over his shoulder. Jack stepped out from his shadowy recess by the wall and snagged him. Half his size, scared more than anything, he tried to twist away and run, but Jack held him tightly by the coat.

"That's when you collared him then."

"Exactly."

"He didn't resist?"

"He gave up, like a fish. I put him in the back of the cruiser, the felon."

"The alleged felon."

"Right, sorry. Alleged, suspected, not yet even charged. So I take him back to the station, then guess what."

"I have no idea."

"The Chief was there."

"In the middle of the night?"

"Right. Rumpled up like he's just out of bed. I'd heard he sometimes does that, he's an insomniac. Anyway, he looks at the guy, our suspected felon, and asks me if he's confessed. I say no but I've caught him dead to rights, it's a slam dunk, and he tells me to bang the guy around a bit until he confesses, clip him hard on the side of the head."

"Oh come on," said Tryphena, "he wouldn't have said that, not in this day and age."

"No, he said it all right but then he laughed and said too bad we can't do that anymore, it saves a lot of court time."

"You wouldn't do that ever, would you?"

"Bang someone around? Not if anyone's looking."

"Jack! It's an abuse of power."

"I'm kidding, I'd never do it, you know that. Anyway, forget it, Tryphie, that was that, what's up with you today?"

"Exams, that's all, studying for next week."

She was in the kitchen in the house where she lived with her mother, on Fitzpatrick Avenue. Her street was insulated from traffic. No one drove down it unless they were lost. As far as numbers, there were just a few more houses on Fitzpatrick Avenue than there were on his street, Garrison Hill, but the houses on Fitzpatrick Avenue were nondescript, all painted dull white or beige or pale brown, as though those who lived there had no imagination, no pizzazz.

They'd talked about it, the sharp contrast between their streets.

"I guess everybody here on Fitzpatrick Avenue is just happy with the life we have," was her opinion, "We don't have to tart it up like you do."

"Tart? That's going too far. Besides, I just rent. I didn't choose the colours. I like both our streets, Tryphie, but mostly I like yours because you're on it. Your street is my favourite."

"Your street's okay too, Jack, I like it fine. Same reason. I didn't pay it much attention before, tell the truth, but now… "

According to the odometer on his personal at-home car, a beaten-up blue Vauxhall, the distance from her house to his was 0.5 miles. In the other direction, it was exactly the same, 0.5.

"You weren't measuring those distances when you were on duty, were you?"

"No. Well, once or twice, yes, I checked it out. It was just a little bit out of my way, and trust me, you never know what you'll find on these streets, patrolling quiet streets like this one of yours, Miss Grandy. It kind of needs special attention. It's part of my job, prevention and surveillance."

"Surveillance?"

"I wouldn't want to see other men, prowlers. Worse would be men with flowers, chocolates."

"None of those, none of those for me."

Usually then, if he was with her rather than on the phone, he'd put his hand on her gently and in a friendly way, on her breast, left or right it didn't matter, or on the belt-buckle of her jeans, or on the small of her back, and he'd pull her in closer and she'd be fine with that or more than fine.

"I'm off tomorrow," he said, "so I'm thinking I could meet you at the park. Late morning? Bannerman Park?"

"Class," she said.

"Skip it."

"I can't do that. That would leave Stan in the lurch. He needs me there."

"Twenty-four other girls and he needs you?"

"I'm his partner, Jack, you know that, it's a fact, there's nothing I can do about it. Tomorrow, he needs my teeth to work on and I need his, that's the way the course works."

Dental hygiene. Who'd ever think he'd care about that? She was at the top of her class, apparently, and Jack was proud, he was proud of her, of everything she did, the way she looked, the way she wouldn't listen to him now when he was asking her to slip away, to not show up, let someone down, because that was not her way.

"I understand," he said, "I'll call you later."

Which he did, near midnight, and she said, "Hey, Jack, guess what, Bannerman Park is okay for me, if it still is for you."

"It is?"

"Classes cancelled. Teacher sick, all-day lab cancelled, freedom after all. We just got phoned. Do not show up, they said."

DUE TO illness, classes at the School of Dental Hygiene had been cancelled. That left Mrs. Henderson with the chance to pull one or two items off the back burner. She'd called an Ad Hoc meeting of the Disciplinary Committee for just before lunch, the first time they'd met this year. After all, as the teachers had often reflected, students of Dental Hygiene were not radical in thought or behaviour. They were peaceful, they presumed little and had few demands.

"When was the last time we held such a meeting, anyone remember?"

"Two years ago? The smoking on the steps? Outside?"

"I think you're right."

They sat informally in the staff room, the three of them, on two soft couches that sagged with age. The school was otherwise empty. They could hear the distant buffing of wood floors down in the Dance Academy, in the basement, and that was reassuring, the buffing and the wax. Mrs. Henderson felt the two disciplines were well-housed together, there on Lemarchant Road. Two clean ships.

"So, Ad Hoc Committee on Discipline, let's discuss it," she said.

"What does that mean, *ad hoc*, literally? I mean I know what it means, we all know what it means, but the Latin," said Ms. Johnson.

"It means *speaking to just this*, I think," said Mrs. Blagdon, "we talk about this, this one time. It's not a repetitive event, thank God. This meeting is just this meeting, this once. Let's get it over with."

"That's right," said Mrs. Henderson, "nothing ongoing. The best thing would be, as a committee, that we never meet at all because we have no disciplinary problems."

"And usually we don't."

"No."

"But now we do, I understand. So, please, Ms. Johnson, describe what happened. Sandra, will you take notes?"

"Sure. Wait. Okay. Go."

"Can I start?"

"Please."

"Last week, in our Cleaning Practicum, the second-year class, an incident occurred between two of our students that caused an unseemly uproar in my classroom. I could not let it pass."

"Describe, please."

"It struck to the heart of ethical behaviour in our field. Let me say that."

"Please, go on."

"I did not overreact."

"No one has suggested otherwise."

"I used it as a teaching moment, turning a negative into a positive."

"Good. Good for you. What happened though, please be specific, why did you want us to get together on this? It sounds like you've handled it already."

"Yes and no. Okay. You know Stanley Grant."

The three exchanged glances.

"He's here on some special programme, through the government. Right?"

"The details on that are confidential, as you know."

"He's the only male student, the first one ever? Was he not granted admission over others better qualified?"

"Privileged information."

"He doesn't fit in my class, he's a black sheep."

"He's not the only student to receive priority admission, Janet, if indeed he was. There's others."

"So listen to this, then see what you say. He was partnered with Miss Grandy. No surprise about that, he's always with her. He had the patient role first, she examined him and cleaned the upper molars. Everything fine. Then it was switch-time so it was her turn in the chair. She lies back, he adjusts the light, and the next thing I see—and everybody in the class sees because we're watching each other—his hands are on her breasts and she's trying to sit up. But she can't, because of what he's doing."

"What do you mean, doing?"

"His hands. He's touching her, unabashedly."

"Surely not."

"Surely so."

"What did you do?"

"I stopped the class in its tracks. I said Mr. Grant, what in God's name. Stop that. By then I could see that the dental mirror had flipped down from her mouth to her chest and was caught in the nap of her sweater and it was that that he was after, ostensibly."

"Where was the dental bib?"

"He'd forgotten it, he said."

"So, really, he was fumbling at the mirror, not the chest, not at the girl's breasts?"

"That's what he said, but I wasn't born yesterday. The way he moved his hands."

"What was the reaction of the class?"

"Not what I'd hoped. Laughter, mostly."

"And Miss Grandy?"

"Not laughing, not upset, just herself. I admit that. She said something to him I couldn't hear and pushed him aside and in about thirty seconds she had the mirror free herself. But by then we were at a standstill. My point today, here, why I wanted this meeting, is that this young man, Stanley Grant, committed an egregious trespass upon the person of a patient, Tryphena Grandy. A mock patient, yes, but in a dental office, in the real world, this would not be countenanced."

"You reprimanded him then."

"In no uncertain terms."

"What did you say?"

"The patient is sacrosanct, I said. Should you drop an instrument upon him or her, it behooves you to act professionally. Seek permission before touching anywhere outside the oral cavity."

"Good. It seems you've handled it well."

"He should be expelled, Mrs. Henderson. Please. He wasn't picking at the mirror, he was caressing the landscape."

"Caressing the landscape? Has Miss Grandy—the landscape if we can call her that—levelled an official complaint?"

"No."

"How long did the laughter last?"

"One minute, two."

"Instruments are dropped daily. I think that this incident falls within the realm of learning, that the class was a success in that regard."

"You're not going to do anything?"

"My vote is no. Sandra?"

"No."

"Two to one then, decision made. No expulsion, nothing on the record. You've taught the lesson and the lesson is over."

"Had you been there to see, you would not be so generous."

"We're teaching young adults, not saints. For saints, you have to go down the road to the Basilica. Can we call this meeting to a close? Get on with lunch? I have tuna fish, more than I can eat. Share, anyone?"

SO THERE they were, Tryphena Grandy and Jack Maher, sitting on the grass of Bannerman Park, facing each other. She looked around the park, reminiscing.

"When was the last time we held such a meeting, anyone remember?"

"I guess you're not aware that you are sitting here with a certified beauty queen, from just three years ago."

When she said the words beauty queen, she teased her blonde hair and frizzed it up like a movie star would, with her fingertips.

"That's my impersonation of a beauty queen, for what it's worth. Miss Multiculture-Canada, that's me, at your service. Actually, to be honest, it was not Canada, it was just this city really, so in a way the crown they bestowed upon me was a lie. Or at least an exaggeration."

"Beauty is skindeep, they say, Tryphie."

"I am aware of the hollow nature of such contests. I bring my accomplishment up shyly but it happened so I might as well tell you. I was carried along by it."

"Don't get me wrong, I can see why you'd win."

He touched the side of her face with his fingertips, brushing away strands of hair.

"It was over there"—she turned and pointed to the northeast corner of the park—"a small crowd, parents and relatives mostly, but there were six other girls and guess what, Jack, guess who I represented."

"Newfoundland, I assume."

"Ha! Portugal!"

"Portugal? Impossible."

"Grandfather was Portuguese, simple as that. He came ashore during bad weather, met my grandmother and bang that was it, he never went to sea again."

"True love?"

"Love at first sight. So they said."

"It happens."

She nodded, she knew. They both knew. They leaned towards each other and kissed.

"Anyway, they got married and forgot about Portugal and the Portugal part got absorbed by the Grandys. Assimilated. In one generation, we all looked the same. But then, four years ago, for the Multicultural festival, the Portuguese Community, small but proud as it is—though you are unaware, Jack, obviously, of the Portuguese community, despite being a policeman who should know these things—they looked around and they had no girls, just boys, and there was a beauty contest and someone spotted me walking home and remembered my grandfather and that was it. They asked my mother, she asked me, we talked, we said yes."

"Like, why not?"

"Right. They gave me an honourary passport, I learned a couple of waltzes on the piano and I was ready to go. They've changed the rules since, it can't be done anymore."

"The Grandy rule?"

"You need closer ties now. Parents, I think."

"And you won."

"Well, I had an advantage. The other girls, they danced to tapes. I actually played."

"Your talent won them over, yes, Tryphie, but you, you're the only one who was you."

"I'm trying to follow that. Thank you, Jack. I still have the passport tucked away. Passaporte, it says, but it's expired. I'll never get it back."

"You could have played chopsticks, or a player piano."

"They dressed me up when I won. I had a sash, a tiara, a wand with blue glitter. The whole Tinkerbell thing. Mother said, don't get carried away. Actually there was work involved, it wasn't just a lark. Chamber of Commerce, you know, cut ribbons at the mall, open new stores, that sort of thing. I can't remember everything I did. Oh, the Santa Claus parade."

"Then I would have seen you."

"You think?"

"Never missed it yet."

He imagined her on Water Street up on a flatbed trailer, waving her silver wand as snow fell lightly, melting on the asphalt street but staying pristine upon the coats, upon the shoulders of those watching. A perfect day for the parade. He must have been looking somewhere else, distracted, not to remember a girl like her.

"I probably saw you, Jack."

"Face in the crowd. That's me. It sounds like you were a good beauty queen."

"I did my best."

"Sure you did. Hey, these are crocuses, right, Tryphie?"

"Yes they are, harbingers of spring. Announcing it."

They were surrounded by flowers, purple and white with yellow stamens, powdery-soft, poking up through the grass. She picked two of them, pinching them off at ground level.

"Sorry, but there are so many of you, and just one of me," she said.

Rennie's Mill Road was just fifty feet away. The traffic was still light though picking up before lunch. Either way, they didn't notice the cars going by.

"Feel these, Jack, how soft they are. Their fragility goes right through."

She twined the two stems together in a loose weaving.

"But crocuses are tough and the park won't miss these two," she said, "there's hundreds."

He said nothing, he just watched her.

"I don't think this little arrangement is going to work."

She put the makeshift mini-garland behind her right ear. It started to topple. He leaned towards her, caught it, tried to weave her loose blonde hair back between the stems. She craned her neck his way to give him access, to help, but it was hopeless, the stems were too pliant, the petals were like velvet, they had no stick to them, no substance. When his hands moved away, the flowers fell in a ragged clump to her lap.

"I'll take them home and put them in water," she said.

He put his hand on the flowers, on her lap, and touched the stems.

"Otherwise, I'll feel bad, picking them," she said.

"It's too late, they're bent, broken and doomed. Look at them."

"They look okay."

"They're starting to flag already, Miss Multi-whoever-you-are, they're irreversibly traumatized by your actions."

"Whoa, where'd you learn words like that?"

"Pathology, autopsies. The longer the words, the better."

"These'll be fine in water, they'll recover."

Then they said nothing for a while, just looked up at the sky and watched the clouds and then he talked about his job again. It was on his mind a lot, even when he was off.

"I'm getting there, with all these nights, one after the next. That's where we get experience, you know, first-hand stuff. We drive around, we walk into bars, we get the feel for things."

He laughed when he said that, and he repeated himself—get the feel for things—and he took the crocuses from her lap, placed them carefully on the grass, leaned towards her and moved his hand under the edge of her dress, which had ridden up slightly over her knees. His fingertips then were on the inside of her leg, and he walked them upwards. She looked down and saw the movement, felt it under the material. She slapped his hand down and away.

"Stop that, not here, this is not where you get the feel for things."

He pulled his hand away and shook it, as though she'd hurt him. "Domestic violence, Tryphie, I've told you about that."

"I'd do it again."

"Top of our nighttime list. Women are not immune to being the perpetrators, as you have just demonstrated."

They were under the crown of a maple tree but far enough

away from the gnarly root system that the grass was thick and dry. Sun filtered through the leaves, dappling them with spots of light.

"Tell you what, let's go to Butter Pot. Tryphie? A picnic, since we have the time. We've been given the time, let's take it, for us."

"How far is that?" she asked, though she already knew the answer.

"Forty-five minutes, maybe an hour, we'll grab some food on the way."

"Let's go then," she said, and she stood up from the grass and straightened her dress, flattened it down with her hands. It was of light blue cotton, worn for summertime.

"I'm game for that, for Butter Pot," she said.

She still had the bent crocuses in her hand, her palm held out, horizontally. At Butter Pot, she knew there were pine trees, a forest, a marsh, a boardwalk, a hill to climb, and at the top, a view for miles and miles.

"Perfect then, it's a good idea," he said.

He looked up at her from where he was. Then he too got up and brushed off his pants and they walked to the street where he'd parked the Vauxhall.

They were close, physically close, anyone could see that. They had their arms around each other. He was a foot taller than she was. She was five feet three inches—a good height for a girl according to her mother who was two inches shorter—though now and then she wore heels to add an inch or two. But not today, not for a walk on grass. Today, in the park, she had on a simple pair of red running shoes.

Oh the luck of it, he was thinking, that he was there with her.

TWICE A day for the next three days, in Bell Harbour, the boy from Grand Falls came to her door and knocked and asked if she was home.

"Rowena," he said, "can I see Rowena?"

He came at lunch and after supper, when the crew was on their break. The first time, her mother came to the front room and Row said to tell him she was studying. Which, in a way, she was, for she had a textbook open, biology it looked like, to her mother, the familiar beaten-up maroon copy which was not a lot different from the very book she'd had herself, twenty years before. The second time, Rowena also said no, and the other times she was out or busy or otherwise occupied, helping with her brothers, or at her aunt's, so she never laid eyes upon the boy from Grand Falls again, and nobody wondered about him much, why he wanted to see her, or how they met or anything, and as it happened the entire crew left town within the week, called away to some other more pressing problem elsewhere. They were called to somewhere where more people lived, where people had jobs and paid taxes and voted for the government, and they left about twenty of the logs blocking part of the entrance to the wharf. Those will be shifted later, the boss said. The bollards were freshly painted though, and the new surface had been nailed down tight for walking and driving, so in a way it was a lot better than before they came. The hurricane patch was closed over, that was good. But the infrastructure—so rotten, they'd all heard—that was too big a job to be done right now. They'd have to wait for that.

First the pile-driver was put up on a flatbed and then the crew drove off in three pick-up trucks, dust blowing out behind them, over the high hill towards St. Jacques.

Row didn't care, she didn't even look up from what she was reading.

"They've left the place half a shambles," her father said at dinner, "hard for cars to get near the store. Mixed blessing, the outside world."

JACK AND Tryphena drove out the TransCanada and now the sky had clouds scattered up high, like puffballs.

It would have been easy for them to just sit and watch the countryside go by, the rocks, the trees and the ponds, and say nothing, but as usual they kept talking.

"Without night-work," he was saying to her, going back to what he was saying in the park—she was close up against him now, as necessitated by the structure of the car, so when he changed gears his right hand slid back and forth along the outside of her left knee—"rookies like me, we'd be even more like babies, we'd know nothing. Parking tickets, that's about it. There's no criminal element in the daytime. Well, almost none, the Sergeant says. Oh, there's shoplifting, petty stuff but right now, this time of day, all the seriously bad guys are in bed, resting up for later on, when they get up to their nefarious activities."

"Nefarious? Another long word. They must have various nefarious activities. Then you collar them, right?"

He laughed, and said to her, smiling, "Yes, various, nefarious, you got it there, Tryphena, you got it, drugs, alcohol, the same old things. They rob, they steal, they push their wives around and then someone calls me, and who am I? Well, now I'm the police. Hard to believe."

They weren't driving fast and there was really no traffic on the road going west.

"Then, in your role as a policeman, Jack, you know you should have your seatbelt on, it's for your own safety, you should set a good example. Which you haven't, so far at least, this morning, in several ways. Set an example."

He steered with his knees for ten seconds and said, "Look no hands this time!" and the Vauxhall stayed steady as a rock as he snapped on the belt. She didn't see his erection, it was pinned down by his clothing, his belt.

"Done," he said.

"Thanks," she said, and then she continued, picking up the conversation where they'd left off, as she seemed to be able to do at any moment, "I bet your various, your nefarious criminals, they have a lot of cavities, right?"

"Cavities like in teeth?"

"Yes, like in teeth. Because listen carefully, Jack, with cavities, your criminals would be various, nefarious, and carious, because carious means full of *caries*—that's the Latin word for cavity—they'd have rotten teeth."

"Very funny, Miss Grandy, very astute, but let me tell you, in the police force we think of other things when we use the word *cavity*, to us *cavity* means a body cavity, it means strip searches and drugs stuffed into condoms, usually in the rectum. Or, in the case of females, of which you are one, undeniably, in the vagina even."

"I've heard of that. You've done strip searches?"

He smiled at her and said, "You know I have."

"I don't count for that, you don't strip-search me thank God, and according to our sociology teacher, cavities in teeth are related to income, to education, to IQ, to parameters like that. The further a person goes in school, the fewer cavities they have. In other words, *caries*, cavities, they're a social indicator. Parental neglect, poverty, conditions like that, they go hand in hand with cavities."

"Same for crime, actually, the same indicators," he said.

"I have zero cavities, zero, while Stan has six. I counted them myself, I found them myself. Part of class. If I did have a cavity, well, my mother has a dental plan so I'm covered but Stan does not have a dental plan. It's not fair. He's on his own."

"I have a dental plan. Through the police."

"I know you do."

She turned in her seat to face him, her knees drawn up. The seatbelt was still doing its job for her, tight around her waist. He thought of Stanley Grant searching her for cavities but he didn't say anything, she wouldn't like that.

"Jack, listen. Maybe if we could prevent cavities, we could lower the crime rate at the same time."

"That's a stretch."

"You think? Why not? Floss and fluoride, simple. Everything's better."

"There's no floss in jails, Tryphie, it's not allowed anymore, it's considered a weapon. Someone got strangled so it's been taken away."

"Go on! You're serious?"

"Think of it. If I was in prison and I was pushed to the limit, I could strangle someone with floss, take them out. I'd double it up, triple it up and just fucking do it, strangle my fucking way out of there, over the wall, out the gate, there'd be bodies everywhere."

He hit the steering wheel with the heels of his hands for emphasis.

"Little white neckties! Fuck 'em!"

Tryphena shivered in her seat, involuntarily.

"That's the way they talk, Tryphie, they say the F-word all the time."

They were more than halfway to Butter Pot by now. She knew she'd be hungry by the time they walked to the top of the mountain. There didn't seem to be much wind, judging from the trees on the side of the road. Leaves were twisting slightly, but the branches were still. No swaying or bending.

"You know we're lucky in a lot of ways that we have teeth, talking about teeth," he said.

"How do you mean?"

"Dental records. Unidentified bodies. It's as accurate as fingerprints."

"I know. I've heard of that. Whoever thinks, when they come to see us, the dental hygienist, and then the dentist for a filling, when we take x-rays those same x-rays might be needed for that. How sad is that?"

Then they were there, to the green sign on the side of the highway that said *Butter Pot*. He turned into the gravel road.

"Here we are," he said.

They drove into the forest until they reached the parking lot, where there were no cars at all.

"Looks like we've got the place to ourselves," she said.

They got out and opened the trunk. They'd bought sandwiches and lemonade on Water Street, and Jack had a back-pack. He shrugged his arms into it, hitched it up, bent forward and back, stretched, tested the weight on his back.

"You're okay with that? I can take some," she said.

"Light as a feather, light as a feather."

He jumped up and down several times to demonstrate the ease with which he moved. The sun was out now fulltime and there was warmth to the forest, and a pleasant dampness or humidity which seemed to rise from the fallen dead leaves that still covered the ground. There were no black flies or mosquitoes.

"Wait a minute," she said, "let me back in the car."

She took the crocuses from the dashboard and walked a short way off into the woods, where there was a slow stream and beyond that a pool of surprisingly clear water that had overflowed onto the pathway. You could see the leaves and pebbles perfectly, as though no water was there at all.

"I think if I just leave them here, this would be the best, for them."

She laid the flowers on the ground, carefully and separately, their stems just dipping a quarter-inch into the edge of the pool. Tall cedar trees palisaded around them, blocking the path of the sun in that one spot.

"I should never have picked them," she said, "that was a mistake."

"Don't worry, let's go."

They left the crocuses behind and set out upon the path into the woods, directly away from the parking lot. They couldn't see Butter Pot itself, the mountain. Calling it a mountain was ridiculous, they agreed, because it was just a big hill. It wouldn't be hard, the walk.

He offered her a hand over some slippery roots.

"They're still wet," he said, "anyone could slip or fall or twist an ankle."

"I'm nimble enough, don't worry about me," she said.

But she took his hand anyway. The path was wide and straight until they came to a bog, a marsh where a wooden boardwalk had been built, presumably to protect the ferns and wild grasses. It snaked along, bearing left, and there they had to walk in single file.

"I haven't been here forever. You know these plants, Jack, look at them, they're different than those out on the shore."

She was thinking of Signal Hill, Cape Spear, Middle Cove, where they usually went for walks.

"It's a different ecosystem here, that's why they made it a park," he said.

Then he said, "How old were you, Tryphie, the last time you were here?"

"Not sure. Four, five? We didn't leave town a lot. My father wasn't into physical exercise, not much of it."

"No?"

"He liked to read, that was his thing. I don't remember if we actually made it to the top. Probably, looking at it, we turned around partway."

"We'll fix that today, we'll get all the way up. Your dad, he couldn't have been entirely against physical exertion, otherwise you wouldn't be here."

"Ha! I guess with that, he must have been okay."

A flock of gray jays jumped around in the pine trees and followed them for a while.

"Saucy birds, those are, listen to them," she said.

"They're whiskey-jacks, they rob you blind when you're out camping."

"They take your money you mean?"

"Actually, yes, but mostly bits of food, bacon, hard-tack, you turn your back for a second and that's it. Hit and run."

The boardwalk over the marsh came to an end and intermittently they found themselves on short steep inclines. Words came to them in fragments. Their sentences became ragged, interrupted by their breathing.

"So," she said, "there's criminals everywhere. Even in the world of birds."

"Crows are famous for robbery, ravens too. Eagles. As an officer of the law, I'd have to clamp them all in irons."

"They'd die like that."

"Oh, I don't know, I see them in cages, they look okay."

"They're not happy in cages."

"They whistle, they sing."

"Sure they do, Jack, but that doesn't mean they're happy."

"They sound happy enough."

"For all we know though, they're singing misery. We think we're hearing happiness, that's what we've been trained to think. Yet it could be sorrow or regret or a million other things."

"That's true enough. I wonder if they get cavities."

"Birds? They don't have teeth. Or gums, for that matter. So no."

"You learn this in dental hygiene?"

"No, I observe. I've had chickadees eating from my hand."

"Pterodactyls had teeth, I've seen pictures."

"They're extinct, Jack. And I'm not even sure they were birds, they were reptiles, I'm pretty sure."

Then they were at the base of the mountain and really, when they looked up from below—as they knew before they started— it was just a rounded hill, one solid mass of rock. There were no dramatic cliffs or drop-offs. But it was steep enough that soil had no purchase there. Trees and bushes began to peter out and they had to lean forward to climb the bare face, over scrabbly stone. The path became less obvious but they could still make out the way because hikers had come there for years, and the rock was scoured by footfalls as well as by rain that had poured down, rivulets that swept away anything loose. Now and then there were black-and-white striped stakes, three or four feet tall, driven into the rocky ground.

"In case of fog," he said, "you walk from one stake to the next. They must have had some kind of massive drill to get those down into the rock."

He listened to her breathing as she walked beside him and he felt his own breath easing in and out and he imagined Tryphena as she must have been years ago, with her non-exercising father who was now dead and gone. Her four-or-five-year-old legs would have been like sticks, hopping, skipping on the lower paths.

"You have pigtails back then?"

"No, why?"

"Just wondering."

"My hair was short."

As happens when climbing hills and mountains, several times they thought they were at the summit of Butter Pot but they weren't. There was yet another rise or prominence beyond them. They laughed about it and carried on upwards.

"A mirage," he said.

"An optical illusion."

"You're right. That shimmer on the highway on a hot day, that's a mirage. Not this."

Finally they were at the top, on a flat open crown of rock. They must have been sheltered from a breeze all the way up, when they'd been climbing up the lee side, because there was a cool and perfect wind they felt right away, in their faces.

"That's nice, and Jack, that little cloud? It looks like a dental pledget."

He shook off the backpack. Where it had pressed against his T-shirt, he was covered with sweat. He looked where she was pointing, at the cloud.

"If you say so. Hey, look down, over there—Holyrood."

A small town, huddled into a cove by the sea. A tall smoke-stack rose above it, releasing a plume of smoke, yellow, hanging in the air as though it were a flag gone limp, a pennant on a mast. Behind the low plume was the bay they'd grown up beside all their lives. Conception Bay. It was as blue as blue could be, bluer than the dress she had on, the dress she'd stood up in when they were back in Bannerman Park. She'd smoothed it out with her hands then, getting up.

"The same colour as your dress, almost."

"Not quite, I don't think. The bay looks different from here, so much smaller."

"Another optical illusion. We're up so high the other side of the bay looks closer."

"Why's it called that, Conception Bay?"

"The Portuguese named it. I'm not sure why."

"It's pretty from here."

"So are you, Tryphie. Mind you, you're pretty from every-where."

"The bay, Jack, the bay is pretty."

They sat down on the bare rock. He opened up the backpack, took out the sandwiches and the cold drinks, the ginger ales, though they weren't cold anymore.

"We should have brought ice."

"Oh, it's fine like this."

She took a long drink, her head tipped back. They ate the sandwiches. Then he got up and walked to the rounded edge of the mountain, the edge being no more than twenty yards away.

"You can see everything from here."

She wasn't looking, she was putting the leftovers into the backpack.

"I can see the path up, part of the boardwalk, the marsh, but I can't see the parking lot. There's no one else around at all, Tryphie, nobody coming."

"We're lucky, we're alone with the sky," she said.

"We should have brought a blanket."

"A blanket?"

She was feeling the sun on her face, the wind, the pleasure of just being there.

"Well, tell the truth, this is one great spot for us, Miss Grandy. If you get my drift."

He walked over to her where she was sitting by the backpack. Her legs were together, straight out in front of her, arms behind her, locked at the elbows, supporting her weight. He bent down and put his hand under the front of her skirt, just as he had done two hours ago in Bannerman Park. This time she didn't slap his hand away. In fact, she bent her right knee out slightly, to make it easier.

"Putting the move on me?" she said.

He kissed her on the forehead.

"I wouldn't call it that."

"Let's put the lunch away first."

The cloud she'd seen still looked like a dental pledget but it was fraying at the edges. She reached for the backpack. He stopped her, he kissed her on the lips.

"Forget the lunch, Tryphie."

"Ants, Jack, ants."

"There are no ants up here."

"There are ants everywhere, even on the moon."

She kissed him back, then pushed him away and stood up.

"Help me," she said.

The breeze had scattered three or four pieces of wax paper.

"Look," she said, "see?"

An ant walked across some lichen, coming their way.

"Okay, you win. It is the moon, we're on the moon. This could be the moon, it could be the moon."

He collected the wax paper and the empty ginger ales and handed them to her and she put them away. She tied up the backpack, firmly.

"There," she said.

"There," he said.

"Now," she said, and with no further ado she turned her back to him and pulled the robin's-egg blue dress over her head and dropped it on the ground.

"I'm game for it now, I'd like to."

She took off her bra and dropped it to the rocks. She turned around to face him and he went to his knees in front of her and put his hands behind her, on her back and then on her buttocks, and pulled her his way. His lips were at her belly-button and then he fumbled with her underpants, pulling them down to her thighs, her knees, her ankles.

"Tryphie take your foot out."

She lost her balance but he had her fast with his hands, his face, his attention and his intention so focused that he could see nothing past her.

"No, no, this one. Now the other. Good."

So there she was, naked on the top of Butter Pot.

He let go of her long enough to strip his own clothes off. They stood straight up together holding hands over Holyrood, high on the so-called mountain, and there was the wisp of smoke and the near forest below and the more-distant sea. But this distant view, he was blind to it now.

"We can lie right down here, it's smooth."

His hands were on her shoulders. He pressed her down. The sun was in the high heavens, so bright that she had to close her eyes. She lay back and the rock was warm, surprisingly so.

"You have a condom, Jack?"

"No, I didn't think of it."

"Be careful then. It's a bad time of the month."

"Sure. Does this feel okay?"

He was on top of her then, blocking the sun. His skin, his weight. "Tryphie, Tryphie," his voice in her ear.

But she also felt a piece of jagged something in her back, a stone. She shifted an inch to her left and the pain went away but then he was inside her for sure, moving.

"Wait, not yet," she said.

She thought she heard the croak of a raven. Funny but she didn't feel that much. Maybe it was being outside.

"Relax," he said.

"Don't," she said.

But he was starting to move a hell of a lot faster and she could feel his shuddering coming on, unmistakably.

"Out," she said.

She pushed at him with her feet and with her hands but he stayed tight to her, she was pinned down on the rock and felt the pulsing as he came into her, three, four, five times.

"Christ, Jack," she said.

How long did it take, thirty seconds all told? She pushed at him again with her legs, her feet now up high against his waist, still under him, splayed out. He was a dead weight.

"Jack! Please."

"I lost it, Tryphie, I lost it. Sorry."

She heard the raven again, for sure it was a raven, a swallowing sound like bottled glass. He slipped out of her and rolled off and away. She moved and the jagged little shard of stone struck again, whatever it was, bit into her shoulder blade. It must be stuck there, like a needle. She sat up then quickly stood up and seminal fluid streamed out of her, down onto her thighs.

"Oh dear God, maybe I can shake it out."

She jumped up and down twice. He turned towards her and shaded his eyes and watched her. He laughed.

"This is something I've never seen before," he said.

"I should hope not."

She bent down and took his T-shirt from where it lay on the rocks and wiped herself down, and away. Glistening on her thighs.

"It's a bad time, I told you."

"You looked so good, I lost it."

He stood up, taking back his shirt. She jumped a few more times now holding his shoulder for balance. Then she turned away and he could see the white pebble-marks on the back of her thighs, her buttocks, her shoulders, white dusting from the rocks. He brushed her off as best he could, still using the T-shirt which was now sticky and damp.

"Get dressed," she said.

She flipped him his underpants with her toes. They flew up into his chest. He caught them and put them on and she put on her bra, her blouse, the dress. Then he put his arms around her from behind.

"I'm in a bit of a daze," he said.

"Get dressed, Jack."

The plume of smoke had shredded some, diffused itself into a thin line over the east side of Holyrood.

"Conception Bay," she said, pointing down to it, "maybe those Portuguese sailors knew something when they called it that."

"Jesus, I hope not."

"My grandfather was Portuguese. I just told you that."

"I know."

Then she repeated herself, saying *Conception Bay*, but this time she pronounced it in a faux-Portuguese way, accented as *Con-sep-see-own* Bay.

He wasn't listening to her anymore.

"My fault, Tryphie, I messed up, I'm sorry."

"What were you thinking?"

"I wasn't thinking."

They walked back down Butter Pot. Where the terrain allowed, he put his arm around her shoulders. Otherwise, he walked behind her and they walked mostly in silence. She didn't know how she felt about what had happened.

"Still, Tryphie, pretty damn nice up there. Right? The picnic?"

"Nice, yes, very nice. Not sure about the ending."

They reached the boardwalk and crossed the marsh and then they were at the parking lot and the car.

"The crocuses, Tryph?"

She didn't answer, she was already in her seat, looking out the passenger window.

"Drive carefully, there might be three of us," she said.

She laughed. She was already happy again.

"There could even be four of us, if it's twins."

"I don't think so, you shook it out, I saw you."

"They don't teach that, jumping for that, in school. Pretty inefficient I'd think."

They left Butter Pot and turned left onto the TransCanada. He apologized several more times.

"Forget it, Jack, I'm fine. You're a broken record. I get it."

Then it seemed they had nothing more to say on the way home. The tires hummed and now and then so did she, a wordless song. There was no parking place in front of her house so he pulled in by the corner, down by Pennywell Road.

"Back to work for me tonight," he said.

She got out of the car and blew him a kiss through the window.

"Call me later then, Jack?"

"Sure, when I get the chance."

But she didn't go directly into the house. She stood on the sidewalk and watched him drive away. His left rear brake light didn't work, but she'd told him that before.

Maybe the whole course of her life had been tipped over by that carelessness up on Butter Pot.

The little girl next door was skipping on the sidewalk. She dropped her rope, came over to Tryphena and grabbed her by the right leg and held on.

"Tryphie!" she shouted.

"Kiziah."

Kiziah's eyes were blue, as blue as her own when she looked at herself in the mirror, as blue as the now-wrinkled dress.

"Hi, Honey," she said, ruffling the girl's hair.

"Oh Tryphie, Tryphie,"—her voice climbing the scale with each repetition of the name—"Tryphie, I love you!"

"I love you too," said Tryphena Grandy.

Those words were easy for her to say there on the street, so uncomplicated, so simple, so true. So easy when she was speaking to this eight-year-old, to her skipping rope, to the chalked squares on the sidewalk, to hopscotch, to childhood unadorned.

INSIDE, HER mother wasn't home but the phone was ringing and she thought of letting it go unanswered but she picked it up.

"Tryphie?"

Stan, from school.

"Tryphie?"

"Hi Stan, yes it's me."

"Have you got a minute?"

"Not the best time, Stan, actually, there's something I have to do."

"Won't take long, one minute. Promise."

"Okay then."

"Studying?"

"Not yet. Soon."

She sat down and put her feet up on one of the other kitchen chairs.

"This book on Egypt, from the library, the one I was telling you about?"

"Egypt's your thing, Stan, it's not my thing. Not right now anyway."

"Wait, give me a chance. I want to describe one of the pictures in it."

She took the pepper shaker and bumped it into the salt shaker and circled them around each other as she half-listened.

"There's a cow and a calf and the cow has long pointed horns, painted white. The horns look like they're a foot long. You wouldn't want to get on the wrong side of this cow, Tryphie, but in this painting—it's on the wall of a tomb and it's over four thousand years old—the mother cow has a newborn calf who can barely stand up and she's licking it. What do you think?"

"Very sweet, Stan. Bring it to school."

"That's what you think?"

"I've really got to go. I get what you're saying. Bring it to school."

"What are you up to?"

"Right now I'm running a bath. The water's running, I have to go. Yikes, I can hear it spilling over. Bye-bye."

Not true. But she hung up, slam! and then she put the salt and pepper shakers side by side like soldiers. Hanging up with a slam made no difference on the other end, thank God for that, it was the same as a gentle cradling, or the pressure from one finger. Okay, Stan hadn't had a nurturing mother himself, not even a family, but it wasn't something she wanted to get dragged into. And why he'd latch onto Egypt for relevance? All he had to do was look up and down any street for examples of mothers, good and bad. Cows, why pick them? How bad could a cow be? On the other hand, who was she to be critical, she had a mother, always had a mother, she'd never gone without.

Butter Pot. In her bedroom she undressed for the second time that day and this time she didn't need help. The blue dress fell to the floor. Then she walked down the hall and really did start to run the water for the bath, turning the taps on, and she sat on the toilet and opened a magazine and flipped the pages. Late afternoon sunshine angled through the small window and hit up against the far wall, on the wallpaper. It formed a slanted trapezoid. Rhomboid? She'd check the proper term later. But more to the point, the jumping up and down on Butter Pot obviously hadn't worked to perfection because a small amount of fluid, slippery, was still seeping out of her. It floated on the surface of the water. She stood up and flushed it down and watched it disappear.

Historically, women often miscarried naturally. But they often tried to help it along, to speed it up, to make sure. They took the opposite approach to nurturing, they tried to stop the life process.

Stan's cow would know nothing about that.

So, join the crowd, Tryphena. Take preventative action. The actual conception, the fertilization of an egg would take a while, it doesn't just happen bang, like right there up on Butter Pot. The spermatozoa had a ways to travel yet. So, what did she have to help her out, close at hand?

Bubble bath. She'd been bubble-bathed a hundred times or more, nearly to extinction, from infancy through childhood. And movie stars apparently used it all the time, they were never seen in a bath without it. So maybe, just maybe, it was for reasons other than modesty and cleanliness.

Try it.

She poured four scoops, the blue-white crystals making an audible swoosh under the rush of water from the tap, and she watched the bubbles form and froth and roll to the back of the tub then climb the sides like a living thing, so suddenly alive that she had to reach in and turn off the tap quickly, sweep with her arm, scooping, trying to keep the foaming suds from rolling up to her, oozing to the floor. She was now on her knees on the bathmat, reaching in. Then, situation under control, she climbed into the tub and Archimedes' Principle did what it always did, water spilled over the side. Bubbles frothing to the floor. Then she lay back and slid herself down like an iceberg, nine-tenths of her submerged, into the warmth. The slow drip-drip to the tiles, that was okay, the heat and steam seeping into her, half-melting her, she could be a baby herself and this the womb. She straightened out her feet slowly and drew her knees back, straightened her legs again, rested her head on the back of the tub.

Then she sank lower and half-closed her eyes and looked through the semi-transparent curtain of her eyelashes and saw the winter wind blowing pack ice towards shore, white on white on gray forever, ice pans to the horizon running seamlessly to the sky, the chrome tap at her feet a gray-metal storm, brewing snow.

She opened her eyes. The room was filled with steam, the mirrors fogged and either she was pregnant or she wasn't. It was as simple as that. How many sperm? Twenty million, a hundred million, she couldn't remember the exact number but there were an awful lot of zeros. Nature didn't leave much to chance and here she was while Jack was at work, his body unaltered. In fact, his body was lightened of its physical burden, the exact opposite, which was nice for him. Could he possibly have done it on purpose? Tried to get her pregnant? The soft breeze, the raven, that little chip of stone under her shoulder. Conception Bay. Some men did that, she'd heard, they did it to their girlfriends to lock them in and tie them down and how well did she actually know him, the policeman? Well enough to know he'd never do that, no way.

She'd ovulated two days ago, that was her best guess. She could feel it when it happened, as though a ghost ran through her.

And speaking of ghosts, what about the sex-education teacher from Holy Heart of Mary, Miss Logan? Uncertain, unhappy Miss Logan in the front of the class, telling them that sperm were like salmon—that's what she'd said—like salmon when they were spawning, climbing over each other with eagerness. Miss Logan had moved back and forth in front of the blackboard wiggling her fingers to demonstrate the desperate wriggling of spermatozoa, how they fought and crawled over each other, looking for the prize, the egg. Of which there was but one. Girls, she'd asked, have any of you ever seen a run of salmon like that? One or two of them had put up a hand. XX chromosomes are baby girls, XYs are baby boys, she said, and she made simple stick drawings on the blackboard. Sex chromosomes, these are called! She had a flair for the dramatic, her voice was passionate, she said that an overwhelming number of sperm head straight for the one lonely target— the egg, and the egg is X, and the X is you, my girls, you are the target, and, afterwards, more often than not, having hit dead center, he who has given you this dubious gift of chromosomes is gone.

Silence in the classroom. Twenty imaginations ran amok, and Miss Logan said it could be a terrible world for women. She'd fanned her face with a magazine and some of the girls were laughing and one of them, laughing or not, must have blown the whistle on the teacher. Probably inadvertently. What went on at school today, dear? Oh Mommy, I don't think I can tell you but we learned about boys and sperm and we're dead-centre targets for it.

Whatever happened behind the scene, Miss Logan was gone within a week. She was no longer teaching anything, not even math, her specialty. Trigonometry, what did that have to do with sex? How did she end up with that class, thrown at her like a grenade? Oh, the nuns, someone up high picked her out and waited.

Tryphena raised up her hips, opened her vagina with her fingers and felt the soapy water run in. She stayed like that for two minutes, her thighs just out of the water.

But look, she could also raise a family with him. A policeman, a dental hygienist, what's wrong with that? It's a good combination, she loved him, she wouldn't have had sex with him twenty or thirty times if she didn't love him. So she put her hips back down into the water and sat up and soap rivulets ran off her neck and chest and down her breasts. The air in the bathroom was colder now. Condensation streaked the mirror. The trapezoid or rhomboid of sunshine had moved higher up the wall and had narrowed, elongated. Most of the bubbles on the surface of the graying water were gone. She pulled the plug out with her toes, playing with the chain.

Girls, Miss Logan said, I was supposed to teach you the science of sex, the sperm and the egg, how fertilization takes place. We've done that here today, and if you've paid attention you know the basic science of it, of human reproduction. Do you agree that you've learned something?

And the girls murmured yes and the teacher went on to summarize, so everybody got it right: XX, XY, baby, simple, not so simple, not so simple at all, and she checked her watch quickly and looked over her class of innocents, row by row, and Tryphena remembered how she then flipped a piece of chalk in the air and missed it on the way down, how it landed on the floor with a click, how the bell rang and no one moved.

Other classes ran shouting into the corridor outside.

One last thing, the teacher said, until this happens to you personally, this communion of sperm and egg, you know nothing, nothing about this topic we've just discussed.

That's more likely why she got the axe, that's where it happened. Tryphena had perfect recall, it seemed, without thinking about it since. Until it happens to you, she said, clear as a bell.

Then it was class dismissed and Miss Logan herself was the first one out the door and it was a shame, looking back at it, how the girls had done nothing for a teacher who had cared for them so much. They should have got together and protested, said something about honesty and love and caring, about Christian values. About Holy Heart of Mary. But they hadn't realized that teachers were human beings, that they had their own lives, they could carry burdens into the classroom and make mistakes and be punished unjustly. Miss Logan was what? Probably Tryphena's age right now, twenty-one, twenty-two, certainly not much more.

As for the Grandys, her mother said to her once over dinner that the Grandys were like rabbits, they got pregnant the first time, also the second time, there's babies everywhere in our family, we're born for it. Which was her mother's way of telling her to be careful, now that she, Tryphena, was old enough to know the facts of life.

Grandys, like rabbits? I don't think so. There's only me, Mother, one baby rabbit in this tiny baby rabbit family.

At which her mother wagged her finger and said that she

herself was the exception that proved the rule, and don't forget, your father died when he was just thirty-four, that we thought we had time for more rabbits but it didn't work out like that for us, we didn't get the chance.

Bath over, bubbles dissolved, Tryphena wrapped herself in towels. She swiped the mirror where she looked like a polar bear, blurred. She bent to the tub with Dutch Cleanser on a small rectangular yellow sponge, and she scrubbed and rinsed and watched the last of the rocks and dust and happenstance of Butter Pot go swirling down the drain.

TWO WEEKS after the wharf, Rowena missed her period, and a month after that, another.

"I think I'll go to the library at school," she said to her mother. She was holding the maroon book, the textbook, at her side.

"Now, Row, why would you do that? It's the summer holidays, I don't even think it's open."

"There's something I need to look up."

"Okay, see if you can get a ride in with someone, I can't take you."

So she sat on a hummock of grass by the side of the graveled road that rose into the wooded hills above town, and in twenty minutes the first car came by. It stopped, they rolled down a window and said, "Hop in, Row, where to?"

"English Harbour, please," she said, knowing it was almost the only destination on the road.

"Why, that's where we're headed," they said, "what a coincidence."

So it worked out well. She was at the school by nine-thirty in the morning but her mother was right, it was locked down for the summer and there was no one there.

Okay.

She walked to the principal's house, cutting across the meadow to do so and the grass there was long enough from the spring rain that it brushed against her legs, and the black flies found her halfway along so she picked up the pace, broke into a run and came in the back door, breathing hard.

"Miss Savoury!" said the principal's wife, standing at the sink, "whatever can we do for you?"

And the principal listened to Rowena and said, "Sure," and gave her the key to the side door of the school.

"Stay as long as you like but remember, if you take out a book, mark it down on the sheet, so we know. And bring back the key, just leave it here if we're not home."

He almost called her *dear* or *darling* but that wouldn't do. Instead he tapped the kitchen table with his hand. His wife stopped washing the dishes. She dried the suds off her hands and together they watched from the kitchen window as the girl from Bell Harbour ran back up the hill, legs bare to the knees, up through the invisible black flies, twitching white butterflies, banks of purple-red lupin, and they wondered, as they had for years, what it would have been like if they themselves had had a daughter run up the hill outside their window like that.

"If all the students were like her," the principal's wife said.

"They're not."

"No."

They finished washing and drying the dishes while, up at the school, Rowena opened the side door and stepped into the hallway. The unnatural echo of her footsteps against the two long walls, the runs of metal lockers. She stamped once, then twice for emphasis. She listened for the echo coming back. The library was down at the end of the hall, where a shaft of light fell across on the floor.

She mused through the card catalogue. Maybe this: *The Human Embryo With Illustrations.* There it was, up high. She had to use the wheeled footstool to reach it. After an hour—half the book was drawings and photographs—she finished it. She ate the sandwich she'd brought with her and walked down the empty hall again. She bent to the water fountain. There was no one to push her from behind. The water was warmer than she remembered, from sitting in the pipes.

So, X and Y, those were the chromosomes that did it. No airplanes or storks or bumblebees involved. How stupid she was. Surely it wasn't possible for her, just the one time, if that's what actually happened.

Then she went back to the shelves, to *Sex Education In The Fortune-Hermitage School District*, a dry summary of the Board's Decision, in 1968, in Hermitage, to delay the teaching of sex education until Grade Twelve. There were dissenting voices, the pamphlet admitted, voices which said that Grade Twelve was several years too late, that unnecessary pregnancies would occur, that they would rue the day if they postponed such critical teaching. But the dissenting voices did not carry the motion, and Grade Twelve was it. If you were younger than that, too bad for you.

She stood up to stretch her legs. From the window she could see the tip of the island in the bay. Those wandering spots of white were sheep. The smaller spots, lambs. They managed without books, sheep did, quite nicely thank you, but it was simpler for them. The grass they grazed upon was greener than it was brown but from here the colours were mixed together, from this distance the texture and shading was that of brushed-velvet. Sixty miles farther out: the near edge of the Grand Banks.

Grand Banks, Grand Falls. Nothing grand about Grand Falls, she'd driven through it once. Used car dealers. Nothing grand about the boy from there either. Leaning on the hard edge of the table to read more closely, her breasts felt a bit sore.

A Bleak Time, by Marion Tripp. This one was a soft-cover book with a nun on the cover, silhouetted, wearing her religious habit, her coif. A girl, pregnant, sat at her feet. In simple prose the author described how such young women (not always young but always women) in Ireland were cast out from their families, sent to work in laundries, often never to return to the *bosom of their families*. How in more enlightened societies there were alternatives. Rowena checked the date in the front of the book, just ten years ago. But that was in Ireland, not here. There were some of those girls who took their own lives, the book said, so devastated they were by their fate, irredeemable.

Then the school door opened and footsteps came down the hall and there was the principal's wife, peeking around the door jamb, holding up her wrist, pointing to her watch.

"Four o'clock, closing time, Row. Your ride's out there."

"My ride?"

"Your dad came. Are you intending to take any of these books home?"

"No, no thanks, I'm okay."

"Leave them there, if you want. I'll put them away later."

"No no, it'll take me ten seconds."

Her father was outside, leaning against the side of the car. The car was running.

"I heard you were here," he said.

He had a quizzical look on his face, as though she owed him an explanation.

"Just reading, doing research," she said.

"Good, it's a great community resource, this library."

He dropped her off at home and turned the car around in the laneway. He had to go back to the store.

"Thanks, Daddy, thanks a lot."

He was whistling behind the wheel, his elbow out the window. "Anytime, anytime."

In the kitchen her mother was sitting alone, reading a magazine at the table.

"Who's home?" asked Rowena.

"Home? Just you and me, right now. But not for long."

The dog was also there, under the table.

"Listen, Mom, listen."

Her mother stopped reading and looked up at her.

"I need to tell you something, something in confidence. Just for us."

"Go ahead, here I am," her mother said.

It wasn't often that her mother sat down at the table and read. There was a pot of something on the stove, simmering.

"It's not so simple."

She'd been standing with her hands behind her back but now she clasped her hands in front of her, as though she were at a recital or in church.

"I think I need to procure an abortion," she said.

Procure, a word she'd learned that day. She wasn't looking at her mother's face when she said it, she was looking at the floor, and out the window, in both directions. Also at the dog. Sweat trickled down her back. The cool breeze from the half-open window made her shiver. The same running shoes that she had on under the wharf were on her feet but the helplessness she felt within them was different.

Thus Row Savoury kick started it all, everything that happened later. Say she hadn't spoken to her mother when she did, what would have happened? She'd have stayed home, walked up and down the road, seen herself grow bigger for nine months like the silhouettes on the cover of the Irish book. Then she'd have had the baby. And they all would have said, for sure, as a family, to hell with the boy from Grand Falls. She'd had enough of him already. He was gone from her life. Then, once the baby was born, she'd be a single mother at seventeen, and what's wrong with that? Nothing much, but it wasn't for her. She'd made up her mind at the library, once she figured it out: the sperm, the egg, the fertilization, the so-called union already visited upon her. The missed periods. Her *friend,* they'd called it, who didn't show up on time.

So she stood there in front of her mother courageously but with really no choice, her mother's face breaking when she heard the words *procure an abortion* and Rowena was sitting in her mother's lap as if she were five years old and they were crying together over some sad story they'd read. Which they'd certainly done many times, crying over stories, though not for years, and not for themselves.

HOW WELL did Tryphena know Jack?

She went to the bedroom and lay down to think. Still warm from the bath. A dressing gown. Her head was on a towel folded on the pillow, her hands clasped on her chest. It had been a long day but she wasn't tired at all and there she was, the picture of repose really, if she could see herself, looking down at her bare feet, gathering her thoughts.

Sometimes you didn't know everything but knowledge had a way of lodging itself in your brain anyway. Or in your heart. And if the heart ruled the head, that's not wise, but that's where she was with Jack and she liked where she was, generally. They just got on, it was as simple as that. A lot more than that, actually, how she felt, her heart, her brain too.

They'd met the previous November at the Christmas Dance, the one held annually by the Downtown Merchants, on Cathedral Street. At the Masonic Temple. And how crazy was that, their meeting? How unlikely? After all, they weren't merchants, they weren't Masonic—whatever that was, she had no idea, the only Masons she knew were jars—so they had no reason to be there. They were half the age of everyone else.

He was with his aunt, who owned The Sandwich Place on Water Street, a last-minute replacement for his uncle, bedridden with the flu. And Tryphena was there at the same dance, the same night, for the first time ever, with one of her cousins, Sandy who owned the Yarn Shoppe. Tryphena anticipated having a pleasant enough time while Jack went with no expectations at all. It was just going to be another party.

There were eight or ten long tables set up for dinner, maybe twenty places at each one, and when Tryphena Grandy settled in and pulled her chair square and looked up, there he was, across from her. He was talking to his aunt. When he looked her way, she was speaking to her cousin. When her head turned again, towards his side of the table, by then he'd looked away, his attention apparently somewhere else. They said nothing to each other during dinner. Conversation flowed around them. Afterwards, when the dishes had all been cleared, the music started. There was no band, just a recorded tape, but it somehow took the measure of the crowd and everybody at their table jumped up as one and moved to the floor. The two of them were left looking at each other. Finally, after two or three minutes like that, over the racket—it was way too loud for words to be heard—he took the initiative. He looked directly across the table to her, tilted his head to one side and opened his hands as though he were about to dance with a partner, though this partner of his was invisible.

She looked at him. Was he asking her to dance?

She guessed yes, and she was right. She tilted her head as he had done and simultaneously they stood up. She had to walk around the table, to the end on his side, and they met there, already moving towards the crowd on the dance floor.

Anyone could see they were good, non-verbally, right off the bat. An hour later they were still on the floor though most everyone else was flagging and falling back onto their chairs. Tryphena was covered with sweat. Her hair was plastered on her forehead, her blouse stuck to her stomach, to her back. He was in the same state. They waltzed and step-danced and shimmied and did whatever the music called for. They couldn't exactly talk without shouting because of the crowd, because of the volume the music had been cranked up to, because of the vertiginous movements of dancers around them.

They weren't fueled by alcohol, they'd only had one glass of wine.

When the music stopped between numbers, he held her lightly by the waist with his fingertips, and she did the same, with hers. They saw their relatives watching them, her cousin, his aunt standing together, looking their way, wondering.

"I like you," he finally said, "in case you can't tell. Actually I can't believe my luck."

His lips were close to her ear. She felt the same, though she didn't say it outright. She was a bit more reserved, at least on the dance floor. But body language says a lot, you don't have to talk if you're dancing. That's why dancing was invented.

Going there, to the Downtown Merchants' Dance, with no expectations, turned out to be the best expectation they'd never had, for both of them.

Two days later he phoned her. "Tryphena? It's Jack, from the dance. Remember?"

"Oh, sure I do, hi."

He invited her to go with him out to the mall, to the new movie that just came in, *Serpico*.

"It's about a policeman going undercover. There's no dental hygienists in it, I don't think. As far as I know. But I don't really know, I haven't seen it, there could be lots of them."

She accepted. They went in his car and halfway through the movie they were holding hands and by the three-quarters mark they had no intention of letting go. When the movie ended, she said, "Undercover life doesn't look so great. You wouldn't want to do that, would you?"

"No thanks, that's not for me. I like it here, being myself."

They agreed—no dental hygienists having appeared in *Serpico*—that there were not enough movies about dentistry and hygiene and plaque.

"There's a lot of potential there, Tryphena, a horror film, maybe needles the size of skyscrapers poking down out of the sky? Everyone running, screaming, spitting blood."

She shivered.

"Want to see where I live?"

At Garrison Hill they dropped their clothes to the bedroom floor. From outside, slanted light came through the blinds, shifting over them, under and through them. Love, sex, desire, youth, carelessness: call it what you will, something they could not resist crept up behind them both that night, covering their eyes with its warm hands, whispering to them, saying guess who?

ROWENA'S MOTHER said, "Oh my God my dear darling."

Then she said the same thing five more times and then, "Rowena, are you sure? How do you know?"

"I looked it up."

"Who, Rowena, who? I can't believe this."

"It doesn't matter who it was."

"It doesn't matter? Of course it matters."

"Not to me."

"You've told me this much, tell me the rest."

"Someone from the work crew."

"Those were men!"

"Not all of them."

"Oh, that boy. Now it makes sense."

"It doesn't matter, it really doesn't matter, it's done with."

"How can it be done with? Oh my God, it's my fault, of course it is, we should have talked about this a lot earlier."

They were arm in arm and their heads were side by side, touching, chins on each other's shoulders. So they spoke to each other as though their heads were one, words reverberating through bone.

"Row, tell me. Please."

She let go of her mother and walked to the sink. There were three juice glasses drying there in the rack so she picked up a dishcloth and polished them and put them away.

"I think his name was Andrew or something. But I don't care."

The wind was sometimes from the north-east and, when it was, the screen door made a bump now and then, pulled open by the draft, then closed again.

Bump, bump, irregularly. *Bump* again.

She lifted the empty dish rack, poured the drained water from the tray into the sink.

"Row, come back, sit down."

Her mother patted the empty chair beside her.

But there were crumbs on the table and spots of jam so she asked her mother to lift up her teacup. She wiped the table in semi-circles and collected the crumbs in her hand.

"I'll just throw these outside first, for the birds, I'll be right back. I promise."

The dog pushed by her, eager and ready to go. Someone had left the front gate open. She closed it, clicked the latch down tight, took a deep breath. She threw the crumbs up into the air and watched them fall to the grass. Birds will come. Then she went back to the kitchen and sat down.

"It doesn't matter who it was, Mom. I don't want to think about it."

"They were men, and that boy was not a boy. Row, it's a crime, you never would have done that on your own."

Bump the door, again. The dog shuffled in from outside as though he could sense trouble.

"Well, what am I saying, of course no one does that on their own. Look, we'll have a cup of tea, I've got to think," said her mother.

There was a long silence while the house creaked and her mother boiled the kettle. She fiddled with some dishes, set out the saucers and then the cups, and poured the tea. Rowena added a cube of sugar to hers and watched it dissolve, then stirred in a second with her spoon.

"He forced you, didn't he?"

"Sort of, I guess so, yes. I didn't have a clue, that's the truth."

"We love you, Row, we all do."

"You'll tell daddy?"

"Give me time, give me time."

Her mother stood up and circled the kitchen twice, looking at the floor.

"Men don't have to know everything. For now, we'll keep this between ourselves."

Bump the door.

"You said *procure an abortion*. Where in the world did you get that idea from, Row?"

"The library."

"Oh, now I see. There's stuff about that in the library? Abortion?"

"Yes, not much but it's there."

"Christ Almighty, someone's not on the lookout at school. But it's my fault, it's our fault, your father's and mine, we let you down. Leave this to me, we'll figure it out. My God, what would my mother say, if she were alive?"

And the rest of the day passed slowly, interminably, and her father finally said, "What's up with you two, you're both like the walking dead."

They said, "Oh nothing, nothing, what's up with you?"

By ten o'clock Rowena was in her bed. The radio was on loud enough downstairs that no one else in the family could hear anything. Her mother called the principal's wife. They spoke for thirty seconds. Then they met twice over the next two weeks, the first time in English Harbour West, at the principal's house, the second time in the hills above Boxey, overlooking the wide expanse of the North Atlantic. Here the waves ploughed in unobstructed to a cobbled beach. They parked their two cars half way up the hill, partly off the shoulder of the road. It was warm enough just for sweaters. They talked, they sat on the grass or leaned against the cars and looked down upon the house in which, ten years before, the principal's wife had helped the local doctor terminate a pregnancy.

"Terminate?" asked Rowena's mother.

"That's what we called it."

"Right here? You did that?"

"Well, Dr. Poole did it, not me, but I helped. Trust me, the circumstances, anyone would have done it, even the College of Cardinals. Well, maybe not them. Anyway, you don't even want to know, and I'm not telling."

It had been a night of high winds, driving snow, electricity out for days. The yellow glow of the lamp, the *shush* of kerosene, the house shaking with the intensity of the storm. It took what? Fifteen minutes? Then they'd washed their hands, calmed their patient down, whispered to her, turned down the lamp and out the door they went. They'd walked two miles bent to the weather. Soaked, freezing, all the way back to where they'd left the car.

"It was a different kind of night," the principal's wife said, "a night for transgression, the breaking of rules. Leave it at that."

"And it worked out?"

"Well, you never heard anything, did you?"

"No."

"There then."

"I guess it's always easier to do nothing, to be paralyzed, than to act, to do something, to initiate action," said Rowena's mother.

"Sure it is, but if we do nothing, then here it's too late. Give Rowena this, ask her what she thinks and let me know."

She handed over a folded magazine, a ten-year-old *Southcoaster*.

"It's an interview with her, with the doctor. Dr. Poole. She's in St. John's now. A psychiatrist, but you know that."

It was so much easier for them to talk outside together on that high hill with the waves rolling in than anywhere else in the world. Sitting above the wild seashore over Boxey, listening to the same waves that had been plied by Odysseus, pounding in relentlessly, rolling, retreating, watching the spindrift, listening to the underlying roar of them, the turning over of stones, waves saying what waves have always said to those who lived by the sea: be brave.

JACK WAS in the Strand Lounge, at the mall. Tryphena was at home, she'd had a bath in the afternoon and was resting so he was at loose ends, on his second beer at 9:30, leaning on the bar. There was nowhere to sit. Lots of people knew him, they'd already come over and said hello and drifted away. The girls with them were the same as ever, nice enough but his loyalty was fully claimed, as they all knew, by Miss Fitzpatrick Avenue, Queen of his Heart, Tryphena Grandy, his girlfriend, yes his *girlfriend*, and a most desirable girlfriend she was, as anyone would say. Miss Portugal, even.

The lounge-band started up, three Irishmen who were all the rage. As usual they sang *falderal-diddley-ay* and slow ballads about love-struck girls wandering through fairs, girls casting their lot with shepherds, lying down in dark woods, dying from poison or hanging, or from the vengeance of crazy fathers. And how realistic was that? Not very, not nowadays. Love— whatever *love* meant—was much more prosaic now, from what he could see.

Then it was break time, already the band was stepping down and he was tapped on the shoulder.

"Oh, Priscilla."

"Yes, me."

And he was happy to see her, Priscilla, she the one before Tryphena. She'd done something to her hair, coloured it like a cockatoo or some other tropical bird, cut it short, dyed it red and blue and green in streaks.

"Nice," he said, pointing to the top of her head.

"Oh that," she said, "that's the only change in me."

They tapped beer bottles.

"Change in the ocean, change in the sea, change in my own

true love, but no change in me," she quoted.

And when she said *change in my own true love*, she tapped him on the chest with her index finger, three times.

He smiled, ruefully.

"Cheers," he said.

"Sort of cheers, Jack."

There was still enough ambient noise that they had to lean towards each other and shout.

"What's up?" he asked.

She was in a play at the LSPU. Hence the hair.

They drank and bought each other another beer but then in a sudden the band was back, the banjo player was tuning up, they couldn't hear themselves think, so he said to her, "Priscilla, outside?"

They could take their beers out of doors, he told her, for he was a policeman, they could get away with it.

Outside it was much cooler. They leaned up against the window of the business next door.

"Be careful, don't lean too hard on the glass, we'll set the alarm off. I've seen it happen."

But there was an alarm of sorts going off in him already because she was looking at him, challenging him with her hazel eyes, and he was standing closer to her than he should.

"How's your denturist?"

"She's a hygienist, not a denturist."

"That's not the same thing?"

"She's fine, she's good. Sorry the way it worked out."

"I guess then she has nice teeth?"

But he didn't want to talk about Tryphena so he moved on.

"What's the play about, Priscilla?"

"Intergenerational conflict, what else. I'm the fuck-up daughter."

He laughed. She had her own distinctive way of tossing off lines like that, smiling at what she said, as she said it. And he felt himself wavering towards her, as wind blows grass in a field, any which way, the prevailing wind his weakness.

"On stage, I have tempestuous love affairs, it's quite rewarding. Real life, not so much."

"So, you're the fuck-up daughter. Like, how?"

Why were they both saying *fuck* to each other? They never did that before. He could see his car over there in the parking lot, sitting there like a life preserver. It was time to leave, to get out.

"I'm impulsive, I do things I shouldn't do, I regret what I do, I regret what I don't do, I change my mind, I've got everybody in the play twisting in the wind."

"I can relate to that," he said.

"I know you can relate to that, Jack."

He couldn't drink and drive. He'd have to walk home, or take a cab. He finished his beer, put the empty bottle down on the sidewalk. She'd hardly touched hers. She was still holding it in front of her, cradled in one hand between her breasts.

"I'm sorry what happened, or at least the way it happened. Tryphena, she kind of swept me away."

"That's her name? Tryphena? What kind of name is that? Spell it for me."

There was a yellow haze over the parking lot from the kind of overhead lights they used there. But through that he could see some stars, or planets or planes, something bright and moving.

"T-r-y-p-h-e-n-a."

"You could have told me, that's all, Jack, I was blindsided."

"I have no excuse."

"I don't want to hear about it anyway, the tawdry details."

"Okay. Sorry. It's kind of late, I'm going to have to run."

"Run?"

"Well, walk, I'll have to walk."

"Okay, bye-bye then," she said, and she brushed by him towards the door of the lounge.

"Good luck with the play."

She stopped and looked him in the eye.

"The play's easy, I'm a messed-up kid in the play, you might say I'm type-cast."

Then she was gone inside.

He crossed to Freshwater Road. He started to walk but fifteen minutes later, at the corner of Merrymeeting Road, she picked him up in her car.

"Jump in," she said, "I got to thinking."

She was leaning from the driver's seat and pushing open the passenger door. He climbed in. Her car was even smaller than his.

"Garrison Hill?"

"No change in me," he said.

They sat in the car outside his place. She turned the wheels to the curb and cut the engine. He wondered what would happen next. He saw her on his bed, naked, as she'd been lots of times before, the usual shadows moving from the sash, the window. If he did nothing now, usually it happened for him. But this night she didn't give him the chance. She twitched her self-confessed, fucked-up multi-coloured head his way. Her face was set. She looked the exact opposite of fucked-up now, actually, to him.

"Get out, Jack, I know what you're thinking, and it's no. That's what I wanted to say to you tonight. No."

He got out and closed the passenger door and she drove away, shifting quickly from first to second, turning left on Queen's Road.

ROWENA TOOK the crumpled magazine her mother had given her and took it to her bedroom.

Dr. Naomi Poole, the headline said.

A photograph of a dark-haired woman, maybe thirty, squinting into the sun. It looked like Chapel Island in the background, but she couldn't be sure. Only a low tip of trees and then the sea, it could have been almost anywhere.

Yes, the doctor said in the interview, she'd been five years in Bell Harbour and the surrounding communities, most of them linked by gravel roads that went nowhere else, and yes, she'd grown up in St. John's so coming there was a challenge. Arriving, she remembered how she'd stepped down from the *Taverner* and was met by the outgoing doctor, an elderly man. All he was carrying was a small suitcase and a Remington typewriter. He said there was no culture there, none at all, it was worse than any village in darkest Africa. He pointed the way to her assigned house and limped as best he could up the gangway. So it was not an auspicious beginning? No. The comment about culture turned out to be way off base but it did make her nervous. As it happened, she was made to feel at home right away. She was out for dinner the first night. Of course, she knew nothing about the practice of medicine then, she was a novice. But she had books with her, and she was willing to learn. She took the boat to Rencontre East for clinics every two weeks. It's quieter there, she said, in Rencontre, it's more protected from the sea, you can actually hear the grass growing. It's not like the bustle here. Bustle? That's a joke. She was surprised that she was expected to pull teeth but the instruments were at the clinic and someone had left hand-written instructions. Some teeth you just rock back and forth, others need a twisting motion. At just two dollars a tooth, she became popular for that.

Then, turning the page, Rowena got to the part the principal's wife had underlined for her, in red ink.

Necessity is the mother of invention. I performed surgical procedures, things I'd never been taught. There were emergencies which left me no choice. I delivered babies at home. I set fractures. I even did a Caesarian section once using local anesthetic. Eventually I trusted myself, I became decisive and I went ahead with things without fear. They worked out. The patients here are resilient, we feel we're in it together, I think that's safe to say. There's not much I didn't do.

The last sentence was double-underlined.

End of interview. Rowena looked at the cover again. The date, ten years ago.

She thought she remembered Dr. Poole. She'd been in bed with a fever and her mother was holding her hand, saying, "This won't hurt." But Dr. Poole was saying, "Well, honey, it might hurt a bit," and she was holding a small silver needle, coming her way.

To procure an abortion, first you had to procure the doctor. That was obvious, she didn't need to read that at the library. And to procure the doctor? That would be the hardest part. But in this she would let herself be guided, now the telling was over. Actually, maybe the hardest part was over, the telling. She was content now to fall into the arms of her mother and the arms of the principal's wife. She had no choice. Realistically she'd be lost on her own, *procuring*. So, later that week, when she was told that she'd have to go to St. John's, and soon, and that she'd be accompanied only by the principal's wife, Rowena said, "Fine, that's fine, I'm ready."

She had no second thoughts about it. She pictured herself somewhat romantically and with sorrow as a pony hobbled, a limping dog, a plaintive gull caught accidentally on a fish-hook, twisting on a cast fishing line, trying to fly away.

Her mother was more direct, calling it *rape*.

"My grandfather, Rowena, he'd go after that young man and break every bone in his body. Even if he had to travel to the mainland to do it. And he'd take along enough friends to make sure it was an uneven fight, just like it must have been for you."

Those times were gone, they agreed, so her mother let thoughts of vengeance pass.

And, several more times, her mother and the principal's wife sat side by side, now just on the front stoop of the house in Bell Harbour, their skirts tucked in, their stockinged feet in the long grass. They looked across the mile of open water to Iron Skull and then at each other.

"I'll take care of her in town as though she's my own daughter. The fewer the people who know the details, the better, because if there's a misstep, nobody knows anything, there's no connections to be made."

"What do you mean, a misstep?"

"You never know, now and then there's a complication, rare but it's not impossible."

"Oh God."

"The procedure is safe, I don't mean that, it's been done countless times. I mean the law, we're breaking the law of the land."

"There's a bleeding disorder in our family, you know, you better tell the doctor that," said Rowena's mother.

"How do you mean?"

"I mean the graveyard's full of us, died in childbirth, go take a look."

"I don't remember anything."

"It's a long time ago. I expect it's worked its way out. After all, I was fine."

"Good, then I'll tell her."

"Rowena, she can be headstrong, you know."

"Teenagers, they're all the same. We'll be fine."

Down at the store, Rowena added up the money from her shift. Eighty-five dollars and some change, not too bad for just a few hours. Take away the three dollars an hour for her, though, how much did that leave for the rest of the family? Not a lot. It would be her last shift for a while. She eyed the deficiencies on the shelves and put out another box of Hershey Bars. That should do it. Then she leaned on the counter and opened up the book she was reading. The heroine was described within as having a *painted face as cold and distant as the moon.*

Cold and distant?

There was a small mirror in the store room at the back. She flicked on the light and looked at herself. She set her features to be as cold and distant as she could, but on her second try the doorbell rang, a customer.

She didn't move. As far as she could see, her expression hadn't changed. *Cold* and *distant* were outside the repertoire of her face. She was the hobbled pony, the limping dog, the caught gull, all of them wounded in some way. That's all she saw.

She turned off the store room light and went back into the harsher, brighter, functioning daylight of the store, and there it was, the non-cold, non-distant smile she had for everyone.

HER FATHER and brothers were surprised that she was going to take a trip to St. John's. She'd only been there one time before, and that was when she was ten.

"St. John's?" they said, "whatever for?"

"To visit Auntie," Rowena said.

"It was my idea," said her mother, "Row might go there to university, it's time to check it out."

"That makes sense but it's pretty sudden. Who'll pitch in at the store?" asked her father.

"I will," said her mother.

"Your uncle there is not a nice man," said her father, "in fact, he's a mini-tyrant."

"Mini?" said Row.

"He's not very tall and he's not very nice. Therefore he's a mini-tyrant twice over."

"I don't remember that," said Row.

"You'll see. Just stay on his right side. Don't say anything controversial."

"Me?"

"Yes, you, Rowena, you. I'm afraid you two, you'll be like oil and water. Don't say anything you think is funny. I guarantee you, he will not think it's funny."

"Auntie's nice, that's for sure."

"Nearly as nice as your mother. How she ever ended up with

that man, I tell you it's a mystery."

A week later, at six in the morning Rowena boarded the coastal boat, the *Taverner*, bound for Terrenceville. It was low tide, the gangway was stretched out pretty much horizontally. She boarded amidst the rattle of metal, the winches and chains off-loading cartons overhead, pallets of lumber, packing cases, even a beaten-up car being swivelled to the wharf. Once through that, she leaned against the near rail and waved to her family. Everyone was there although her father was at a distance, on the steps of the store. He waved from his vantage point.

"Be careful in town," her mother shouted.

Down the rail was the principal's wife, also going to St. John's.

"Share the cab, you two," her mother shouted.

"Of course!" the principal's wife shouted back, "of course we will, we've already talked about it!"

She moved along the rail to the girl and put her arm around her shoulder. Rowena had on a thin cotton shirt. The early morning breeze was cool, the sun coming and going behind clouds.

"Row, your sweater!"

"They did a nice job here, on the wharf, didn't they?" someone said to Rowena's mother.

It was true, the bollards were now painted a dazzling red, like lipstick or toenail polish and the planking was solid, all the former rot, the sponginess and bounce, seemingly gone.

"Your sweater!" her mother shouted again, and she saw Rowena nod, and the principal's wife say something to Rowena, smiling.

Then the lines were released and pulled on board and the pitch of the engines changed and the *Taverner* reversed itself, churning the water at the stern into a jumbled white. It eased away from the wharf. Children got back on their bicycles. Men lifted cartons, walked to pick-up trucks, girls and women took small parcels, other men wound rope and flipped cigarettes into the sea. Dories and skiffs, pushed by the same shimmer of breeze that ruffled Rowena's hair, swung in unison from their moorings. The *Taverner* wheeled, slowed, then bow-first picked up speed. The wake roiled out behind as she made the turn towards Chapel Island. All the hills bent Rowena's way, saying goodbye to her. She saw her mother walk away, the last to leave.

There's the barasway, there's Iron Skull.

Smoke from the stack swept down. She felt the dry taste of burnt diesel on her tongue. It was even colder out here once they cleared the harbour because the sun had shifted to the other side.

"Let's go in," said the principal's wife.

They walked into the warmth of the passenger cabin. Four other travellers were playing cards already, strangers they didn't know, from somewhere else. Rowena pulled her sweater out of the suitcase and they opened the door to the port side where yes, the sun was bright but still no competition for the wind and chill, so after fifteen minutes of that they ended up back inside, sitting and reading most of the way to Pool's Cove, then to Rencontre East.

"What's that you're reading?"

Rowena laughed.

"About a girl as cold and distant as the moon."

"Cold and distant? Sounds like she's headed for trouble," said the principal's wife.

"She's beginning to warm up, she's met someone."

After Rencontre they were out from the shelter of small islands, into the open for the last leg of their journey, Fortune Bay and the Atlantic now unencumbered by intervening landfall so there was a heavy swell, a pitch, a yaw, a roll. They felt queasy, they put their books away, wrapped themselves in their coats and buttoned them to the neck. They went back out to the rail. The air was crystalline now, the diesel smoke whipped overhead and out behind.

They felt better out there, they agreed.

The hills were now on their port side. They were lower, even more barren than at home, stubby trees from this distance bent by easterlies, the rock sheared of soil where the wind hit, balding the surface. Close to shore—and they weren't far off—terns stalled, pinwheeled and plummeted.

"Could you live in a more beautiful place?" asked the principal's wife.

Her hair was blowing all over her face.

"No," said Rowena.

But how would she know, Rowena, because she was only sixteen years old and had never lived anywhere else.

They arrived at the harbour in Terrenceville, the boat settling into calmer water. Deserted low outbuildings were shut fast, given over to birds. Herring gulls strode the guano-stained roofs, patrolling the wharf like soldiers, cocky but ill-trained, marching in whatever direction they liked. The engines reversed, the same white churning in this different harbour, the soft bump port side against heavy wooden planking. Two men with orange gloves materialized. The military gulls took off, complaining, and the men with their gloves caught the lines easily, made them fast, and down came the gangway with a slide and a metallic clatter. Rowena and the principal's wife were the last ones off, taking their time.

A car pulled up, the taxi, unmarked. Rowena climbed into the front seat, slid to the middle and the principal's wife followed her and sat by the window. In the back, two more men and a woman piled in.

"The more the merrier," the woman said, "and the cheaper too."

Ten dollars, Rowena calculated, would make up her share of the cost.

"Don't you ever worry about money," the principal's wife whispered to her, patting her purse, "I've got it here."

The woman in the back seat touched Rowena on the shoulder.

"I've been on this trip a thousand times, more than enough to pay for the cost of a brand-new car twice over, but look, my dear, this wreck of a car he's still driving. I'm thinking of getting my own vehicle."

"No, Mary, no, we fear the consequences of that, you, your own car, you'd never pass the license, never, oh praise the Lord for the safety of this world, let that not come to pass," the taxi driver said.

There was a clamour of agreement from the back, the general opinion being that Mary and the rest of the province was better off the way things were. So the back seat kibitzed and laughed and the journey began.

The initial road, of gravel, was partially washed-out in sections. Rowena leaned against the driver then fell away as the car turned and straightened. After twenty minutes they got to the blacktop and turned left. Stunted spruce climbed the hills on both sides of the road. Now and then the solid woods broke up and were replaced by grass, bulrushes, water lying in ditches, a series of ponds or small lakes reflecting the same scudding gray as the sky. The sun had gone now behind clouds. Waves in the larger ponds rushed towards the road and hit up against the shoreline ten or fifteen or two hundred feet away. Now and then there was a small cabin off in the distance. Then the low forest closed down again or there were rockfalls from small cliffs here and there, and gravel pits, and Mary in the back remembered the time they hit a moose.

"It must have been about here," she said.

"You're right," said the driver, "and I got myself this car out of that poor animal."

That was a fine trip, they both agreed, for everybody but the moose.

"That was a long time ago. We were lucky, weren't we?"

"Oh yes, oh yes."

From the back seat, Mary reached up and tapped Rowena on the shoulder again. "What's a pretty girl like you going to be doing in town, such a young thing?"

"Visiting my family, my aunt and uncle," Rowena said.

"Good for you," said Mary, "that's lovely."

Now the taxi was rolling quietly along the four-lane TransCanada Highway and there was a pleasant smell of damp wool in the car.

The principal's wife said she was doing the same thing as Rowena, visiting family and shopping. Everybody in the car assumed that she and Rowena were related, that they were mother and daughter.

"Lovely, you two, you and your girl," said Mary, "girls your age, honey, you should travel free, don't let this grouchy man charge you a penny."

As they approached St. John's, traffic built up. More cars whizzed by.

"Okay, front-seat ladies, where to?"

"Gower and Prescott Street for us," said the principal's wife.

"I got one stop first then, for Mary," he said, "because Mary here, she's for the Monkstown Road."

To get to Monkstown Road, they had to dip down into a valley, then up again past the largest houses Rowena had ever seen. Then a park that was bigger than Bell Harbour. The grass there was a deep green, the trees were in full leaf, the sun was back out. Traffic slowed and stopped for some reason.

Mary said, "Bannerman Park, that's nice, now how'd you like to be young and in love and sitting in Bannerman Park. Oh, the things they have in town, including men. Let me out please, with this traffic I might as well walk the rest of the way. Which means ten percent discount on the fare, Skipper, for nondelivery of essential cargo."

She stepped out without paying.

"Catch you later, dear," the driver said, "and now for you two."

It was high noon by Rowena's tiny watch when the taxi dropped them off at the northeast corner of Gower and Prescott. These were not main streets, not really, so only the odd car was going by. She waited with the principal's wife on the sidewalk while the driver opened the trunk, extricated their suitcases, separating them from the others.

"There you go," he said, "that'll be twenty dollars for you two."

The principal's wife pulled a bill out of her purse and handed it to him.

"Your mother gave me money, don't worry."

Then the taxi left, heading west. The two men in the back seat waved goodbye to them, smiling and friendly, their shared experience over, at least for now.

Gower Street ran along the upper side of the hill overlooking the harbour. It ran east to west but Prescott dropped precipitously down.

"You know where you are now, Rowena?"

"Not really, it's been a long time."

"Cross the street here and go up the hill, it must be on the far side, number 71."

But Rowena couldn't see the house as she remembered it, white with flower-boxes under the front windows. The road curved as it climbed, obstructing the view higher up.

"I still don't see it."

"It has to be up there. 71."

They walked together partway up the hill and then Rowena saw the flower-boxes.

"Okay, there," she said, "there we go."

"Tomorrow night then, Row, right here at 9:45, we meet."

"Should I bring anything?"

"No, just you."

"It'll be dark then."

"Nearly dark, close to it."

"We're going to walk?"

"Yes, we'll walk, it's not far. I'll see you then."

She touched the girl on the shoulder and watched her as she crossed Prescott Street, carrying her suitcase up the hill. Then the principal's wife went back to Gower and turned the corner, heading east.

Row found the small house—it was only fifteen feet wide—in the line of row houses that curved its way up the block. There were the flower-boxes, the screen door, the push-bell.

"They'll be expecting you, Row," her mother had said, "they love you, they're family, but they have no idea why you're really there."

She put her suitcase down on the narrow sidewalk and rang the bell. She couldn't see the ocean because of the same curve in the road that had hidden the house. There was a constant background humming in the air, an industrial low-pitch whine or grind or throb coming from the harbour, below. She could see the top of the far hills which were not as high as Iron Skull, she didn't think, but they were wider, they looked endless, left to right like a distant wall across the lower half of sky.

She heard feet coming to the door and then her aunt was there, saying, "Rowena! Rowena!"

Her aunt came right out onto the sidewalk to hold her and to look at her, and then to hold her again.

"Oh my, such a sight for sore eyes, I'm telling you. Look how tall you are! Rowena! You've grown up! And you're in the front room, upstairs, it's all ready for you."

She picked up Rowena's suitcase and whirled it into the house.

"Where's Uncle?"

"He's out, still at work."

Up the stairs they went. She put the suitcase on the bed. Row thought she could see tears in her aunt's eyes. Indeed her aunt dabbed at her eyes with Kleenex from her sleeve.

"Oh sweetheart," she kept saying.

They unpacked together, putting Rowena's things in the small dresser.

"There, you're set. Are you hungry?"

"Sort of, a bit, yes Auntie."

"I thought we'd go to the mall right away, we can get a bite there."

"Sure," said Rowena.

The bedroom was as small as hers at home. She had to turn sideways to get along the far wall, squeezing by the bed. She put her book—the girl with the cold and distant face—on the bedside table. There was a tiny lamp there, for reading.

They took the bus to the Avalon Mall and Rowena bought postcards. For lunch they had tuna-fish sandwiches and ginger ale. Her aunt leaned across the table as they finished and asked her what she was doing in town, apart from visiting them, "And about time, Rowena, that you visited us, by the way," and she looked across the table at Rowena with such fondness that she reminded Rowena of the principal's wife, who sometimes looked at her in the same way. But her aunt needed her Kleenex repeatedly, she dabbed at her eyes and blew her nose and Rowena replied that she was thinking about university, she wanted to check a few things out.

Thus she lied to her aunt, hiding her true agenda, and her predicament lodged in her chest as a sorrow, a swallowed stone, as though she were dragging her aunt down with her, unsuspecting, to a place she wouldn't want to go.

"You can live with us, here, Rowena, come university. I might have to twist Walter's arm but I miss family, it would be a dream come true for me. We tried to have children, but it didn't work out."

"I'd love to stay with you, if it's okay with Uncle."

"Family's not something he's ever known."

"No?"

"He's got a bit of a chip on his shoulder."

"That's what I heard," said Rowena, "sort of."

"He had to fight to get anything. Your mother never hit it off with him, it's too bad, but it's water under the bridge and today, with you here, I'm the happiest woman in the world, guaranteed."

She looked at her niece from Bell Harbour, sitting so straight and willowy before her, so polite. She reflected that although her younger sister had been blessed with four children and she herself had none, her sister's love must perforce be divided into quarters while she had Rowena to herself, right now, which meant her love could be whole, one hundred percent.

And Rowena, looking back at her aunt, could see her mother there, the same eyes, the same curl and wave in the hair, missing only her mother's composure. Though the truth was, her aunt's lack of composure, her need for tissues, was because she had been thrown for a loop by Rowena's presence, so happy she was to have a child, even a grown-up one like this, here, for herself, under her care. It had never happened to her before.

"Let's shop," said her aunt.

"Okay, sure."

But by shopping, her aunt meant window shopping, not actually buying anything, which was fine with Rowena, who had no desires except for postcards, and they were back at Prescott Street by four.

"I'll start dinner."

"I'll help, Auntie."

"No, honey, go upstairs and rest, you've had a long day. You can help with the clean-up. All I have to do is heat it up anyway, it's all prepared, there's nothing to do."

Rowena fought it but she fell asleep. Her book slid from her chest to the bedspread. She'd never felt this tired before. Then she was awake, and she could hear music coming from the rest of the house. She was groggy, disoriented. Her breasts were even more sore, day by day.

She jumped up and ran downstairs.

"Sorry, I fell asleep, can I do anything?"

"Just visit with your uncle, Row. I'm fine here."

She was taking a casserole out of the oven.

She whispered, "Rowena, go sit, talk with him, make friends. He's in the living room."

"Welcome to town, Missie," he said, and immediately he started to play records for her, one after the next.

"This is Merle Haggard, this is Waylon Jennings, how about this, you like this one? Rowena? How about this one? Wait, this is Tammy Wynette."

She listened to the music and said, "Yes, I like it, it really rocks."

"No, it doesn't rock, Rowena, that's the point, it's country and western."

She was sitting on the other end of the sofa. He moved back and forth as the songs ended, carrying albums, spilling them even, still in his uniform from work.

"You should move to town, Rowena, little Miss, you and your whole family, I don't know how you stand it out there."

"Stand it?"

"There's nothing to do in Bell Harbour. Nothing. Remember I've been there once. Oh, listen now, this is a famous singer too, Jim Reeves, it's called *Four Walls*."

Jim Reeves' voice was deep and the tempo was slower than the other ones he'd played so far.

"He sounds kind of sad," Rowena said.

"Sure he does, that's the whole point of country music, it's sad, it's supposed to be sad, it's heart-breaking music, it's known for that. Maybe it's not for kids."

"Oh I like it, I like it."

"You're not old enough to understand. Not yet, but you will."

At dinner they talked about the mall, about how far apart the bus stops were in Mount Pearl, the timing of the buses, how poor scheduling sometimes led to speeding "but don't tell that to the supervisors because they don't listen, they don't care about anything but being on time, even if all your passengers are thrown to the floor. Oh, and this stew is the best, thank you, thank you. We get fresh meat here in town, not frozen. And Rowena, how's that mother of yours? Still reading all those books, still got those ideas?"

"Ideas, Walter?"

"Oh, you know, she lets her children run all over the place, do whatever they want, raising them wild."

"Walter, she does not raise them wild. Look at Rowena, see how she's turned out."

Her uncle winked at Rowena. "Well, I'm just going to have to reserve judgment on that, aren't I?"

After he finished his apple pie, he went to the living room and turned on the TV.

"He likes his programs," her aunt said, "I like them too. Want to join us?"

"Sure, Auntie, I'd like that. At home, we only get two channels, now and then, with bunny ears."

Thus they passed the evening together. None of the programs were all that great, but she laughed when they laughed, for it was funny enough, and during the commercials they talked about work and school and fishing and not-fishing, and her uncle put another record or two on and said, "Listen to this, both of you, this is what life is really like."

It was Merle, Merle Haggard again. She recognized the voice and he confirmed it.

Inevitably, the evening stretched out in its own comfortable way to bedtime. Then she brushed her teeth in a strange bathroom, lay in a strange bed, fell into a strange hollow. Strange mattress. Despite her afternoon nap, she was still exhausted. She read for only fifteen minutes, put her watch on the bedside table, turned off the light and lay in the altering semi-dark. Cars went by sporadically on Prescott Street, their headlights flickering a dull yellow through the closed curtain.

Unlike her parent's house, which stood alone and shifted and creaked and bent with the wind, her aunt's house on Prescott Street, in St. John's, anchored on both sides, was still.

IN THE morning of the day that was to be her day, the morning of the evening, the morning of the night, Rowena didn't want to be the first one up. She stayed in bed until she heard her aunt on the stairs, then in the kitchen. She quickly made her bed and was downstairs in a minute, helping with breakfast. She cracked eggs into a bowl, whisked them, poured them into the frying pan, started to lay down strips of bacon around the edges.

"How many, do you think?" she asked.

Her aunt was now sitting at the table, watching her.

"Two for you, one for me, three for him."

"Six then," said Rowena, "six it will be."

The bacon sizzled. Upstairs, they could hear footsteps and the toilet flushing.

"You look like you know what you're doing, Row."

"Experience, Auntie, I do it at home."

"You got the moves."

Rowena acknowledged this with a shimmy of her hips. It was true, she had economy of movement and a certain style with the frying pan.

"I have Bingo tonight," her aunt said, "I hope that's okay."

"Sure it's okay, I'm visiting friends, I'll be out late anyway."

Then her uncle was coming down the stairs, singing *I'm a truck-drivin' man.*

"Oh Uncle, bus-driving I thought it was, not a truck."

"You're right! And actually, my girl, the bus is harder than trucks. You have to stop, start, turn, check your mirrors, punch tickets, keep your eye on the silly ones, you can't just sit and watch the white lines go by. Can't turn on the radio and zone out. It's a demanding job."

"What route are you on today, Walter?"

"Mount Pearl. Same as ever."

"Bus drivers," said her aunt, "don't get immortalized in music like truckers do, but Walter's right, it's harder. He's done them both, he knows."

Rowena thought for a minute and sang out loud *"I fell in love with a pretty girl, dropped her off in old Mount Pearl."*

Her uncle laughed and said, "Hey you're not so bad, you're all right, but all the pretty girls I see, they get off my bus before they should. Except for one, this one here, thank goodness she stayed on for the duration."

He grabbed his wife around the waist as she tried to sit down. Then he let go and drummed his hands on the arborite.

"Yes, I'm a bus-drivin' man."

Toast jumped from the toaster.

"I'll get it," her aunt said, reaching for it.

"Bingo's just once a month for me, Rowena," she said, "and we don't do it for ourselves, we do it for fundraising."

"That's good," said Rowena.

"We raise money for the Sally Ann, and for the Grace. Over the year, last year, we raised over a thousand dollars."

Her uncle was tucking a large napkin into the collar of his shirt. The coffee was perking, the aroma filled the kitchen mingling with that of the bacon. Her aunt put Walter's eggs on a plate and put it in front of him.

"Looks delicious, ladies, thank you, but did I hear something about a thousand dollars? That's the first I heard of all that money."

"Yes, Walter, a thousand dollars, we raised it for those in need."

"Really! I'm flabbergasted. You and your lady friends can ill afford to give that much away. You and I can ill afford it too. Charity begins at home. I don't see the pepper."

"It's behind you there, on the windowsill, Uncle."

"Well I'll be damned, so it is."

"I'll get it for you," his wife said.

It was out of reach for him, that was true, Row noticed, but her aunt had to get up and walk around the table to fetch it, though she didn't seem to mind. The way they interacted, her mother and father had exaggerated about the so-called mini-tyrant. They seemed happy enough together in the morning warmth of the kitchen, the stove, breakfast, and it must be strange for them, her being there.

"If twenty women," he said, waving his fork, "raised a total of one thousand dollars playing Bingo, how much is that per person?"

He didn't stop eating but looked up at the ceiling to calculate.

"Fifty dollars," said Rowena.

"A thousand divided by twenty is like a hundred divided by two... equals, you're right, Miss Mathematics, it's fifty dollars which, the last time I looked, is about two months' city taxes thrown away, and that doesn't count the IODE and all the other things you do, and besides, I bet not all those women donate, some of them keep the money. Knowing your friends."

"That's not true, Walter."

"Sure it is, you told me once."

He stabbed his fork into the scrambled eggs, twice. "This is a bit underdone, and to say you play Bingo for the sake of others is a stretch. It's a gabfest, that's what it is."

"Once someone kept some of the money. Once, Rowena, once out of hundreds of times, Sarah did, maybe fifty dollars, and that was just to keep the wolf from the door. We were fine with that."

"That was no wolf, that was her drunken husband. Wolves got better manners. Also, eventually, they go away."

Rowena poured a cup of coffee for him and got milk from the refrigerator and brought it to the table.

"Thanks," he said, "and sugar please too, and what are you up to today, in the big city, girl, what are your plans?"

He picked up his last strip of bacon in his fingers.

"Tonight, I'm meeting a friend, so I'll be late."

"You have friends here?"

"No, she came from Bell Harbour too, we came together, she's visiting too."

"Taking in a movie?"

"Maybe, I'm not sure yet."

She brought him the small bowl of sugar.

"Kids your age, usually they hang around at the mall, where they get into trouble."

"Walter! That's not invariably true."

"I drive the bus, I see what I see."

"Some kids, Walter, not all kids."

"They're only interested in two things, and need I tell you what they are?"

"Don't say it, Walter. Not this morning, not now."

"Drugs and sex. Oh, and let's not forget about getting on the bus without paying, that's something they like to try."

"Then that's three things they're interested in, not two," said Rowena.

"This coffee's good," he said, reaching to the side and taking Rowena by the arm, "and my advice is to go to a movie tonight, little Miss Math, Miss Algebra, you can count your numbers real fine but living where you live, I don't know what you do there for fun, so go to a movie, any movie. When was the last time you saw one anyway? You know, a film from Hollywood? They pass light through it, it projects on a screen?"

"Walter."

"We show movies all the time in the Orange Lodge," Rowena said, "once a month at least."

"Once a month? That's not all the time. And the Orange Lodge? My dear, I've seen that place and it's not the same. I mean in a theater, a real honest-to-God theatre, with seats made for movies. Seats you don't stack in the corner after."

"I guess," said Rowena, "then, that would be the last time I was here."

She turned to her aunt.

"Remember, *A Hundred and One Dalmatians?*"

"Oh do I remember, we went together in the afternoon, and walked all the way home."

"You could ride the bus with me today if you want, you could see the whole city that way. Well, Mount Pearl. Ride shotgun."

He pulled the napkin from his chin.

"Why in the world would Rowena want to ride a bus all day?" her aunt asked.

"To see the city. Simple as that. No better way. It's modern here, it's not tumbledown, there's roads, there's a vibrant community with jobs and a future. In other words, it's not Bell Harbour, it's not full of government make-work projects. I could go on and on, why ride the bus. You, Rowena, you've never seen anything like this city in your life."

There was silence around the table. Rowena put her toast down on her plate. Her aunt leaned over and turned on the radio and they waited for it to warm up.

"Just telling it like it is," he said.

"It's true," said Rowena, "I never have seen a city like this. But actually, Uncle, we do have a road at home."

"You do? Where does it go?"

The truth was that the road at home went almost nowhere and to get anywhere near the TransCanada you had to drive through hundreds of miles of wilderness. The other truth was that that road had just been built. It was maybe two years old.

"It goes to Bishop's Falls. It's the start of a road. It's not paved yet."

"Okay you have a road of sorts, but my offer still stands."

He stood up.

"I think," said Rowena, "I'll just walk around town a bit and get my bearings, go down to the harbour. There's plenty for me to see without the bus, though thanks, Uncle, thanks anyway."

He sat back down and looked at his watch.

"I'm in a bit of a hurry, but my bus, you know it always waits for me so what the hell, listen: I can't tell you how lucky we are, my dear niece, that we live here in St. John's. That we're here, where there's movies, doctors, health care, transportation. Why without St. John's your own aunt sitting there would have bled to death."

"Walter, that's not true."

"Sure it's true, look at her, Rowena, she had her appendix out and they couldn't stop the bleeding."

"I'm fine," her aunt said looking back at Rowena and rolling her eyes.

"Sure, roll your eyes, but Missy, you should know she would have died without the doctors being right here. Though sometimes, what with the Bingo for fundraising and orphans and cripples and God knows what else, all the money she and her friends throw out the window, I wonder whether I should care if they saved her or not. Sometimes it gives me pause. Like now."

"Oh Uncle, that's a terrible thing to say."

"How long are you going to be here, Rowena?"

"Two days, today and tomorrow. I'm sorry, Uncle, I shouldn't have said anything."

He moved towards the coat rack in the corner.

"Well, two days is long enough, and I know where you get that lip of yours, it's from your mother. She's way too easy, she's lost control over her entire brood. The wolf pack. God knows what you'll get into here."

He rummaged in the refrigerator and pulled out a lunch bag.

"Whatever it is I want no part of it. Forget the bus. Do whatever you want, it's the modern way."

He put on his bus-driving jacket.

"That's a real nice uniform, Uncle, we don't have those at home, anything semi-official like that. Just ordinary clothes. No buses either for the nonexistent roads."

"What are you saying to me?"

"Nothing. Sorry, I take it back."

"Sorry? I hope you're sorry."

"Stop it you two!" said her aunt.

He bent down and kissed his wife on the forehead and went out the door.

"Oh Rowena, he's not like that most of the time, he gets in a mood, he goes off, he hates Bingo for some reason and the rest of it comes from there, he didn't mean what he said."

"Auntie, I'm sorry, Father warned me."

"He did?"

"He told me not to say anything, like I just did. I'm sorry. At home, we just laugh about things like this. Bingo, everybody goes to Bingo."

"Oh, poor Walter, poor me, I don't know..."

Music stopped on the radio and the weather report predicted rain in the late afternoon.

"They're usually wrong, Rowena, but take an umbrella, there's an extra one in the closet."

For a minute they sat and listened together as the regular programming resumed, and the music started again.

"He's a real good bus driver," her aunt said.

"I know, I'm sure he is."

"Not one accident in fifteen years."

They cleared the table and washed the dishes. Then they went their separate ways, her aunt to work at the Grace Hospital—"Come see me later, I'll be at the gift shop all day, take your raincoat"—and Rowena walked down Prescott Street. On Water Street, buses went by her in both directions, no Uncle at the wheel. No Mount Pearl, not there.

At the harbour, the ships were bigger but they still moved through the water in the same way as the boats at home. Nothing different. They pulled up to the wharf in the same way too—well, more carefully because this wharf was solid concrete, nobody could ever break it up or get underneath it. The ropes, the hawsers were the same but thicker, snaking over the sides, being pulled tight. The sky, the gulls, the lap of water was the same. Well, not quite, the water here was dirtier, browner, near-opaque. Still.

She should never have said anything at breakfast. That was a big mistake—not that she would have called it *lip* but it was rebellious, smart-alecky, everything she wasn't supposed to be. Real nice uniform? She'd have to tell her mother and her mother would say to her, "Rowena! How could you? Write a letter now and apologize!"

So what to do? She walked and walked. She walked along Harbour Drive and Duckworth Street to the base of Signal Hill. She walked up Quidi Vidi Road. She walked around a large lake also called Quidi Vidi. She walked towards the university but stopped at the library, at the Arts and Culture Centre. There she sat and leafed through a magazine for half an hour, not reading the words. She felt a slight pressure on her chest, like an elephant's foot, delicately applied. Strange that, but a deep breath and it was gone. Then, nearby, she bought a sandwich in a building full of students who were a few years older than she was. Nobody said anything to her or looked at her. She did not exist for them, she was too young to be noticed.

By then it was afternoon and there was nowhere else to go but back downtown. She doubted anybody had ever walked so aimlessly, and for so long, before. Eventually she stood beneath the shadow of the Roman Catholic Basilica and wondered if, under the circumstances, she should cross herself, what effect that would have on what was to follow. But she didn't even know how to do it, technically—how to cross herself—whether she should move her hand from left to right, or from right to left, and up and down, or down and up. So she didn't try. She moved on, taking a shortcut down a street called Garrison Hill. The painted houses were lopsided, built on just one side of the road. On Duckworth Street again, she needed to pass some more time so she listened to records in a record store. Outside, a mist was in the air now but it was still dry enough to sit and rest by the War Memorial.

She was hungry but the principal's wife had told her not to eat after lunch. She thought back to the Basilica and moved her hand tentatively from left to right across her chest, then back the other way. Maybe that was it.

Fat bees bumbled by her in the air. There must be a hive nearby, maybe in a tree. She looked at the cars of the city and then out through the Narrows to the Atlantic. It reminded her of home in an inexact way because there, on the left side of the Narrows were small wooden houses, even some stages and flakes on wooden supports over the shore, and then the open ocean was reaching up, up, its waves, then slipping back down the shore rocks.

By her Timex, only four o'clock. The pressure feeling was back on her chest.

She rose to her feet and went east to Battery Road. There she turned to her right at a convenience store that looked nothing like theirs at home. This one had bars on the door. A clamour of metal came from the shipping below, loading something aboard. She passed a large house hidden in trees, a lone black chicken pecking by a fence. Then the road dipped and the houses became smaller and smaller and some of them looked like they were nailed or velcroed to the side of the cliff. So yes, this was more like it, like Bell Harbour, she could hear the slow repetition of waves on rock, also familiar, and here the pavement eventually stopped and turned to trodden grass, as it did at home.

How had it come to this?

She passed an offshore rock with a signal buoy drilled into it, then concrete bunkers from the war. *Fuck you*, one of them said to her in graffiti.

That's how.

Blueberry bushes were everywhere, flowering, and the path clung to the side of a cliff. Here was a chain to hold onto, drilled into rock. She climbed higher and higher until she overlooked the ocean and distant headlands and she figured that Iron Skull must be even higher than where she stood now, it had to be, but it was hard to compare because the view of the ocean to the east was so much wider here. No islands below. It goes all the way to Ireland, the ocean. The nuns from the book could be looking her way now. Waves were hitting like they were mad, hundreds of feet below her, one low boom after another. A grey light shifted on the choppy sea.

She had no idea what the principal's wife was doing.

She clambered to the top of the hill over rocks and bushes to the tower, to the parking lot. Eight or ten cars there and by then it was nearly six, her time was coming closer. She was tired, she must have walked twenty miles. She rested for a while on the stone wall that overlooked the sea. Storm clouds but no storm. She crossed thirty yards to the city side, her raincoat and sweater tied around her waist. A cooler breeze there. Across the Narrows was a lighthouse and above that, from what she could see, was wilderness.

So Uncle, you're not living that far from nowhere yourself. Here in your bus, your civilization not much more then skin deep.

She took the road down, easier than the way she came up. Cars went by her, then a tourist bus. One of the cars offered her a ride but "No, I'm out for the walk," she said, "I'm doing fine, I'm okay."

Thus she ended up back where she started, at the War Memorial. She put her sweater back on. Luckily, so far, the rain was holding off. She thought about Sunday School and the Basilica and how they sang, in church when she was small, *If God so loves the little birds, I know He loves me too.*

Funny, singing that song, whispering it to herself, slowly tapping her foot on the broken pavement, how she took solace from it though she believed not a word.

THAT SAME afternoon, the principal's wife had walked from Gower Street to Quidi Vidi Road with her raincoat over her arm and an umbrella in case the sky opened up. There was an electric-ozone smell in the air, as though lightning were hovering overhead, clouds of cumulonimbus piling up slowly over the southside hills.

She took a passageway down the right side of a house. A hedge, a small tree obscuring the side entrance. In the shade, below the darkening sky, she could just read the small brass sign no larger than a business card, affixed at eye-level on the door: *Naomi Poole, Psychiatry.*

So here she was. She pushed on the door and went in and there was a waiting room, empty, a hand-printed sign on the inner door saying *Quiet, we're in session, sit and wait, thank you.* So she hung up her coat on one of the line of hooks—a windbreaker already there—and sat down in the light from the window. No voices, no footsteps. There were a few magazines on a low coffee table and a loose piece of paper on the floor, which she bent down to pick up.

Dear Dr. Poole,

Thank you for agreeing to see Stanley in consultation. As we mentioned, briefly, on the phone, he is a student here at Brother Rice, presently in Grade 12. One week ago, on November 18 he was rescued from drowning in George's Pond, on the west face of Signal Hill. He had fallen through the ice and it was only by chance that he was saved.

The principal's wife stopped. She shouldn't be reading this. It was private, something fallen from a chart or an envelope. Let's see, it was dated two years ago. But, in the stillness of the waiting room, hearing only her own heartbeat and already on edge, the easy distraction this letter offered was too much to resist, so she continued.

I have attached the newspaper clipping, although I know you've already seen it. Our concern here, at the school, is that he may have attempted to take his own life in this bizarre fashion. If so, he nearly succeeded in doing so. Hence this referral to you.

Some background: He lives in a foster home on Campbell Avenue with five other children. This is apparently his fourth placement since birth. His mother was unable to care for him— we don't know why—but, from the records, he lived the first six years of his life in the Battery under the impression that he had been adopted, when in fact he had not. Since then he has moved from placement to placement. This instability is not because of shortcomings of his own (to the contrary, he has invariably been described as friendly and attentive, as he has been since entering our school) but the system, as you know, is not perfect so he's been bounced from pillar to post. Not sure how meaningful this is.

You'll like him; we all do. Thanks again for taking him on with such little notice.

There must be another page, a page not here, with a signature, a closing, but she could see nothing else on the table or the floor and that was good, she was feeling guilty already for reading it.

That said, Stanley, whoever you are, I hope it worked out for you.

So, this is what she does, Dr. Poole, this is a glimpse of it. A shred. Compared to what she herself does, at home, day in and day out…what exactly does she do? Make the bed, wash the dishes—not many of those with just the two of them— sweep the linoleum, watch her reflection grow older in the window-glass. Beyond the window-glass the sea which from that distance was usually characterless. She wasn't educated for the great things, as her friend the doctor was. But they'd hit it off right away when they met the first time because they believed, didn't they, in the same things. They were equals philosophically, if that's the right word. Mind you the doctor actually got to practice what she preached because she had the education, the training, she didn't just have what she had, herself, vague yearnings. The education, the degrees, they'd given the doctor the stamp of approval.

The inner door then opened and there she was, Dr. Poole with a young man, ushering him out. He smiled and the smile moved from the doctor to include her, still sitting there.

"Till next time," the doctor was saying.

And the principal's wife wondered if this was the boy, from the letter.

"Thank you, Dr. Poole," and he acknowledged the principal's wife too, again, with a little bow from his waist as though he were a courtier from long ago, half-jesting with her, half-acknowledging that, by their mutual presence in this unusual and obviously therapeutic place, they shared something. A vulnerability most likely, so she nodded back to him.

Then he was gone and the two of them hugged and she gave the doctor the loose piece of paper, the one from the floor.

"I found this, fallen here," she said.

"This?"

"I didn't read it."

"That was careless of me. I guess I had the file when I answered the door. Thanks."

"Actually I did read it. I couldn't help myself, I read it."

"You did?"

"It took my mind off things. I guess that was him?"

"Yes, I guess I can say that, that was him. Confirmed. But we have our own problems, come on in. Problem, I mean."

It was warmer inside. She must have turned the heat up against the rain, expected. There were two armchairs more or less facing each other, and they each took one. The principal's wife spun in hers, back and forth, not all the way around but she wasn't spinning out of happiness.

"I have to tell you, I'm not happy with my projected role in this, with our plan. Our tentative plan," the doctor said.

"I don't like it either," said the principal's wife, "but she's determined to get it done, come hell or high water. What was I to do? She's done a lot of reading, what she could find anyway, what was available to her down home. She's definitive, she's made up her mind."

"That doesn't mean it's up to us. There's the official route, the abortion committee at the hospital."

"Oh come on, you know how that works, it doesn't work at all."

"I'm not so sure of that. Really, how you described it, it was a crime, a rape. I think they might go for that."

"They never have before."

"True enough."

"Dilly-dally, dilly-dally, they wait, they dither on purpose, and then it's too late."

At the far end of the room was a window, then the street. Sheer curtains half-open. A grandfather clock ticked. Cars went by, a walker. Books lined the wall behind the doctor, from floor to ceiling.

"She's eight weeks."

"That's the okay part but I don't like it."

"Of course you don't like it, nobody likes it."

"I'm wavering, in case you can't tell."

"I can tell, I understand, I feel the same way but having done it once, and the circumstances are much the same—not quite as bad I admit—but anyway, either we have our principles or we don't. I remember what you said back at Boxey: *this is what we have these skills for.* That's what you said. You never regretted it, that time."

"No. But that was Boxey. And skills you say? Skills I haven't used in a long time. Ten years. They're no longer skills, they've gone to rust."

"Oh I don't think so."

"I'll put the kettle on, that's an easy thing to do. Any fool can do that," the doctor said.

She went through another door into the inner house but was back in a minute.

"Here's my problem, or part of it. Boxey was a long time ago, when I was working as a real doctor. Real, like not a psychiatrist. Technically my hand was in and I was more idealistic to boot and I didn't have any sense of caution. I was not yet doing this"—she waved her hand in a circle at her desk and the wall of books—"and I had more faith, if you could call it that—I guess you can't really call it that but I'll call it that anyway— faith in what I believed. It's not so certain to me now. I see six or seven sides to every square, every circle. Not only that, forgetting whatever principles we had and whatever ideology, the whole fabric of the community back then was on our side—or would have been had they known about it—which I'm sure is not the case here, because here, today, in St. John's, let me tell you it's different. Here we would be pariahs."

"Oh I don't think so."

"You don't live here. Who knows about this, how many people?"

"About Rowena? No one, just her mother. And, technically, if I remember right, you said a pregnancy at eight weeks is easy, straightforward."

"She's healthy?"

"Oh yes, she's healthy, she's fine. I'm not trying to force your hand, I wouldn't do that."

"You are forcing my hand. Of course you are."

The kettle was whistling now. The doctor excused herself and the principal's wife rose and went to the wall of books and ran her hand along the spines. Carl Jung. Thomas Szasz. Names she'd heard of but hadn't read. The other names she didn't know at all.

"Sugar, milk?"

"Both thanks. She's adamant, Naomi, she actually said she'd go and do it herself if it came to that. I'm not so sure she would, of course, or how, but that's something else she's taken, I gather, from books."

"God. She reads too much then. What's her name again?"

"Rowena, Row Savoury."

"So, one of them, the Savourys. She's sixteen? I didn't deliver her then, that was before my time."

An hour passed and the grandfather clock chimed six o'clock and the principal's wife finally said goodbye and left. The hashing of the situation was over. Outside, the rain and the lightning had never materialized. She walked down Quidi Vidi Road, tapping her umbrella like a cane. With each step she swung and tapped as though she could be blind, which in a way she was because she'd forgotten about the bleeding disorder that ran in Rowena's family, forgotten about the graveyard full of young women, forgotten because the disease had "worked itself out," because Rowena's mother had been fine through childbirth, because the principal's wife was too tired and unsure of herself now to be aware of the possibility of a tragedy still to be played out. In other words, despite her intelligence and compassion and conviction, despite the long hours at home watching the meadow and the sea and her face reflected in the window and the wildflowers bent to right angles outside in the wind and the school painted white—where rational thought theoretically prevailed—this afternoon, in St. John's, she wasn't thinking straight at all.

BACK AT the office, Dr. Poole was dealing with a familiar feeling. She was somewhere she didn't want to be. She was in over her head. But she'd have to deal with that and do her best and the game would go on. It had its own momentum. Her old friend was right, you either had ideals or you didn't and actions always spoke louder than words so now wasn't the time to back off. Stand up, be counted. She couldn't wish the sixteen-year-old girl to go away, she was too real, she was here and needed help.

The fallen letter from the Catholic School Board was still sitting in front of her. She shouldn't have dropped it. Too much of a hurry. Nor should her friend have read it when she picked it up.

She opened the file, the name STANLEY GRANT neatly written on the tab in dark ink. She reinserted the lost piece of paper, her carelessness, clipping it to the top page of her handwritten notes, the first session. Neatly organized, she was certainly that. Psychiatry was no easier than surgery, her teachers had told her, lives were on the line in both fields. But that was not quite true, the comparison. In surgery there was visible bleeding, cause and effect jumped out and you had to be quick, direct, merciless even for the best results. Whereas in psychiatry, it was like playing with plasticine, a lot of massaging and moulding required. Gentle is the byword. Even then, who knows what would happen. Tenderness was no guarantee.

Boxey. The things we're trained to do. We don't want to do them, given a choice we would not, but we go ahead and do it anyway because no one else will. Then we forget it, we repress it, we amnese it (is that a word?) we put it away until something like this comes up, and then we remember.

She shuffled through the earlier notes, remembering how the young man came to her, neatly dressed in a shirt and tie and smiling despite the fact he'd nearly drowned the week before. Spotted up on Signal Hill, on George's Pond, jumping up and down on the ice one afternoon in late November. Jumping up and down until he went through and disappeared. But there was a dogwalker who saw it happen and that was the lucky part because the dogwalker then ran across the intervening thirty yards of rock and snow and scrub-grass with his Black Lab and in went the dog—trained just for this— under the ice, like a submarine, gone, and out he came thirty seconds later with Stanley Grant, the boy, hanging onto his neck. She had this from the newspaper. The boy wasn't able to tell her, or had so far chosen not to tell her, why he'd done what he did. Testing the strength of the ice or of me, I don't know which, both maybe, but when the dog came it was like a visitation from the underworld and he was so persuasive, the dog, he had his teeth on my collar, Stanley told her, so I grabbed on. More or less, that's all he said, even now.

The photograph she'd saved from the newspaper was tucked in there, under the referral letter. Stan, not identified by name in the paper, flanked by his two rescuers, all three smiling like nothing had happened. Well, the dog wasn't smiling but it looked as happy as a dog could look, it was certainly pleased with itself, you could tell. The whole scene looked posed, like a family photograph rather than the record of a near tragedy. They were all soaking wet and the boy had a blanket around his shoulders and in the background was a thin covering of snow, a hump of bare rock, probably a grey sky. *Signal Hill Drama* was the headline. It turned out—as the letter from the Board had said—that he'd been fostered here, there and everywhere and was essentially alone in the world. Hence the irony of the rescue photograph, emanating as it did an illusory happiness, a fiction. She'd pointed this out to him, that he was smiling happily in the picture, as she circled cautiously around him that first day, avoiding direct questions. The November sun came through the window. It was unseasonably warm out there, judging from the short sleeves on the passersby outside the window, so she took a chance. She suggested they walk up the hill together, to George's Pond itself, a fifteen minute walk during which they both took off their jackets and slung them over their shoulders. They looked a casual pair. The snow and the ice from the newspaper photograph had long since melted—it could have been spring instead of fall—and she asked him if everything was okay at Brother Rice and apparently it was. He said there were no skeletons falling out of closets there, nothing like that but he knew what she meant. The brothers, the priests? Nothing like that. He said that something had just come over him, that he was not acting out of conscious volition. He used words like that, *volition*, as though he'd spent a lot of time with a dictionary.

Rowena. Books for her too. Books could be a problem

though she loved them herself. They could be the quickening, the end of innocence.

Home was okay too, he said, he was used to his status as fostered, he knew nothing else, his brothers and sisters from all over now ranged from four to fourteen. He was the oldest.

That first day, when they got to the pond of his near-drowning, the water was ravelled by wind and populated by four or five cheerful ducks instead of flat ice and he said something like, well here we are, here's the scene of the crime, hard to believe, I never thought I'd be standing here with a psychiatrist, and it was like Bell Harbour for her all over again, a *déjà vu*, talking to patients outside, to patients who became friends, chatting by the roadside or on the wharf or at the store, brushing hair from her eyes, shading them from the sun as she did that day with this young man who was certainly troubled despite his mask of, mostly, cheerful insouciance. A woman passed them going uphill with a small brown dog on a leash. Lucky, he said, it wasn't that dog going by when I went under, that would have been the end of me. Actually, the ice had felt solid to him, he felt it through his feet, from the shoreline out, like slate, like a parquet floor. He'd been surprised when it happened, when it gave way. He spoke to her with a maturity beyond his years, with none of the usual hesitations and space-fillers she heard from teenagers. He said he was actually happy now, that it was nice being there with her, even though she was what she was, a professional caregiver.

So their relationship had started out nicely, she felt, on the right foot. They'd broken the ice (so to speak, he laughed at that) and since then he'd moved on with his life, graduated from high school with decent marks, went into dental hygiene—dental hygiene? strange choice but it was practical, he figured, he'd end up with something useful to do, sort of like a trade without the muscle work, like welding in miniature, and he'd get a plaque with his name on it, and could make a living. He was actually more interested in Egyptology, he confessed, but let's be practical, Doctor, I'd have to go to the mainland for that and that's something I could never afford to do, no way. I'm not the scholarship type. Not academic in the sense of studying and marks. Why Egyptology, she'd asked. Good question. He'd seen pictures in a magazine and those Egyptians, they knew how to live and die and they had pyramids where the same air sat for centuries. Trapped molecules. He could go for that, the stillness, but also he liked Egypt for other reasons. They valued children, he could see that from the drawings, how children had simple toys, how they got along with animals. Most sessions, once or twice, up would come the Ancient Egyptians and how they lived. It was a motif for Stanley Grant. Or a way to divert her attention from him, from the real problem.

She picked up the chart, now intact, and filed it away in the cabinet behind the desk.

That day, the sun had gone down fast. They'd had to put their jackets on for the chill. They headed back down at a good clip and went their separate ways at the bottom of the hill.

Last session, she'd asked him if he wanted to stop coming but he'd said no, not yet, he wasn't ready for total independence, not really, not quite yet if she didn't mind. He was resistant to the leaving part. Obviously not something he wanted to do. And it was okay with her to keep it going. He seemed open to her but was he really? Still an enigma.

He and this girl, this Rowena Savoury. Passions of the young beggared those of adults. Trouble ahead. She remembered it herself, kids who knew everything and nothing at the same time, their sadness and hers overwhelming.

"FUNNY TO think of her there in St. John's alone," Rowena's father said, "well, not alone, but not here with us. With your sister who hardly knows her, and that man."

Dark clouds hovered over Iron Skull, which they could see

straight out from the kitchen table, and the heat was unusual. The air was still. *Sultry* was not a word often used in Bell Harbour but she went ahead and used it.

"It's sultry today, isn't it," Rowena's mother said.

"Sultry? Sweaty, yes. I wonder if they've locked horns yet."

"Who?"

"Walter, that unhappy man, and Row."

"It might happen, I admit."

"Anyway she's not here and it's not the same without her."

"Someday we'll have to get used to that."

"I know. Remember Back Cove?"

Parents when alone discuss their children. That's what they do. Rowena's mother and father could hardly ever talk about Rowena without one of them bringing up Back Cove, because Back Cove summed up Rowena for them, what she was like then, at eight years old, and she hadn't changed a lot since.

"She scared us that time."

"She sure did."

That's all they had to say. They didn't have to spell it out for each other. All they had to do was look out the window with an unseeing gaze, the view no longer there, and remember how she didn't get home that day from school, when she was just in grade three, and how they wondered where she was, without concern until five o'clock, but then the first bit of worry came at them and they walked up to the schoolyard but she wasn't there either, the grassy yard was empty, swings hanging there, the teeter-totter forlorn. They took separate routes back home, calling for her all the way, covering their bases, knocking on the doors of her friends and her friends were all home safe and sound and accounted for but they knew nothing about Rowena. They hadn't seen her. By six it was full-out panic mode, they had the whole town roused and out looking, combing the hills as far as the trees and the forest beyond, through the meadow, the cemetery, all around the school again. You see any strange cars? No. Boats up and down the shoreline, and two of their friends set out for the barasway, past the dump where once or twice there'd been a bear. Dozens of people were now looking for her, all shouting the same thing. *Rowena. Rowena.* They rang the school bell and the church bell. Under other circumstances, charming. The Legion emptied. By seven o'clock still nothing, by eight the uncaring sun was well behind the hills, darkling-time, treetops silhouetted against a fading pink-yellow slash and there were no more shadows, just the soft ground where every hump and growth looked alive and ominous, and nothing, still nothing, no sign of her until there she was, a small dot moving down on the upper road from St. Jacques where Hilda Cluett was the first to spot her. Ran up to her and picked her up right off, I did, Hilda said to them all pleased with herself, and where have you been, my dear, my dear Rowena Savoury, you've got the whole town turned upside down, we're tearing out our hair for you, where have you been? Back Cove, Rowena said cheerfully, holding up a torn topographical map she'd found outside the school, apparently half under the steps and half out. I was going to Back Cove, here, it's on the map, and it didn't seem like all that far but it was. The girl's face was bleeding in rivulets from black flies and her arms and legs were scratched like she'd been wrestling with large cats. I'm thirsty, she said. But otherwise she was fine. So before Hilda Cluett walked her home, she gave her a long drink of water from the garden hose. Taste good? Yes, thanks, Mrs. Cluett, thank you. You little prodigal you, Hilda Cluett said, wiping the girl's face with a washcloth, you can't go home looking like this. It turned out that finding the map, reading it, exploring, going down the steep heavily wooded hill to Back Cove was easy enough but the return was much harder, the trees had grown in so tight down there and there was no path, she must have lucked her way down to make it in the first place but coming back up it was like a wall of needles or knives in her face, she had to pick her way squeezing through the low branches, branches tearing at her. But she knew where she was, she said, she just kept the noise of the ocean to her back and aimed upwards, knowing she'd hit the road sometime because she had the map and there's the road. See?

"She's independent, always has been," her father said.

"I'm not so sure of that, not in everything," her mother said.

"She'll find St. John's interesting, I think, compared to here. I don't suppose she'll want to live here forever."

That was a given for the children in the town. They'd leave and go away, somewhere else.

"We don't have to think about that now," Rowena's mother said, "though she's growing up fast. Real fast."

"Girls her age in town, I guess they're going out with boys."

"That happens everywhere," her mother said, and she let the moment pass, fanning herself in the sultry heat, almost but not quite telling him the reason Rowena was in St. John's, because that would drive him crazy and he wouldn't wait for the next boat, he'd try to go himself, borrow a speedboat or something and try to head across Fortune Bay, which was not wise. The radio had storm warnings, the marine forecast said stay at home, the weather was turning. She couldn't muster the courage to tell him the truth, yet.

They themselves never talked about sex. They went ahead and did it, sure they did, and they knew what they were doing but then they moved on and did something else.

THE COOL mist finally drove Rowena from the War Memorial to a little tea-shop on Water Street, but the staff closed it down at nine. Daylight was starting to fade. She headed slowly back up the hill on a strange street, tired, feeling all the walking she'd done. She thought of trying to phone her mother but she only had three dimes and at the phone booth on Duckworth, someone had broken the door half-off.

Forget it. She'd be home tomorrow night and that would have to do.

The mist was fog now, it was prickling her face but that was okay, she was used to it, it actually made her feel more comfortable, more at home, like she was looking out the Reach with nothing on her mind.

At 9:45, at the corner of Prescott and Gower, she met the principal's wife, as arranged.

"I think it'll be raining when we come back, that's my feeling," said the principal's wife.

She had her umbrella. She swung it like a cane or a sword, nervous circles in the air. No longer tapping with it, more energized now.

"How's your aunt, Row, and your uncle?"

"They're fine. They're not expecting me back till late."

"Good. You ready?"

"Ready."

"Let's go, but don't pay attention to where we're going."

"No?"

"I don't want you to know."

"I get it, I won't look."

But as they walked, Rowena could easily see that they passed the big hotel which wasn't far from the record store where she'd browsed earlier, and before that they passed the War Memorial and she could smell the faint odour of sewage that she now associated with proximity to the harbour.

"You can't see much in this fog but I know where we are," she said.

"You do? I hardly know myself."

"I was here already. It's Quidi Vidi Road. Who could forget a name like that?"

And in fact soon they were at a street sign that said the same, that very name—Quidi Vidi—though the fog was dense enough that they had to stop and peer upwards to read it.

"End of secrecy then," said the principal's wife.

"Is this going to hurt at all?"

"No."

"I'll never tell anybody."

"I know you won't. Anyway, no one's going to know."

Then it started to rain suddenly, as though it had been waiting in the wings. A cloudburst. The principal's wife opened her umbrella.

"Quick, tuck in here with me, Row. You want to change your mind?"

"No."

Rowena was bone-thin, next to nothing physically. Two Rowenas could have fit with her under the umbrella.

"I can still smell the harbour, even from here," Rowena said.

A few cars passed them going half-speed, crawling in the rain.

"You can change your mind anytime, Row. Most people would never go through with this."

"I know. Let's get it over with."

"We've done it before though, the doctor and I, you know that?"

"Mother told me."

She was holding tight to the principal's wife's arm now, gathered in by her.

"Just checking, Row, just making sure."

A hundred more yards up Quidi Vidi Road, then down the side of a darkened house where they knocked, and the door opened, and there they were, sitting together, three of them, the doctor in her chair straight across from her. There was a desk between them.

She knew her, this was the same doctor who'd given her the childhood needles, the doctor from the magazine article. Older now but the same, for sure.

"Dr. Poole," she said.

"I don't remember you, exactly, Rowena, but I know we've met before. Now here we are together again, but the circumstances, I gather, are very different."

"I know, I'm sorry."

Her hands were folded on her lap. She wasn't fidgeting.

"So, tell me, please, make it clear, tell me exactly what you want me to do for you."

"I'm pregnant, and I don't want to be."

"You know what you're asking?"

"Yes, I'm asking for an abortion."

"How far along are you?"

"Eight weeks."

"Do you have any reservations at all, any concerns?"

"No."

"There are ethical issues in this for some people, religious issues, moral issues..."

"I've already considered those."

"You don't mince words, for someone your age."

"I knew what you'd ask, I've thought about it. Though I didn't know it would be you. What happened, it was a mistake, and this is the only way it can be corrected. I know it's not easy for you."

"No, it's not. And some women will regret this later, having this done."

"Not me."

"Not many, actually," said the principal's wife.

The two older women looked at each other.

"Well then, decision made. Do you have a history of any medical problems?"

"No."

"Anything that runs in the family?"

"No."

"What we will do takes just five minutes but first you need to take these. It's called pre-medication."

She reached across the desk with two pills and the principal's wife, at her right side, handed Rowena a glass of water.

"One's for pain, the smaller one is a relaxant, a sedative."

"Pain?"

"Very little of that, five seconds. You probably won't even feel that."

Rowena swallowed the pills and they led her to a narrow stretcher-like bed behind a curtain. Maybe it wasn't a bed, maybe it was a table. It was firm, covered with a thin sheet, not much wider than her body. There was an antiseptic smell in the air.

She lay and looked up at the ceiling. No cracks in this one, not like the one at home.

She heard them talking, then a few metallic sounds like cutlery rattling and she was drifting away.

"I'm taking your clothes off, from the waist down."

She felt hands under her, her skirt, her underpants gone, the table or the bed swinging back and forth under her like a boat in a soft swell.

"A needle in the back of your left hand," someone said.

Iron Skull, the barasway, the wharf, the dog, the grass, her mother's voice.

"Rowena?"

Voices far away, hands close to her, touching her.

"Come down a bit. This way. Now, your legs."

Her legs were taken from her, up and out, her feet secured. Wrapped at the ankles? Then something cold slipped inside her and it was lights out, Rowena Savoury.

And the principal's wife was thinking and remembering, as the doctor proceeded, carefully, methodically, as best the doctor could—dilators and curette in hand—how they'd come to this point, here, tonight, where no sane woman would ever want to be. Remembering they were here because of men, careless men, men of legislature, men of government, men of authority, men of religion, men of wandering tribes on horseback, men everywhere, men on ships or in caravans, dories, men with knives and sulphuric acid and stones and men of harsh rectitude, of harems with concubines, men of principle, lawmaking men, and all of these men could go ahead and proselytize and argue about this forever, they could talk all night for a year while women remained silent but those men might as well tell the waves to stop breaking on the shore because not all women were listening to them, some were listening to themselves.

THEN ROWENA was awake again, coming out of it, a heaviness. She saw the doctor first, leaning over her, then the principal's wife, on the other side.

"Everything's fine, it's finished," said the doctor.

Rowena felt a patting on her left arm.

"Good, you were good, Row, everything was fine," said the principal's wife.

No pain, nothing. She was still on her back on the narrow table. Her legs were straight out, together, no longer where they were before.

"You'll need this pad," one or both of them said to her. It was hard to tell where voices came from. The room was shifting. Then she felt her waist lifted, her legs moved apart again, something firm and bulky pushed up between her thighs.

"Some bleeding still."

"That's normal."

"More than in Boxey."

"It's normal, nobody's the same. This is okay."

"Good."

"Rowena, soon you'll be able to sit up. Rowena?"

"I feel dizzy."

"That's normal, that's the medicine. It'll wear off."

Was it actually over, was it this easy, could it be this easy? Over and done with like this?

"That's it? That's all?"

"Yes, that's it. In five minutes we go home. Well, not home. Prescott Street."

"Thank you," said Rowena. Her head was beginning to

clear. She looked around to see the familiar bookshelves, and the two floor lamps on, turned low. Those she hadn't seen before. No sign of any instruments, nothing surgical, just her lying on this table in the middle of the living room. The two women not hovering, moving around her.

"We can leave?" she asked.

"Yes. As soon as you feel up to it."

"I feel up to it now."

"Wait. Wait five minutes."

So she lay for another five minutes on her back, feeling good, feeling very good, like she could be walking through air again, uncompromised, light-footed, in just a few minutes time.

"Okay, try to sit up now. No wait, we'll check the pad again."

"Some bleeding, some, a little bit. Still normal."

"Change it for the walk home?"

"Might as well, it's easier to do here."

The hands again at her waist, the bulk between her thighs.

"Okay, Rowena, let's give it a go."

She sat up, swung her feet over the side and jumped to the floor. No more spinning now.

"I feel good, I feel better than I have in a long time," she said.

No more boy from Grand Falls, no more of him.

"Go then," said the doctor.

And Rowena and the principal's wife stepped slowly from the living room to the waiting room, then into the rain coming down. The door closed behind them and they walked up the side of the house in the dark to the street. The principal's wife let the umbrella snap open.

"There, come in closer, Honey, good for you. Hold my arm. How do you feel?"

"Good."

But there was a wetness, undeniably so, a warm wetness

spreading down her, onto her thighs, maybe to her knees, the inner side of them, inside the jeans. The thickness of the pad stuck there was strange.

"I'm bleeding, I can feel it I'm pretty sure."

"That's normal she says, that's expected. Not for long. The sooner we get back, the better. Get you resting. Okay?"

They went towards the harbour where the fog had cleared because the rain had incorporated it, subsumed it, had become one with it, ushered it to the curbs and the sidewalks and the shining street. Small rivers were running down every curb to the harbour. But the visibility was still not good, the street-lights were muted by the downpour. No one else was out and about. Her feet, her ankles were already cold and wet from the rain. The burst of energy she'd felt when she jumped from the table was gone.

"Wait," Rowena said. Her legs were trembling.

"We can't stop here, Row, it's the middle of nowhere."

"How far?"

"Maybe a half-mile. You know, we walked it."

"Okay, sorry, let's go."

"Plymouth Street? I think we'll go this way, a short-cut."

Past the hotel, the girl was still holding the woman's arm but the rain if anything was picking up and it was impossible for them both to stay dry under the umbrella. The principal's wife held it out over Rowena, trying to protect her, cold rain running down her own neck and getting under her sweater, soaking her hair, her shoulders soaked too, but the girl seemed to be getting weaker rather than stronger by the time they got to the lights at Military Road.

"Not so far now, hang on."

"I don't remember this."

"Sure you do. Hang on, hold onto me tighter. Is the rain okay?"

"The rain? The rain's fine, I like the rain."

"You like it?"

"Sure."

She couldn't possibly like the rain, she wasn't making sense.

"What do you like?"

No answer.

The dark stains she could see on the front of Row's jeans, that's all they better be, rain. She looked at her own legs and they were much the same, maybe worse. Drops were hitting the asphalt so hard that they were bouncing back up, almost knee-high.

"This is our street, Rowena, this one here. Gower Street. See?"

"I think I should rest."

Now that made sense, good.

"Once we're across the lights. Come on, Row, it's green"

By the wall of the nearest building they took semi-shelter. Huddled together but they couldn't stay there like waifs, they had to move on. Then damned if Rowena didn't almost fall down. The principal's wife had to hold her up with two hands for a second and the umbrella splayed out to the side and twisted to the ground and she had to pin it down with her foot.

"There's something tight around my neck," the girl said.

"No, no, there's nothing there."

She bent down and recovered control of the umbrella.

"You sure?"

"I'm sure, I'm looking. Feel this, this is my hand and I'm feeling your neck and there's nothing there."

They either walked or stumbled and were only fifty yards from Prescott Street, almost to the principal's wife's boarding house, when the very first car they'd seen in the storm passed them, coming from behind. Then it pulled over to the curb in front of them.

"A police car, oh Jesus, this is all we need."

Rowena didn't respond.

"And he's getting out. Pull it together now darling, stand up straight."

The young man towered over them, asking them if they were okay, did they need a ride, the car was warm, they looked like they needed a ride. Outside was no place to be, not a night like this. Unusually solicitous.

"No, no thanks, Officer, we're fine, we're almost there."

Was he looking at them as though they'd done something wrong? Well of course they had done something wrong, hadn't they, they'd broken the law of the land even if the law itself was broken past repair, but there was no way he'd know that. Impossible.

"You're sure you're okay?"

"Absolutely sure. Look, we can see our place."

She would have pointed to it but Rowena was again hanging onto her, onto her left arm, and the umbrella still had a mind of its own, hard to control. Now it flailed in front of them. She was trying to ward off the worst of the rain but down it came nevertheless and still the damn policeman was curious, he didn't seem to want to leave. He turned a flashlight on Rowena, trying to get a better look at her. He bent down, asked her if she needed help.

"No," Rowena finally said, though you could barely hear it.

She pulled herself up then, Rowena did, summoned the strength from somewhere and let go of the principal's wife and that seemed to satisfy him, finally.

"Okay then, good night," and he was gone back to the cruiser and the cruiser was gone, pulled away, and gone was that particular danger.

"Nice policeman," Rowena said.

"Nice? Something we don't need right now. Good riddance to him."

And praise be the girl laughed and agreed, so maybe this was passing, whatever the weakness was. Sill the medication, nothing worse.

"Nice policeman," Rowena said again.

But she was touching her throat with her hand again. Even

though the principal's wife had reassured her, she felt something there, a tightening like a string or a necklace too small for her. A cord, someone pulling on it.

Then the principal's wife half-lifted and half–walked her through a river three or four feet wide coursing down the curb from higher up the hill.

"Here we are, Prescott."

The water came over her ankles. *Double soaker* they called it at home.

"Cold."

"It's the medication, Row, don't worry."

It was 11:50, later than they expected to be. And Christ Almighty the door to the aunt's house was locked. The principal's wife tried to turn the door knob, once, twice.

"Did they give you a key?"

"No."

"You told them you'd be late?"

"I guess."

So the principal's wife had no choice, she knocked on the door firmly and said she had to go, she really didn't want to be seen there.

"Listen, I'm going to run, I'll see you at noon down at the corner. For the taxi. You'll be fine. Rest. Take this, there's pads in here if you need them. The pills are for pain, you take two."

She handed her a small plastic bag, kissed her on the forehead and left, crossing the street, and as she did she was wondering if they'd made a serious mistake. She and the doctor. Something was amiss here, nothing like the last time.

But Rowena would be with her aunt, she wouldn't be alone, and the die was cast, the deed was done, it was over. She felt scrambled, close to distraught, but why should she feel that way? Turning theory into practice, not so easy. Had to be done. At the rooming house, she'd get to sleep. One last look back and there was a light going on over the door and Rowena was where she'd left her, leaning against the door jamb.

Row was shivering, trying not to. Then there was a blaze of light over the door and it opened. Her uncle, in his pyjamas, obviously waking up just for her and he wasn't pleased. He ran his fingers up over his face, unshaven, then both hands through his hair in a mocking gesture of disbelief.

"Out to all hours, I see."

"Sorry, Uncle."

"You made it just in time. After midnight, Rowena, it's not like back home, Rowena, this castle here, the moat's closed at midnight, the drawbridge is pulled up at midnight, slam the portcullis. Pumpkins stay out. Understand?"

Then he stepped back and shouted up the stairs, "Cinderella, she's home!"

"I'm sorry, Uncle."

Such an effort to stand straight and look at him. Pulling herself off the side of the doorway and stepping inside.

"Go to bed, you're leaving in the morning. The sooner the better."

He watched from below as she made the hard climb up the stairs and he heard her walking down the hallway and locking herself right away in the bathroom.

Drugs or alcohol, this princess, she's no different.

She undressed and there was blood on her jeans, it was the wharf and the barasway all over again but more this time. The pad they'd put on her was soaked through. She changed it which left her, one-two-three, three of them left and surely that would be enough. Please. She stuffed the old one into the plastic bag and, holding the package tight under her arm, she unlocked the door and went back down the hall. Her aunt had turned the bed down. The low nightlight was on, plugged into the wall. She was way too tired, too dizzy to read. She lay down and pulled the sheet and blankets up to her chin, then over her head. She turned to her side. A towel, she should have one to put under herself. She huddled, shivering, still the cold.

If her mother were here.

Then she must have fallen asleep because she jerked awake and the ceiling was on the move, coming closer and drawing away again like it was breathing and her tongue was dry and again she felt, between her thighs, the stickiness. Distant rain was drumming on the roof. Somehow she'd have to haul herself back to the bathroom and she managed it, locking the door, *click*, changing the pad, washing the blood from her hands, from her fingertips, from the washcloth, hiding the evidence. Pink the streams down the drain. Into the hall again past the silence of the other bedroom and her aunt and her uncle sleeping and her mother a hundred miles away. Closing her door, waiting please for it to stop.

Her uncle almost made it back to sleep after she came home but damn it, he never quite drifted off. He checked the bedside clock, turned left and right and stayed awake for what felt like three hours but wasn't. He heard her make another trip to the bathroom. Then he said fuck this to himself and to the sleeping body of his wife and went to the bathroom himself to look around. Everything was good. No smell of booze and he was good at that, smelling liquor or beer, the breeze of it on the drunks who got onto the bus, smiling and holding on. So she must have taken something else, a chemical. Yes, there was something in the air not quite right.

He came back and nudged his wife with his elbow, gently. Her back was to him. She always slept soundly because she was guilt-free, she said, and she smiled when she said that, celebrating the innocence of her long, pure nights.

"Hey."

No response. She could wake up though, all he had to do was whisper, usually.

"Hey wakee-wakee," he said a little louder,.

He gave her a push in the back, enough she'd have to feel it for sure, and this time, yes, she rolled his way, her arm bent back over her head.

"You awake? Your sweetheart's home."

"Under the B, twenty-seven."

She was talking in her sleep, playing Bingo, no idea what she was saying.

"Beth! Listen to me!"

"Walter, what time is it?"

"One, two in the morning. Something like that. She came home an hour ago."

"Rowena? Good."

"But Beth, listen!"

He poked her side again.

"She came home late, big surprise, and now she's flushing the toilet every fifteen minutes and who can sleep through that?"

"Flushing the toilet? What do you mean?"

"Here she goes again, listen for yourself."

They heard the girl open the door from her bedroom and step down the hall, the squeak of the boards.

"Third or fourth time," he said.

"What do you mean?"

"I mean this is the third time or the fourth time your little visitor has been up already, which makes it impossible for me to get sleep."

The bathroom door closed, water ran from the tap, the toilet flushed with a swoosh and then there was a prolonged silence before her footsteps again, slowly, trying to be quiet no doubt, cast a shadow under their door going back down the hall.

"And, there's a funny smell in the bathroom too."

His wife sat up.

"Maybe she's sick, Walter."

"Sick? She's sick? I'm going to be a basket case in the morning. That's who's going to be sick."

Now both of them were fully awake and it couldn't have been ten minutes before they heard her again, the footsteps, the shadow under the door, the tap, the flush, the pause, the return trip, the creak in the boards and the different creak of the mattress from the bed in the front room, and then the kind of stillness that meant no one could possibly sleep in that stillness, because they were waiting for the silence to crack open again.

"I'm her mother now, right? Walter?"

"It's what you always wanted. If this is what parenting is like, I guess we've been lucky."

"I'm not so sure of that, how lucky we've been in that regard."

She sat up and felt the floor with her feet, for her discarded dressing gown. She stood up, put it on, put her feet into slippers and went down the hall to the bathroom.

He was right, there was something in the air, a cloying.

She looked around and nothing was amiss. She sat on the toilet to think and there it was, on the side of the sink facing her, a fingerprint, actually two of them and maybe a hand-smear as well and it was blood, no mistaking it, and what in the world did that mean?

Down the hall she went to Rowena's room. She carefully opened the door, just a crack.

"Row?"

The girl was there all right, under the covers.

"Rowena, are you okay?"

No answer, no movement. She opened the door enough to squeeze into the room.

"Row, it's me."

And the girl rolled her way in the bed and said, "Mommy, I don't know, I just don't know."

Her aunt stood over her. The girl spoke again, her eyes staring up at her directly, and she called her *Mommy* for a second time.

"Walter! Walter, come right away!"

And Walter came right away and leaned on the doorway,

irritated, and it was then he heard Rowena say what he later told the police she said: *"Mommy, I'm sorry, the abortion, there's something gone wrong with me."*

"Did I hear that right?"

"No, you did not hear that right."

His wife was sitting on the bed now, her arm over the girl.

"She's delirious, she thinks I'm her mother for God's sake, she doesn't know what she's saying. Call the ambulance, Walter, call right now. There's something wrong with her."

"Now? In the middle of the night?"

"Rowena it's me, your Auntie."

She turned towards her husband again.

"Walter! Call the ambulance!"

"Yes, dear. Right away, dear. Whatever you say, dear."

He went downstairs. He was moving pretty quickly, for him, and she heard his voice on the phone, the urgency in it.

"Row, honey, we've called the ambulance. Excuse me, sweetheart, I need to look."

She pulled the covers down slowly until she saw the blood at the girl's waist pooling there and Walter's footsteps were coming back up the stairs so she pulled the covers back up to hide what she'd seen, bent down to her again, held her tight through the covers, through the blankets, the sheet and the bleeding.

"I called them," Walter said from the doorway, "I called them but not the ambulance, I called the police."

Row by then was unconscious so she never saw her aunt bending over her, crying. Nor did she hear her uncle cursing and moving up and down the stairs in frustration and, five minutes later, she was unable to hear the police car pulling up outside, the heavier footsteps of the young policeman, how he spoke to her, bending over her in the same pose that had been struck by her aunt, how concerned he appeared to be, how water fell from his raingear to her face, nor was she aware of the siren coming their way from Gower Street and the subsequent clattering of the ambulance attendants up the stairs and the ride hell-bent to hospital where doctors came running to do what they could.

What could they do? They poured blood into her as though she were an empty vessel, four units, five units, forcing them into her under pressure, trying to bring her back where she belonged. They called the youngest doctors in to watch, pulled them out of their beds and off the wards and out of the cafeteria bleary-eyed, and they said, look, doctors, this is why you went to school.

THE FIRST morning of his double-shift, Jack was refreshed. He'd actually slept for four hours, from two till six, his feet up on the arms of the couch back at the station.

"This happens once in a blue moon," the Sergeant said, "I can't remember the last time."

"It's my aura," Jack said, "I have the criminals shit-scared. I have to say though, I feel good."

"Well the party's over. This just came in. Not too taxing from the looks of it. The hospital, there's somebody down there needs watching. They might need you, a transfer to the Mental."

So he rose from the couch and stood and stretched and washed his face downstairs by the lockers and found the assigned cruiser where he already knew it was, and that's how he found himself, bright-eyed, ten minutes later, in the Emergency Department, standing just inside the swinging doors with the Head Nurse, Miss Harris.

"False alarm, Constable," she said, "he's calmed down. We're okay I think. Want a coffee?"

"Sure," he said, because he was starting twenty-four hours straight duty and who knew what the day and the night would bring. Coffee now would be a good idea.

The morning shift-change was underway. Nurses in white uniforms flew by. In one direction, they looked tired, ready to leave, and in the other direction, incoming, they were cheerful, laughing.

Then a shout came from outside, from the waiting room, and the swinging doors flew open, towards him. A man staggered in, covered with blood. Blood on his pants, his shirt, blood hanging in shreds from where his left arm should have been. The arm was missing, it wasn't there anymore. He had his right hand, the only hand he had left, swung over, holding tight onto the stump, what was left of the lost arm, squeezing hard.

He semi-focused his eyes on Jack and said something like, "Officer" or it could have been a groan with no formed words at all, and then the swinging doors came back full force upon him, knocking him to the ground, to his knees.

"Watch out," the Head Nurse said.

She took off, ducking into one of the small side rooms just as the man, off-balance, released his hand and the stump of the severed arm glistened for a second then pumped volley after volley of blood splattering *spit-spit-spit* first on the floor then up the left wall until it fixed itself on Jack, aiming at him, strafing him left to right across the chest of his uniform, then back again right to left, then lower across the front of his pants. Jack just stood there. Then the supply of ammunition diminished, the spouting lost its force and the amputee toppled to the floor, his face slammed sideways on the tile, a face as white as porcelain. His eyes were staring nowhere, sideways.

"Okay then, here we are," said Miss Harris, at Jack's side again, still spotless in her nursing whites, stepping into the midst of the carnage. She was quick, she danced through the congealing pools of blood and applied a cuff she had already commandeered, wound it briskly round the base of what remained of the left upper arm.

"Hit a hundred and sixty," she said.

"Me?"

"Yes you. That button."

He pushed it, they heard the cuff swell and tighten. What was left of the bleeding stopped.

"There you go," said Miss Harris, "now we're in control."

"Oxygen," she said.

Nurses and orderlies were everywhere. A stretcher appeared.

"Grab him by the coat and pants, keep his head down and lift," said Miss Harris.

"Call Housekeeping. Call the surgical resident."

She spoke efficiently, she rubbed her hands together. If she had a drop of blood on her, Jack couldn't see it.

"Good work, Constable," she said, "you did a good job, good work. You don't look so good though, sartorially speaking, he's done a number on your clothes."

She was laughing. Doctors and orderlies were now whisking the patient away, deeper into the hospital.

"He'll be all right?" asked Jack.

He looked down at his uniform, his pants sodden, stains and streaks turning a visibly darker colour now, scarlet-brown.

"Don't worry, that'll come out easily enough. Cold water, elbow grease. Next thing though, we need the arm. Can't forget the arm."

"The arm?"

"The one he apparently doesn't have anymore. Maybe they can re-attach it."

Two cleaners arrived with buckets and mops. The Head Nurse strode out into the waiting room.

"Okay, which one of you came in here with the man who made this mess?"

There was only one person there. He raised his hand like a schoolchild.

"Okay, where is it? Where's the arm?"

"Back in the woods, back in the woods."

He said the same thing twice. There was no blood on him at all either, he was as spotless as the nurse was.

"In the woods? What were you thinking? Constable, go with

this man, get the arm. Wait, we'll get the cooler from the back."

"It was a chainsaw," the man said, "out Indian Meal Line."

There was the cooler now, sloshing with ice.

"Saline, and this plastic bag, the arm goes in this, then the bag goes in the ice and all of it goes in the cooler. The faster the better. Go."

So Jack, bloodied, was back in the cruiser again driving north out of town with the man who was, as it turned out, the brother of the victim. But this brother was undamaged and was now struck dumb, saying nothing.

But he nodded yes, he confirmed it, Indian Meal Line, that's where it was.

"What happened?"

Finally he spoke, "He cut his arm off. That's all."

The lights were flashing, the siren was going flat-out and they were into Torbay in record time, ten minutes. Cars pulled off the road for them. The man smiled, seeing the effect of the siren, and looked over at Jack for the first time.

"Look at them skedaddle out of the way, look at them! Hi-de-ho!"

Then he said, "Oh, turn left right here."

Indian Meal Line ran away from the sea straight into the low boreal forest, miles and miles of scrubby woods on either side of the road, twisted conifers, pine, spruce, jumbled rocks, a hydro line scalloping pole to pole. Jack had to weave the cruiser along because in many places the asphalt had fissured and collapsed down into the ditch, narrowing the useful part of the road.

"Look for a culvert," the man said.

But there were culverts everywhere.

Then the brother finally opened up, the cruiser weaving slowly now, the brother too looking out his window. "We were cutting firewood up here. There's a stream, a culvert. We got a red bandana in a tree, look for that."

They drove on, looking.

"I told him hold it with both hands but he never listens to me, he's the smart one, at least the smart one till now, and it caught and slipped I guess on one of the branches, you can see the alder's thick in here, you gotta get past those before you get into the real stuff and the saw must have slipped, the next thing I know he calls out and his arm's on the ground and he's kicking the fucking saw with his foot, with his boot, he kicks it right into the river saying fuck you this and fuck you that and he was holding on with his hand to the cutoff part and the saw was jumping around in the river like a fish until the motor cuts out and I think I fainted then."

"You fainted?"

"He's stronger than I am. We sharpened it the night before. Cut through steel, this could, he said, that's exactly what he said last night and look, it did. Well, bone."

Jack spotted the red bandana half-hidden up a tree.

"That it?"

"Yes. Buggers steal the wood, you don't hide the marker."

Jack pulled partway to the side of the road, into the loose gravel. He turned off the siren but kept the lights flashing. The brother was out and hopping over the ditch and Jack followed but the lid of the cooler was loose and ice-water sloshed down his leg. The trees were so damn thin they looked pretty much useless for firewood. Why bother in the first place, he wondered, cutting anything in a place like this.

"Not here, not right here, no, everything looks the same. Oh, there's the trail!"

They angled deeper into the woods.

"We tie the flag too obvious, it's easy for them, off they go with what we cut, the bastards."

They could still see the cruiser, the pulsing lights. That's how thin the trees were. Jack put the cooler down for a rest then lifted it again. They picked their way farther into the forest and then they were into a small clearing with a stream about three feet wide burbling right to left.

"Here," the man said, "this is it. See?"

Indeed, there it was, the blade of the chainsaw sticking out of the water, midstream. Jack reached and pulled it out by the tip, ice-cold but clean as a whistle. There were brown spatters all over the leaves which were thick there on the forest floor, and there were gouges and slashed roots where the saw must have jumped around before it hit the water.

The brown spatters the same colour as the spots on his uniform.

"So where is it, the arm?" Jack asked.

They were both looking around and saw nothing.

"It was right here, I swear."

It should have been easy to see a severed arm. There wasn't much there but the roughed-up carpet of leaves and a few rocks, and the brook going by.

"The fingers were moving and clenching themselves. They were in their death throes, I'm telling you it was right creepy. I came to, he was kicking me."

They walked thirty feet up and down beside the brook and the water was bell-clear and the arm was not there.

"I know I should have picked it up."

"Would've made it easier, that's for sure."

"But I couldn't do it. He told me to, I tried but I couldn't do it. And he sure as hell couldn't."

Jack spilled the contents of the cooler out.

"Looks like we don't need this."

"God I fucked up. Wherever it is, it's not here."

"No one's perfect, don't blame yourself. This could happen to anyone," said Jack, though he didn't believe what he said because he knew it would never have happened to him or to anyone else he knew. They'd have taken the arm along, sure thing.

On the way back to the hospital, the brother became even more talkative.

"Given my druthers I'd work for the Department of Highways. They got the benefit plan, I heard, just as good as the police force, I bet."

"It's true, a highway job's a good job," Jack said.

"My brother, he's tough as nails. I'm kind of not. But Highways, I could do Highways. Maybe they hire people with one arm? Both of us, we could sign on. I've seen them standing around plenty, they're sure not doing much even with two arms and he could hold the sign, one hand's good enough for that. Benefits, sick days, think of it, that's a dream. Sick days! I'm telling you, you call in you say you got a fever and what do they say? Stay home, stay home they say, rest till you're better. Time off paid, never happened to me, or my brother, once."

Back at Emergency, Miss Harris raised her eyebrows but the surgical resident shrugged and said, "Well, chainsaw cuts, they're not the easiest to reattach anyway, they chew up tissue like hamburger."

He changed his uniform at home, back at Garrison Hill. He took a minute to call Tryphena and tell her about it. She must have been sitting at the kitchen table, filing her nails, because he could hear the *scuff-scuff*, her nails, her breathing, the phone crooked on her shoulder, close to her mouth.

"What do you think?" he said when he was finished, "where did the arm go?"

"I have no idea."

"I figured it out, Tryphie. Listen. An animal took it, a fox. Like it was take-out, like KFC or pizza."

"A carnivore you mean? That makes sense. I could see that happening."

"Or voodoo."

"Oh that's likely. Common here, voodoo, spirits everywhere."

"I missed my coffee. You finished with your studying, Tryphie?"

Scuff-scuff.

"Yes, pretty much, I'm prepared. You're working through the night tonight, right?"

"I'll try to call later."

"Good."

She made a quick kissing noise through the phone.

They hung up and she saw in her mind's eye a thin ragged fox, a carnivore, a mother, running up one of the low hills on the Indian Meal Line. She loped along the shoulder of the road, wary and alert. She pricked up her ears, sniffed the air with her nose, stopped, turned right, jumped into the cover of the forest. Then just a minute later she reappeared roadside with something substantial in her mouth but from this distance it was hard to be sure what it was. But it had to be dinner, something to eat. Why else drag it out? And how lucky was that for the fox, for the baby foxes back in the den? Kits, they're called. Was it the right time of year for kits? She wasn't sure. It didn't matter. A meal like that coming out of the blue would be appreciated, those baby foxes would nibble first and then tear in all directions with their little teeth at whatever their mother brought home. Even if it were that poor man's hand, his cold clenched hand, those fingers blue or dead-white or whatever colour they were after lying in the forest, those kits would pull the flesh off bit by bit until there was nothing left but bone.

That's what mothers did, they took care of their young. They couldn't be choosy, they'd take whatever nature offered them and run with it. It was a hard place, the forest.

Mothers, fathers, kits, babies. Forget about those foxes. She reflected further on the story Jack had told her. Too bad about the uniform. She saw him splattered head to toe. Bizarre, yes, but still, over all, she was impressed with him. He'd gone and searched for the arm in vain but he didn't blame the useless brother or even make him feel bad. Add it up? He had the right chromosomes for fathering, if Butter Pot came to that. Well, the voodoo, that was too much but that was a joke. She liked that too, his jokes, even if they were as crazy as that.

She smiled. She finished buffing her nails and idly drew a cross-section of a tooth on a paper napkin. She used a pencil and when her mother came in a few minutes later, she peered over Tryphena's shoulder and said, "What's that, a tooth?"

"Yes, the cross-section of one."

"Imagine you, a full-blown dental hygienist. It won't be long now."

Tryphena crumpled up the napkin.

"Crudely drawn," she said.

"Oh not so bad, I knew it was a tooth. How's Jack, how's our Sheriff?"

"He's fine, but he told me yesterday, no more calling him Sheriff, he finds it belittling."

"Belittling? He can't laugh at himself anymore?"

"Not right now."

"Your father, he could always laugh at himself. He wasn't perfect but he could laugh at himself."

That night, Tryphena lay in the dark and quickly fell asleep, dead to the world. She wasn't much of a dreamer but she soon found herself sitting at a video lottery terminal, somewhere she'd never been, at one of those one-armed bandits. The lights were bright around her and there was a racket of music, a clamour like a midway, a din, a carnival atmosphere, a calliope playing, a merry-go-round whirling over there. And Jack was with her, pressed up against her right shoulder, behind her, urging her on. He handed her money. Here, here, he said, you do it, and together they put money in the slot, his hand on hers, and together they pulled the arm of the one-armed bandit down but instead of seeing a row of red cherries or yellow lemons, up came three shiny white teeth on the screen. What are those? he asked. His voice was loud in her ear and the word *those* reverberated like a rock song. Molars, molars, I think we've won, she said in her dream and Jack jumped up and down and she could feel the metal of his belt-buckle biting at her shoulder. Stop, she said, and she moved her shoulder forward, out of the way. Then a rush of silver coins cascaded out of the machine, first to her knees, then to the floor. All of that money! She should have been happy but she wasn't. Melancholy shrouded her, enclosed her, swallowed her whole. She looked around and Jack was gone, his belt was gone, the carnival atmosphere was gone, even the coins were gone. On the floor, by her feet, there was nothing but a small pool of blood.

Oh, it's my period at last, she thought as she woke up, but when she checked, in the bathroom, there was nothing there.

A ROUTINE day and routine things happened. He wrote fourteen traffic tickets in the afternoon, calmly deflecting the praise showered on him by the miscreants.

"I know how you feel," he said, "I'm not a policeman twenty-four hours a day. Tickets, I hate them worse than you do. We're together on this."

Then he'd snap the ticket under the wiper blade or hand it to them.

"Nothing personal," he'd say.

Back at the station, the Sergeant suggested that Jack take a few hours to himself. There wasn't much happening that couldn't wait and it was going to be a long shift, the upcoming night on top of the day he'd already had. The Sergeant joked too about the severed arm, saying, "It was good of you to try to give them a hand."

When he stopped laughing at his own wit, he said, "Just be back in an hour, an hour and a half max."

So Jack walked outside to stretch his legs and decided, what the heck, sure, why not drop in on Tryphie, surprise her. She'd be at home. Rather than walk, he took the cruiser, and even though her mother had asked him not to park it near the house—it excites the neighbours to see it there, Sheriff, they push their curtains aside and they're bored and they're nosy— he parked it just two doors down. Her mother wouldn't like it but she wouldn't be home in the middle of the afternoon anyway.

He walked back to the house, past that damn little Kiziah who was always skipping on the sidewalk like a wound-up toy, singing, and he rang the doorbell and heard her footsteps running down the stairs. She opened the inner door—it had one of those tear-drop windows—and she stood there just an inch or two away, breathing through the mesh of the screen. He pretended to consult his little flip-pad of notes, leafing through it.

Then he said to her, "Police."

She affected an air of puzzlement and said, "Funny, no one put in a call for the police, as far as I know."

"Regardless, Ma'am, we're looking for a former Miss Portugal. We have received information, down to the station, that said Miss Portugal may be residing at this address."

"Your information is wrong, or out of date. It's true that once years ago I was Miss Portugal, briefly, but those were the old days. I've been supplanted by three or four younger ones since. Maybe you want one of those."

"No, you're the one, you're the one I want for sure. Tryphie, let me in I have an hour off."

She pushed open the screen door and looked out and said he shouldn't have come in the cruiser, her mother wouldn't like it, he was already upsetting the neighbours, probably. He stepped inside and kissed her, up against the hall radiator. She closed the inner door with her left hand, distracted, and by then he was touching her breast, the left one, through her sweater.

"Wait," she said.

"We've had reports that Miss Portugal is running a common bawdy house here on Fitzgerald Avenue."

"It's a lie. You know it's a lie."

"I know but I'm afraid I have to execute a search warrant."

"On me?"

"Who else is here?"

"No one, not right now."

"Then it's you, and thorough the searching should be. I have half an hour."

His hands were behind her now, trying to unsnap her bra but as she was still pushed back awkwardly against the radiator and the wall, it wasn't easy. She twisted to the side, away from him, and said, "Wait. You're behaving in a way inappropriate to an officer of the law. When on duty."

"We have our methods."

"Jack, stop. Drop the policeman."

"I'm thinking of a total body search."

"Not here you're not."

Hand in hand they took the stairs to her bedroom where she sat on the bed facing him.

"Not sure I'm up for this right now," she said.

"You are Miss Portugal, aren't you?"

"Let's just be us."

"This is a bawdy house, Miss Portugal, maybe with just one customer but regardless of the paltry numbers, I must be thorough, I must examine you for evidence."

"Evidence of what?"

"Sexual misconduct."

"Good luck with that."

"How much does it cost here, for your favours?"

"Nothing," she said, "I charge nothing. That's what they're worth."

"Not so sure of that."

He unbuckled his heavy leather belt. He'd been in her bedroom twice before. She had stuffed animals on the bed, combs and brushes on the dresser, what looked like a small bottle of perfume. Seeing those tokens of her life, he realized how little he knew of girls and women, except for this, what they were doing now. Her curtains were pulled back but no one could see in unless they were on rooftops across the street.

"Some policemen," he said, "are no doubt more experienced than I am at this. Some may even be jaded. At interrogation."

He leaned down to her and they kissed.

"But this is new, for me, this one-on-one, this type of search."

She had her hands on his belt.

"And it's quite exciting to me, as perhaps you can see."

She unbuckled his belt and then she pulled up her sweater, taking it off over her head.

"Yes, I can see," she said.

"Tell me your name, suspected felon," he said.

"Tryphie," she said.

"Not good enough."

"Tryphena Grandy."

He touched her bare shoulders, reached behind, found the clasp and undid it and then flipped the bra over his shoulder, pinwheeling it.

She finished undoing his belt and he pushed his trousers to the floor and stepped out of them still in his underpants, now tented out by his erection, nearly in her face.

"A condom?" she said.

"I don't think so, you're probably pregnant. Let's be realistic."

"The verdict's not in. No more chances."

She touched the hardness coming at her through the white cloth, with the fingers of both hands.

"My shaft," he said.

He was almost falling into her, pushing towards her now. "There's a small opening at the front there, Tryphie, pull it open, pull it open."

"Jack, once without a condom is enough."

"Why bother?"

The tent-pole slid past her ear, first on the right side, then the left.

"Tryphie, try it, just like this, no condom needed for this. Tryphie, please do it."

She looked up at him and with one hand pushed him away.

"Actually, this is not the best time or place, this your shaft or not," she said.

"No condom is needed."

"If we do nothing, Jack, then we don't need a condom for that either."

"Tryphie."

"Not now."

She looked away from him and started to put her sweater back on. The bra was still on the floor, out of reach without her bending right past him. So she decided to leave it there.

"Tryphie, what the heck?"

"I don't want to do this now, that's all."

He was rocking on his feet in front of her.

"I'm tired of being the sacrificial animal, Jack, we have sex and I'm the one living with the results, I don't feel like it right now."

"Christ," he said, "sacrificial animal? What's that?"

"I'll decide when and where, that's all I mean."

He sat beside her on the bed.

"Christ," he said.

"Sorry. Get dressed. Mother will soon be home anyway. How'd you like her to see you like this, your penis sticking out of you like a Bomarc missile?"

She got up and left the bedroom and went downstairs. He looked down at himself, his missile fading away.

Well fuck this.

He dressed, he followed her down. By then she was standing in a see-you-later pose against the teardrop door which was wide open, ready to bid him goodbye. Her back was up against the door, her nipples under the sweater, both hands behind her on the doorknob.

Somehow this visit hadn't turned out the way he hoped.

"I'll get condoms, next time," he said.

"That's a good idea."

She stretched up and kissed him on the cheek.

"I'm not mad or anything. Timing's bad. By the way, you did a good job, the guy with the arm. I thought you were nice with the brother, from what you said."

"Oh, that guy. What a loser."

"But you didn't tell him that."

"No."

"That's what I mean, you were nice to him."

"Tryphie, look, I'm sorry about this."

They were both in the open doorway now and he could hear the rhythmic snap of the skipping rope, the little girl, not far away.

"I'm not familiar with Portuguese courting customs. Would that help, if I said that?"

"Go ahead, try it."

"Sweetheart, I'm not familiar with Portuguese courting customs."

"I forgive you then."

"I'm new, I'm learning."

"So am I."

She shrugged her shoulders in the particular charming and heart-rending way she had of shrugging her shoulders and she smiled.

"Bye-bye for now," she said.

The screen door swung shut. He walked alone back to the car, but she called after him, "Hey, call me later, when you get a break, anytime."

"Sure, Tryphie, sure, thanks."

And there was the girl with her rope going *snap-snap snap-snap* on the sidewalk. Shiny plastic-looking red shoes. One foot, then two feet alternating. Rope blurred over her head. Her head wasn't moving at all. She looked at him with her eyebrows folded down, like he was obviously the enemy.

"You think you're smart, Mister Policeman, but you might get a ticket yourself, parking there, no matter who you are," she said, never missing a beat.

WHEN STAN returned home from school to Campbell Avenue, he

was surprised to see, sitting on the front porch steps, a small replica of the red pyramid at Snofru. He recognized it by its smooth sides. This one was made of plastic and was only six inches tall whereas the original would have flattened eight or nine houses on both sides of the street.

Meant for him, obviously, no one else would have a clue.

He reached down and picked it up. *Made in Japan*, the sticker on the bottom said, $4.75. Someone had sprinkled fine dirt there, on the step, to take the place of sand.

He stepped inside to a stillness, strange within the usually rowdy house. He thought he heard whispering. He toed-and-heeled his boots off and hung up his coat and then there was suppressed laughter from the kitchen and the door opened and "Happy Birthday, Stan!" shouted from multiple pitches of voices, a disorganized chorus, a mixed cacophony, and four small pseudo-Egyptians herky-jerked their way out of the kitchen, coming his way. These were his brothers and sisters—for now anyway—the other fostered ones who had come to Campbell Avenue from various agencies, with their various troubles, but now they were dressed up as best they could as small grain-farmers, yellow-gold sandals, arm bracelets probably from the dollar store, paper skirts rustling as they walked sideways, caricaturing the postures he'd shown them in photographs of vases. But they couldn't keep their faces straight, though they tried, holding them in profile yet sneaking glances his way.

"Hey, that's great! You look great!" he said.

"Happy Birthday!"

The children couldn't keep up the masquerade for long. They laughed and the mock parade fell apart. One of the girls had a plastic snake dangling from her T-shirt. Cleopatra.

"Stan, we're Egyptians!" they said.

They rushed to him and held onto his jeans and shirt while the foster parents hung back, waiting, watching, feeling that it was unlikely that it could get any better than this, their complicated lives, maybe it could but with the ever-changing cast of characters they lived with, with the good and the not-so-good, they were damn lucky right now with this particular crew.

"The cake, the cake's in here," they said.

In the kitchen, the walls were half-covered with long blades of grass that must have been pulled from the vacant lot across the street, scotch-taped helter-skelter.

"Let me guess, these are banks of the Nile?" asked Stan.

"Yes, the Nile, the Nile!" the children shouted and they broke out some green ice cream which they all insisted was crocodile, and they lit twenty-two candles which he blew out, almost not finishing them off, on purpose. This was a first for him, a birthday celebrated, a happiness, he thought, that to most would be an every-year occurrence.

Later that night, at bedtime, the kids said, "Stan, please, start where you left off, please, please."

"I'm supposed to be studying."

"Stan, you have to!"

"Okay you win. Twist my arm. Sit tight. Where were we?"

"By the river."

"By what river?"

"The Nile!"

"Where's the Nile?"

"Egypt!"

"Almost right."

"Ancient Egypt!"

"Okay now you got it. Here goes. Turn the light down. Sally? Hold onto my arm. Now I remember…The four Ancient Egyptian children were frightened because the sun was going down. They looked at each other but nobody talked. Nobody admitted they were afraid. It wasn't chilly but it wasn't as warm as it used to be. At home, they'd be starting a fire with papyrus chips, with branches fallen from the palm trees. But here they had nothing and only Aqbar was tall enough to look over the reeds. Take a look, Aqbar, they said, and someone had to do it, to find the way out back to…where, Sally?"

"The Magic Cave."

"That's right, the Magic Cave, so Aqbar stood on his toes and parted the reeds with his hands and the low rays of the sun glanced off the reeds, the greenery, and maybe, oh dear, was that a tiger there? Why were the reeds, those ones right there, moving by themselves? There was no wind. Why were they moving?"

"Stop, Stan," Sally said.

"No go on, go on!" from the chorus.

"Then there was a low growling and stripes of sunshine, yellow, and the stripes of the reeds, dark, merged into the eyes of a tiger crouched just six feet away. Lashing his tail. Run, run, Aqbar said to the others, I will stay and fight the beast, and the last thing he remembered was the blur of the tiger coming his way, the scattering behind him of his brothers and sisters, how he pulled from his waist his rope of hemp and paraffin and ducked and slipped the noose over the neck of the tiger as its claws flew overhead, and how he hung to the rope still shouting Run run! And then the hot breath of the beast turned on him, scorching his face with its fetid breath, its long curved teeth…"

"Stan, stop!" they shouted, though the oldest one said, "No don't stop!"

Looking at the face of the youngest, he stopped.

"Till tomorrow then. It's too scary, and besides, I have to study," he said, "and thanks, thanks to you all, that was one great party we had. Shokrun."

"Shokrun?"

"That's *thank you*, in Egyptian."

"Shokrun, shokrun," they all said as Stan turned the light out and went to his own room to study. Or to try to study. Trying was easier than doing, that's for sure.

HIS NIGHT-SHIFT started out easily enough too, no hint of what was to come.

"Patrol up and down Water Street," he was told.

For two hours he walked back and forth between the bars and restaurants and closed businesses that lined both sides of the street. He went twenty minutes one way, twenty minutes back, strolling, sauntering, from nine to eleven. He wore his rain gear as rain came and went in gusts, in sheets, in waves. He walked most of the time with his hands held behind his back. Now and then he turned into the vestibule of one club or another to let the water stream off, to say hello to the staff in the nine-tenths-empty place. Canned music outside of some of them, speakers high over the doors. Then he'd go back out into the weather and walk some more. He saw a good-sized rat run from left to right across the street, stop and look around, then duck up an alleyway. He waited for it to come back. But the rat had its own agenda, it did not reappear. It must be tucked into a hole in the wall, or gone all the way up to Duckworth, looking for cast-off fries. No hands or arms or fingers under there, though that would be a treat.

Eleven o'clock. The wind picked up some more, the foghorn from the Narrows kept tolling away and the rain started up even more heavily and he contacted the station.

"All quiet down here," he told the Sergeant.

"Then drive around, there's no point in getting soaked through."

The roads downtown were near-empty, just the odd taxi-cab flicking its lights to him, saying hello there, policeman, fellow denizen of the night. "Don't flick back," the Sergeant had told him, "you're the boss, you just cruise along. Keep your distance."

He patrolled Harbour Drive, Water Street, Duckworth, and then, on Holloway Street, so steep that the near-vertical sidewalk was cut into steps, he picked up an old guy wearing nothing but a hat, walking sideways, slowly down the incline so he wouldn't fall.

"Oldtimer, you need a ride?"

No, he didn't need a ride, he was fine, he was going shopping.

Jack put him in the back seat and covered him with a gray blanket from the trunk and took him back to the station.

"My only arrest so far," he said, "no resistance."

"We'll keep him overnight, phone around in the morning" said the Sergeant, "maybe we'll hear from someone. Good. Come with me, my friend."

Up Barter's Hill, right on Lemarchant, Military Road all the way to the hotel, then back along Gower Street. The rain wasn't slacking off at all.

There were two women on the sidewalk, on the north side. He slowed as he passed them because one of them, her open umbrella held uselessly out to one side, seemed to be trying to hold the other one up. He pulled over to the curb and looked back in the mirror. Now they were walking his way again but the mirror was streaked on that side. He could hardly make them out.

What the hell. He buttoned up the top of his coat and got out. Yes, they were walking towards him but the smaller one was barely making it.

"Everything okay?" he asked.

The one with the umbrella was middle-aged, the other one just a kid, a teenager in a raincoat, hanging onto the older woman's arm.

"We're okay, thanks."

Nothing from the young one.

"She's got a fever, a cold, we've only got a block to go, don't worry about us, she's just a little weak. It must be the flu. We've been to the doctor."

The umbrella was tipped down in front and it was hard to see the young girl's face even though she was only three feet away.

"You need a ride? I can give you a ride."

"No, we're almost there."

The teenager finally said something and it sounded like no. No? No what. He wasn't sure.

"Did she say *no*?"

They were leaning on each other now, the two of them.

"Yes, that's what she said. She said we're fine."

"It's late for you to be out like this."

He looked at his watch. 11:30.

"Not that late," the woman said.

He walked with them for several steps and by now they were up to where he'd stopped the cruiser. The inside lights were on, the motor was running, the heater was kicked in.

"You're sure? It's warm and dry."

"Honestly, it's just a block, really, we're fine, Officer, you're very kind but we're already home."

"Okay, your call," he said.

He drove away, back down towards the harbour, taking a last look at them over his shoulder. They were a dark shadow on the north side of Gower, moving. When he turned left, taking Prescott down to Water Street, they disappeared from view.

Then the rain really kicked into a higher gear. It drummed and danced off flat surfaces, off the asphalt, off the hood of the car. Waterfalls poured off the awnings on Water Street.

"Come on in," the Sergeant said, "might as well take cover from the storm. Even the worst of the worst are holed up on a night like this."

He thought one more time about the woman and the girl and the rain and the wobbling umbrella. It was late for them, no matter what the woman said, that was a bit weird, but they'd be inside by now so forget about them, why not?

He headed the cruiser back up the hill to the station and then ran from the parking lot to the front door. He was still warm and dry. The gear they had was the best. He could have stayed out all night, if push came to shove and he'd be fine in this.

Paperwork on the old guy, now asleep on a bench. He wrote a quick paragraph, it didn't need much.

Tryphena, he was thinking, how he kind of messed up with her today. Butter Pot too. He'd take that back if he had the chance.

Priscilla, messed up with her too, didn't do right by her. The way her hair was now, multicoloured, the fuck-you new attitude, the actress thing, admit it, still a temptation. Hard to let go, greedy and how stupid was that with Tryphena the way she was. Desire, he seemed to have no shortage of that. He could feel it as he sat there, welling up inside him, that he had in spades. His daily fix of her, Jesus, needing her more and more, not less and less and there was no tiring of her, never. Falling into her, not just the sex though, everything she brought. She was happy, that was it. She had no guile. Only a fool would think past her, towards anything else.

"Jack!"

"Yes!"

"Daydreaming?"

"I guess so, yes, sorry."

"Action time now, wake up. Something weird going down on Prescott Street, check it out. It sounds like a domestic, number 71. Police, police, that's all he said. Usually they say more than that."

Rain was still streaking the headquarters' windows. He put his gear back on, shook off the cobwebs, turned the key in the squad-car and it started without a problem, a nice contrast to his own little car, the Vauxhall. Touch and go to start, the Vauxhall, always had been. Cheap, fourth-hand. Hey, Tryphena, get in the driver's seat, he'd say to her and he'd push it down the nearest incline, either on Pennywell Road or Garrison Hill, wherever they were, and she'd release the clutch and the car would dip its nose and cough a few times, then go *vroom* and she'd be laughing with the pleasure of the improvised start. Something loose, she'd said the first time, and when he smiled at her she said, No, not me, Jack, I mean the car, the starter, the battery, the cables, something loose under the hood, you figure it out. The ignition.

She could have been an actress too, a comedian. But she wasn't into that, there was nothing public about her.

He'd already been on Prescott Street once tonight and it was just two minutes away. He turned right and passed his own place, Garrison Hill, everything dark there, everything fine. Left on Bond Street, right on Prescott. No rush, nobody said rush. There wasn't a lot of penetration from the headlights in rain like this so he had to go slowly. There was a downhill curve ahead.

No red flashers, that wasn't part of the drill for domestics. Keep a low profile, stay cool, stay calm; that's the secret, boys, when you find yourself in the beating heart of families after the witching hour.

Witching hour? Well actually now it was closer to dawn. 3 AM. If it weren't for this rain, in a couple of hours he'd see the faint light of the sun gray-lining the summit of the hills to the east.

He crept downhill looking for numbers. 71 would be on the right. The wipers were maxed out now, smacking back and forth like maniacs and the drumming on the roof ratcheted up even more. He leaned forward so his chin was over the wheel and there—a light cast onto the street from an open door. That must be it. He pulled up by the curb and got out of the car. The light from the open door barely made it to the sidewalk. Curbside, a river, turbulent, three feet wide, was pouring down the hill and he'd say to her later, calling her on the phone, as she'd asked him to do, Tryph, I had to step over runnels of water. Runnels? she'd say. Yes, runnels or a runnel, I'm not sure which, but it was there. A river.

One big step and he was over it, and another step to the open door. He checked the number, the paint wearing thin but he was in the right place. Didn't care about the rain because he had the raincoat on, collar turned up, the clear plastic cover for the hat. He was used to this, the weather, day after day of it sometimes so tonight was the same, and as for these row houses, he'd been in them lots of times and he knew the layout, he could walk into them blindfolded.

So he stepped in and just inside the tiny vestibule with its two or three hanging coats was a man sitting on the bottom step of the stairway, his head in his hands, tufts of gray hair stuck this way and that. An armless white undershirt complete with holes. Gray pyjama bottoms.

He looked up at Jack. "Officer! I called you!"

He stood up and said his name was Walter something-or-other but Jack missed it, the last name. Get it later.

Bright lights on in the hallway, and the hallway opened straight back to the kitchen where the lights were also turned up high. Lights everywhere downstairs. He could see straight through to the kitchen table, neat as a pin, a doily in the centre with a vase of perfect red and green flowers. Plastic, they had to be this time of year.

Rainwater ran off him to the floor. He stepped back into the vestibule to shake it off on the linoleum and a voice came from upstairs somewhere, a female voice, wavering, "Up here please, up here."

The man at the bottom of the stairs was now running his hands through his hair, smiling.

"Police," Jack said.

Identify yourself right off the bat. If you don't do that, you'll be unpleasantly surprised by what people see, what people don't see, even when you're standing there all decked out in your uniform, even when they were the ones who'd called you in the first place. Because they've forgotten they called you in the first place. They're in some primitive alternate world where everything's a threat. You're nothing but a stranger in their house and who the hell are you? is what they might be thinking.

So, "Police," he said again, "is everything here okay?"

From upstairs the same voice, "Please!"

From where he was standing, he could see nothing of the second floor. There was no smell of alcohol in the air so already there was a difference. Domestics and alcohol, they were dance partners rarely separated.

"Officer," the man said, "you can arrest her now."

"You're the one who put in the call?"

"I did, yes, I called you. Like I said."

The man was calm and controlled and smiling as though he were Jack's best friend, standing at the bottom of the stairs, his arm easy on the banister.

"What's the problem, please, Sir?"

Sir. Show respect. Costs nothing.

But there was something in the man's stance, how he'd positioned himself at the bottom of the stairs, something potentially obstructive going on, like he was standing in his way.

"She's broken the law, Rowena has. Too smart for her own good and now this."

"Rowena?"

The man pointed upstairs.

"She's had an abortion."

A woman in a nightgown ran halfway down the stairs. She was crying, beckoning him up. He'd been there at least a minute and still knew nothing.

"Quick, quick," she said.

"Excuse me," he said, "I need to get up there."

"She's bad and now this," the man said, keeping his arm where it was, like a gate.

The woman was turning away, she had slippers on and she was half-stumbling her way back up the stairs.

"Rowena, she has no respect. Now she's in the trouble she deserves."

"Your daughter?"

"No fucking way. My niece. She's only been here one day."

So, Jack, it's time to move, drop the protocol. Forget politeness, forget the drills.

"Move," he said.

He didn't wait any longer. He pushed the man aside and took the stairs two at a time to a small landing. It was much darker up there, only a low light from the front bedroom. He moved quickly down the hall and looked in.

A thick, heavy odour, a pungency to the air, not sure what that was.

A plug-in nightlight low on the wall by the bed. Sitting there, on the bed, on the near side, was the woman from the stairway, in her nightgown, her hair every which way, bending over someone under the covers, someone small. He felt for the light switch and flicked it on and the small bed jumped out and nearly filled the whole room. A bedside table, a dresser jammed into the corner.

"She needs an ambulance," the woman said, "she doesn't need you. Please call the ambulance."

He slid along the wall by the foot of the bed, then along the far side, knees tight against the mattress. Now he could see down better. There was a young girl lying there, her face up, dark hair on the white of the pillow, her own whiteness frightening, pale, as if she'd been folded into the colour of the sheets and become part of them. As pale as scrimshaw, he'd later say to Tryphena. Scrimshaw? Yes, you know how white that is, Tryphie, deadly white. Scrimshaw is ivory and ivory is dead.

"Call the ambulance! Please! Not the police, not you, she's bleeding, she's delirious, she doesn't know what she's saying."

Then the man from downstairs was in the doorway, saying, "There she is, that's the one you're looking for."

"Okay," Jack said, "stand back, clear the room, and you, Ma'am, up please, I need to have a closer look. How old is this girl?"

Her eyes were closed. Good, because eyes open meant dead. Her hair was pasted down, straggled onto her forehead. She was so thin she was hardly there, a child. He bent over her and moved the woman's arm off the girl's chest. A drop of rain fell from his hat onto her cheek.

"Excuse me," he said, though she hadn't moved or felt anything, she was long past that.

"She's sixteen, she's my niece. I'm phoning the ambulance myself then, please stay with her, I don't know what's wrong with you men."

She headed for the doorway but her husband was still there, blocking her.

"No you're not, the police are here, they'll take care of this."

Jack touched the girl's shoulder. She was breathing shallowly, rapidly. He reached down and pulled the covers up and out from the near side of the bed. From her waist to her knees, on her nightgown, there was nothing but blood. She lay in it, she was drenched in it. Blood bathed her.

Christ.

The man in the doorway still hadn't moved. He couldn't see what Jack had seen because the policeman had the covers held up, a curtain between them.

"Get out of the room," Jack said, "and call the ambulance now."

With his free hand he reached down to pull up the slip or the nightgown or whatever it was, so flimsy, so unsubstantial but for the weight of the bleeding. It could have torn from the heavy weight but it held. On her thighs there was blood, nothing else to see. He let it down.

"It's her own fault," the man was saying.

He let the covers drop down too. Small, this girl. He tried to feel her wrist for a pulse. Nothing. But his fingers were cold and the girl was cold and there had to be a pulse there, obviously, she was breathing.

"Call the ambulance," he said towards the doorway, "I'm not asking you again. Do it now."

But the man didn't move and the woman couldn't get by because he filled the doorway in front of her. He had his arms across it, stretched out to either side.

"Okay," Jack said, "this is what I'm going to do."

But he was still trapped against the wall, his knees tight against the bed so he took one step up until he was on the bed too, the foot of it, ducking for the ceiling, two more awkward steps till he was down to the floor and knocking the man's arm out of the way. Then he was down the stairs three or four at a time, flying he could have been, and in the squad-car he was on the radio back to the station.

"Sergeant, we need an ambulance pronto, 71 Prescott."

"What is it?"

"I'm trying to figure it out but it's bad, get them here fast."

He ran back inside. A few of the houses nearby had their lights on. They were being watched, the usual.

"Take her away, it's okay with me," the man said.

He was standing on the lower steps again.

"We have other priorities now."

"Abortion's a crime."

"Get out of my way, you're in my way."

"She's from Fortune Bay, that says it all."

Jack pushed past him and took the stairs again, double-time. It must be the blood that caused the smell, so much of it in the room, in the air pouring through and over them. He was sweating under his uniform even in the cold and damp and the open door downstairs and the chill of the street, now at last he was sweating.

Jesus, this is something else.

The woman was now lying on the edge of the bed near-side, her arm over the girl. Not crying, not now.

"Is this true, what he says? Abortion?"

"No, it's not true, he's gone crazy, look at this poor thing, look at her, she's just past being a baby herself."

In the distance, finally came the siren of the ambulance. The hospital was only three minutes away, everything was close. He counted the girl's respirations. Ten in fifteen seconds. Which meant forty which was high, super-high.

"Who called us, who called the police?"

"Walter did."

A whirling red cut through the still-closed curtains, the siren was expiring now, low-pitched outside. Then the metallic clattering at the front door and Jack went to the top of the stairs.

"Up here," he said.

There were two ambulance attendants, a folded stretcher between them.

"Oh, Jack, hi."

They knew each other from other times. Together they tipped the stretcher up and angled it to the bedroom.

"No pressure, no pulse, I can't feel anything," said the first attendant.

"Move it out faster, let's go," Jack said. "Grab the sheets, we'll lift her in these."

"She's my niece," the woman said to the ambulance men.

"She'll be fine, we'll get blood into her, she'll be as good as new."

The attendants were cool, efficient. They didn't panic, they'd seen everything. They tipped the stretcher with the strapped-in girl down the stairs and Jack was out in front to lead the way.

But there, at the bottom, there he was again, the man of the house.

"You can't take her to the hospital, that's not for her."

"Get out of the way," said Jack.

He was bigger than the other man and he was young and he was trained and fuck this he thought and he grabbed the man by the front of the undershirt, lifted him off his feet and slammed him up against the wall.

"You're obstructing an officer, you're under arrest. Get out of the way."

The stretcher squeezed by them and out the door. A painting of a schooner popped off the wall by the man's shoulder and fell to the floor. The glass frame shattered. Jack got his handcuffs out, he'd practiced, he was good at it. One or two quick moves with the wrists and it was done and the guy was shouting, "What the hell, what the hell," as he was pushed into the cruiser.

"Sit there, do not move, and shut up, you're waking the dead."

Now the stretcher was in the back of the ambulance.

"I have to say that was good," said the driver, "actually it was great, what you did, it was great, it had to be done."

Jack wanted another quick look at the girl so he climbed into the back of the ambulance. Doors slammed up front. He stood over the girl's face, bent down and looked at her. Water dropped from his hat onto her face again, more like a stream this time, a steady trickle.

"Every second counts," said the attendant, crouched, "get out of here, Jack, we better go. Do we have a name?"

"Rowena something."

"This is how people die outside of hospitals," the attendant said, "by dilly-dallying."

"Okay then I'm out of here, sorry, let her rip, go boys."

He jumped out and the doors closed behind him and up the hill the ambulance went with the siren magnifying its own echo off the jammed houses, the precipitous hills. The lowered sky was still as dark as midnight. He went back upstairs to check and look around. Nothing there but the smell, the thick pungency of it. A novel on the floor. Two heavy plastic bags under the bed, and he opened one of them and it was filled with a pad and the pad was filled with blood.

Evidence, so bring it along. Who the hell knows what's happened here.

He took the stairs down, one at a time now. The need for rushing was over. He offered the woman a ride to the hospital and she put on a thin coat and closed the front door of the house, not bothering to lock it. She got into the front seat and looked back at her husband through the glass-and-wire partition.

"So," Jack said, "she's your niece?"

"Yes, she's from the south coast. From my sister."

From the back seat came the voice saying, "What the hell am I doing here?"

The woman had her purse in her lap and she looked at the policeman. She was together now, in charge.

"Thank you for what you did," she said, "it's ludicrous, this abortion thing, whatever he said he heard."

She turned and looked into the back seat.

"Walter, you've got hearing problems, you know it, women get periods, we have a problem in this family, we bleed too much."

There was a red light at Gower and Military Road and Jack looked both ways. Nothing was coming so he drove straight through it.

"The same thing happened to me, I was her age," the woman said.

"Was she out anywhere tonight, your niece?"

"No, she was home all night with us."

"Not true," the voice from the back said, "she was gone the entire evening and she came home late. Like she's Cinderella."

"Walter, for God's sake. You're being ridiculous."

"She came home late, she was acting like a dope-head. I let her in and two hours later she says to us *I've had an abortion,* clear as a bell, and I'm the one who's ridiculous?"

The woman looked at the policeman uncertainly.

"Okay, she was out for the night, but the rest of it, he didn't hear right."

"Later," Jack said, "don't worry about it now."

He dropped the aunt at the hospital and then he looked in the back seat and thought about all the paperwork this guy would entail, all the step-by-step crap he'd have to go through.

"Tell you what, I'll give you a break on this, we'll take you home. We'll drop the charge."

"Thanks for nothing," the uncle said, "but since I did nothing, I guess that's fair."

At the station, he ran it past the Sergeant and the Sergeant said he already heard about it through the grapevine, the ambulance guys were talking it up and it was fine with him, he'd back him all the way. Men like that were scum anyway, they had their priorities screwed up. As far as he was concerned, it was the best kind of policing, including dropping the charge.

"Now it's out of our hair. Win-win."

Jack wrote it up, a new file: *71 Prescott Street*. In the middle of a long paragraph he mentioned the abortion claim. He could hardly leave it out. Somebody might read it and somebody might not and if the girl was lucky no one would read it. Then he could forget it too.

Looking outside, the rain had stopped. The day had fully broken. Tryphie, she'd be getting up and his long shift was nearly over.

Was it too early to phone her, ask her, well, Tryphie? Any sign of anything?

She was sick of him asking, sick of it, sick of it. And her mother would still be in bed, so yes, it was way too early. Anyway, after tonight it felt a bit crass, his own personal stuff. His own concerns so petty compared to Rowena Who-ever-she-was, sixteen years old.

He put both hands on his head.

All he was worried about these days, it seemed, everywhere he went, it was the same: blood, bleeding, girls.

SHE REMEMBERED nothing about her trip to the hospital. She was as close to death as life could be and still be counted amongst the quick. Her body, breathing, lay in the night ambulance as it shot up Gower Street with the accelerator to the floor, siren ripping off the walls of the clapboard houses on both sides of the street, but she was insensate to all of that.

The ambulance turned hard left at the hotel, throwing the attendant holding the oxygen mask almost on top of her.

"*A whiter shade of pale,*" sang the attendant to himself, sitting forward. He couldn't see the colour of her face anymore because of the mask. His practiced hand was in the way. It wasn't in the patient's interest to take the oxygen off and have a look at her. That wouldn't do.

They braked, they sped up, they slowed, they sped again until they were there and the back doors of the ambulance peeled open and they ran, pushing her on the wheeled gurney into the Emergency Department, straight to the resuscitation room. Her respirations—recorded on the chart Jack eventually obtained by court order—were exactly as he had counted himself, forty per minute, she was "hungry for air" and her blood pressure was zero.

But just as her age had made her vulnerable, under the wharf, here it worked for her, giving her the resilience to survive. The bleeding stopped, mostly because there was no blood left to lose, and the new units of blood she received, so different from her own, clotted as blood is supposed to clot. Thus she was saved, in large part because of the policeman who had received the call to her aunt's house. He didn't waste time once he figured out what was happening, where the danger lay, what really mattered. He flew down the stairs when he could have walked, he pushed the obstructive uncle out of his way when he could have reasoned with him, he said fuck you to him—or thought it and didn't say it—instead of being slow and icily polite, and he radioed for the ambulance from the squad car with his voice dead certain, saying hurry, quick, fast, step on it. Pronto, he said.

It could be as simple as that, saving a life. After two hours of transfusions, the girl was transferred to the ICU, alert, talking and following instructions.

She had just one visitor, her mother, and that was nice for her and for the staff who could rejoice with the mother and her good fortune. Then, as she was stable as can be, they thought of transferring her to a ward. She was no longer in danger. But the doctors were struggling with the diagnosis and they were afraid to let her go.

Some kind of clotting deficiency? they wondered. They drew blood and sent it off to Montreal for a detailed analysis, but how long would that take? Another week, two weeks? And, after all, her blood now was mostly somebody else's, it had been transfused into her and was not her own, so even then the results, when they came back, might be skewed.

However, being doctors, they could make an educated guess. They conferred together over coffee in the cafeteria and the one with the reputation and the position of authority said, "Von Willebrand disease. A heavy period in a young girl, nearly exsanguinating in a few hours, that's the most likely diagnosis. Any other possibilities?"

The students shook their heads at the question. They had no idea, that's why they were students.

Now the same man, the gynecologist-in-chief, was holding Rowena's wrist by the bedside in ICU, taking her pulse while three young students stood by, observing.

The patient, to them, looked fine in every way. Freckles, feisty even. She'd already been up and around and sitting in a chair by the bedside. Now she was resting on top of the bedcovers. She did have bruises at the front of her elbows, where the IVs had been.

But, riffling through the morning chart for new results, what's this? There's the pregnancy test. It's positive. That puts a new spin on things. The nurses already knew this, but they'd let the doctor find the result himself.

"You were pregnant?" the gynecologist asked her, as though he couldn't believe it, looking at her. She didn't seem old enough. Yet he'd seen everything in his twenty years of caring for women and for girls and for those in between, like this one.

The students stood straighter and leaned forward, more interested now, and the gynecologist looked at her wristband to remind himself, to double check.

Rowena Savoury, her birthdate, yes, she was sixteen, plenty old enough. Thirteen's old enough, unfortunately.

"Miss Savoury here is sixteen years old," he said, "and any female over the age of twelve is pregnant until proved otherwise. Remember that, you won't go wrong. Forget it, one day you'll look like a fool. That's why we order the test, every time."

"You were pregnant?" he asked her again.

Rowena was ready for this. She showed no sign of embarrassment or discomfort.

"Yes I was, but I'm not anymore."

"That's true. Not any more absolutely for sure. How long, students, before the positive pregnancy test reverts to normal after a miscarriage?"

"Three days?"

"Good enough. Some are longer than that."

"I thought I was pregnant but I never did a test. So, now I know for sure, thank you."

"When was your last period?"

"You mean other than this, this one just now?"

"Yes."

"I can't remember. A long time ago, they're so irregular, I never know."

"This is often the case in young girls. Their hormones haven't kicked in like clocks yet so again it's possible to be fooled. But there's one certain feature about pregnancy and it's always there, available, in the history. What's that, Dr. Murphy?"

"Sexual intercourse, I would expect."

"That's it. But that part of the history is often not forthcoming. And why is that?"

"Reluctance on the part of the patient to reveal her sexual history."

"True. That's something we all share. Being open about sex is not easy. For example, Dr. Murphy, when was the last time you played soccer?"

"Three nights ago."

"And when was your last period? Don't answer that. You won't answer as easily as you did about soccer. You'll tell me that it's none of my business and you're right, but I'll tell you that under any other circumstances, a doctor-patient clinical examination, it's a question that has to be asked. No matter how awkward you feel. And one more thing. Never trust the answer. Order the test even if they say yesterday was my last period, Doctor. Ask them about sexual activity, don't hold back. If someone's pregnant, then you don't really have to ask because we already know, at least the facts if not the circumstances. Most circumstances are good, but not all. So you can ask about that too, if you're not sure."

He turned back to Rowena.

"Have they always been heavy, your periods? Heavier than average?"

She shrugged her shoulders.

"I never talked to anybody about periods. Nobody talked to me. My friend, we call it, that's all I know."

Medically the gynecologist knew that there were two possibilities: one, she'd spontaneously miscarried and bled to excess; two, she'd had an abortion somewhere in the streets of St. John's and it had gone to hell in a handbasket.

"We'll discuss this at rounds," he said, "and you're right, you are no longer pregnant, Miss Savoury. I'm not sure if I should express my regret."

"It's okay, it's better than okay."

"Ten percent of pregnancies, it happens. A spontaneous

miscarriage. So in a way, what's happened here, to you, is perfectly normal. But for the extent of the bleeding."

"I wouldn't know."

"No, you wouldn't. Is there a father for this...your situation?"

He made a vague motion with his hands, as though her situation had wings and was flying out the window.

"There is no situation, now," she said, "and there is no father."

A minute ago she seemed so young that pregnancy was impossible, and now she seemed older than her age. A chameleon, this outport girl.

"We still don't understand the bleeding, Miss Savoury. You'll have to stick around until we do."

The police had already asked him when they could talk to her. They'd been at the scene and had been instrumental in getting her to the hospital on time. But he'd put them off, saying she wasn't ready, she needed to recover her strength, she'd need a few days for that. Now, with the pregnancy test back, maybe in fact they wanted to do more than just say hello to her.

If they knew. It wasn't up to him to tell them anything.

So what he wanted to say to her, now, to his patient, with some urgency, just to her, without the students, privately, was this: get your story straight, little Miss Savoury, because the police are coming your way with possibly more awkward questions. Different than these medical questions.

He'd run this whole issue past the young doctors at break. A good teaching point this was, the sudden loss of a pregnancy, the legal and the illegal causes. Bring in confidentiality too, what we can and cannot divulge to the authorities. The patient is primary. The patient is primary. Never forget that. You couldn't say it too often.

But now in fact their primary patient seemed pretty sure of herself. She even looked happy.

"When can I have more visitors?"

"Anytime, if they're family. Oh, one more thing. There'll be a psychiatrist coming, probably this afternoon. By the latest, tomorrow."

"For me? A psychiatrist? Why?"

"Ask one of these young doctors."

"Why a psychiatrist?" said Row Savoury, scanning the trio at the foot of the bed.

"Post-traumatic stress," one of them said.

Rowena laughed. "Me?"

The gynecologist said, "Someone scares us like you did, yes, we want them to talk to you. You've been through a lot. Post-traumatic stress, a bugaboo they're starting to worry about. I'm not so sure it exists but it's protocol. You nearly died."

"I don't feel stress, I feel the opposite of stress."

"There you go. Still, it's routine, we pick whoever's on the duty roster and we give them a call and they come and see you and all the bases are covered. Then we don't worry. Okay?"

"Okay sure, whatever you'd like. Thanks for everything you did, Doctors."

She included the students in her wave goodbye as they trooped back to the nursing station. There the gynecologist looked at the on-call list, clipboarded to the wall.

"Let's see...Dr. Poole, Quidi Vidi Road. That's not far. Give this guy a call please, we need a psychiatric consult for our little girl."

"Miss Savoury?"

"That's her."

Psychiatrist? Send in the clowns you mean, thought the nurse. That girl needs no one but her mother, and she's got her already.

"Dr. Poole? Actually, Dr. Poole's a she," she said.

"Better, better, even better. Better a woman for this, probably."

"Oh, and Doctor, the police, they're still phoning. Twice already this morning. They want access. Access, that's what they call it."

"They'll have to wait. Soon though."

Thus came to pass the coincidence of Dr. Poole being consulted on her own convoluted case, asked to give advice on the situation she partially created herself.

And when she got the call, she sat down until her heart resumed its normal pacing, which took five minutes, and she wondered if the chickens were coming home to roost. From Boxey or from here, how far back would the police go if they had suspicions?

Well, one thing: relax. Her name was on the schedule and no one could have engineered that. A coincidence. The world's wired for coincidence, she knew, and there's another example.

"I'll be there as soon as I can," she'd said right off, "what's her name again?"

In the cafeteria, young Dr. Murphy was saying to the gynecologist, "You said that under some circumstances we should ask about the circumstances of pregnancy—how it happened—that most were good but not all. But you, we, we never asked this young girl what her circumstances were. Why was that? At her age, maybe they weren't so normal, so good."

"Good question. She's better, she's happy, she has the psychiatric visit upcoming for that. Let sleeping dogs lie. We don't want to turn over every stone every time. Tell you one thing, we'd never finish our day if we did."

AT NOON on the morning after the procedure at Dr. Poole's, the principal's wife was waiting by the curb on the north side of Gower Street, across from Nunnery Hill. Her suitcase was at her feet. The sun was out, the pavement was drying in a hurry. Feathers of steam rose from the middle of the road. She unwrapped her scarf, put her gloves in her pocket and paced twenty yards this way and twenty yards that way and still there was no sign of Rowena. She closed her eyes, counted to sixty slowly, then opened them again. Nothing. Now Row was actually late. She wasn't there, there was no sign of her. Goodness, she hadn't even turned the corner from Prescott Street yet so where was she?

The taxi pulled up and the side window rolled down and the driver leaned over her way.

"All aboard! Where's your girl?"

He got out to pick up the one suitcase. The back window then rolled down too and there was the same woman who'd come to town with them. Mary, that was her name. Her head was partly out now, hand shielding her eyes from the sun.

"Where's your little girl?"

"I don't know, I'm at a loss."

"Sleeping in I bet," said Mary, and the driver opened the trunk and put the suitcase in.

"No, she wouldn't do that."

The driver looked at his watch.

"Listen, I'll pick up the others, it'll take me fifteen minutes and I'll cruise by again, we can make up the time on the TransCanada. But after that, fifteen minutes, then time, tide and the Terrenceville taxi, they wait for no one. We'd miss the boat."

The car left, heading downtown, and the principal's wife had no choice but to walk the forty yards to Prescott Street, to the aunt's house, and knock on the same door by the bedecked flower-boxes full of red geraniums. She double-checked, number 71, the same place she'd knocked last night and now she'd have to do it again.

Knock-knock. She did it. There.

Footsteps came to the door right away and, through the screen was a middle-aged man, tired, his hair dishevelled, in a torn undershirt.

So, this is the uncle.

"Yes?"

"Perhaps you could help me. I'm from the taxi, we're looking for Miss Rowena Savoury and this is the address she gave."

"She's not here. She's in the hospital."

"The hospital?"

"We've been up all night with her, yes, she's in the hospital."

"Which hospital?"

"The General. I phoned in sick myself this morning. First time in years. Christ Almighty."

"She's sick?"

He laughed but he wasn't amused.

"I don't know I'd call it that, *sick*."

He was rubbing his face with both hands, yawning. The principal's wife felt the sidewalk shifting under her, destabilized. She touched the door frame.

"So she won't make the taxi."

"No, she won't make the taxi, I can guaran-fucking-tee you that."

"I beg your pardon?"

"She's not going to make your taxi."

He started to close the door but she said, "Wait, what in the world was the trouble?"

"You don't want to know."

And this time he did shut the door and she walked back to Gower Street and sat on the front step of one of the anonymous houses. She pulled her knees up to her chin, trying to compact herself, to feel solid. And then the taxi was there again, back faster than she thought it would be, full now but for the front seat which was waiting for her and Row.

"I'm sorry, I can't find her, I'll have to have my suitcase back," she said.

Those words skimmed out of her. What else could she do? The driver turned the key off, got out and pulled her suitcase out from the others.

"There you go. She's all right?"

Nothing seemed to bother him, this man. He was still on time. Unconcerned.

"Sorry."

"It happens, it's not the first, it won't be the last."

He gave her his card with the phone number printed on it—Terrenceville Taxi, the logo with fir trees and a moose, rampant—and she took it, even though she had already had two of them in her purse.

"I'll call as soon as I can."

"No trouble. Listen. Any Monday or Thursday, I can be here, same time, same station."

Then the cab was gone eastward up the street, not dawdling, and the principal's wife was already on her way back to the boarding house. There, in the communal bathroom, she threw cold water on her face and tied her hair back tight, tight, then tighter, a lump in her throat making swallowing difficult.

What to do now, what to do.

"It looks like I need to stay another night or two," she said to them downstairs.

She left and walked to Quidi Vidi Road, to the doctor's. There she knocked on the back door again. She was knocking everywhere she went it seemed, and tentatively too as though she were timid, afraid, scratching more like a mouse. Back home, nobody knocked, they just opened doors and walked in because knocking meant trouble. So nobody knocked.

No answer here, not this time.

She couldn't sit and wait. She went back up the side of the house to the street, turned towards Forest Road and walked past the cemetery to the hospital.

"I'm sorry, it's not visiting hours."

"Where is she, please, Miss Savoury?"

"Savoury? Let me see. Is that Rowena?"

"That's her."

"She's in ICU and I'm sorry, that makes visiting even more difficult."

"ICU? I'm her mother."

"That's different then, honey. Mothers, they get a free pass. Down that way, up the elevator, I hope she's okay."

She had to wait twice for the elevator. It was too crowded, too many young people in white coats. She hung back. She couldn't go in there with them. Her mouth tasted as dry as dust but there was a water fountain across the way and she bent to it, she drank and then the elevator was there, empty this time. Up she went. The doors opened.

Whatever I find, I find, but please let it be good.

She thought about taking the elevator straight back down but no, she couldn't do that in a million years. She followed signs for the ICU and identified herself.

"Oh my, you're the mother! Some lucky your girl is, you're here, come in, come in!"

The one who said she was Rowena's nurse took her by the arm. Then she was pulling some curtains back and smiling and saying, "Your mother's here, your mother's here, Rowena."

God, she's fine, she's sitting up.

The principal's wife put her purse on a chair and then put her arms around the girl.

"Darling," she said.

The nurse was rattling on, "My, it was touch and go last night but look at her now."

"I guess we missed the taxi," said Rowena.

"Yes we did, but never mind that."

"They had to give her blood last night, multiple units of packed red blood cells," said the nurse.

"Blood?"

"Lots of it. About as much as you can get. That's what they said in report."

The lower section of the window to the outside was levered open. A breeze came through it over a gravelled roof.

"It was a heavy period, they tell me," Rowena said.

"Now girl," said the nurse, "tell your mother everything."

"Everything? I don't remember."

NICHOLAS RUDDOCK

162

"It was the police who brought her here. And there's more to it than just that."

Rowena was surprised. She let go of the principal's wife.

"The police?" she said.

"Let me take your blood pressure. Yes, the police, and you are one lucky lucky girl, what with your condition and all."

And the principal's wife was thinking, police? condition? She sat on the chair while the nurse pumped up the cuff and put the stethoscope in her ears and wrinkled her forehead, her nose, and wrote some figures down.

In a pinch someone could squeeze through this window and take off across the gravel roof and jump to the ground and run. But she and Rowena didn't have to run, they just had to sit tight, say nothing, and then go home, none the wiser.

The relief she felt now was like heaven and Row could have been dragged to the hospital by the four horsemen of the apocalypse for all she cared, let alone the police, because look at her, she's okay and that's what matters.

"Your blood pressure is perfect, one hundred over sixty. You're certainly out of the woods, Miss Savoury, and you'll be out of here in no time. And, by the way, that's a lovely name, Savoury, I love it, you two are lucky. We don't see Savoury much around here. Kind of reminds me of Christmas, happy times, everything looking up, although I don't know why. Know what I mean?"

"Savoury's a spice. Most people do like it," Rowena said.

THE CHIEF picked up the file. He read it through for the third time—it only him took five minutes, it wasn't long—and then he called the Sergeant and asked him to come up, please.

The Sergeant stopped what he was doing at the front desk and came down the long hall, and the secretary ushered him in, and he sat down in the single chair, uncomfortable in his bulk because the Chief was as thin as a greyhound and worked out every day.

The Chief said to him, "What do you make of this?"

The Sergeant was nonplussed, or pretended to be.

"Make of what?"

"Our new constable. This Jack Maher. This report here. He writes well, this 71 Prescott Street thing, he summarizes what happened, he mentions in the middle of this report how there was a suggestion—he calls it that, a suggestion—of an abortion having taken place, yet, come the summary, also well written, there's no mention of it—the abortion— just the ambulance, the girl goes to hospital, the uncle's arrested, he's unarrested, not really pro forma but we have no issue with that. My question is, what happened to the abortion charge?"

"Well, Chief, he hasn't been able to follow up yet, the girl's in ICU and we have no access to her."

"Not my point. My point is this: the constable should have highlighted this issue in the summary, not buried it. It makes it look as though it were buried on purpose."

"He worked a double-shift, maybe he was tired. I read it, I thought it was good. Everything's there."

"Talk to him, Sergeant. Send him back to the hospital as soon as we get the go-ahead, talk to her, talk to the family. Minimizing crime, turning a blind eye, we don't do that."

"He doesn't think anything happened. No crime, just a crazy uncle blowing off steam."

"How many years of service does he have, and how many do you and I have?"

"I get your point. He's been with us three months."

"Stay on him, I want this resolved without any more pussyfooting. This is our official take on it: it's a fucked-up illegal abortion until proven otherwise. We've seen enough of those in our time. Oh, and one more thing, unrelated. We have a request from a force out west—this is not for general consumption—they'd like someone for undercover."

"We're shorthanded now. That's why the double shifts."

"We cooperate now, they cooperate when the time comes. Who comes to mind, here?"

The Sergeant mulled it over, running through the new recruits, and he pointed to the Prescott Street file. He leaned forward and tapped it with his finger.

"You could do worse than Jack. He's good, he's smart, he doesn't stand on ceremony. I could see him doing that."

"Smart? You say he's smart? You need a different kind of smart for undercover."

"Like cagey? Jack could be that."

"Is he single?

"He has a girlfriend."

"La-di-da. I wonder what that means, a girlfriend? What's it mean these days?"

"You know better than I do, Chief. Girlfriends mean different things to different people."

And the Chief laughed, as the Sergeant knew he would. The Chief had been married three times. He came around the side of the big mahogany table, laughed some more, clapped the Sergeant on the back and said, "Dismissed, dismissed, get the hell out of here. Girlfriends! Why there's girls all over the country, last time I looked. Am I not right?"

And the Sergeant had to agree, it was the truth, it was one of those certainties of which there weren't many in their line of work. There were, indeed, girls all over the country.

"Same parts, same everything," said the Chief, "now get out of here."

THE STUDENTS were looking at the posted results of the exam they'd just written. Tryphena Grandy was there in her accustomed first place with 98% but Stan had just scraped by, rock-bottom.

"My God, look where I am. 62%," he said.

"Not great but you passed. You'll graduate and then no one will care about this mark. Ancient history."

"I'm a bottom-feeder, a dragger. While you are the *Bluenose*, Tryphena. You skim the surface of the sea."

"I think they're fixing the *Bluenose*, Stan. They're always fixing the *Bluenose*. It's falling apart."

"It is?"

"I think so. It's been a sinkhole for money. Compare me to something else."

"I can't. Either way, my marks are subaquatic while you're walking through air."

"What did you expect? You hardly studied."

"Not true. I did but I studied the wrong things."

"Egypt?"

"Ancient Egypt. How'd you guess? I got side-tracked when it came to the properties of tooth enamel. That got me thinking of pottery, that got me thinking of Egypt and the kids wanted another bedtime story and there were sabretooth tigers in the story and one thing led to another. That led, maybe partially, to 62%."

Other students were crowding around now, pushing them off to the side. There were moans, cheers and groans and oh-my-Gods which could have meant anything from extreme happiness to despair.

"As it turned out, though, I discovered that the Egyptians knew a lot about teeth. But they didn't ask for any of that knowledge on this exam. It's disappointing."

"You have to learn from your mistakes. This is how you're going to make your living. Prioritize."

"For example, Ancient Egyptians strengthened their jaws and teeth by chewing papyrus. Did you know that?"

"No."

"Was it on the exam?"

"No."

"That's how they made paper, Tryphena, by chewing."

"I have to go to my locker."

"I'll go with you."

They walked away from the crowd and took the stairs to the basement.

"I learned that skull studies have shown that Egyptian molars were twice the size of ours."

"That can't be true."

"Why not? Those were different times. That's what I said to the kids, about sabretooth tigers. They were scared, so I said that those were different times. Look at the jaw muscles of the tigers, I said. Look carefully at the ancient drawings."

"Study the curriculum, Stan, our curriculum."

Their lockers were next to each other and she bent to her combination.

"I can do that for you," he said.

"You can?"

"I've watched you spin it, I know it off by heart."

"Stay out of my locker, Stan."

"I would never touch your locker. Or the lock for that matter."

"More useless knowledge for you then. You're the king of that. Oh, and Stan, since you're the king of useless knowledge, and speaking of Egypt, I might as well tell you this."

She paused and pulled a book from the top shelf of her locker. But she didn't open it, just put in her backpack.

"Wait," she said, "let me remember. I'm thinking."

"I'll wait, no rush, I have all day."

He'd be happy if they never moved, if they stayed by their lockers for a millennium.

"Stan, do you know why sabretooth tigers are extinct?"

"No I don't."

"Then you didn't study enough, even in your own field. They're extinct because of pumice stone."

"Explain that, Tryphie. You got me there."

"The sabretooth tiger hunted in the reed beds of the Nile River."

"True."

"For its prey. But the underlying bedrock there is made of pumice."

"Maybe true, I don't know."

"The Nile River originates in the Congo a thousand miles away."

"True."

"Stan, the Nile River scours down through pumice for a thousand miles and small animals drink from the water just like you and I drink from the tap. Or from the fountain upstairs. But the Nile water is filled with invisible granules of pumice. Jam-packed with it. So gradually these small animals become saturated with pumice stone, they slow down, they become easy prey for the tigers lurking on the riverbank."

"Go on."

"So they get eaten by the tigers. Over years, the tigers have their teeth ground down, relentlessly, by the tissue of their prey, laden with pumice. Those long sabreteeth are ground down to useless nubbins."

"Pumice is an abrasive, you mean."

"Exactly. Imagine it, those poor tigers. Evolutionary advantage becomes a disadvantage."

"So they died."

"No ripping or grasping teeth anymore, so yes, they died. Not right away. But that's why we don't see them anymore, sabretooth tigers."

That's why Stan loved her, for what she said and talked about, not just for the daily sight of her, though honestly that would have been enough on its own.

"Can I lock that for you? Your hands are full."

"Sure. Anyone can do that. Just don't open it without permission."

"I would never do that."

"Thank you."

He inserted the loose end of her combination lock into its receptive opening. He pushed it closed, deeply, and he sighed. He looked at her but she didn't respond. She'd missed the obvious metaphor of the sexual act, or ignored it, or both, or neither.

That was as far as he could ever get with her.

They climbed the stairs and walked out to Lemarchant Road.

"I guess, Tryphie, you've got all the answers. Tigers, everything."

"I have problems too. I don't talk about mine."

"I'd listen. For you I have all the time in the world."

"Goodbye," she said.

"I'll tell the kids about the pumice, that's a darn good one."

They went their separate ways. He went home to ponder his future and she went directly to the doctor's, out at the mall. There she sat with a *Reader's Digest*, and she was given a plastic container with a screw-on top, and sent next door, holding it, to the lab, for the pregnancy test.

Irony, she felt, looking at the *screw-on top*—its relevance to Butter Pot. And fifteen minutes later she sat in front of the doctor who said, "Yes, it's positive, so come back in ten days and we'll get the ball rolling, Miss Grandy."

He never asked her what she'd like to do with the fact that her life had changed, never asked her whether she was happy or not. He assumed. He assumed, he was a cheerful man.

"Ten days, Miss Grandy," he repeated.

Girls reproducing themselves, the next generation. It was simple for him, centuries of women like this.

"Good for you," said the nurse, cut from the same cloth.

She took the bus home. She thought about the baby she was going to have. She thought about the father. They had chemistry together, for whatever reason, she and Jack Maher, an interesting fact because there was no explanation for it, really. He didn't pay her the same devoted attention that Stan did, for example. Stan was a nice guy. She was lucky to have him in her class but there was no chemistry, no magic there. Nothing kicked in for her, day to day. Whereas with Jack the chemistry—call it that—had knocked her over, she could hardly stand up, the first dance. Without his arms around her, she'd have had to hold onto chairs. Her knees weren't the same that night, they were made of rubber.

Chemistry, atoms and molecules that surged through the blood, throwing caution to the wind, chemistry that brought them to where they were now.

ROWENA STILL in the ICU. The activity level hummed along on a twenty-four-hour basis, unchanging. There was no downtime. Lights were hardly ever dimmed, or if they were dimmed, then suddenly they were up again and feet were running past her. All she had to separate herself from this was a lightweight beige curtain which hung from a wheeled track on the ceiling. It opened with a swoosh. Telephones burbled, nurses spoke to themselves and metallic trays fell to the floor with a clatter. But she was feeling fine physically. She had no bleeding at all.

"Why can't I get out of here?" she finally asked.

There was no rush, there was a bed shortage on the wards, they'd had a bus accident with non-life-threatening injuries, beds were full.

"Not the Mount Pearl bus," she said.

"No, somewhere near Ferryland."

Then, in the afternoon, finally something of interest.

"Rowena? The psychiatrist's here for you."

She put her magazine down.

"Yikes," she said, though she'd been warned.

"We don't see much of them here, they're rare birds in ICU. Getting more common though, it's the modern age. Sigmund Freud, that's all I know. His name."

"Wait a minute, let me think."

"Sure, she can wait. No rush."

"She?"

"Yes, it's a she."

But first the nurse put a thermometer in Rowena's mouth and disappeared around the curtain. A minute later she came back and took it out and gave the satisfied look, the nod she had. She shook it down with her wrist.

"Hmm, good, ninety-eight degrees, normal, everything's fine, Miss Savoury. Okay, so it's time for her now. You okay?"

"Yes."

"I don't think you're a mental case. None of us do. But that's our opinion and in the grand scheme of things around here, our opinion carries no weight. Zero. So, the psychiatrist."

Then she was back with none other than Dr. Poole herself, Dr. Poole looking so different in her white lab coat, clipboard held to her chest with both arms, smiling professionally— though she was forcing that smile upon her face. It looked unnatural, implanted there.

Surely they would notice her, this actress pretending.

"So, let me introduce myself, I'm Dr. Poole," she was saying.

But no, to everyone else she was relaxed, friendly. She gave a separate smile to the nurse.

Rowena nodded to her.

"I'll leave you two then," the nurse said, "shout if you need anything."

And she left and the doctor pulled the curtain around, sequestering them. Now it was just the two of them, a window half-open to the outside, to a gravelled roof, then a gap for the street, then the tops of distant trees. Greenery swaying.

The doctor pulled a plastic chair closer to the bedside and then she paused, waiting for the nurse's footsteps to recede.

"Rowena," she said.

Row was sitting in the middle of the bed, still in her hospital gown but she swung her legs to the same side as the doctor.

"Rowena, I apologize to you. I've made the biggest mistake a doctor could make."

She was speaking so quietly, her voice couldn't have gone anywhere. She was bending forward at the waist, almost whispering.

"Rowena, they called me to see you."

"So you're the psychiatrist?"

"That's right. Me. That's what I am on my better days. Can I sit down?"

She was now speaking in her normal voice and the girl gestured her to the chair.

"It's my turn on the call system. So they called me. Here I am."

"I'm glad it's you."

"Really?"

"It could hardly be someone better."

The doctor sat down, the clipboard now on her lap. Rowena's legs were just a foot away, as bare as they were last time.

"I've been castigating myself, I made a mistake, I should have been more specific in my questioning. I'm out of practice in clinical medicine, I should never have let you go home like that."

"It's okay, it worked out, look at me. I'm fine."

I'm fine, she said, just as she had said to the principal's wife, *look at me*, and she held her arms up to illustrate her recovery, her vigour, her health.

"Still, there's no excuse. Forgive me."

"The doctors are talking about some kind of bleeding disorder. I lost so much blood it couldn't have been normal, they say. How could you possibly know about that?"

"By asking. By asking more specifically. Maybe something in your family?"

"You did ask. I said there were no troubles. As far as I know, that's true. Without you, Dr. Poole, I'd still be where I was, so I'm grateful, I'm nothing else but grateful. Look at me."

She moved her arms up and down again, as though she could fly.

"Okay, I see, you're happy, that's good, I'm relieved. You look better than I feel. So. Down to brass tacks now. I'm supposed to talk to you about your mental health. Forget mine. I need to write a report, a consultation, so let's talk, we'll talk. This is something I can do, I can talk and write with the best of them."

"What do we talk about?"

Dr. Poole was taking a pen from her purse, testing it on the paper on the clipboard.

"Start with your family, Miss Savoury. Oh, no, first tell me where you're from. Tell me as though I know nothing about you. And that's not far from the truth."

They were alone for an hour, murmuring behind the curtain, unintelligible to the outside world. The ICU staff shook their heads. Apart from suicide attempts, they hadn't seen a psychiatrist on their floor for years.

A uniformed policeman came into the ICU. He too wanted to see the girl.

"We heard she's okay now."

"Grand Central Station," the nurses said, "wait your turn."

"Who's with her now?" Jack asked.

"The shrink."

"Oh, she needs a shrink?"

"Someone thinks so. Maybe we all need them, maybe they're indispensable."

They smiled. The policeman was young and good-looking, there was nothing to not smile about.

"I can see her then, when he's finished?"

"The doctor is a she. Third time I've had to say that."

"When she's finished?"

"I'll stick my head in, they've been there a long time. I'll ask."

Jack saw the nurse do exactly that, put her head through the curtains. Then she looked back at him and nodded.

So, it would be okay. Access at last. But what was he going to ask her?

Rowena was saying, "I don't know what to say to them. The

police? They brought me here, I know that."

Dr. Poole was drawing random lines on the cover of her notebook, now closed. They'd covered a lot of ground, enough for her to write something convincing. Massage it here and there and the consultation has been thorough, it's finished, and the girl will be okay from a psychological point of view, she's over this, just let her go home when the haematology is complete. When she's safe. That's what's important.

"Here's an idea, Rowena. About the police. Do you know what amnesia is?"

"Amnesia? That's forgetting."

"That's right. Have you heard of retrograde amnesia?"

"Retrograde means backwards."

"Correct. So retrograde amnesia is forgetting, backwards in time. It's a known medical condition. It happens mostly with head injuries but it can happen with any major trauma. You've had major trauma. You're a prime candidate for retrograde amnesia."

"Meaning I don't remember what happened?"

"Yes, and for some time previous too. Memory loss in a retrograde direction. For example, you might have forgotten the whole day before, or most of it."

"I see what you mean."

"All you can remember is leaving the house. Your aunt's. After that, nothing."

"They'd believe that?"

"They'd have to. It's science, it's documented. Assuming it's true. I'll put it in this report too, if it's true."

"I do remember leaving the house."

"You do?"

"I remember everything, actually. All night."

"Maybe you do, maybe you don't. Maybe you're confabulating, filling in the gaps. That's also a normal psychological response to stress."

"I went out from the house in the morning. I walked to the

harbour and I walked a lot of places and after that, now that you mention it, it's all gone blank."

"Really?"

"I thought I remembered but now there's nothing there."

They both smiled.

"This is going well," said Dr. Poole.

"Yes," said Rowena.

"In fact then, from my examination, it appears that you do have retrograde amnesia. This will be one of the pillars of my report. A defence mechanism, a protective device for the long-term health of the psyche. Otherwise we'd be tormented by negative experiences."

"Not negative for me."

"I'm finished then. I'll come back again, once, to make sure you're okay."

"Great, thanks, thanks for coming."

"Well, they called me. That was lucky. You've been through a terribly hard time. I'm sorry."

"They told me I had blood transfusions, enough to start my own blood bank, they said. But now I don't remember any of it. All of that is flown away."

"Do you remember me?"

"Sure I do. Once from back home, that's all. Years ago. Then just now, right now."

"There you go then. So I'm going. I'll write this up. Not much to go on because of the amnesia, but we've made strides. I'll check on you, probably tomorrow, and before long before you'll be back home safe and sound, and all of this will be over. Miss Savoury, it's been a pleasure to meet you."

She stood up and whisked the curtain open on its rails, pulling it wide. Now they could see the nurse's station and the policeman who was sitting there watching them.

He in his dark uniform, everyone else in the purest white.

The psychiatrist, Jack could see, was a woman—as they said she'd be—maybe forty-five, thin and brisk, a clipboard in her arms tucked tight to her chest, and she first looked his way, bent back to the girl, touched her on the shoulder and spoke to her again. Then the girl actually reached up and hugged her as though they were the best of friends.

Fast work. So they were close already, closer than usual.

Then the psychiatrist came over to him directly. He stood up for her, hat in hand, and she stood in front of him. She was feeling stronger now. She was the hunted one but aware of it, he the hunter, unaware.

"She's all yours," Dr. Poole said, "Miss Rowena Savoury, but don't push her on anything please, she doesn't need that. I'm Dr. Poole, by the way."

She held her hand out and they shook hands.

"Constable Maher," he said, "I'd never push her. There's just a few questions."

"He's the one who brought her in," one of the nurses volunteered.

"Oh," said the doctor, "nice to meet you then. If you have a minute, maybe you can tell me what you found, where she was. She remembers nothing. The whole day's gone blank for her. Retrograde amnesia, it's called."

"In fact, he saved her life, from what we heard," the same nurse said.

"That's an exaggeration," said Jack, "but she wasn't in great shape."

"Post-traumatic amnesia, retrograde for some hours. We see it frequently. After what I understand she's been through, it's doubtful she'll ever remember. Was she at her aunt's house when you found her?"

"There's an investigation, we're not really at liberty to discuss the case. But yes, that's where she was."

"Can you tell me anything more?"

"No and yes. After all, we're on the same side. Bleeding vaginally, unconscious. Soaked pads under the bed."

"Oh my God."

"But all's well that ends well. From here, she looks okay."

"She is. She's better. But why exactly do you have to see her? Why is there an investigation?"

The policeman walked halfway back to Rowena with the psychiatrist, so they could be alone.

"There was a question at the scene, a comment about a possible abortion. Did she say anything to you about that?"

"My turn to be confidential. But no, no, there was nothing like that. The fact is, she can't remember anything anyway. So who knows."

"Thank you. My turn then? Nice to meet you."

"Yes."

She nodded and left the ICU and he sat down in the same chair she'd been in and introduced himself to Miss Savoury and said he'd seen her the first time under much more difficult circumstances.

He put his hat on the bed. Whenever she moved her legs, it moved, a bounce, a shift.

But she didn't remember him, she didn't remember him at all, not from the house or from the ambulance.

"But I heard you're my saviour, that much I know."

"I helped, that's all," he said, "it was the medical people who saved you, not me."

She shook his hand in a formal way. She was a bit thinner than Tryphena, and younger, but otherwise the two of them had a shared happiness that rose out of them unforced, he could see it right off, a contentment even here in the ICU, after all she'd been through. Physically though, all of these girls and women, counting the doctor, were nothing. They could break as easily as sticks.

"So, hello again," he said.

He was proud of what he'd done for her but now, sitting there, he was also worried about what he was supposed to do next.

He took notes—as the doctor had done—but in his case he

had just a small notebook propped against his knee. A pencil.

"Age, name, address, please?"

"Rowena Savoury, 16, Bell Harbour, Fortune Bay."

"You have brothers and sisters?"

"Three brothers, that's all. No girls but me."

"Your father, what's he do?"

"We have the convenience store. He runs it."

"Your mother?"

"She takes care of us. She helps out in the store. So do I."

"I hear she's visited you already. So she's in town?"

Rowena laughed and moved her legs and feet and the policeman's hat wiggled on the bed.

"That's not really my mother. That's the principal's wife, from home. She lied about that to get in here, said she was my mother though she's not. Without her, I'd be alone. White lie, she says."

"Her name?"

"Alma Fiander. Mostly we just call her the principal's wife."

"Why's that?"

"I don't know. Like that forever."

"How did she know you were here?"

"We travelled together. Boat and taxi. We were supposed to get the taxi back, I guess it was this morning. I've lost track of time. Maybe it was yesterday? Anyway I missed it, she tracked me down. Came to see me right off and they didn't ask for her ID."

"Her identity remains safe with me."

"My real mother, she'll be here soon. The boat's tied up for weather, we heard."

"Storms pass, mothers will come."

"I hope so."

"Now if you don't mind, there's a few other and harder questions I have to ask you, Miss Savoury. You don't have to answer any of them if you don't want to."

"Go ahead."

Be direct when you start questioning a suspect. Don't pussyfoot around.

"We heard you were pregnant. That's the fly in the ointment, that's why I'm here."

"Where did you hear that?"

"I can get the medical records, to confirm, by court order, or what the heck, you can just tell me, if you know."

The girl looked straight at him and said, "Yes, I was pregnant, so they tell me, but now I'm not."

He made a few quick notations in his book which were actually just hand movements. Sometimes, Tryphie, he'd say, when I'm talking to a witness—not that I've done it a lot—I pretend to write, I move my hand along, or I actually write words down but they're nonsense words. I rub them out later, it gives me time to think.

"Miss Savoury, how far along were you in this pregnancy?"

"Eight weeks more or less, something like that. A guess."

"And the purpose of your trip, here to town?"

"To check St. John's out for university. My marks are good. And to see my aunt."

"How do you like it here?"

"I liked it before this happened. Not sure I like it now. But it's a big place. Do you like it?"

"I never lived anywhere else."

"I think I walked as far as the university."

"You remember that?"

"It's more a feeling. I think I saw it, or part of it."

"That's a ways from Prescott Street. But now, back briefly to the pregnancy then, if you don't mind, were you okay with it?"

"No, I was not okay with it. The opposite, I was horrified."

"Horrified?"

"I'm happy it's gone."

"You've been told that? It's gone?"

"Yes. The doctors said."

"Who is the father?"

"As far as I'm concerned, there is no father. There was just a mistake."

"So what were your plans? What were you going to do?"

"What do you mean, do? Do about what?"

Ask her outright, get it over.

"Did you make plans to terminate your pregnancy? In other words, have an abortion?"

She surprised him again.

"Yes," she said.

"Yes?"

Pencil hovering over the page, waiting.

"As soon as I figured out what had happened, I thought about it. I read about it. But I didn't have the faintest idea how to go about it. So I could not make an actual plan."

"You did nothing."

"Correct."

"I wouldn't know how to go about it either," he said.

Don't tell them anything about yourself. Be a cipher. Tryphena would be at the doctor's right about now. He looked at his watch. Actually, not quite yet. This same dilemma might soon be coming his way, almost for sure. If he timed it right, he could pick her up, pretend to arrest her in the cruiser.

"You came here by taxi?"

"By boat, then the taxi, yes, from Terrenceville."

"Tell me what you did, in detail, if you can."

"What I did here?"

"Since, say, the first morning. That's two days ago by the way, not one."

There was something about the girl that was familiar and it wasn't because she was happy—as Tryphena was happy—she was too young to remind him directly of Tryphena.

"I remember my uncle asked me if I wanted to ride the bus and I said no, I'd just walk and explore and I left on my own and walked all over the place. Oh, I sat by the harbour for a long time."

"That's it?"

"That's what I did."

"Your uncle. Do you get along with him okay?"

"Yes and no."

"Meaning?"

"My mother says he's a chauvinist. He doesn't like my mother, and that makes it hard for me. I love my aunt though, she's the best."

"But he's a reasonable man?"

"I wouldn't say that. He thinks I've got attitude. That may be slightly true. Why do you ask?"

She smiled at him. No attitude towards him, not yet.

"Because he said at the house, I heard this when I was there, when I was there,"—he made a show of flipping a few pages of his notes—"your uncle said, to me, on the night that you were...sick...here I quote, this is what he said... *she was out late, she came home in a terrible state and outright said she had an abortion.*"

There. Cards on the table. How much fun is this? None.

The girl was looking directly at him but the warmth was gone.

"Abortion? Oh, so that's where you heard it, from him."

"Yes."

He stood up and pulled the curtains around, completely enclosing them. No other eyes. And the Sergeant, if he were watching, he'd say, good move, Jack, empty gestures like that, they maximize the nerves. It's like truth serum.

The girl though, it didn't fizz on her. She was still sitting there on the centre of the bed, prim and proper.

"I can't remember a thing after the harbour," she said, "I've tried and tried, I draw a blank."

Rowena protecting herself, protecting the principal's wife, protecting the doctor, her mother and everybody she cared about.

"Nothing?"

"Maybe one thing. I was at the War Memorial in the afternoon. There were bees there."

"What kind of bees?"

"Fat bees. Bumblebees. I said the same thing to the psychiatrist. The one who was just here."

He consulted his notes.

"Dr. Poole?"

"Is that her name? Dr. Whoever, she was really nice. She says I must have amnesia."

"She told me that too."

"So, here I am. I'm not going to be much help, it looks like."

"Well, you never know. Things might come back. Or we get information from other sources. Clarity closes cases, they say, but right now there's no clarity here. Around this case there's fog."

"No fog for me."

"No?"

"Not really. The doctors say that I have something that prevents the proper clotting of blood and that's why I bled so much. They say that although I was pregnant, I miscarried, and that ten percent of the time that happens normally, in any pregnancy, and that it could have happened to anyone, what happened to me."

"Ten percent miscarry? They said that?"

"That's what they told me. So there's clarity for you, if you want clarity."

Now she had the attitude.

"I'm writing that down. One last thing though, and this is more like a generalization, not really to do with your situation, it's really a personal question, off the record."

He closed his notebook and sat forward, towards her.

"There's strong feelings about abortion in the community, some say it should never be allowed, never done at all, and as you said you'd thought of it, abortion—though you had no idea how to go about it—so, would that have been a problem for you, the morality of it, if you'd been able to find a way?"

"No one's asked me that."

"Not the psychiatrist?"

"It didn't come up."

"You don't have to answer."

"I don't mind, actually. I've thought about it. I'm okay theoretically with the termination of pregnancy."

"Termination?"

"That's what they call it in the books. *Termination*. I think we should be in charge of own bodies, women, when things happen to us. Especially if it's not our fault."

"That's your view?"

"Shared with a lot of others. Is that all?"

"I'd like it to be, yes. But I might have to get back to you. My superiors, they'll probably want to know what happened during the missing hours."

Then for some reason, because she liked the policeman, and telling him could make no possible difference, and the conversation was over, she said, "It was raining, I do remember that. It was raining and wet, my legs were cold."

The words *wet* and *raining* triggered it.

The two women on Gower Street, in the side mirror, in the rain. This is the younger one. Almost falling over, leaning onto the other one and holding on. For dear life? Maybe it was dear life. Christ, he was slow on the uptake. The lowered umbrella, the slanting rain, the reassuring okays coming from the older one, the older woman saying we're fine, we're fine.

He didn't twitch or show his hand.

Tryphena, I was so cool, he'd say to her.

"Your amnesia then is not total?" he said.

"Maybe I'm wrong."

"No, you're not wrong. It was raining cats and dogs that night. Torrential."

She shrugged her shoulders. Not in the same lovely way Tryphena did. More perfunctory, dismissive of him now.

"Who knows, the mind plays tricks," she said.

He stood up.

"Mine doesn't, not for long, anyway," he said.

He picked his hat up from the bed and said goodbye to the girl and to the ICU and to the nurses. He walked out into the fresh air and checked his watch and he had fifteen minutes to spare.

Pick her up and get the news.

But he had time to take the route back along Gower Street, stopping where he'd stopped before. Now it was in sunshine, daytime. The street was not as empty as it had been and he got out of the cruiser, as he had on that night, and stood in the road. He looked up and down the street and imagined them coming his way again and there they were, the unmistakable little Miss Savoury from the hospital, her retrograde amnesia starting to develop holes. Like Swiss cheese, mice eating away at it.

Easy to admire her though. Sixteen, and so much more sure of herself than he was. Clarity, she'd jumped on that. She had clarity for herself, somehow. Hats off to her. Whatever happened, so far she's doing okay.

But the Chief, and maybe the Sergeant, they'd want to know who the other woman was, the older one. He could hear their voices saying who the hell was she, Jack? Find out, investigate. Why, Where, When, Who, all those Ws, the other questions, the routine. Get the answers to all of those, Constable.

What in Christ would he do with Tryphena, if she was in this situation? Pregnant.

Maybe he could and should say to her: look what the girl in the hospital did! What girl, what hospital, she'd say. He'd have to tell her the whole story, the umbrella, the rain, the aunt and the uncle and no way that jerk uncle could have made that up, the abortion, the word he heard. Uncle Whoever didn't have the brains or the imagination so it had to be true. What would Tryphie think of that?

Well, don't discuss active cases with anyone, not even wives. They were told that on the first day, in no uncertain terms. You could be suspended for jeopardizing an investigation. Fine. Understandable. But hey, Tryphie's not my wife, she's my girlfriend and she can hold a confidence. Did they say anything about girlfriends? No they didn't. How could he leave her out of this, this predicament, this moral dilemma?

Leave the girl alone, that's what he'd do. Miss Savoury from Bell Harbour. She's suffered enough. If he were in charge, this case would be closed. Dismissed. Retrograde amnesia, strange but true. Look, it'll even be in the psychiatric report, for sure. Read it. Leave her alone and move on.

Back to his own life. He checked his watch and checked on the radio and he was free and clear so he picked her up, Tryphena, waiting for her for just two minutes outside the doctor's office.

"Positive," she said right off, sliding into the front seat, "we're screwed, Jack. Not just me, both of us this time."

But she was laughing, she kissed him on the cheek, she reached over to him in the strangeness of the police car and held onto him a little longer than usual.

Then she let go and leaned back against her window.

"More room in here, this beats the Vauxhall," she said.

He drummed his fingers on the wheel.

"Christ, Tryphena," he said, "what'll we do?"

"Drop this car off, let's go back to your place," she said.

TRYPHENA STAYED the night.

"What'll your mother say?"

"She'll be all right with it. She trusts me."

The next morning they were still there, lying in bed on Garrison Hill. Morning light came through the half-closed blinds. The good news was, since the pregnancy test came back positive, they hadn't needed condoms. She was cuddled up to him and they were talking about incarceration, being in prison.

"It must be hard, all that time without family," she said.

"They chased the wrong prize, Tryphena. That's what the Sergeant says. They get little sympathy from me."

"And without sex. Months and months. Years."

"Not sure about that, Tryphie, they find a way. Trust me on that. Plus they have conjugal visits."

"Conjugal? That's what we're having, right now."

"Sort of. I think this is more comfortable."

"Bang-bang I bet, under those circumstances."

"I've seen the room. It's like a bad hotel. Institutional green."

His left arm was under her neck, his index finger in her hair, idly twirling.

"You know what?" he said.

"No, tell me."

"I'm investigating a possible abortion at work."

She turned her head towards him.

"Here in St. John's?"

"Yes, right here."

"Wow, tell me about it."

"I'm not allowed. It's an active investigation."

"Tell me anyway."

"Okay. Twist my arm. This is it, Tryphena, in a nutshell. The other night, the heavy rain, I'm out driving down Gower and there's two women walking west and something made me take a closer look. I get out, it's pouring, there's an older woman and a young girl and the young girl seems like she can hardly walk. What's up with this, I think. I offer them a ride. No no everything's fine they say, and the younger one perks up and she's now standing on her own, she looks nearly normal, they say they're almost home, so I leave."

"Gower where?"

"Near Prescott. Anyway, I don't think of them again. Later that night, though, three in the morning, I'm called to Prescott

Street and there's a girl in bed bleeding vaginally. She's unconscious. The man of the house, who seems like a major asshole, claims she's had an abortion. I can't deal with that because the girl's almost dead, we call the ambulance, she goes to the General, she's saved."

"Good."

"Right, good, so I write it up in my report and the Chief reads it, he's always prowling around it seems, he sees the abortion claim—I could hardly leave it out—and he wants me to pursue it. Be a mad dog on crime, he says. He sends me back to the hospital to talk to the girl, and don't be too nice to her he says, but the girl, when I get there, she can't remember diddly-squat because she has amnesia for the whole night and day. I'm thinking we could just let this rest. The doctors say it was a miscarriage, the girl's been through a lot already. So that's what I'm thinking I'll write in my report. Then I remember, hey idiot-fool, this is the girl from Gower Street, the one with the older woman and I put two and two together. What do you think?"

"I don't understand. Two and two meaning what?"

"An abortion. The uncle said he heard the girl admit it, before she passed out. But the aunt says no, she was delirious, she wasn't making sense but you can tell, the aunt's in protection mode, she'd lie at heaven's gate."

"So, what do you think happened?"

"Miscarriage, abortion, either's possible. So I ask her, I'm in the ICU—the girl—what she feels about abortion and she's upfront with me, she says she's thought about it, she'd have done it if she knew how to do it but she didn't know how, and now the whole night's gone blank for her. Then she looks at me and smiles with her freckles because she knows, and I know, that without a memory, she's free and clear. Oh, she's sixteen, younger than you are. Put your leg up, Tryphena, over here. Press in."

"Like this?"

"Yes. Good."

"So she was pregnant, you mean?"

"Apparently. But no more. Anyway, the upshot is this. I think she had an abortion but do I care? I have to care because the Chief cares. He considers her a criminal. Go get her, he says, more or less."

"Abortion's a crime, right?"

"Outside the hospital it is. But they make it hard, it's next to impossible to get it done legally so inevitably some end up in the back street. The law says arrest her, arrest the doctor, arrest everybody. Apprehend them, that's the fancy word for it."

"Arrest the father too?"

Jack laughed.

"No, not him, he goes scot-free."

"Male privilege, I've heard of that."

He stopped twirling his finger in her hair and moved his left arm down lower, behind her back, pressing her even tighter to his side, her left leg bent up and over his.

"I haven't told anybody what I saw on Gower Street."

"Just me."

"Just you. I think there was an abortion, Tryphie. Why else would she be out there walking and falling and not accepting help? She had it done somehow, whether she remembers it or not, and my money's on the Battery, somewhere in there. So this is my dilemma now, because if there's an abortionist and I find him and arrest him and throw him behind bars, then our little hospitalized, nearly dead girl—Rowena's her name—she's charged too. Everybody who helped her is charged."

"That doesn't seem right."

"Tell that to the Chief."

"Jack, you're doing the proper thing. That's good. Don't say a word. Do your best, don't find anything, let it blow over."

"That's dereliction of duty. We don't make the laws, we enforce them. We're not supposed to look the other way."

"She's sixteen, you said."

"So you'd be okay with it, my saying nothing?"

"More than okay."

"Kiss me."

She did, on the side of his neck.

"I'm with her, Jack, whatever drove her to do it, that's good enough for me."

"Tryphie, I guess we should be getting up?"

"Soon."

It was a weekend. They'd already planned to go up the Southern Shore on one of their jaunts.

"Tryphie, wait, does conjugate mean the same as conjugal?"

"Close, I think. Want to try again?"

He turned to her and she to him and they pretended, briefly, to be incarcerated, to be hungry for love despite the institutional room with the spare furnishings and the green paint and the guards outside listening to the moans and groans, unsuppressed.

Bang-bang-bang it was over.

"That was really good," they both said.

"Can't wait till next month," said Tryphena.

"See you then, biker babe, be good out there," said Jack.

An hour later they'd showered and were up and away in the Vauxhall.

"Find some gannets, Jack. But let's stay away from Butter Pot."

His car had cost only eight hundred dollars but it was reliable enough. She'd protested the first time she'd seen it. Stupid Vauxhall. Tires look unsafe, they're as bare as a peach or a tomato, she'd said, no tread at all. Tryphie, not true! Touch the tires with your eyes closed, they're like braille, they've got bumps. She closed her eyes but wasn't satisfied so at Canadian Tire he had new ones put on. No worries now in that department, they could jaunt about the countryside as much as they liked.

"Cape Race? Tryph?"

"That's a ways."

"So what, we have all day."

"Oh, the sweet days of summer, the days so long, that's true enough, we won't be cheated for time today, there's at least sixteen hours of daylight left. So okay, Cape Race."

She had binoculars and a bird book open on her lap.

"I want to see gannets. Gannets, gannets and more gannets."

"Nothing satisfies you. Sometimes less is more."

"Not with birds. The more the merrier."

"Gannets, those I know. Other birds I'm not so sure. Small birds look the same to me."

"According to this book, gannets dive as deep as sixty feet. Imagine that. Then they rub their beaks together when they come back to the nest, saying hello."

"That's true, I've seen it."

He took the turn up the southside hills towards Petty Harbour, saying, "We'll take the scenic route."

Five minutes later the ocean appeared on their left. The sun was so bright they lowered their sun visors simultaneously. Tryphena put on her sunglasses. There was barely a shimmer of wind but the storm swell was still there. On their left, maybe fifty yards away, the sea was breaking on the shoreline. They rolled down their windows, then rolled them back up against a slight chill.

"Mist is rising," she said, "I love those little mist pockets. Water evaporates from the forest floor, I think."

Now and then, if the road dipped low enough, the sun managed to slip behind one of those pockets, creating a local pearl-like haze.

"Mist goes up, fog comes in sideways. That's how you tell the difference," he said.

"If there's a lot of it, it's fog. That's a good general rule."

"Probably true. The girl in the hospital? From Bell Harbour.

There's more fog down there than anywhere else in the world. They say there's a machine that makes it off the Grand Banks. They can go a month or more without ever seeing sunshine, Fortune Bay. They live in grey, or black and white. The damp seeps down on everything."

"How do you know that?"

"I knew a Mountie who worked there. He came back stark raving mad for the sun."

"I wouldn't like that."

"But for us, no fog today, none on the marine forecast. I checked. It's clear like that usually, after storms."

There was almost no traffic. Two or three pick-up trucks came by in the opposite direction. Then the Vauxhall had to tackle a long incline that did not appear to be steep, but nevertheless he had to downshift to make it, trembling, to the top.

"Not a lot of horsepower," he said.

She tapped the dashboard fondly.

"Good enough, good enough. I like this, spring and summer's good but actually fall's the best for me. Kicking leaves."

"What about winter?"

"Too dark, too long."

They listened to the hum of the almost-new tires. They passed eight or nine small towns and it was fully two hours before they were to the point where they'd leave the highway and make the turn left, towards Cape Race. The forested hills by now had disappeared. They were in barrens, endless on both sides of the road. Low vegetation, scattered ponds, ridge-laced runs of bare stone, scrabble where nothing grew, scree, low jumbles of rock turning brown-green with lichen and moss.

"What's the difference between lichen and moss, Jack?"

"I have no idea."

"Lichen grows on rocks, moss grows on organic material."

"Rocks are organic material."

"No they're not."

"Ask any rock, they'll tell you."

Finally they took a break, stopping by the side of the road. She waved her book in the air and said that there were supposed to be caribou. But there were no caribou when they got out and looked, just an otter fooling around in a pond. It ran along the shoreline, dove in, looked at them, climbed out and ran away.

"I thought otters lived in the ocean, in saltwater," she said.

"They live in both places. They like to slide off rocks, organic rocks mind you, into fresh or salt water. They're happy in both places. Be an animal, be an otter, that's what I'd be."

There was a frizz to her hair. It caught the sun like the mist pockets had, back in the forest, and haloed it.

It was still cool so he put his arm around her shoulder and pulled her closer. She put her arm around his waist.

"My turn to drive now," she said, "okay?"

"Sure."

He sat in the passenger seat and took off his shoes and put his feet up on the dashboard.

"I told Stan about my sabretooth tiger theory," she said, laughing.

"The pumice?"

"The pumice."

"Don't talk to me about Stan. I can't figure that guy out. Girls do dental hygiene. Why would a guy go into that?"

"He's not much different than you are, Jack."

"Meaning what?"

"He's a guy, he likes cars and sports."

"He's a guy, he wants to jump your bones, Tryphie, that's all, don't delude yourself. That's what any guy would want. To my knowledge, he has yet to succeed in his desire."

He nudged her in the ribs.

"Joking," he said.

"Jack, you could be friends."

"Guys should not do dental hygiene. It's hard to get past that."

"La-di-da, la-di-da, you're stuck with stereotypes. He's okay. And no, he has not succeeded in his desire."

"But you have felt it, coming from him."

"Desire? Maybe a bit. Mostly he struggles, he's not that happy."

"I'm happy, Tryph. Today I'm happy."

"It's easy for us. Not so easy for him."

"Because he's adopted, you're going to say."

"Fostered, Jack, not adopted. There's a big difference."

"Fostered is worse?"

"I think so, yes."

"Adopted, fostered, happy, not happy, here we are, let's forget him. It's Saturday morning and here's the turn. Left here, Tryphie."

The road to the Cape was soft, too soft. Half of it was gray sand, the other half scattered with fist-sized rocks. Even the new tires couldn't get much purchase. They picked their way for about a mile, sliding through washouts. She used first gear, even reverse. Jack got out twice to push. Then the loose rocks increased in size. Streams of water coursed across the roadbed, and the road itself went up and down like a roller coaster.

"With a Jeep, maybe we'd be okay," he said.

"No sign of a Jeep dealer."

He pulled a map out of the glove compartment.

"We shouldn't push our luck, we might not make it back out."

"We'll stop then, this is nice enough. What the heck."

They were only twenty yards from the sea and the sea was a deep blue because the clouds up high had shredded and blown away and the sun was high in the sky. A slow, soft swell broke casually against the shoreline. She pulled the Vauxhall half-off the travesty of a road, onto the side grass, which was hummocked and relatively dry.

"Fancy this, it's more like the Caribbean today," he said, "but there won't be any gannets, this doesn't look like gannet territory. No cliffs."

"We'll see them later."

They went through wild grass, nearly knee-high, to a small drop-off. A ten-foot scramble down an incline of loosened rock. He scuffed his way down and turned and offered his hand and she slid down into him. For miles left and right, nothing could be seen but the ocean, the shore, a patchwork sky in blue and white. Sun broke on the surface of the water further out and the waves were still high and crashing but even they looked happy. Full of energy.

"What's that smell?" she asked.

Kelp, saltwater, fish but there was something else in the air too, a heaviness. Down on the beach to the west, fifty yards away, a large tubular mass lay on the shore, parallel to the water's edge, as though it had been spun there.

"A whale," he said, "beached."

They weren't the first ones to notice it. Someone had already cut a thick rectangular chunk of flesh out of the dark body, down near the tail.

"Dead for some time. Stand upwind, Tryphie, come over here."

Though the wind was barely perceptible, she did, she walked over to his side.

"Someone's been having fun with a cutting knife, why would they do that?"

"Beats me," he said, "It's a pilot whale. They run ashore a lot, so maybe they're not really the greatest pilots ever, maybe they're misnamed."

Flies darted and scrambled over the carcass, particularly around the eyes, the mouth, and they were also clustered in the deep cut made by the knife. Tryphena picked up a small bleached piece of driftwood and whipped it back and forth.

"Shoo, buzz off."

But the flies paid no attention. The whale's head was waist-high to them, a dried leathery look to it, the mouth half-open with rows of small gapped teeth a golden colour in the sun, staccatoed there like nuggets along the line of the jaw.

"He's been here a while, Jack, more than a few days. If he's a he. Do you think this is a natural death?"

"I expect so, why not? They get caught in nets, they drown, they beach themselves. End of story."

"Whales are cetaceans."

"Yes they are."

She crouched and touched the pilot whale on the nose and then picked up a rock smaller than her hand with a streak of quartz, white as milk, circled through the waist. The rest of it was black. She put it in her pocket. They walked another two hundred yards up the beach until the whale was just a dark shape behind them. They sat on two boulders, half-facing each other, looking out to sea. They ate their lunch, they drank the ginger ale, the sun beat down on them, hot.

"You know, I might take a swim," he said.

"Here? Not me, it's way too cold, I'll pass."

He stood up and shielded his eyes. The shoreline was low, the shallow intertidal zone stretching out for fifty, a hundred yards before the roiling ocean itself.

"All I really need is some place where there's no kelp or seaweed, I can do without that. And protected."

He walked away, leaving her behind, picking his way along the shore. It was low tide and he was able to walk a hundred yards, then another hundred yards skirting the edge of the water all the way until he came to a small peninsula, a shelf of rock. In some places water rushed in through crevices and he had to jump out of the way. But the sun was drying off the highest ridges and there it was, a spot with an entry point, clear water eight to ten feet deep. A starfish in orange at the bottom. He looked back and Tryphie was very small in the distance.

Leaving her could be like this. He'd just keep on going till he was gone and she was gone and looking back there'd be nothing to see but gone. There'd be nothing on the shore.

He waved to her from the vast distance and she lifted her hand in reply. He took off his clothes and dove in, the cold surprising him, the shock of it, his immersion time less than five seconds.

Jesus the water is cold cold cold.

He dried himself with his sweater and was soon back with her, but shivering.

"You didn't stay in long."

"In and out like a bullet. What are we going to do, Tryphie?"

"Do?"

"About this, about us. About you."

He touched her on the abdomen, where the baby was.

"We're not sixteen, Jack, we don't have to *do* anything. We did what we did, it's done. Now we make the best of it. I love you, that's the truth."

He took his hand away from her.

"I love you too," he said.

But he wasn't sure. He was throwing words out like a hangman's noose and he could have been speaking her grandfather's Portuguese. Or Swahili.

"Like the swim, it's a bit of shock, all of it," he said.

"Shock or not, it's the way it is."

On the way home they stopped at a curved beach covered with cobbled rocks. Waves rolled in, smooth combers cresting, breaking.

"Hey, there's your gannets."

Birds with golden heads hovered over the water, folded their wings and dropped straight down and disappeared only to emerge a few seconds later again, back up into the air.

She put her arms around him from behind.

"You're a good policeman, Jack."

"You think?"

He leaned back into her, gently.

"You find things. Gannets even."

"They're easy, they're everywhere."

"You found the girl and you saved her. What's better than that?"

"That was pretty good, I admit it."

"And you'll never tell them about what you think happened, right? Jack?"

"Nope. Decision made. That's what we decided."

"You and I."

"You and I together. Yes, and thanks for that."

"Not telling is no big deal, because we don't know anyway."

"We suspect, right, we do not know."

He was still looking out to sea. He leaned back into her. She pushed back, they held each other up. The wind was getting colder now.

"You could lose your job."

"You testing me?"

"Just checking. I think you got your priorities straight."

"I agree."

"I wonder how they see their prey under water, those gannets. Look at them."

"They have sonar like bats. Like dolphins."

"Jack, you lie, that's not true!"

Zip went the golden heads, their wings so white yet tipped with black, birds who rubbed beaks together at the nest, who mated—her book said—for life.

They watched the gannets and the waves for another half-hour. The horizon had a half-ragged edge to it, as though it was torn from a stretched-out piece of wet paper, as though another storm was brewing, or this one had a ways to go yet.

Jack, you lie, you lie, he kept hearing her say to him.

IT WAS Saturday morning at the convenience store. The storm that had stopped the coastal boat from coming seemed to have passed and the wind had died to just a breeze. From the side window Rowena's father could see waves rising and then falling back against the beach, frothing up the cliff-face on Chapel Island.

He wasn't busy, which was bad. Not busy meant there was no money coming in and they had a lot of expenses. Four kids, maybe a mistake but they weren't thinking about money at the time of conception, were they. The store never made much, he'd never had packets of dollar bills coming home in a wheelbarrow, staggering up the road. Just a trickle of dimes and quarters but that sure beat nothing and this morning it was nothing. Zero.

But today the silence was doubly bad because it allowed him to frown out the window and stew over the phone call he'd just received from Hilda Cluett.

To hell with this. He couldn't wait until lunch. He poked his head out the door and looked up and down the street which was empty of commerce. He looked at the empty wharf, the pile of logs, and he closed the door definitively and hung the sign on the knob which said "Back After Lunch." Then quickly he walked up the hill, the sea sheltered there, quiet on his right, and at the house he went through the back door into the kitchen and there was his wife, her travelling suitcase on the table.

"What the fuck is that? And what the fuck am I hearing?" he said.

"I beg your pardon? The boys! Don't use that word!"

"The boys aren't here, I saw them up the hill."

"Don't use the F-word, we don't use that here ever."

"Okay sorry. What's the suitcase for, honey-pie, and what's that I'm hearing, sweetheart? Why am I the last to know anything about anything?"

"What are you talking about?"

"Mrs. Cluett phones me down at the store and not only does she cancel the fucking order for a box of soft licorice which I ordered in special for her and her dentures, but she tells me cheerfully, as though I should know, because I'm the father after all, that she heard through the grapevine, through the telephone operator, so already thousands know, that the taxi left St. John's without our Rowena and without the principal's wife. Though the principal's wife was there and ready but Row didn't show up."

"That's why the suitcase. I was going to tell you. I'm going to town first thing, soon as the boat comes. It's in English Harbour now."

"What in the world's wrong with Row?"

"She's sick, she got sick. She got way too sick for the taxi."

"Sick with what?"

"Female trouble. She's a girl, maybe you noticed."

"What does that mean?"

"We buy her baseball gloves and soccer balls and a boat and a motor. We should have paid more attention to her. Simple as that."

"I don't get it. What's happened?"

"Female trouble, bleeding, that's what female trouble usually is."

"Oh."

"Enough that she had to go to hospital, and that's where she is now."

"She's okay?"

"Sure she is. But she needs one of us and I think it should be me. I'll be back in a day or two."

His wife was still stuffing clothes into the suitcase and didn't seem to be paying him the fullest attention.

"I'm the one who told her babies came from storks. I put her off, I'm the fool," she said.

"Babies? What's that got to do with it?"

"And you're the fool too, we said nothing to her. Her friends told her babies came on airplanes. She's the smartest girl in the world and she didn't have a clue."

"What are you saying to me?"

"Alan, she got pregnant. Someone took advantage of her. It's as simple as that and it's not her fault and now she's the one to pay."

"Christ almighty."

"That's right, Christ almighty, that's how I feel. Now the baby's lost, thank God that's a blessing."

"The bleeding, you're talking about. That's what it's about?"

"Yes."

"God. I can't believe this. Who should have talked to her? Me?"

"Both of us. We failed her. We fucked up."

"Now you're using the F-word. When did you find this out?"

"The principal called. You were down to the store, I was about to pick up the phone to tell you and then you charge up here as though I've got nothing on my mind."

"Sorry. Jesus."

"That's okay, I shouldn't have snapped your head off either."

"I don't know much about girls. That's the sad truth."

"Stay home with the boys. There's soup, some fish, it's all in there."

She gestured to the refrigerator and closed the snaps on the suitcase.

"Let's go down and wait for the boat. I got no appetite," she said.

"Neither do I."

"The storm's over."

"So they say."

An hour later Rowena's mother was tucked into the cabin and the *Taverner* was rolling past Chapel. Pitching and rolling and everyone else was happy as clams but holding on for dear life while Rowena's mother sat at the small table, holding on too, resting her unhappy head on the suitcase that previously hadn't moved out of the attic for ten years.

Everybody else on board would know why she was going. That's how the telephone worked. News spread like the tentacles of an octopus. They'd know where she was going, but they wouldn't really know why.

"Share the taxi with us?"

"Sure, please, count me in" she said.

"Rowena, she's sick?"

"She's better now. That's what I've heard."

"She'll be fine. Lucky you are, with her, Rowena, a girl like that. Does all the math in her head, I get something at the store. Amazing."

"Thanks, I know. That's thoughtful of you. I'll just rest my head now."

"Sure, you go ahead."

And that's how she stayed until Terrenceville, her head down on the suitcase, her hair sweating against the leather and the chatter of the others until the dock, the taxi, then what seemed like an endless trip to St. John's.

BECAUSE HE saw Dr. Poole just once a month, and because he often thought of Dr. Poole, because his head was full of ideas, Stan had taken to jotting down notes, reminders, things he wanted to cover at the next session. And when he was notified—as he just had been—that his birth mother had reached out through the Children's Aid to find him, to meet him, to say hello, well, that was a powerful moment to say the least. Always he had been the motherless child. Now he could be born again—non-theologically!—but, just as easily, he could be once more abandoned. There's danger everywhere, nothing was simple.

So he wrote down a few things—*a powerful moment*, for example—and thought about a few more, including her responses.

Dr. Poole, should I meet her?

Of course she'd say yes. Keep your heart open, Stanley, some mantra like that. She'd say, that's a strength of yours, your resilience, but he wasn't so sure, he could fake resilience. Watch me smile, he thought. What feelings could my real mother have for me, possibly, after twenty years? Well, that's opening a can of worms, Dr. Poole will say, I expect your mother's feelings will range from love to anger, love for the obvious reason, anger directed at the living symbol of her guilt, the abandoned ship, and that's you, Stanley, sitting across from her. Psychologically that's possible. Why would she love me now, Dr. Poole, if she didn't then? Maybe she'll be acting out of curiosity, we've never spent time together. Wait, that's not true, for nine months we were inseparable, then I was born and five days later it was goodbye, I was packaged up, wrapped in blue swaddling—that's my guess—and given away or taken away or cast away. Castaway, a word of its own. Five days? You were five days old? Stanley, how do you know that? They told me, the Children's Aid. If that's the case, she needed time to think about it and that's not rejection, it's sorrow, regret, helplessness, God knows what the situation was for her. Dr. Poole, you have no children, everything you know about maternal love comes from books, it will be hard to face me, won't it, for her? I may appear as the Grand Inquisitor, I'll be a dagger in her heart. If she has one. She's brave to do this, Stanley, to dial up the agency and identify herself. Amnesia would serve her better. In Ancient Egypt, Dr. Poole, lasting judgment of crimes was reserved for the final Court of the Dead. I have a kindly disposition towards my mother because of that. Christians too believe in a reckoning, ultimately, all societies do. I've managed a sort-of-life without her. Maybe she'll be warm and generous, maybe she'll look to me for generosity, having had little herself. Who knows about her. I've imagined this a thousand times. I forgive her, I forgive her, I forgive her, I forgive her. I can say that a thousand times. This is not likely to help my studies though, I've been distracted. I've taken to copying out all the hieroglyphics from the Rosetta Stone, trying to memorize them. I write them on paper, on cloth torn from sheets. Once, nobody knew what they meant, those symbols, now we do. The text itself is not interesting but the calligraphy, the exercise is.

Moving on. Dr. Poole, they had a nice birthday party for me at home. My brothers and sisters. We're not related of course, except by the fact that we are not in any way related and therefore we play a charade. Nevertheless, it brings us together. Some of us have lived in the same house for five years. So, at the party, they all dressed up as Egyptians and gave me a pyramid. It's on my desk, a toy. The youngest, she's a real firecracker. But she can lose it sometimes. She has healed scars, physical ones, cut marks on her arms, though not the self-administered kind, I don't think. They're random, crisscrossing. She says she fell through a window when she was two. I believe her. I've told her about you, maybe some-day, who knows, she could talk to you. Anyway, they put on paper skirts and togas and got Egypt mixed up with Rome but their hearts were in the right place. It was my first real party, really, just for me.

Let me read you a note I've written out in full. You might think this is about Tryphena but it's about me, when it comes down to it, yours truly.

He stood up from his desk in the quiet of his upstairs room and read aloud:

If I lived in a better climate I would build her a garden. I would populate it with the things she loves. Birds. She loves birds, she knows their names. They don't just fly by her, anonymously, as they do for the rest of us. If I could sculpt from sandstone I would stay on North Head and carve for her the likeness of, let's say, a gannet. Curious onlookers would shake their heads at my persistence. I'd stay nights in a small tent, with my tools, with small fires for warmth, if that's allowed up there. Or, if not a bird, then a plant or an animal. Two known facts: she likes gannets, she likes the carnivorous pitcher plant. She's drawn one of those on paper, the pitcher plant, she showed it to me at her locker, with a fly hovering near the opening, waiting to fall to the nectar. That's me, the fly, I saw that right away, an obvious analogy though she did not mean it, it never crossed her mind. To her, the fly was just food. She's a straight-ahead thinker. If I could touch her emotionally, reach her, I already would have. I'd do anything for her, even prepare a wedding feast when she marries the policeman. Cutlery will shine on linen. Food will come from the sea. I will swallow the spiky outer shell of the sea urchin and let it tear my throat. I will make no sign of discomfort. She will marry him, I know she will.

He sat down with the paper still in front of his gaze. Stanley, that's morbid, she'd say. Granted. So then, I will not read this to you after all, Dr. Poole. I will spare you this. After all, you discourage my attraction—delusional, you say and you're right—to my classmate. That's what you call her now, my classmate, rather than referring to her by name. I don't blame you for this, you're on my side. I'll study harder to be with her anyway. I'm my own person, I'll walk her to school if that's allowed, I haven't asked. Six blocks but why should she be alone that long. I'm getting closer to her, we can talk for five or ten minutes on the phone. She's not as distant, she listens. Of course she's stuck with me anyway, I'm her partner in class until say a Granger comes along, slipping alphabetically between Grandy and Grant, but without this Granger, we're a pair, inviolable till the end of the school year. Which, unfortunately, is not so far away. The chances of this, this Granger person, appearing, are slim. The class is full, there's little to fear in that department. You'll tell me—as you have told me before, Dr. Poole—that there are other girls in the class for companionship, many of them unaccounted for, romantically. How true that is, and how irrelevant. There's no one like her.

I'm besotted, I admit it, I'm sorry. Let me give you an example of why. The other day I told her I thought we were like dentures, the two of us, upper and lower, Polidented together. Explain, she said, distractedly. Okay, I said, we function together during the day, stuck together by name and circumstance but at night we're apart, separated, like dentures, placed by our esteemed elders into an artificial medium, either hydrogen peroxide or water. Imagine, I said, if we actually were those dentures, then we'd be drowning within sight of each other, helpless, but here I overstepped, Dr. Poole, because I said, blowing my cover of insouciance, Tryphie, that's sort of how I feel with you, I'm drowning. Now, she knows nothing of what happened up at the pond. Nothing. Anyway, immediately she scoffed and said that we were way too young to be compared to dentures, that dentures can't drown, they're inert, that even if they weren't inert, they bubble at night in peroxide so maybe they have gills, they're breathing when they're underwater, no one is drowning, Stan, she said, don't be so morose, don't think that way. I said, Tryphie, please, I can't help it, you're breaking my heart. I am a fucking idiot, I said to myself privately but I was unable to stop. What did I do next? I asked her whether she'd like to take a walk downtown with me, look at a few storefronts, and she said, no, storefronts weren't her thing and besides, she couldn't do that, she had to wait for Jack. Storefronts aren't my thing either but I didn't know what else to say. What to offer her. Then the policeman pulls up in his Vauxhall, she comes alive and I'm forgotten and off she goes. This Jack of hers: heartless people wear a disguise and the disguise is fixed, fixed to their face by invisible nails. You never know till they take it off and then you see them, you see the bleeding. That's a warning about the policeman, what I see about him, which I cannot say to her.

Dr. Poole. I know you are busy. These are my thoughts for the last few days. You can see I'm actually moving forward. I'll excise the last part, the Tryphena part. Stay positive! Sure, it's venting, but it helps. You don't have to say much, Dr. Poole, I know what you think.

A knock on his bedroom door. He put his pencil down.

"Stan?"

"Come in."

It was his sister, the firecracker one with the healed cuts, the scars. She usually wore a sweater with long sleeves and she had one on today.

"Can we look at the picture, Stan?"

"Again?"

"Yes, again."

"Sure, why not."

He'd cut it out of National Geographic, from the issue on Ancient Egypt. The drawing of the cow, the calf, the tomb drawing.

"How old is it?"

"Four thousand years."

The cow must have just given birth to the calf, she was licking its arched back and the calf was pushing back with its infantile legs against the strength, the rasp of the tongue. The cow was painted white, the tongue a vivid orange, the calf was a patchy black-and-white and the intervening centuries had crumbled portions of the surface away.

"We can't see her face. The cow's."

"No," said Stan.

"I'd like a copy of that, for me."

"You can have this one. There's others, I'll find another for me. Here, take it."

"Really?"

"Sure. It's yours."

"When do you get to see your mother? Soon?"

"I'm waiting. Any day now, I think. They're going to call."

"It could happen for me, right?"

"Sure it could. That's why we're here."

"I don't think so."

"Don't cry about it."

"I'm not crying."

"Maybe a bit you are."

Twelve years old, not even in high school. He touched her on the shoulder, on the sweater.

"Sorry," he said, "look, take the picture."

"ANYTHING NEW from the hospital?" asked the Sergeant, "this Rowena Savoury?"

"No, we talked but she doesn't remember a thing. Retrograde amnesia."

"That's convenient, for her."

"It's a well-established condition. According to her, that's what the doctors told her."

"Well, I'm no psychologist, Jack, as you know, but it's very convenient, memory loss, it kind of lets her off the hook. And I don't even have to run it by the Chief to hear what he's going to say about it. He'll say it's bullshit. Amnesia, that's bullshit. That's the way his mind works."

"Meaning?"

"Meaning there's no point in telling him what you just told me. He's already said he wants to push on with a two-pronged investigation, no holds barred. So we proceed. Actually you proceed, you're the chosen one. First prong, talk to all the parties involved again, see if we can't find something, some inconsistency, particularly some idea where she was that night. Was she by herself, for example? Was she on her own? Unlikely, I'd think. Second prong, you'll like this one, Cindy Whistle."

"Cindy Whistle?"

"She's in the typing pool, downstairs. Got the most beautiful dark eyes, you could fall into them. You'll see."

The Sergeant was smiling, enjoying himself, thinking of Cindy Whistle.

"And?"

"Jack, here's the truth. There's an abortionist out there. Finding them is the easiest thing in the world, it's usually a piece of cake. They may be burrowed away like rats in a hole in the wall—the Chief's analogy, not mine—but given a case to solve, a policing problem, what's the easiest one in the world? Finding abortionists. She's already done it twice, Cindy has, she smoked them out. That's also the Chief's expression, smoking out the rats. Twice she's done it. All we did was this: ask her to walk up and down Water Street, mope, cry a bit in cafés, say she was pregnant, she didn't know what to do, single, jobless, at her wits' end, you get the drift. Don't hold back on the drama, Cindy, play it by ear. Say you might kill yourself, you should say that, even. She was agreeable, she was having trouble making ends meet, we gave her a bonus for the time and effort. Off she went."

"She has children herself?"

"No. Within half a day, both times, case closed. Unbelievable. Cindy did her thing like she was born to it. She cried in a café for all of ten minutes and the women there understood, they sympathized, they're soft-hearted, they're willing to share secrets, they slipped her a name and a phone number. Here's a guy they said, he'll help you out. We sent her in, an old-fashioned sting operation, she clasps her hands in the waiting-room and bats her eyes and it's over. Game, set, match. First one was a doctor, the other one a so-called political activist, a do-it-yourselfer. Go talk to her. This whole thing, it's yours, run with it."

Like he told Tryphie, Prescott Street was not just going to go away.

He went down to the typing pool. Looking through the door, there were three women there, all wearing headsets. Only one of them was young enough play the role of a pregnant damsel in distress. He asked her to step out into the corridor with him. She shared a look with the others. Their six hands had never stopped moving since he entered the room. *Clickedy-click, clickedy-click.* She wore no rings on her fingers. She stopped typing, she came with him. Luminous eyes? Not really but they were nice in their way, for sure. The Sergeant wasn't far off.

"Cindy Whistle?"

"That's me."

"I'm one of the new constables, Jack Maher."

"Hi. I'm sure I've typed up a few things of yours. I know I have."

"I thought that happened by magic."

"Not really, just these fingers."

She wiggled them, an imaginary typewriter, laughing.

"I'm here kind of officially. The Sergeant says you've done some special work for us in the past."

"Oh, God no. Don't remind me. On Water Street?"

"I think so, yes."

"I wish I hadn't. I wish I hadn't done that."

They were standing in the corridor which was narrow but brightly lit. Their shadows brushed against each other on the wall. He was a lot taller than she was, his shadow more defined.

"The Sergeant would like you to do that again. He said you were great."

"Being pregnant, you mean?"

"Yes."

"I can't do that again, I'm sorry."

"You can't do it again?"

"Okay. Here's the thing. I did it then, yes, I did it twice but I can't say I'm proud of it now. I'm older. Women have the right to do what they want. I'm not out to make things hard for anybody. I type, that's all I do. In fact, I wish I hadn't done it, back then."

She spoke fast and with conviction.

"Oh," he said.

"Girls have enough troubles," she said, "without laying traps for them."

"Point taken," he said.

"Is that all you want?"

"Yes, that's all, I guess. There's certainly no obligation. I understand."

"Sorry," she said.

She turned and went back to work and no doubt the two older women raised their eyebrows and God knows what they shared in there, together, at break-time. Everything or nothing. Either way, they were all sworn to secrecy, they couldn't take their jobs home either.

"Sergeant, she said no. Turned us down. Total failure," he reported, "she's switched sides, reversed herself politically. She almost convinced me."

"Jack, give me a break, you just fell for her."

"Not true. She's had a change of heart."

"Can't blame you, those eyes, they're like kryptonite. Never would have thought though, Cindy Whistle, like she's a feminist, you mean?"

"Outright refusal. An expression of regret about the past."

"Well, we'll just get someone else then, leave it with me. Do the rest. Recheck the cast of characters."

"How do you mean?"

"Go back, talk to the aunt and the uncle. They hold the key. Find the taxi. Talk to them. It's police work, beating the bushes for grouse. Guilty parties."

So Jack went back into the city, in the cruiser, and there he was again at 71 Prescott.

"Oh Christ, you," the uncle said.

But he stood back and let Jack in and turned down the record player so they could talk.

"What little Miss Rowena said was this, clear as a bell: *I've had an abortion. A-bor-tion*, and if someone tells you anything else, they're pulling the wool over your eyes."

"You're sure about that?"

"Christ Almighty, you asked me a question, I gave you the answer. Whose side are you on anyway?"

Then he went to the Grace Hospital, to the little shop the volunteers ran. There was no one there but the aunt standing behind a counter with some home-made get-better cards, some stuffed animals. Also a fine selection of crucifixes and rosary beads.

"Abortion? That's ridiculous! Rowena said nothing of the kind. She was delirious. You saw her. She was out of her mind. She was not capable of forming sensible words. You were there, Officer, you saw her! You were as worried as I was! And Walter, he needs his hearing tested. He never hears a word I say. And there's this, Officer, I'm sorry to say this but you've seen it yourself, Walter took no shine to Row and he's a vindictive man, stubborn too. I love him over the years but now, this is beyond the pale, it's ridiculous, Row's family, she's not some girl off the street, it's ridiculous, the whole idea of some crime being committed. She's barely grown up, she's sixteen! Why in God's name are you pursuing this?"

He had no good answer to that. He thanked her and left and next he talked to the ambulance attendants.

"Jack, she was unconscious, we heard nothing of the kind. And that was the best thing you did, we still talk about it, pinning that guy against the wall. Love to see that again. You know, if you can, why not forget it, Jack? Let it go, she had a miscarriage, that's what we heard, and if you go and push it further, then that's a miscarriage too, a different kind of miscarriage, this time of justice. Right?"

"I know what you mean but as police, we have to take another perspective on it," he made himself say.

Next the doctor who'd been on call in the Emergency when she came in.

"Leave her alone, what the hell does society have to gain from this?"

It seemed everybody had strong feelings on the subject of Miss Savoury, one way or the other. Mostly one way.

"Can I ask you something unrelated, Doctor?"

"Go ahead if it's fast."

"If someone has an abortion, are there any after-effects?"

"No one had an abortion."

"I know, but hypothetically, what are the long-term effects?"

"Physically? None. Mentally none too, that's what we were taught. Not that I've been around for long. Now I have to go."

Jack checked with the taxi service. Lo and behold it was his lucky day. They'd be on Gower Street in ten minutes, if everything was running right, so he waited there curbside and there they were. He flagged them down. There was only one passenger, a woman in the back, and she and the driver both looked concerned, getting out of the car, asking him what the trouble was.

"I'm on a schedule, Officer, did I do something wrong?"

"The boat in Terrenceville, it waits for no one," said the woman, "whatever he's done, Officer, please, give him a break, he's a family man. Though he's not a good driver, he does manage to keep on time."

"This will only take a minute," said Jack.

The Sergeant said never say anything about investigating a crime. Tell them that, Jack, they'll clam up, they won't be on your side, they'll lie outright.

"Do you remember, either of you, a recent trip, it would have been two or three days ago, no more than a few days back, coming in with a very young girl?"

"Sure I remember, school age, and by the way this is Mary," said the driver, "she tags along. You and I, we pay for most of her fare, this one, every ride, through government taxes."

Jack nodded to her.

"Payback for all I've done," said Mary, "rightly so too, and don't we pay the fare for politicians too, the crooks, and yes, Officer, I remember her very well, plain as day, she with the freckles. With her mother. They sat in the front, well away from us. A lovely thing. Rowena, that was her name. With her mother, like I said, sitting beside her by the door."

"Did they speak of the purpose of their trip?"

"Shopping," said Mary, "why else would they come to town?"

"And," said the driver, "to visit relatives."

"Officer," said Mary, "let me be clear with you. She was quiet and shy, she was a lovely girl, polite like an angel. Why in the world would you be interested in her? Some mistake?"

"She lost something," said Jack, "we're trying to find it."

"Oh well, that's different. What'd she lose?"

"Nothing important."

"What, a scarf? They didn't have much, a couple small suitcases. Lose something, they call the police? You think I was born yesterday? You ever studied human nature? Officer, I been around and I can tell you this. That Rowena, that girl, she is incapable of doing wrong, she is one of the sweetest things I have ever laid eyes on, that ever walked the face of the earth."

"She's done nothing wrong, we know that," Jack said.

"They're from Bell Harbour," the driver said, "that's where they live. Terrenceville to here. It was the first time I ever saw them or had them as passengers. The girl missed her pick-up but that happens all the time. That's why I'm not retired."

He looked at his watch.

"So if you don't mind…"

"No, that's fine," said Jack.

"No tickets, no nothing?" asked Mary

"Free and clear. On your way."

"Find that scarf, get it back to her now."

"Mary, you be quiet. Thanks, Officer."

And Mary climbed into the back seat, smiling and waving back as they took off.

Back at the station, Jack said to the Sergeant, "Nothing to show, just the vindictive uncle frothing at the mouth. The positive pregnancy test. The taxi ride, nothing special. That's all we have."

"Where there's smoke, there's fire."

"Where there's smoke this time, there's a sixteen-year-old with freckles that everybody seems to love."

"Jack, those are the worst kind of criminals, the saintly ones. I quote the Chief again. Anyway, we have a new Cindy Whistle. Come here, I'll introduce you."

Marion Chipman, twenty-two, from Kilbride. Planning to join the police next year, if all went well. She was anxious to please and she'd already agreed to hit the streets with her own variation of the single-mother story.

"Mom and Dad would want me to do this," she said, "they have strong feelings on the sanctity of life."

"That's important," said Jack.

"Makes me nervous though."

"Of course it does."

Priscilla with her fancy-coloured hair could do this, professionally, without breaking a sweat. She could act anybody, anything, change her face, her personality, make you believe it in a second but she'd never take on this role either. No point in asking. And Tryphena Grandy couldn't do it, couldn't play a wolf in sheep's clothing if her life depended on it. What you saw with her, you got.

"Marion, thank you, they say it's easy. It won't take long."

Marion Chipman walked down first Duckworth Street and cried—thinking of her first dead puppy could still bring the tears on—in both a music store and a book store, the same stores in which, by coincidence, Rowena had passed the time during the long afternoon of waiting. Staff and customers saw poor Marion, they patted her on the back and whispered to her and on their advice she took the next bus up to the Student Centre at the University. There she was even more alone, confused, abandoned, frightened and unsure. Her puppy had been a Golden Lab, six months old, the car that hit her a

Pontiac, and the driver kept saying he was sorry, sorry, covered her up with a blanket. At the Student Centre, she met firebrand women, some of them not much older than she was, and much older women too, with wild gray hair flying out on all sides. Their eyes blazed with the passion of their convictions. What can I do? What can I do? she asked them, and her new friends told her that two years ago there was a doctor in town but he was caught by the police and imprisoned and now the medical community was polarized, paralyzed, and no one was willing to stick their neck out for girls or women. No one? If they knew anybody they would set it up, they sure as hell would, but as it stands, she'd have to go to Montreal. Montreal? Marion cried softly. The women searched through their purses and found a crumpled address and phone number in that far distant city, in French-Canada. A Doctor Morgentaler, they wrote down. They weren't sure of the spelling. He's courageous, he's politically committed, he's in the vanguard of women's rights. I can't afford to go to Montreal, Marion said. It's a shocking state of affairs, they said to her, we're sorry but that's the way it is here on the island.

She took the bus back to the station, having been under-cover for less than six hours.

She reported to Jack, "There is no illegal abortionist at work in St. John's."

"That's kind of what I thought."

"It wasn't easy, lying to people trying to help me. I did get a phone number though, a doctor in Montreal."

She started shuffling through her purse.

"He does abortions, they say, and everybody there turns a blind eye. They don't prosecute."

"No?"

"Here it is."

She handed him the piece of paper, the name, the address. He put it in his pocket.

"Good work anyway, Marion, not everything pans out," he said.

And he was about ready to go home when the Sergeant said, "Jack, go see the Chief."

"Now? Want me first to tell you about Miss Chipman?"

"I heard. We struck out, I'm surprised. But yes, he wants to see you. So go now."

The Chief was sitting behind a mahogany table almost big enough to play snooker on.

"Sit down, please, Constable, and bring me up to date."

"There's no one, Sir, no active abortionist, professional or amateur, in or around St. John's. The last arrest, two years ago, chilled the activists."

"Chilled? I like that. But I wasn't born yesterday, the girl had an abortion, we just haven't found the missing link."

The Chief leaned forward. There were several files on the desk in front of him. A gold-braided uniform hung neatly on a coat rack in the corner, and there were three different photographs of the Narrows, taken from different angles, on the wall behind him.

"So, our usual method of inquiry has not done the trick. This makes us pause but we're the police, Jack, we backtrack, we investigate. How did she come to town, from—" he shuffled to the front page of one of the files—"Bell Harbour, Fortune Bay? I've never been there, have you?"

"No, Sir."

"It's way the hell and gone. She probably had to get here by boat, which then means a taxi, which means records. Did she come alone or did she have company? There's lots we haven't done to get to the bottom of this, the hunt is just starting."

"I found the taxi. They know nothing."

"Strike them off then. But there's my hunch to go on, and usually I'm right. That's only half of what I wanted to talk to you about, though. Let's put this aside for now."

He closed the file in front of him, pushed it away.

"Now, nothing to do with this, with Prescott Street. Have you ever thought, Jack, about undercover work?"

"No, Sir. Only in passing. We talked about it in school."

"The Sergeant has recommended you, he said you'd be a good fit."

"For undercover?"

"Yes. We're being asked for help on this, from another force."

"I've never really given it a thought."

"You should, you should. It's an opportunity. It would be a feather in your cap, a feather in all our caps, you being one of us, if you see what I mean. There's no rush but I want you to think about it."

"Undercover. Okay, I can think about it."

"You have a steady girlfriend here?"

"Yes, Sir, I do."

"Is it serious?"

Jack raised both hands from his lap and wiggled his fingers back and forth, as though to say, wordlessly, *so-so*.

The Chief understood, he smiled.

Thus, not quite as Judas betrayed Christ, but similarly, with a simple gesture, Jack betrayed his love, his girlfriend, Tryphena Grandy. Their whole life together, the wiggle-waggle of his fingers, a gesture that spoke to his Chief and said indifference.

"Where would it be, this undercover?" he asked.

"I can't say yet. Confidential. But you'd be gone from here. It would be like, *poof*."

The Chief made a vanishing upward movement with both hands, like a genie leaving a bottle.

"You disappear, you get struck from the register of your own life."

"Oh."

"Mull it over, think about it."

"How often would I get back?"

"You don't get back, Constable, you disappear, that's the only way."

"*Poof*," the Chief said again, moving his hands less dramatically this time, carelessly.

"*Poof*," Jack said.

He walked out of the station. He was still in his uniform but he was finished for the day. He got into the Vauxhall and it started this time with one turn of the key. It was too early to pick her up, he was forty-five minutes early so he drove up to the top of Signal Hill. The city was semi-socked-in, one of those also so-so days. Clouds hung a few feet over his head. He thought about how he'd wiggled his fingers in front of the Chief, saying so-so, betraying her as though she were a memory already, a passing fancy, not a real girlfriend. Oh no, she's not a real girlfriend, no one I'd stay around here for, just somebody I knew, we had sex a few dozen times and I ate dinners with her mother and she was almost a dental hygienist, if I remember right. Oh, and then there was Priscilla, her picture now up on posters all over downtown, on the lampposts. Her play must be doing okay, because it was *HELDOVER!* Half-forgotten, half-remembered, all those girls he used to know in St. John's, before undercover.

He got out of his car. On the oceanside, everything was flat and gray. He walked across the parking lot to the town side, doing what Rowena Savoury had done herself a few days earlier, what thousands have done before and since and will do forever on Signal Hill. Waiting for something, waiting for something to clear their sky.

No boats were coming in through the Narrows. He looked over the city. He'd lived there for twenty-three years, all his life. He couldn't see the street Tryphena lived on because it was blocked by a series of yellow and red houses. But down a bit, through a gap, he could see the building, the School of Dental Hygiene. They'd noticed the gap before, as though a tooth were missing in the landscape. She'd said, Look, Jack, there's school, down to the right, just there, from the Basilica. I can see it, Tryphie, he'd said.

That day, he did love her, he remembered how he loved her, he even loved her school and how stupid was that?

HER REAL mother finally arrived from Bell Harbour. She came in with the principal's wife and Rowena introduced her to the nurses and nobody cared about the subterfuge.

"For you, Rowena, it's allowed. You can have two mothers. You can have some quiet time together, all three of you."

The nurses left them alone. The women huddled by the bed, the three of them in an embrace.

"Row, honey, I'm so sorry we couldn't get here earlier. Your father stayed home. Someone has to mind the store and feed the boys. He sends you his love, though, you know that."

"You told him?"

"I told him part. I didn't tell him about Dr. Poole."

She was whispering and the principal's wife was also whispering, saying, "Some things men are better off not knowing. They lose their heads."

The gravelled roof outside was under an inch of water from the storms but the wind had died down and the little wavelets, which had rippled there for two days, had flattened down to nothing. Now it was just a grey mirror, reflecting sky.

Then her aunt came in so she actually had three visitors behind the curtains, bustling about in the confined space, then sticking out their heads, looking for chairs.

It was still okay with the staff. They had two empty beds plus Rowena, who really didn't need to be there, so it looked like a quiet day for them. Though they would never say this out loud—it's a quiet day—because that bred trouble in the form of car accidents, fires, drownings, you name it. So they spoke not a word as they checked the equipment, reorganized the crash cart, as they wrote more detailed notes than were necessary about the patients they actually had.

Along came the chief gynecologist and his troupe of minions. He asked the women to give him and his students and

Ms. Savoury a few private moments, so out they went into the hall and waited while he said to her, "Quite the crowd today, I see. Now, when you go home you'll have iron pills to take. One a day for three months. And monthly, somewhere, somehow, you need to get your blood checked."

"When can I go home?"

"You live in a very remote place, we don't want any surprises. Let's say two days."

"I'll hold you to that."

"Also, birth control pills," he said, "Dr. Murphy here will prescribe those. They'll make your periods lighter. That's why. Not for birth control, really."

"I get it."

"But it's up to you, they do both. Oh, you passed the psychiatrist's report with flying colours. You're a pillar of stability, apparently. How'd you like the psychiatrist?"

"She was okay, she was nice. Dr. Poole."

"Good, then all our bases are covered. Students, any questions for our patient?"

No, they had no questions, certainly no questions in front of the mother and the other two women. Off they went en masse.

"A policeman came to see me," said Row, "but he hasn't been back."

"What did he want?" asked the principal's wife.

"He says they might have to look into it, what happened. He asked me a lot of questions but I said I couldn't remember."

"Is that true?"

"Not completely but close enough."

"What did he look like?" asked her aunt.

"He's the same one that was at the house."

"Oh, him. He's nice. I gave him a piece of my mind though, when to meddle, when not to, and this is a not-time-to-meddle and off he went. He came to see me at the Grace."

"He saved my life, everybody says. Everybody but him. He says no, it was the doctors."

"That's to his credit. He seems a nice man, like I said."

"Listen," said Rowena's mother, "I brought Monopoly along, let's just put the board down here and pretend we're in New York and buy some serious real estate and put our minds on something else."

None of them had been to New York, they agreed. That didn't mean they couldn't play, of course they could.

Finally, in the late afternoon, the orderlies and nurses moved Row and the women and the Monopoly board, undisturbed, to a ward. Outside the new window now was a straight drop down to the parking lot, then a distant hill and sky. After getting the GO TO JAIL card twice—and being able to laugh about it without feeling sick inside—the principal's wife excused herself to go shopping. Row's mother, distracted from the game, had fallen deeply in debt and left with her, happy despite her losses. Her aunt Beth was the last to go. Adjusting the many residences she'd accumulated on Park Place, she announced that she had dinner to prepare and would have to forgo her newly acquired wealth. Walter would like this, there was sure a lot more money in Monopoly than in Bingo.

"All's well then. See you later, Rowena. Bye-bye. I doubt that nosy policeman will ever come back."

Row was putting away the game when the psychiatrist, Dr. Poole, also came by.

"I ran into your mother downstairs, fifteen minutes ago. Haven't seen her in years. By the elevators. Everything still fine with you?"

"I'm going home tomorrow, maybe the next day."

"Good. I told her to go to the lab. The haematologists wanted some blood work for family studies."

"My aunt too?"

"I don't think so. I don't know. Your mother was alone."

"They're still trying to figure out the exact cause."

"Maybe we'll never know, not everything. Hope we don't.

Anyway, I don't think I'll have to see you again, so this is good-bye for me, Miss Savoury."

They shook hands, the psychiatrist smiling ruefully.

"Thanks for everything, and for the good report," said Rowena, "the doctors just told me I passed your exam with flying colours. Those were the exact words."

"Yes, you did. You actually did, no sign of problems. Wish I could say the same."

"Thanks for everything, everything," said Rowena.

That night she was unconnected to lines or monitors and she moved restless limbs against cool sheets, and the window that was open a crack to the night air let in the sound of crickets and she slept dreamlessly, waiting to leave.

"WALTER, HOW many years have we been married?"

"I can never keep track, Beth, you tell me."

"Twenty-two years. A long time."

"Hey! Have you seen the album cover for this one?"

"Which one is that?"

"The new one. *It's Not Love, But It's Not Bad.*"

"I think it fell behind the radiator."

"Jeez, you're right. Thanks."

"You sure love Merle Haggard, don't you, Walter?"

"Sure I do, who wouldn't?"

"You have the whole collection, right?"

"Every single one."

"That's what I'd like to talk to you about, Walter, sort of."

"Go ahead, I'm all ears."

"First turn the volume down a bit. I can't hear myself think. And it's not really about Merle Haggard, not directly, it's actually more about Row."

"Oh Christ. I don't want to talk about her."

"Walter, that's exactly my point. Because Merle Haggard would want to talk about her, if he were here instead of just his picture on that album cover."

"I don't get it."

"Well it's like this. He would talk about her, Walter, because she's family and Merle Haggard cares about family. Listen to the music, that's what you've always told me. Listen to the words. Secondly, Merle Haggard would talk about her because she's a young girl and inexperienced and he'd never turn his back on someone like that."

"Where are you going with this?"

"I'm getting there. Thirdly, even if she did break the law, do you actually think that Merle Haggard, who wrote those songs you like so much, would report his own flesh and blood to the authorities? To the police? Walter? Well?"

"You're mad at me."

"I've never been so mad."

"Sit back down. Let me think."

"What I'm saying is this. Row is our family. She's our niece. She's my sister's daughter. Say she robbed a bank, say she didn't pay a parking ticket, say she was raped and had an abortion, what the hell are you doing talking to the police about her?"

"I don't know. Maybe because of the things she said. You heard her, in the kitchen."

"You're a grown man, you goaded her into it. Also you picked on me about Bingo and Merle Haggard would never do that either."

"Don't be so sure. He's divorced."

"So will you be too, if you don't change your tune."

"What are you saying?"

"Stand with us. You, me, and Row. Stop telling what you heard to the police, or we're through. After twenty-two years, there's not too many things you can't do to me, but this is one of them."

"It's not a lie what I said, it's the truth."

"Walter, that truth of yours is far, far worse than a lie. That's what people like Merle Haggard understand and that's why he writes those songs. There's a greater truth, and greater truth can have lies in it. It can be full of lies. That's what you need to learn."

"Are you serious?"

"I am deadly serious. Walter, we need to stand together on this. We are through if you don't fully take back what you said."

"I'm already on record. How can I take it back?"

"Say you lost your memory, say you lost your mind, say anything, say what you heard was wrong. That's what I did, that's what we both should do. Then there's no more problems for Row."

"So you admit it, you heard it too."

"Yes, I heard it too."

"I knew I was right."

"But I would stand before God and deny it a thousand times until the gates of heaven came crashing down on the Mount Pearl bus before I would tell the police anything that would get Rowena into trouble."

"God, you're serious."

"So where do you stand, Walter, with us or against us?"

"Us?"

"Me and Row."

She pointed to the record player.

"And your friend there, because he's with us. Merle. You know that, if you think about it."

"Are you threatening me?"

"It's not a threat. I love you but there are limits to my love. This time you've crossed the limits."

"You want me to stand up and say to the police, fuck off?"

"Yes. Maybe not exactly those words."

"I can see what you mean. What I did."

"You do?"

He was looking blindly at the liner notes on the back of the album.

"You're right. I'm ashamed. I never should have done it. It was a mistake."

"Yes it was."

"A cowardly mistake. A bully."

"Yes."

"Listen. Maybe I didn't hear what I thought I heard. I'm sorry. Come over here now. I kind of like you when you're mad. You're fiery, you're feisty. And you're pretty too."

"You think so? Still?"

"Pretty all the time but prettier when you're mad."

"Now that sounds like Merle Haggard. Did he write that?"

"No, I said that."

"So what you need to rehearse is this, Walter: I did not hear Rowena say anything about an abortion."

"I have to say that?"

"Yes. Say it."

"I did not hear Rowena say anything about an abortion."

"Say it again."

"Rowena, she said nothing about an abortion. I misheard."

"Good. That's it."

"Beth, please, come here now."

"I have to turn the oven down, Walter. Wait."

When she returned, he was still sitting on the couch but he immediately put both arms around her and buried his face in her waist and then he moved one hand under her dress and moved it upwards.

"Walter," she said, "I think we should go upstairs. My sister could be back any minute."

"I did not hear Rowena say anything. I did not hear Rowena say anything. I did not hear a damn thing, I heard nothing."

His voice was muffled into the front of her clothing, face pressed into the material, but then he looked up at her.

"Twenty-two years, Beth, sure, but I never get tired of you."

"You'll change what you said?"

"I already have."

"And Row?"

"She's a sweetheart, always has been."

"Oh, Walter. I love you, despite…"

"Move this way, Beth, a bit more, turn a bit."

"Oh, Walter."

"Nice?"

"The record's over, it's skipping."

"Forget the record. Let it skip, we'll go upstairs."

"It's Merle Haggard."

"I have no interest."

"Have to be fast, we haven't got much time. Oh, Walter. The pork roast. Be quick."

"Quick? That's never been a problem."

THE DENTAL hygiene instructor, Ms. Johnson, stood at the front of the class. Tryphena was sitting in the back row, rotating a pencil through the fingers of her left hand, rolling it first one way then the other. Her goal was to become as ambidextrous as a centipede, but she wasn't far on the learning curve. Whenever her attention drifted, the pencil fell on the floor.

"Now class," Ms. Johnson said, "down the hall we go, to the clinical practice room."

That brought about a stir of expectation. The practice room meant dental chairs, sterilized instruments, hands-on training. Tryphena slipped the pencil back into her purse.

When she stood up, there it was again, a queasiness, the taste of the apple she'd eaten half an hour ago.

It'll pass, it did before.

They walked down the hall to the room at the far end. Sunlight poured through the windows. Once it had been a warehouse or a loft of some kind. Sails, barrels, ropes, it could have been anything in the old days but now ten dental chairs— old ones, nearly antique, they still had to be foot-pedalled up and down—were set up along the length of the room in two rows of five. Stainless-steel stools for the hygienists, trays of sterilized instruments which swung in from the side. Over-head, despite the sunlight, each chair had an individual spotlight suspended from the ceiling.

"Pull the blinds down please," the instructor said, "pair up as usual. Stan, you're still with Tryphena, if that's all right with her. After last week I wouldn't be so sure about that."

She looked at Tryphena. Tryphena nodded. Everything was fine with her.

"Mr. Grant, none of your nonsense this time," said the instructor.

Of course she was referring to the infamous past event, when the mirror fell and the handle got snagged in the nap of Tryphie's sweater. He'd fumbled after it, compounding his mistake. Stop at once! the instructor had shouted and the whole class had turned their way to look. Do not touch that instrument, Mr. Grant, do not touch the sweater! The instructor had then come over—as Tryphena extricated it herself—and said, Don't ever let me see anything like that again, and she had reported him to the head of the school, saying, ridiculously, that he had taken liberties with the bosom of his patient.

"Excuse me, Madame, may I publicly address the incident to which you allude? May I speak on my behalf?" said Stan.

"I'd rather you not."

"For those present who are unaware, what happened in this class last week, which you decry, was reviewed by the Disciplinary Committee and I was found blameless. This should be public knowledge."

There was silence in the room, as though no one knew what to think. Only eyes moved.

"Blameless? You were blameless? Yes, it was reviewed, Mr. Grant and yes, no action was taken. That's not the same thing as blameless. I was overruled."

"A physical error, compounded by inexperience. I apologize to all present for my clumsiness, but not for my intent, which was honourable."

To Tryphena, it had been either an honest mistake or slap-stick comedy and she didn't care. His hands were on her breasts for a tenth of a second, fumbling, and he was contrite. The strongest man in the world, he said to her later, would shake and drop things when in such close proximity to her. As Antony shook before Cleopatra. Or some such nonsense, Egypt again, Antony drunk on beauty, entranced.

"Enough of this. The fact is that the Disciplinary Committee was overly kind and turned a blind eye to your deceit. Patients, please, into the chairs now."

Bustling filled the room and the tension lifted.

Stan doffed an imaginary hat to Tryphena and bowed at the waist.

"No, this time you go first," she said.

"Fine."

He hopped up into the seat where the faded green upholstery was so worn in places that, particularly on the armrests, off-white fluff poked through dried cracks in the leather.

"Hygienists, what do we do now?"

"Pump up the chairs to the proper height," said one of the students.

"Good, proceed."

Ten chairs rose together.

"Next step? Ms. Grandy?"

"Adjust the headrest for comfort."

"Good, proceed."

Then each girl adjusted the overhead light and focused it and the instructor said, "Proceed now, girls, and remember, try not to breathe directly on the face of your patient."

"Tryphie, you can breathe on me."

"And girls, most importantly, your shoulder muscles, if you've been doing your abduction exercises at home, you will have no postural difficulties, you will not let your hands or your forearms or God forbid your bosoms lean upon the patient's arm or torso. Remember the Latin phrase *noli me tangere*, that's Latin for what?"

"She's obsessed by bosoms in a very unhealthy way," said Stan, "and who says bosoms anymore?"

"Mr. Grant? Did I hear you speak? I think I did. Answer the question then!"

"*Noli me tangere* means *don't touch me*," said Stan.

"Well, I'm impressed, perhaps you learned something last week after all. Mirrors, girls."

Clattering throughout the room.

"Light your Zippos, your lamps."

Each hygienist had a small alcohol lamp on the side-tray, and each lit the wick with a Zippo, obtaining a gentle blue flame.

"All set? Warm your instruments carefully."

Tryphena passed the dental mirror through the tip of the flame, a quick swing three times, to warm, to cool.

"Why do we warm our mirrors? Girls?"

"To avoid fogging, Ms. Johnson."

"You can lean on me a bit, Tryphie, if it makes it easier for you."

She inspected his lower molars, at the back.

"Your teeth look pretty good, Stan, you've been flossing."

"Make small talk, girls, yes, put your patient at ease, talk to them but don't expect to have a conversation."

"Flossing is new to me, Tryph. Floss is a girl's name."

"Now, girls, time for suction! Oral secretions can be most uncomfortable, so we need to suction them. How often?"

"Every three minutes, Ms. Johnson, or when the patient appears to be having swallowing difficulties, whichever comes first."

"Good."

"I shall be the perfect patient today. I shall not say anything suggestive to you about suction," said Stan.

"Appreciated."

And he was very good. He complied with each nudge she gave him, turning his head an inch or two this way or that at her bidding. His eyes remained closed. The warmth of the overhead light bathed them mutually. His breathing was soft and gentle and his often-restless arms did not fall accidentally onto hers.

The bliss he was in, this class, this experience.

She finished her inspection and removed the mirror.

"Finished? Change places now, all of you."

She released the chair and he descended to earth. His turn now. He opened a new set of instruments and pumped Tryphena Grandy one-two-three, high, high, higher, rhythmic his foot as the chair responded, and because he was so much taller than she, he also had to lift and adjust and fix the tray with the alcohol lamp, and the overhead light had to be raised and swung away, and lifted, and swung back and readjusted.

"We won't forget the bib this time," he said.

She lifted her head as he passed the small chain around her neck, and the bib was then in place, upon her chest.

"I'm watching you, Mr. Grant."

"Then my marks cannot help but rise as quickly as this chair."

He passed the mirror through the flame and leaned towards her and sat back and pulled the stool closer and got off and spun the seat upwards, re-adjusting the light as though he'd been doing it for years.

"It's still in my eyes too much, Stan."

"Okay, sorry, how's this?"

"Better."

"Hygienists! Begin!"

"Okay, open up now, honey."

He must have been chewing a peppermint Lifesaver. His breath upon her was fresh and aromatic. But suddenly the instructor was there, no more than two feet away, and she was shouting or coughing and choking with indignation and saying, "Mr. Grant, damn it, Mr. Grant, I'll have none of that! You called her *honey*, I heard you!"

Tryphena opened her eyes and Stan swung the light away.

"Honey? I said that? I don't think so."

Could he have called her that? Could he have had the nerve?

"I can't believe it, Mr. Grant, after what happened last time. I'm asking you to leave this classroom now."

"You must have misheard me, Ms. Johnson."

"Ms. Grandy, did Mr. Grant, or did he not, call you honey just now, loud and clear?"

Tryphena sat up, holding onto the armrests. She looked at Stan and she looked at the teacher.

"*Honey*? I don't think so. *Bunny* maybe, he sometimes calls me Bunny."

A few of the other students laughed.

The teacher threw up her hands and said, "Bunny? You expect me to believe that? Okay you two, I don't know, but count your lucky stars, Mr. Grant, that your patient here is very fast on her feet on your behalf, and Miss Grandy, I'm surprised at you, your powers of invention, because I know what I heard and I warn you both, stay away from saying anything like *honey* in my class again or I will smack you both like a bee, and not a honeybee but a wasp! So!"

She walked away. Tryphena put her head back on the headrest. Stan adjusted the light.

"Thanks, Tryphie. Did I really say that?"

"Yes."

His mirror touched her lower teeth, gently. The instructor was four chairs away, looking out the window and Stan realized that if thoughts could kill or destroy, the row of stores across the street would be in flames.

"Your lips and teeth are perfect."

His breath was of peppermint, yet the strange taste of apple she'd tasted earlier returned to her, the sour apple rising, stinging her throat.

He touched her tongue with the mirror like a feather. She swallowed once, twice. He started to place a cotton pledget between her cheek and the upper molars when she vomited. It came up in a rush with no warning, projectile, a hot stream like lava over his hands, his wrists, his buttoned shirtsleeves.

"Oh Christ, Tryphie."

But he didn't jump away, not with the instrument in her mouth.

She sat up, gagging, she tried to turn her head, wiping at her face with her hands. He was almost as quick. He took the mirror out of the way with a flourish and it fell to the floor because he needed both hands now, she was leaning forward, she struck her forehead on the edge of the tray. He grabbed it and pushed it out of the way. She was trying to spit out the pledget. She pried at it with her fingers while her mouth was still streaming, salivating or spitting, half-vomiting still down onto the useless little bib.

"Tryphie, are you okay?"

"Mr. Grant! Do not go anywhere near those bosoms!"

But his hands were on her back, patting her like a baby, then on her shoulder.

"Are you okay? Tryph?"

"Ms. Grandy!"

She shook her head, no, she was not okay. She couldn't get air enough to speak. Up came more semi-digested tuna fish or whatever she'd had for lunch, soured, over the bib, down onto her lap. Tears filled her eyes.

"Ms. Grandy?" said the instructor, now close beside them.

"Hang on," said Stan.

He wiped his hands on the only part of his shirt that was clean. He undid the bib, hands under the back of her hair. Then he took her by the arm and helped her, half-lifted her up.

"You can stand?"

"I think so. I'm cold."

Sweat was pouring down her face, her neck.

"I'll take care of her," said Stan, "I'll take her down the hall."

Tryphena was wiping her lips now on the back of her wrist.

"Is that okay, Ms. Grandy? You want to go with him?" asked the instructor, motioning to Stan with some distaste.

"Surely one of the girls would be more suitable? Ms. Grandy?"

"No," she was finally able to speak, "Stan'll be fine."

"Bunny," he said, "come on."

He left her at the women's washroom and in the men's, adjacent, he stripped off his shirt, ran hot water over it, wrung it out, put it back on. It was already cold and clinging. Then he went back into the hall to wait for her. He heard water running. He sat on the floor, his back against the wall of the corridor, waiting.

Inside, in front of the sinks, she'd taken off her sweater, her blouse, her skirt. She was standing in her underwear on the cold tiles, face bent to the rush of the tap. A sour dampness surrounded her, in the air. Another wave of nausea. Quickly she turned to one of the stalls and she was down on the floor, on her knees, vomiting into the toilet. Then for five minutes she lay with her cheek on the side of the porcelain bowl.

Stan put his head into the washroom.

"You all right? Tryphena?"

"Not really," she said.

She shivered.

"There's a sweater and a blouse in my locker, I think."

"I'll get it. I know the combo."

She made it back to the sink and wrung out her blouse as best she could, took the mass of wet sweater and spread it out on the window ledge. Then she washed her face with her hands and the water was ice-cold and she brushed her hair back and rinsed out her mouth, spat it out, bent over the sink with her weight on her elbows, then stood up and looked in the mirror.

First trimester, the vomiting. Hello.

She put on her skirt, twice now the weight with all the water.

Stan knocked on the door.

"Got it," he said.

"Come in."

Pale as any living girl could look, the sodden skirt, her brassiere, the dim light fighting its way through opaque glass up high to the outside.

"Here you go, put this on."

He was handing her the blouse when the door opened again with a rush and the instructor was there, her eyes narrowed.

"Mr. Grant! What now? What are you doing! This is the girls' washroom! Do you recognize no boundaries?"

"Now this, Tryphie."

He handed her the thin pink sweater he'd found scrunched at the bottom of her locker. V-necked. Warm and dry.

"I asked him, Ms. Johnson," said Tryphena, "there's no one else here."

"Never in my born days. You two will hear about this. Now, Mr. Grant, get out of this washroom! And Ms. Grandy, put on some clothes!"

"Tryphie, I'll be outside."

"I'll be there in a minute, thanks."

Stan leaned outside and took a drink from the water fountain. Ms. Johnson exploded back through the door and without looking at him returned to the classroom. Then Tryphena came out, her hair tied back. Fetching as ever despite the circumstances, some colour returning to her face.

"God, how did that happen?" she said.

"I'll walk you home?"

Something he had often suggested, never accepted.

"I think I can finish the class. I'd like to try. I'm emptied out."

"I'm in trouble again with that woman."

"Looks like it. Pervert in the bathroom, that's you."

"Right. Found out. Glad to help you though, Tryphie."

"Thanks, Stan. I'm sorry."

"I couldn't ask for a better way to end my career here. Guilty as charged."

After class, which they managed to complete without further incident, he did walk her home. She said yes when he asked the second time, and it was just six blocks and ten minutes to Fitzpatrick Avenue where there was a little girl playing hopscotch by herself on the sidewalk, and Tryphie thanked him again and put the key in the lock and that was as close as he would ever get to her, he knew, that moment, the smell of green soap and vomit, the sight of her so damaged yet still commanding and beautiful, her hair tied back. Wan. Sad, tired.

Which reminded him.

"One thing, Tryphie" he said, "I'm meeting my birth mother soon. She contacted me."

"Really? That's great. That's good for you."

"Through the agency. I hope it's good."

"Tell me how it goes, don't forget."

As though he could forget her at all, for even an hour or two.

"I have mixed feelings about my mother," he said.

"Tell me how it goes, Stan. Right now though, today, this is enough for me. Bye, and thanks again for the help."

The door closed. Yes, she'd looked wan and sad and tired and sick, commanding, beautiful, all those adjectives he could muster up for her, and what was he but lonely. Shirt still wet, he shrugged his chest inside it, picked at it with his fingers to let the air get in, and set out for home.

JACK SAT at the kitchen table on Garrison Hill with a map of the city. He'd decided not to say anything about the girl and the rain and whatever she did but that didn't mean he couldn't satisfy himself. Check it out. See what he could find. Be a sleuth. That's why he went into the police.

So he took the city map and unfolded it and stretched it out in front and flattened it on the table. He stood up and bent over it.

Here we go, here's Gower Street, Prescott, everything east is over there.

Thus beginneth the investigation, by yours truly, Sherlock Holmes of Garrison Hill, St. John's, active police officer.

Let's see now. Rowena Savoury and the woman who turned out not be her mother, the one with the umbrella, they were walking here, west on the north side of Gower when I saw them, right about...here. That being the case, no point in looking further west, west is out of the picture. Unless they were doubling back, but they weren't in shape for that. No reason either. Plus the rain, plus no one around, so why would they do that? They'd be taking the shortest route home, it just made sense, so look to the east for where they came from.

Deductive reasoning. That's what Holmes was famous for.

So, moving on, looking to the east for the scene of the crime. For fun, we'll call it a crime. And that should be easy, there's not much over here, in the east end. A few small neighbourhoods, the hospital, the high bare hills, the Battery, then the sea and the sea is out. Not under suspicion the sea, impersonal, implacable, a mind of its own. Not capable of planned evil.

He went upstairs to get his old protractor from high school and with it made a semi-circle in red pencil, with the epicentre on 71 Prescott, right about...here, the radius from Gower Street to, oh an educated guess, say about this, a mile, seeing how they were walking, more like staggering, they couldn't have come from too far, so we'll set this radius to the tower on Signal Hill. You can't go any further than that, which is right here.

The resulting neat half-circle went all the way past the hospital, up into the hills, surrounded Quidi Vidi Lake and took in all of the Battery and the far side of the harbour.

So this has to be ground zero. Let's put our money on the Battery. It's another world there, dark at the edges, dark inside it too. Something about the way the lights were strung out along the roads irregularly, sparse, the corners and the roofs of the houses and the dark pockets formed within, and that's where he'd set up shop, personally, if he didn't want to be noticed.

Next step, get the Yellow Pages. Turn to *Physicians and Surgeons*. Assume the abortionist was a doctor but if this doesn't pan out, remember the assumption, go back and change it. There were two pages of physicians listed in the telephone book.

He opened it and went through the list, one by one. If the name was outside the red semi-circle, he crossed it off. If inside it, he put a small red dot on the street, at the approximate address, saying to himself right...there!

Hey, funny. Here's the psychiatrist from the ICU, Dr. Poole herself. Down she goes, she's this red dot here, close by the hospital. Quidi Vidi Road. That makes sense, if you're on call, you'd want to be close.

When he finished his list—it only took half an hour—there were nine dots, so nine possibilities. Doctors on Forest Avenue, Forest Road, Circular Road, five on Water, one on The Boulevard. No doctors in the Battery so his own early preference wasn't panning out, not yet.

Next step: Who has the technical skills for this?

Someone with a surgical bent, someone who knows what they're doing, an obstetrician, a gynecologist, that's the most likely.

And here we have, let's see: our friend the psychiatrist, an ear-nose-and throat surgeon, six GPs and an internist. But all doctors are trained for the simple things, I think, and abortion is a simple thing.

Say he and Tryphie decided not to keep the baby. No that's not quite right, say Tryphie decided not to keep the baby.

Really it's up to her. Nothing to worry about because it's safe, simple, no physical or mental complications afterwards. Hop up and go. The Savoury girl, what happened to her, that's a fluke.

Undercover. The Chief was going to get back to him about that any day now. Poof, what the hell, he might not even be around.

Why would a doctor do this, for money?

No, too high a risk, too little return. A philosophical motive then, a belief, which narrows the field. Who exactly has abortions? Women do, women have them. Who sympathizes with women, who might bend the rules for women? A woman would do that more likely than a man. And how many women are there on this list? Already know the answer to that! Just one, exactly one, our psychiatrist who's been walking about this case already with her clipboard and white coat and little smile. She who hugs the patient so warmly. Could it possibly be? Not likely, psychiatrists are bullshit artists, they're not practical, they have no experience, they're the last ones to do anything technical, you'd think. Smiling at him, shaking his hand in the ICU, clipboard like a shield, saying yes, you can talk to her but don't push her, it looks like she can't remember a thing, amnesia, too bad. Butter wouldn't melt in her mouth.

So look into her first, right now.

He phoned the Newfoundland Medical Board.

"Hello, I'm new in town and looking for a female psychiatrist. For my wife. I see in the book, can you tell me please about this Dr. Poole, on Quidi Vidi Road?"

"Tell you about her?"

"Does she take patients?"

"I'm looking. Hang on. Yes, I believe she does."

"Her background, whether she'd be right."

"Oh, we don't have much, just a thumbnail sketch on our doctors. We have those for everyone."

"And? Please?"

"She has an office on Quidi Vidi Road, as you already know. She's been a psychiatrist for ten years. Prior to that, she was a medical officer on the south coast, in Bell Harbour. That's all we have."

"Bell Harbour?"

"That's right, Bell Harbour. A long way away."

"Thank you."

He hung up and took his protractor and jammed the sharp metal tip of it into the map, sticking it down through Quidi Vidi Road, through the roof of her office to the basement to bedrock, sticking her like he would a butterfly or a moth, or a rat. A rat, that's what the Chief would call her.

Got you fair and square, sweetheart. A perfect package, all of them from the same place, four of them! Who'd believe this? The girl, her mother, the other mother, and now this one, the psychiatrist. The south coast cabal.

The other eight doctors he'd dotted on the map? He scanned over them one more time, but why bother? There was no point. He put the map, his protractor, the red pen, the list of doctors into the drawer of the kitchen table. Tucked away where it was safe.

He walked the five minutes to Fitzpatrick Avenue. She was in the kitchen.

"Tryphie! Guess what? Guess who is already establishing himself as a brilliant investigator?"

"You, I suppose."

"Correct, Miss Grandy!"

He described his deductive reasoning, his protractor, his list, his phone call to the Medical Board.

"So you see, I have almost certainly unrooted the cabal."

She looked at him across the table.

"But you haven't told anybody. We agreed."

"No, no, this is just for us. But maybe it can work for us."

"For us? How do you mean?"

Say you decide not to keep the baby, he started to say, but

he only got as far as *Say you decide* when her mother came through the front door with groceries. She was having trouble with the screen door and one of the bags ripped and a can of soup fell to the floor.

"Jack, good, you're here, how about a hand with these? Tryphie?"

So he never finished the sentence.

"Sure," he said, "let me help you, hang on."

"They pack them too heavy. Grab this quick."

"Got it. There."

"Thanks. We're a team, Sheriff," her mother said, "working together, everything's so much easier. Wow, so glad you're here."

So, instead of having the talk with Tryphena, he unloaded groceries and put cans in cupboards and time flew by and chit-chat this and chit-chat that until they were all eating spaghetti together like a family and then it was too late to say or do anything.

Tryphena said goodbye to him at the door.

"Talk later," she said, "kiss-kiss."

THE NEXT morning he was called by the Chief's secretary before he even took his hat off.

"Me? Now?"

"Yes."

The Chief sat behind the vast gleaming of the giant desk. Reflected in it, upside-down. His secretary walked in with Jack, put a file on the desk, then left and closed the door.

"Sit down, Constable. Please."

He waved to one of the chairs.

"It's Calgary, as it turns out, the undercover situation."

"Calgary?"

"Bears, skiing, cowgirls. Calgary. Oh, let's not forget the Stampede. Off the top of my head, that's Calgary. But what you'd be doing there, it's none of that, it's drug-related."

"You mean there's a firm offer? For me?"

"As of this morning. They had files, they looked them over, they chose you. Feather in our caps. This helps us, as a force, because when they choose you, they're saying they have confidence in us."

"When would this be?"

"Next week. Thursday, Friday. They need a few days to create an identity."

"Mine?"

"Yes, yours. Brand-new life, like we said."

"Poof, you said, actually."

The Chief laughed, "Right, I did say that. Poof it is."

"And for how long?"

"That's anyone's guess, it's open-ended. Having second thoughts?"

Jack tried to remember what he'd said before. The last meeting, had he actually committed to this? All he could remember was wiggling his fingers, his so-so relationship, his girlfriend, the two-faced coward that he was.

"No, not exactly. It's just come on quicker than I thought."

"Good then. Here's what you do, Jack. Take a few days off, that's part of the preparation. You need to shed your skin, tie up loose ends. Banks, mail, family, but don't say a word where you're going. Then just wait for the call. Calgary, there's mountains close by. My first wife came from there. Did you know that?"

"No, Sir."

"Before your time. A fish out of water here. She didn't fit in, she didn't like the music, the weather, the stores. What could I do? Totally unpredictable. Jesus she even went skinny-dipping in Windsor Lake, Jack, just off the road and that's illegal, as you know. Free spirit."

Jack was only half-listening. Tie up loose ends? How would he do that?

"So we parted amicably and she went home. That's the

way it is with women. My advice, don't take them out of their comfort zone."

If he was gone he was gone. Loose ends? Torn to shreds, to tatters.

Now the Chief was sitting back in his chair which was also tilted back and he was looking blindly over Jack's head.

"Windsor Lake. I'm driving by—I was a constable then just like you are now—and there she is, my own wife coming out of the water. Her clothes folded on the shore. Cars honking. You can't become Chief of Police with a wife like that. Not that I was thinking that way, I wasn't ambitious then, I was sorry to see her go. Half-sorry anyway."

"Yes, Sir, I would think so."

"Attractive she was. Clothes, no clothes. No denying that."

Then the Chief sat forward and pulled himself closer to the desk.

"But forget her, she's a long time ago. I mention her only because of Calgary. In undercover, Jack, no assignment is easy. It's not like walking a beat or patrolling or working overtime at concerts. Way different, way harder than that."

"I imagine."

"Harder even than cracking cases that don't want to crack. Like Prescott Street, come to think of it. Why, here's the file, right here. Maureen brought it in at my request. Jack, what's up with this?"

"Sir?"

"Where are we with this file? The Sergeant said we're nowhere."

"I guess that's a fair assessment. So far, nothing's come up."

"Is that what you think? You're sure? You've gone over it carefully? Worked the angles?"

"With a fine-tooth comb, Sir."

Tryphena, darling, if you could see me lying, you'd know I could do undercover, you'd be proud of me. My conscience, my co-conspirator.

"No one saw her anywhere, earlier?"

"No, Sir. Rainy night, no one out and about. By the way, everybody I talk to, even the taxi, they say she's the sweetest thing, she's an angel, etcetera etcetera. They all want to vouch for her character. Funny, how they bring it up. It's not like I ask."

"So she's sweet, big deal, what's that got to do with it? And forget her character, character's for sentencing. It doesn't enter into the fact of guilt, it doesn't dissuade us from laying a charge. Even Jesus Christ was charged with something. That's why Pontius Pilate, the crucifixion, that's what I was taught, so don't tell me what she's like, I don't care what she's like. She could be Alice in Wonderland and Mother Teresa and Shirley Temple all rolled into one, the Queen of England thrown in. I know something happened, but they've drawn the wagons around her."

He opened the file on his desk and shuffled through it.

"It looks like this case, obvious though it was at first blush, is slipping through our fingers. When does she get out of the hospital?

"Later today I think."

The Chief rose from his desk and put on the jacket, the one with the gold braids. Then the hat with gold trim.

"Tell you what, son, let's go right now, you and I together. We'll talk to them, the aunt and the uncle. Sometimes, when I get dressed up, they get rattled. The braid, the stripes, you know. Come along, but don't say anything, leave it to me."

Jack drove, the Chief beside him in the cruiser. They didn't get far before they were held up for five minutes on Harvey Road. They watched as an ambulance, parked askew, picked up someone from the street. There was glass strewn all over the pavement and a smell of gasoline in the air. They could hear distant sirens. A bicycle lay by the curb, its front wheel twisted and bent. A young policeman directed traffic around the scene.

"Who's that?" asked the Chief.

"Charlie Rose, we started work the same day."

"I can't keep track anymore, the new people."

Then the Chief said, "Fuck this, we can't wait forever."

He put his braided arm out the passenger window and Jack eased past with the left wheels up on the sidewalk.

"Executive privilege, one of the perks. Just walk on by, like the song says."

Jack turned right at the light at Rawlins Cross.

"Slow down now, we're almost there. Jack, I want you to think about this. Who's the weak link in this case? Not the aunt, from what I read, from what you wrote, so it's either the girl or the uncle and I put my money on the uncle. Why? Because what kind of guy would call the police rather than the ambulance under those circumstances? Who would do something like that? I'll tell you who. Somebody vindictive, somebody mean, and in my experience, once you're mean, you're always mean. You never change."

They parked at the fire hydrant across the street from 71 Prescott.

"Jack, you knock. Use those knuckles."

The aunt recognized him right away and said, "Come in, come in, you saved her life, you don't have to knock ever, walk in anytime."

And, to the Chief, she said, "My goodness, Sir, aren't you dressed to the nines, like a soldier. Come in, please do."

Looking at Jack, she raised her eyebrows.

Her husband was behind her and he too was making welcoming noises. There was a record playing with the volume turned up pretty high.

"Merle Haggard, isn't it?" asked the Chief, "I recognize that voice."

"None other," said the uncle, crossing the living room to turn it down.

"Don't turn that down for me."

"No?"

"Well, maybe a bit. Miss Savoury now, she's still in hospital?"

"Not for long, we're picking her up in an hour. Right, Beth?"

"That's the plan. Please, please sit down, both of you."

She motioned to the couch and Jack and the Chief sat side by side. The aunt and the uncle were in the armchairs.

"I'd offer you tea," the aunt said.

"No thanks, we'll pass on that. You don't mind if the constable takes notes?"

The Chief held his braided cap on his lap and sat forward to the edge of his seat.

"Here's the truth. We still have this case wide open and it looks like your niece is in a considerable bit of trouble. More evidence has come to the fore."

Jack was writing and watching faces and wondering what the new evidence was and, as instructed, saying nothing.

"Oh, I think I know what you're talking about," said the aunt, "it turns out she has a bleeding disorder. That's what the doctors figure. Why should that cause her trouble with you? Von Willebrand's, some name like that. I think I have it myself."

"You do have it, Beth. Tell them."

"They don't want the gory details."

"Sure they do. We almost lost her. First her appendix burst and then she was bleeding inside like a tap and it was touch and go. Three years ago now."

"Four."

"No, three. The dog was sick and died just after, remember?"

"Sparky, little Sparky."

"What a guy."

"Regardless of that, please, moving on," said the Chief, "Miss Savoury's circumstances are quite different than yours. And from the dog's. She had a positive pregnancy test, for example, and foetal tissue was found microscopically in the pathology samples."

"Foetal tissue?" asked the uncle.

"That means there was a baby. Not much of a baby but a baby nevertheless," said the Chief.

The aunt looked at the uncle and the uncle looked back at her.

"You're surprised?" asked the Chief.

"Wait a minute," said the aunt, "whatever the hospital found with their so-called testing—and remember this, they've made plenty of mistakes in their time, we read about it every day in the papers, all their mistakes—the reason Rowena was hospitalized was bleeding, as the doctors confirmed. That's the reason."

The Chief ignored her. He was looking straight at the uncle now.

"Sir, you heard her say that she had an abortion, you're on record testifying to that, and you called the police rather than the ambulance. You must have had a good reason for your actions on the night in question."

"I'm glad you came here today," said the uncle, "because the truth is, I need to unburden myself."

"Go ahead, please."

"It's this way. I misheard. It was a mistake, a total mistake on my part. I should never have called the police. All I did was delay the necessary treatment for Rowena. As for what I thought she said, the word *abortion*, that's what I thought she said, but now that I look back upon it—I've thought about this a lot, as you can imagine—it was the middle of the night, this constable was here, he can testify to the confusion, the anxiety, I realize what I heard was wrong."

"You heard wrong? That's what you're saying now?"

"Maybe she said *contortion*, or something like that."

He smiled.

The aunt was also sitting forward, sharing the same eager position as her husband. Her hands were folded in her lap. She smiled too, as though sharing a confidence.

"Let me summarize this for you," she said, "what we finally figured out, Walter and I. He did not hear it right, he was excited, he jumped to conclusions. He was stressed from lack of sleep, he got confused. It could happen to anyone. He knows he shouldn't have called the police. It worked out okay because of this policeman here, but it was a terrible, terrible mistake. Not one an uncle should make. He's going to apologize to Row himself. I hope you'll be able to be there to hear it."

"That's right," the uncle said, "Row, she reads a lot, she uses big words, she could have said anything, I could have heard anything. Anyway, she'll forgive me, knowing her, and that's all that matters now."

The Chief changed course, as any good investigator would.

"How do you account for the fact that your niece was pregnant, and that she lost the pregnancy?"

"Well," the aunt said, "Sir, it's certainly not up to me to account for anyone's pregnancy, let alone Rowena's, I have no idea about Rowena, how she got pregnant, indeed if she was pregnant. But for damn sure, if she was, I'm sure she's not the first sixteen-year-old ever to be in that condition, and, for all I know Row was taken advantage of or she was forced, which is a crime worth investigating—look at her, she's the size of a stick, she couldn't fight off anyone—and if she did have a miscarriage, if that's what she had, then that would be a blessing, it would be God's way of fixing a God-awful terrible mess."

The Chief sat back on the couch.

"God's way?" he said.

"Nature's way, God's way, take your pick."

"Where was your niece all night, before she came home?"

"We didn't ask. We didn't care. At a movie, drinking coffee downtown, dancing, singing, riding the night bus, take your pick."

"She knocked before midnight, I let her right in," said the uncle.

"What exact time was that please?"

"I didn't look."

"That's when you expected her? Midnight? Was she later than expected?"

"No, right on time. Punctual. Beth and I, we have no natural children of our own."

"No unnatural ones either, Walter. Just Sparky."

They laughed together, sharing it, looking at each other fondly.

"Our little joke, Sir. So finally, after twenty-two years of marriage, we finally had a child to take care of. For just one night. I couldn't sleep and Beth couldn't sleep, we talked, then we heard Row call out and after that, well, you were here, you know the rest. I was overtired. I behaved badly, I know."

"Yes you did, Walter."

"Row's welcome here anytime. She's a sweet kid. Does long division in her head."

He reached for his wife's hand and held it and now she was dabbing at her eyes with a handkerchief.

The Chief made a gesture of disbelief. He pursed his lips and blew the air out.

"Please, these crocodile tears, Ma'am, go ahead but we know what happened. No amount of perjuring yourselves will change what happened."

"Crocodile tears? No one's crying false tears here. And perjury? The truth shall out. You say you know what happened? Then go ahead and prove it."

She swivelled and pointed her finger at Jack and said, "This man here, this saint in uniform, he saved her and now you want to ruin her life? You want to prove she did something like a common criminal? Go ahead and try but you won't be able to. You'll certainly get no help from this house come hell or high water, I absolutely guarantee you that."

The Chief looked at the uncle.

"Well?"

"You heard her, you heard the little woman."

"Don't call me that, Walter."

"You heard the wife. That's enough now. Maybe you should go."

When they left, walking across the street to the car, they heard Merle Haggard with the volume pumped back up through the half-open windows. The Chief didn't look happy.

"That didn't go so well, she got to him. Sorry about that, I might as well have whistled into the wind."

The Chief took off his braided jacket, folded it carefully and placed it in the back seat.

"Drive, Jack."

"Back to the station?"

"Yes. We could chase her down to Bell Harbour, I guess, try to get to her in front of her family. That works sometime. A direct accusation in front of the parents and they break down. Intense emotion rattles the soul, spills the beans. Crude though, for someone that age."

"She's smarter than those two, and they did okay."

He pointed back over his shoulder. The Chief sighed.

"Can't win them all. What the hell, we tried. I can see what you're up against. Still, for you, Jack, there's Calgary, so not everything's a lost cause today."

To which Jack said nothing, but his silence sounded more to him like assent than refusal.

"They're like foxes, these fucking people, their fucking lives, they'll drive you fucking crazy if you're at this fucking job long enough. I don't blame you, Jack, I take back what I said earlier. It's not your fault. They've fucking covered their asses here."

He'd find a place to talk to Tryphie. Undercover. Cut the ties, shed his skin like a snake. Where could they talk? How about the steps that ran through the weeds, the broken concrete stairway off to the side, below the Basilica. Nobody went there, nobody knew it existed. He could talk to her there.

"Chief, where'd you get that information about the pathology, the foetal tissue?"

"Made it up. By the time we get the records, it'll be there. You know, people are crazy, they're nuts. My wife, in Windsor fucking Lake, Jack. No clothes, a water goddess. Ten degrees Celsius, air temperature. I covered her with a blanket from the back. She was shivering. I just couldn't keep her happy here. You figure it out, I can't. Women. That guy back there, look at him, he's been ass-whipped. This job, sometimes, thank God we got pensions coming our way, thank God for that."

SHE WAS surprised that her uncle was there when she left the hospital.

"Hello, Rowena," he said, "can I carry that?"

It was just a small plastic zip-bag with her toothbrush, a brush and comb, some Kleenex. It wasn't even as big as a purse. He even offered her his arm.

"Why, thank you, Uncle," she said, "but I'm okay. This is nothing."

"Give it to me anyway, dear, that's what I'm here for. Pack horse Walter. I took the day off, happy to do so."

Her aunt smothered her with kisses. Her mother and the principal's wife were there too, but they were more reserved.

"Row," they just said, "Row."

The nurses treated them all with special deference, imagining themselves with their own daughters, leaving hospital after a grave illness.

"You're so lucky, to have so many mothers," they said to her, laughing.

They patted Rowena on the back and they hugged everybody else, including Walter.

"Now these are your iron pills, dear, in this container. Take them twice a day till they're gone. And these, this circular package, are the other pills, remember? Oh, and Rowena, do you have all your things?"

She pointed to the bag her uncle was carrying. He was standing, waiting, watching the women and the nurses fuss and smile and mill about like the seagulls on Harbour Drive.

Then the chief gynecologist passed by, without his students. He stopped and shook her hand and said, "Goodbye, Ms. Savoury, congratulations on your stay. We'll be in touch by mail, when all the results are in."

"Thank you."

No hugs that time.

The psychiatrist, Dr. Poole, was there too, the one who'd been called in to counsel her in the ICU.

"Goodbye, Ms. Savoury, call me if there's any problems. You promise?"

The nurses couldn't help but notice how long Rowena and the psychiatrist held onto each other. Now that's a hug. Nothing perfunctory about it. Afterwards they commented, they'd been impressed. Did you see that? they said, maybe there's more to these shrinks than meets the eye, we need to take their roles in here more seriously.

Then, like it was some sort of play or production in which all the cast members had to appear, who was next but the policeman. The one who saved her life. There he was in his uniform, tall and handsome and still the only one in black or dark blue. As though he knew she was leaving, which maybe he did. He didn't try to talk to the family, he just nodded to the aunt and to the uncle, both of whom acknowledged him with a friendly wave. He seemed to be more interested in the principal's wife, looking at her, then looking away, then looking at her again, but she had her face averted, it seemed, she was talking to Row's mother or bending down to tie her shoe or, finally, she stepped back out of the room to the corridor.

But no matter, he knew. She was the one with the umbrella, struggling in the rain. No doubt about it, and a charitable interpretation of her behaviour now was that she was trying to avoid him out of shyness. Not so charitable, out of guilt.

"Who's that" he asked one of the nurses.

"One of her mothers."

"One of them?"

"She has two. We thought she was her only mother, but she isn't. Really she's just a friend of the family. Her real mother, that's her over there. A whole troupe of mothers, she's lucky that way. All from the same town, maybe it's the outport way."

The psychiatrist had her arms around the girl too, joining in the emotional departure, unaware that he'd jammed the point of his protractor down into her house, through the roof, catching her between her shoulder blades and pinning her to the floor. Hardwood, probably.

Then the doctor let go of the girl and moved off to the side. She was just watching as they all left the room and walked as a group down the hall. The uncle pressed the button for the elevator.

Jack went over to Dr. Poole, just the two of them together now against the far wall.

"Hi again."

"Hello."

"I'm Jack Maher, remember? The policeman on this case. We met a few days ago in the ICU."

"I remember."

Sure you do, sure you do. Smiling and as friendly as can be, no nervousness.

She held out her hand, as she had once before, and they shook hands.

"Quite the nights and days for our Ms. Savoury," he said.

"I'll say. Thank goodness it's over. She's been discharged. Going home."

"Still no sign of her memory returning?"

"No. Not likely to. All's well that ends well. The amnesia actually serves her well, absolving her from whatever happened."

"I've been impressed with your involvement in this case, Doctor, from day one."

"Day one? I think it was day two or three."

"Maybe so. You're very close to her, obviously. I watched you hugging her like a long-lost friend."

"That happens. As psychiatrists, we should guard against it but with her, so vulnerable, there's no harm in it, showing physical affection."

"You used to live in Bell Harbour, Doctor. Where they all come from."

He gestured to the family. She was suddenly distracted. She turned her head from him as the elevator doors opened and the uncle was the first to step in.

"I'm wondering if you didn't know them before. You must have."

They were all in the elevator now and Row was waving back to them, waving goodbye, watching them standing together until the doors closed and she was gone.

"I knew the mother, yes."

"From Bell Harbour?"

"You've been doing research on me."

"We look into everything. It's routine."

"You know, Officer, you seem like a nice young man. I know you were instrumental in saving her and everyone's grateful to you, myself included. When I was in Bell Harbour though, as your research will tell you, I was young too, probably your age, not much older. Down there, we had the RCMP for the police. They learned what to see and what not to see, how to get along, that not every little infraction was a crime."

"Little infractions, of course not. You did surgical procedures there, I expect?"

"Of course I did."

"Wide-ranging skills, you must have dealt with everything from birth to death."

"What are you implying?"

"An observation we've made about this case. From our perspective, we see a young girl who was one day pregnant, and the next, not."

"Lucky for her, the miscarriage. Nature intervenes. She didn't want it anyway."

"Nature? Let's hope that's all it was."

"I understand what you're saying. I practice psychiatry now. Your exhaustive research should tell you that."

"You don't do anything else?"

"Nothing like I used to. I'm so far out of practice. The fact is I wouldn't recommend my care in any other field to anyone. Nice talking to you though."

She walked away down the hall.

End of investigation. At least now she knew that he knew. Even if no one else did. Well, Tryphena, of course she knew too.

He had some time on his hands. From the hospital parking lot, he drove over to Quidi Vidi Road and stopped the cruiser outside her office. He sat there for fifteen minutes. Shoppers went in and out of the small grocery store, Belbin's.

A middle-aged woman in a flashy orange raincoat walked down the side of the doctor's house. Then he lost sight of her, where the hedge intervened. The doctor must have beaten him back to her lair, the short walk from the hospital.

If this were a movie, the curtains to the street would now part ever so slightly and someone would look his way and the curtain would drop back down. But nothing happened.

He shifted in his seat and took out his wallet. He uncrumpled the paper with the phone number of the doctor who flouted the law, his name, the address in Montreal. Thank you, Marion Chipman, for this. He could go there, no one would know him, so it would be a bit like undercover. His first try at it. Set up something there for Tryphie. A termination, poof, problem solved. Tempting though it was, he couldn't do anything here on Quidi Vidi Road, no way, it was too close to home. He could probably persuade this woman, in light of his knowledge, to do it. But that would be blackmail.

He pulled away from the curb.

The Chief had said, take a few days off, Jack, tie up loose ends. Well, there's a whole tangle of those.

Change out of the uniform, go talk to her now. Take the bull by the horns, my boy.

Why do I feel so bad about this?

STAN SCREWED up his courage. He knocked on her door, 7 Fitzpatrick Avenue.

"Yes?"

Her mother. It could have been worse, it could have been the policeman if he was that far advanced, if he had door-answering privileges here, which, considering his other assumed privileges—let's not think of those—was not impossible.

"Mrs. Grandy? My name is Stanley Grant, I'm a classmate of Tryphena's. Is she home?"

"Sure she is. I've heard of you. Hi, Stan. She's upstairs."

"May I talk to her?"

"Hang on."

She disappeared and Stan heard her calling, "Tryphie? Tryphie, someone from school."

Her footsteps on the stairs.

"Stan! Oh, hi."

"Good morning, Tryphie, I hope you don't mind my coming by."

She was leaning against the door which had a tear-drop window set into it, and she was looking a lot better than the last time he'd seen her, after the vomiting. An elasticity to her as always, the way she moved, even the way she leaned against the door frame.

"You're feeling better, I can see that."

"Good as gold now. What's up?"

"I'm wondering, if you have a few minutes, we could talk?"

She looked at her watch.

"Jack'll be here."

"This will take ten minutes. It's about my mother. Then I'm gone."

"Your mother?"

"Remember I said, the big reunion?"

"You met her?"

"Come out, please, just down the street. I'll show you something."

She stepped out onto the sidewalk and closed the screen door.

"Look," he said, "look down there, what do you see?"

"Nothing."

"Look harder."

"Okay, the street. Kiziah. The end of the street. Traffic on Pennywell Road, nothing unusual."

"See that red car?"

"The sporty one? Right there?"

"That's mine. Actually that's my mother, that's what she's turned into."

"Stan, I'm sorry, I don't get it."

"Jump in, sit down."

He opened the passenger door of the flashy red car and he beckoned her to sit. Then he moved quickly around the front of the car and sat in the driver's seat.

"I can't go anywhere, Stan."

"We'll just sit. Five minutes."

"I didn't even know you had a car. These are bucket seats, I think."

"They are. So, Tryphie, yesterday I finally get the word to meet her at Velma's, the restaurant. Yesterday. It's so fast, I'm taken aback, I'm nervous so I get there early and no one's inside, the place is empty. I go outside. I lean against the wall, waiting for her. I have not seen her these twenty-three years. My mother of course I mean. In my pocket I have several good-luck charms from my little sister, we'll call her that, including, foremost, a copper penny. Then this car, this red

Camaro, this one we're sitting in, pulls up and there's a parking spot open and she kind of backs into it but the car's still three feet from the curb. She gets out. Stan? she says. I agree with her, yes it's me. She's crying already and I don't know what to say except, look, let me park that better. So she takes my place and I take hers and I park the car better, good enough anyway, and I hand her back the keys. She's got grey hair, the same age as your mother I would guess, a nice coat and hat. Certainly no bag lady, which was one of my concerns. Thin, made-up, some of that. She buries her face in my windbreaker right there on the sidewalk, still crying. I put my arms around her and pat her on the back. Cup of tea, I hear her say. It's surreal, I feel nothing. We go inside, we're the only customers. She sits down opposite me and stops crying as fast as she started and then she sips tea, and I do too. Stanley, she finally says, not the name I'd have chosen. Me either, I say, but it was out of my control. Stan, she says, it sounds better in short form. Then, no other words pass for a couple of minutes and she just looks at me and looks away. Cat's got my tongue, she says, I was afraid of that, she says. Tell me what happened when I was born, I finally say because if I don't outright ask her, it looks like I won't find out. I'm actually thinking, Tryphie, the way she's looking at me, maybe she's got some kind of mental problem. Am I talking too fast?"

"No, go ahead."

"Mental problems, they can be hereditary. That's not good from my vantage point. But she says nothing except the cat's got her tongue. We finish the tea and the waitress is standing there and my mother, though it's hard for me to call her that, to think of her as my mother, pays with a five-dollar bill and the waitress runs off to get the change. Wait a minute, wait a minute, I say, tell me, tell me something about you and me and what happened. If I could talk, if I could let go and express myself, she says, we wouldn't be here now, we'd have been a family all along. Try, I said. She pulls herself together and says more or less what I thought she'd say, nothing surprising, that she was young, she didn't even know what hit her, and as she talked she kept her eyes down and moved sugar around in the bowl with a spoon and said she's sorry she had to give me up, her parents, something about them, now she lives in Halifax, she has a husband but no other kids, and she's not living with my birth father, he could be dead."

"She said that? Dead?"

"She did. The reason she looked me up, she said, was to say hello, she felt bad needless to say, to apologize though it was too late for that. Her counsellor had said, talk to your boy but the damage will be done. I pretended not to agree with her there, saying she didn't have to apologize, not to me, no damage has been done, there are times we do things we have no control over, etcetera, etcetera, I'm not sure exactly what I said but I felt I needed to support her. She was awkward. It's not your fault at all I said, repeating myself five or ten times though actually I believe it is her fault, I've seen other children raised by single mothers and they're doing okay. But she's weak, you can tell. Then she says as though it would have no effect on me, Stan, I see a resemblance. Oh, really, I thought, because looking at her I didn't see myself at all so she must be speaking of the father, whoever that man was, a fly-by-night I guess, who might, she has already told me, be dead. I let that pass. Resemblance? I didn't even want to know. But still. Tryphie, to summarize, my expectations for this visit were way too high, my unknown life and my potential was being slaughtered before my eyes."

His hands were on the steering wheel as though he were driving. Not clenched or anything. Tryphena reached over and touched his right hand.

"So, yes, I was expecting too much. Then she gives me the keys to this fucking car, says it's mine, the paperwork's done but for the insurance. Keep it, Stanley, it's a present from me, inadequate but it's all I can do. Her lips are having trouble forming words. This car, she says, please accept it, a small price to pay for all the years, la-di-da, la-di-da, we have this other car, we don't need this. I said, I'm not looking for material things from you. I'm sorry I can't say more, she says. Effectively she's jerking me around, if you ask me, emotionally, not on purpose but because she doesn't have the resources herself to go beyond a reflex conversation. Okay, suck it back, Stan. You're the way you are because of this, look at her. I'm telling you, Tryphie, if you scripted what happened, you couldn't have come up with this."

She took her hand back and put it in her lap.

"She says she's going. I realize the waitress has been standing there with the change for God knows most of this conversation, if you can call it that. She looks at me like I'm the sorriest dog on earth. Then I realize, hell, this is Abigail, from our class. She waitresses on the side. Okay, I'm public knowledge now. I was too stunned to see it was her before, I didn't look, I was too focused. Hey Abigail, this is my mother. I introduce them and then I walk my mother to the front door and we go out to the sidewalk and a black car, a Buick, is waiting there and the car picks her up and she's gone. Driver in the front seat a big heavy guy. Nova Scotia plates."

"That's it?"

"Almost. Abigail comes out and says nice things to me. Like, that couldn't have been easy, Stan, that's actually the first time you met? Sorry I overheard, I never knew this, that sort of thing. It's okay, okay, I said. She was nice, I never talked to her before. I didn't care she knew. So, here we are, the mother thing's over, and this car, Tryphie, this is my mother now, in a way. More reliable though."

"It seems to be a good car, Stan. Feel it."

She wiggled her hips around in the bucket seat. Shimmied in it.

"Twenty thousand miles, that's all. It's got some pep. Reunions, from what I read before, they're not always great. To the contrary, often they're not great."

"So you were prepared."

"Yes and no. I gave my sister her penny back. She could tell how it went, she didn't need to ask. We went for a drive, Dairy Queen."

"What's that on your sleeve?"

"Here? Nothing, I copied out the hieroglyphics from the Rosetta Stone. I can almost do it off by heart. A burgeoning talent of mine."

"In ink."

"Yes, ballpoint."

"Don't wash it Stan, it'll smear."

"I know. It's my exam shirt now, I'll wear it for that. It will help me concentrate, that's my plan."

"You know, Stan, it looks like she wouldn't have been a great mother anyway."

"No."

"From what happened."

"She wanted to be nice but she couldn't be. Nice was smothered up in her or choked out of her or she never had it."

"Did she say she'd see you again?"

"No."

"You're doing okay?"

"At the Dairy Queen, my sister says some people should never be born. This she says with a vanilla cone in her hand and obviously she's thinking about herself. How sad is that?"

"The one with the penny?"

"Yes."

"And what did you say?"

"I agreed with her but I didn't say it. I have some responsibilities as a human being. I said that's crazy, Maudie, look at us, we're doing okay."

"Good, Stan. Listen, I think I better go now, duty calls."

"Sure, thanks for listening. That's over. Now don't get sick again."

She let herself out of the car. He watched her grow smaller in the mirror. He turned the key and the motor started but he didn't drive off immediately.

Might be a hole in the muffler, the noise, the throatiness of it. Get it checked.

Kiziah was sitting on the curb.

"Who's that, Tryphie?" she asked.

"A friend from school. His name is Stan."

"That's a nice car he's got. Nicer than the policeman's."

"I guess so. But don't judge people by their cars."

"Noisy though. Want to skip, Tryphie?"

"No time. Not today."

"You're saying that more and more."

"I am?"

"Yesterday and the day before that and the day before that, you said you were too busy."

She thought of Stan's mother in the restaurant.

"Well then, five minutes, Kizzie, I can do five minutes."

"QUITE A nice tight crew this time," said the taxi driver.

Just Rowena, her mother, and the principal's wife, no other passengers. Row and her mother were in the back. They watched the landscape slide by, the outskirts of St. John's petering into the knuckled rock of the Avalon.

"It seems a long time ago we came in," said Rowena.

"I guess you had a real good time, then," the driver said, "you kept us waiting a few extra days."

"Sorry about that," said Rowena.

"The boat wasn't running anyway. Not much lost."

"That's what I heard."

"She's thinking of going to Memorial, for university. Checking it out takes time," her mother said.

"Her marks are good enough for anything," said the principal's wife.

"You're finishing high school?" said the driver, "I still might go back myself, get my high-school diploma, why not? It would sure make my mother happy, God bless her soul. Sure, she's been dead these twenty years but she knew the value of an education. As does your own mother, obviously."

He looked back at them in the mirror, scanning them.

"We all value education," said the principal's wife.

At one point the highway actually lived up to its name, the *high way*. It crossed a ridge of land, a narrow isthmus with ocean on the left and right, the two bays almost touching, the road clinging to the spine of land between. Huge rocks had been thrown or dropped at random and lay over the landscape of grass, juniper, berries, ponds, gravel pits.

"Wind's up, but not too much up," said the driver, "it'll be a fine day on the water."

He had the radio on low, voices talking, laughing, indistinct, a background buzz, and Row fell asleep against her mother's shoulder. The taxi hummed its tire-song until they were back at Terrenceville. Five days flipped by on the calendar yet the martial-looking gulls were still there, strutting and patrolling the wharf as though nothing had happened. The same terns dove in total ignorance of what she'd been through. The men with their orange gloves laughed in the same way and looked at her with the same lack of interest. Too young to think about. They loosened the giant hawsers and threw them snaking aboard and the *Taverner* departed into moderate seas. Reaching open water, they rolled and beat their way west through Fortune Bay, spray lashing the port side. On the starboard side though, it was warm enough to stand in the sun, protected. Rencontre East, Pool's Cove, then Bell Harbour.

"There's father," said Rowena.

They waved back and forth and the ship touched the side of the wharf and the gangway came down and the three of them walked off together and that was it. Rowena's holiday in town was over.

But the memory of her trip was not over, because Dr. Poole was alone in her office, thinking of her. She could see through the sheer curtains, see through them easily from where she sat, right out onto Quidi Vidi Road. Shoppers walked past, a slow woman with a cane, the usual sparse traffic, and, for a while, a police cruiser stopped by the curb across the street. This was the second time she'd seen it. The same officer, the one from the hospital? She couldn't tell. He never got out.

Psychiatry, her calling, patching people together like a raft from twigs. And here come the high seas and the wind's in a fury. The phone call from the principal's wife coming out of the blue, Bell Harbour, Boxey, the night with the kerosene lamps haunting her again, Rowena Savoury, and here in town lonesome boys jumping on ice with layers of sadness that make no sense. You do the best you can and what do you get? Police cars outside your window, and everything you touch turns perilous.

The doorbell rang, her next patient.

"I'm a few minutes early, Dr. Poole."

"That's fine, come in."

It was time for her own problems to fall away. So what if you're unhappy, stripped of confidence and a suspect in a criminal case.

The next time she looked, half an hour later, while her patient was putting on her coat and saying goodbye, the police car was gone.

TRYPHENA WAS in the kitchen with three or four books in her arms. She smiled when she saw Jack, his head poking through the door. She waved with half a hand but then the books began to slide. She lifted one knee, bent left, right, stood on one foot, then bent backwards. She recovered, she pulled it off, she averted disaster. The books settled back into place.

"Whoa," she said.

"What are you doing with those?"

"Taking them upstairs."

"I'll give you a hand."

"You have the car?"

"Outside, yes."

"Maybe I'll take them to school then."

"You've read all of those?"

"Committed to memory, Jack. The gist of it, not every word."

In the Vauxhall, she kneeled on the front seat and spilled the books as carefully as she could into the back.

"I'm hungry," she said, "I'm eating for two. Let's go back in."

There was a plate of Ritz crackers and a jar of peanut butter on the table.

"Judging from the crumbs, a family of mice has been at this already," he said.

"Ice cream too, I think, in that bowl."

"Tryphena, we have to talk about this."

But her mouth was full. She nodded, she knew.

"So, can we go for a walk?"

"What's wrong with here?"

"What's wrong with here is that your mother's always showing up. Does she have some kind of spy satellite in the sky? Focused on us? I give her maybe ten seconds."

He held up his watch.

"One, two, three..."

"Hardly fair that, Jack. She does live here."

"Some kind of high-alert system, like the DEW line or what the Russians have."

"Okay then, I get it, let's walk."

Outside, the neighbourhood girl was skipping on the sidewalk as usual.

"Does she never sleep? She's part of the spy system, that one," Jack said.

"Oh skip with me, please Tryphie, you're the best. Please!"

"Tryphie's busy, we're going downtown. Tell her, Tryphie, we'll be back. Time for that later."

Tryphena patted the girl on the head.

"Later, honey," she said.

"Okay then, go anywhere you like, I don't care."

She twirled her rope in one hand and watched them as they walked to Pennywell Road. Jack's arm was now looped over Tryphena's shoulder and her arm was around his waist. Young lovers in bright sunshine. They walked hip to hip, he in a T-shirt and jeans and looking nothing like a policeman and she in the same blue dress that got them into trouble in the first place, the one she took off so easily up on Butter Pot.

"So," he said, "here we are, we're pretty happy together, since we met, aren't we?"

"Yes we are."

"Then it's time to talk."

"Not quite yet. I think I know what you're going to say and I'm not sure I want to hear it. Let's walk first, talk later. I promise."

Her arm was still around his waist. They walked on until they were below the police station, heading downtown, stepping off Long's Hill, dropping down towards a scrabby little neighbourhood of fenced-off empty lots and small houses. Cars flew by behind them, now high above. Ten or twelve steps of cracked concrete had been built for the rare lost walker who came down that way. A bent handrail on one side, a narrow field of weeds overgrown to the right. In the distance, sunlight flashed on the water in the harbour. Beyond that were the shadows, the looming bulk of the southside hills, the distant backdrop of their lives. That's where the view closed down. Beyond that was the Atlantic, which could not be seen except through the tiny slot, the Narrows.

"If we had a laser, Tryphie, we could blast through those hills and see more of the ocean. We wouldn't feel so boxed in."

"That's how you feel? There'd be no harbour then, Jack, nothing protected, so we wouldn't be here at all. No harbour, no St. John's. Without those hills, we're nothing."

They were still on the crumbling stairs.

"I need a breather," she said.

"Fine, this is fine here. We can sit."

The steps were warm from the sun. She felt it on her legs and the back of her thighs through the dress. Dandelions and other weeds poked up through cracks. She tore one off and then another.

"You have to get the taproot," he said.

It was impossible, her fingers didn't have the strength, the concrete pinched down onto the roots like a vise.

Then he started to talk to her—as he'd already imagined—but his words stumbled and there was no flow to what he said.

"Tryphena, listen, the whole point is this, it has nothing to do with us, it's just the timing of it, where we are now in our lives."

She continued to pull at weeds.

"A termination of pregnancy, despite what happened on Prescott Street, the girl there, the medical procedure itself is perfectly safe and easy, it's been done thousands of times and then what? We resume our lives, just as they are now."

"Tryphena, are you listening?"

"This," she said, "is now a dandelion salad. If we had Thousand Islands dressing, we'd be set."

"I'm talking to myself I guess," he said.

She looked off into the distance into those hills, the ones he wanted moved. So he too started to pick at weeds. He had to bend and reach but he added a few to her pile, tossing them in from a foot away.

"Ordinarily, Jack, this isn't the nicest place, but today it's the absolute worst of all places. I hate it."

"Jesus, Tryphena."

"I can't believe you're talking like this. I have no interest in what you're saying, even less in what you're going to say."

She had a lump in her throat as though she were going to be sick again but it didn't feel the same as before.

He stood up and took two or three steps down so now his head was more or less on a level with hers, where she was sitting, and he turned to face her and delivered a sentence well-rehearsed.

"Tryphena, since this happened, I feel we've been under a bit of a cloud."

He was calling her by her full name, Tryphena, Tryphena, Tryphena, rattling on, repeating himself, saying the same thing over and over. She remained mute. Finally he sat down beside her again on the same half-broken step. He put his arm around her shoulders but felt nothing but stiffness so he took it away and leaned back on his elbow. She was sitting straight up and not moving. She brushed a strand of hair off her forehead, from over her right eye, in a familiar gesture that once had made his heart fall and turn but now left him just watching, observing. He pulled out a long blade of grass and put it between his lips and tried to whistle. All he blew was air.

"Tryphena, you're not listening to me."

"I'm afraid I am."

Then she cupped her hands in circles over her eyes as though she had a pair of binoculars and was searching the distance. Or she was crying.

"Are you okay?"

"Not really."

She wasn't crying. Her voice was steady and so were her hands.

"What do you see?"

"Not a lot."

"Tryphena, please listen. We're not the first to have this conversation. We could plan our life better if we went at this differently. That's what I'm saying."

She dropped her binoculars, her hands.

"Plan our life? I didn't realize I had to plan our life, Jack, I didn't plan you and I didn't plan sex. And obviously you didn't either."

The sky was a pastel-blue over the harbour, over the southside hills, but the hills themselves were dark, sheer rock, water dripping down from the high bogs, a few oil tanks carved into the upper reaches.

She finally turned her blonde head his way and looked directly at him.

"I just don't feel the same way about this."

"Come on," he said to her, trying to remember to get his points across, starting in again, Tryphena, Tryphena, Tryphena, the drone of her name. They were too young, their lives were unformed, he was just getting started in the police, she wasn't even graduated, neither of them had any money, in fact they had debts, don't forget that, and if they made the right decision, together, they wouldn't have to go ahead with the whole cavalcade.

"Cavalcade? Say what you mean."

"Sorry I don't mean cavalcade. Bad word."

"Say what you mean, Jack. I'm ready now."

And he almost said it, the baby, the crib, the toys on the floor, the bottles of milk, but seeing her there, the way she was with the life he'd always valued drained out of her, he couldn't do it, he backed off and it was his turn to say nothing.

He stood up and stretched but then the demands of the silence egged him on again.

"I'm not exactly sure what I mean."

"So I see. But I get it actually. You don't want us to go ahead with this."

"Tryphena, that's it. Yes. In a nutshell."

She stopped looking at the distant hills and the harbour. At her right foot was the pathetic salad of weeds they'd built together.

"I've checked into it, it's not so hard, in fact it's easy, we fly to Montreal."

He reached into his wallet and pulled out the piece of paper.

"Address, name and phone number, right here."

"I've never been off the island," she said.

"We go together, stay in a hotel, stay a few nights, fly home and no one's the wiser."

She stood up and straightened her skirt.

"I will never go to Montreal, Jack, never. I will never do it, there are no circumstances under which I would do it, not for anything in the world, so forget it."

"Christ, I'm glad we're having a dialogue on this."

"It's too much for me. Can we forget it for a bit, just be ourselves?"

He shrugged his shoulders.

"Okay, Tryphie, whatever you say."

How hopeless this was.

They stood up and resumed the walk downhill together, not touching. But eventually, by the time they got to the Newfoundland Hotel, she put her arm around him again. Why not? Who else could she put her arm around? He did the same thing after five steps and they cut down to the Battery and walked like that, fused, out to the end until the road ended. Somehow the sea breeze, the waves, the cries of the gulls washed away some of the way they'd felt. They turned around, retraced their steps out of the Battery, past the cliff-hanging houses, the bright colours, the dips and falls in the road, the patches of long grass, the cars jammed here and there, the last old house on the right with the chicken loose, pecking at pebbles.

One day, Jack Maher and Tryphena Grandy would look back at it, this walk, how they put their arms around each other when they were at their bleakest moment. When they fell apart on the crumbled steps, when they couldn't talk, agree, or feel desire. When he kicked their pathetic salad of dandelions over and watched it tumble and scatter and said out loud, *okay, whatever you say*. When he backed off and shut up yet was drawn to her again despite his treachery, his duplicity, the ticket to Montreal he already had in his pocket—take a few days off, Jack, tie up those loose ends!—and they walked in this fragmented state back to Fitzpatrick Avenue where they sat in his car and there was his voice bringing it all up again, as though she'd change her mind.

"Tryphena, please, think about this just one more time. It seems kind of funny—not funny-ha-ha but funny-strange—that you could come down so decisively on the side of some anonymous outport girl with freckles who most certainly had an abortion, actually tell me to lie about it, yet not consider the same thing for us. Same situation, I don't get it."

Then that damn little Kiziah ran over and thumped on the side of the car and pressed her nose against the window and Jack pointed his finger at her.

"For the love of God, get rid of her."

Tryphena looked out the window and banged back, not very hard, not hard enough, with the heel of her hand and the girl jumped back for a second, laughing, leaving a smudge on the window, and in four seconds she and her nose were back, no quitter she, more banging on the car, her nose flattened out and then more of her face, like a ghoul.

Tryphena rolled the window down and said, "Honey, I'll be there in a minute, give me a second with Jack."

"Close the window, Tryphena."

"Tryphie! Don't close the window!"

"A minute, honey, wait."

"Lock the door," he said.

At which point Kiziah pulled open the back door and jumped in and grabbed Tryphena by the pony-tail and pulled.

"Kizzie no!" her hands thrown behind her head defensively.

Kiziah stopped and clambered over the seat and sat on Tryphena's lap, squirming, twisting.

"It's entirely different, Jack"— hugging, squeezing the girl—"that girl's situation, my situation, our situation, they're entirely different. We're not the same girls."

In the rearview mirror, Jack could see other kids playing, like a schoolyard. No shortage of children on this street. Bicycles hopping curbs, hockey sticks.

"Tryphie, what are you talking about?" Kiziah asked.

"Nothing, honey, here, I'll let you out."

She opened the door and half-rolled, half-supported the little girl back out onto the sidewalk.

"Take your rope. Here."

She left the door open.

"In Quebec they understand it better, Tryphena, they're French, they look the other way."

But now her arm and shoulder were being pulled like toffee.

"Tryphie, Tryphie, Tryphie, Tryphie."

"I'm going in, Jack, there's no point in rehashing this."

She leaned towards him to kiss him but Kiziah was pulling too hard the other way. She didn't even get close, she blew the kiss in the air and was out of the car. He put in the clutch and turned the key and when he stopped at Pennywell Road, in the rearview mirror, she'd gone inside her house. Kiziah must have gone with her because she wasn't there either.

Tryphena, get your priorities straight.

He wasted the rest of the day at home. He re-heated pizza. He watched television for three hours. He stood by the living room window and looked out over the lights that were his city, the splash of darkness that was now the harbour and here's the crux, he figured: he could forget all those times with her, the dancing and what the dancing had become, jaunts in the car, her birds, her gannets, her binoculars, stories from school, the way she carried books and leaned on doors, the nights on Garrison Hill. Her mother the spy. He could do that, he could cut and run—poof—and go to Calgary and never see her again, push her away, peel her body off his skin, untether her like tangled string knot by knot, touch by touch, thought by thought but if he did that, really, what kind of a man would do that? Send money for the baby? Not the kind of man he'd like to be. Christ, could he do that? Actually, he was so fucked up that he'd like to call her now and listen to her voice and fall in love with her all over again.

Well, he had the ticket to Montreal. Actually he had two tickets but one of those would go to waste. Hers. But still, he had two days off so he'd check it out.

Tryphie, they'll do it for us. What do you think now? Airport.

"YOU CAN'T be serious," Mrs. Henderson said.

"Oh I'm decidedly serious," said Ms. Johnson, "because despite last time, when the disciplinary issue I raised— Mr. Grant's openly touching Miss Grandy's bosoms—was passed over lightly, this time he has gone beyond the pale. The reputation of the school is at stake. Perhaps even its provincial license."

"That's an exaggeration. Keep this in-house, Janet, whatever it is."

"Okay. Then I formally request another meeting."

"The Disciplinary Committee, you mean?"

"Yes."

"For the second time in two years, the second time in a week?"

"Yes. For the sake of the school. If we act together, as a formal committee, then we shall be found faultless by any inquiry."

"Inquiry? Don't be ridiculous. Again you are exaggerating."

"Twenty girls left these premises yesterday with twenty different versions of what happened in my lab. Twenty girls will talk, and rumours will fly like crows."

"Crows! My goodness, call Mrs. Blagdon then, I'm quite fascinated."

"I have called her already. I think I hear her footsteps."

The door to the staff room opened and in came Mrs. Blagdon, Secretary to the Ad Hoc Committee, holding some wool and knitting needles.

"I'm here. Now what in the world."

"Sandra, hello. Another meeting, please take notes."

"Really?"

"Put down the knitting, yes. Ms. Johnson, you can now go ahead."

"Thank you. Sandra, ready?"

"Proceed."

As before, the committee sat on the worn-out sofas in the staffroom, undisturbed by the presence of others.

"To begin: I would like to make it clear, in the minutes, that I regret having to raise these disciplinary points, but I do so in the best interests of the school and of those students of ours who study so hard to become dental hygienists."

"Duly noted," said Mrs. Blagdon, her pencil racing, glancing at Mrs. Henderson, then down again at her page.

"So, in my last Practicum, on positioning and cleaning, subjects of paramount importance, the same student, Mr. Stanley Grant, called his partner, Miss Tryphena Grandy, then playing the role of a patient, by an endearment."

"What exactly did he say?"

"*Honey, open your mouth.*"

"This is going to jeopardize the reputation of the school?"

"Let me go on. He inserted the mirror carelessly, stimulating her gag reflex. She vomited helplessly upon him, her semi-digested lunch over his hands and shirtsleeves and of course upon herself, and he proceeded, as he had last time, to take liberties with her body. Subtle liberties made more despicable by the guise of helping her, movements of his hands on her neck, her back, patting her here and there, once unmistakably again upon her bosoms, I believe, down through the dental bib."

"You saw all of this."

"Yes. Done no doubt to make mock of my previous complaint. As though he knew that once again I would be helpless. That we as a committee had already granted him privilege by our silence."

"*Honey*, you heard him say? That's bad?"

"In the context of the dental office, it's unpardonable."

"What did Miss Grandy say?"

"She covered for him, as usual. *Bunny*, she said, some call me Bunny, and that was so ridiculous that the class laughed en masse, as though they were watching a sit-com. I was mortified."

"Merriment then broke out in your class."

"Yes. I pointed out the boundary issues again. That shut them up to a degree, plus the obvious distress Miss Grandy was in. Genuine distress provoked by the amateurish examination of Mr. Grant. But that was just the start of it. Here, Mrs. Henderson, is why I felt obliged to call this meeting. Miss Grandy, pale and shaken and soaked to the waist, then asked permission to be excused, to go to the washroom. Of course, I said yes. But Mr. Grant quickly and brazenly volunteered to escort her to the Ladies' himself, a deeply inappropriate, gender-insensitive suggestion."

"It is unusual."

"I asked Miss Grandy—so quick to *Honey* and *Bunny* on his behalf a moment before—if it would not be more seemly for one of the girls to accompany her. No, Stan's fine, look at him, he needs cleaning himself, she said. Or something to that effect. And the two of them disappeared down the hall as the rest of the class, totally distracted from their work, tittered and raised eyebrows—the gall of that man! they were thinking— so, after a minute or two of attempting to restore order, I told the students to sit and contemplate what they had seen and I followed the two of them down the hall. By then they had disappeared. To my horror I could hear his voice echoing from the tiles in the Ladies' washroom. I assure you, both of you, that nothing like this has ever happened in our school before. I pushed open the door, fearful of what I might find, and my fears were more than answered for there he was, nearly shirtless himself, with Miss Grandy dressed only in her bra and underwear, handing her a dry tattered shirt and sweater, the two of them sorrowful yet patently guilty in their complicity, and he called her *Bunny* to my face, rubbing in his arrogance and disrespect, and here I am today to demand that we take some action on this, or I shall lose control of my class, and, even worse, should this incident become common knowledge, woe betide the reputation of our school."

"Are you finished?"

"Yes. Well, almost. I would also like to say that upon Mr. Grant's shirt cuffs were markings that meant, to me, but one thing. A crib sheet in preparation for cheating on the upcoming exam."

"Now that is a serious charge."

"Yes it is."

"The most serious charge a teacher could make. You were able to read what it said upon these so-called crib sheets?"

"No. They were unintelligible. From what I could see from my vantage point."

"Perhaps you've jumped to conclusions, Ms. Johnson."

"Mrs. Henderson, please, I preceded you in this school by some years and I am no fool."

"Nevertheless a charge like that needs one-hundred percent proof, which is lacking. So we can put that issue aside. Mrs. Blagdon, do you agree?"

"I agree."

"On the other charge you have brought to our attention, did Miss Grandy evince any discomfort from being in the washroom with Mr. Grant?"

"No. But it doesn't matter, it's the example it sets to others."

"Mrs. Blagdon, what do you think?"

"It's irregular, yes, but under the circumstances his presence might be considered a gesture of kindness, Mrs. Henderson, rather than an act of defiance or a boundary issue. We do have to be sensitive to boundary issues though."

"Thank you. That is my interpretation too. Ms. Johnson, the Disciplinary Committee, two of us anyway, finds that the behaviour of your students is not censorable. We do not fear outside repercussions from a display of common courtesy between young people. That said, I respect highly your work as an instructor and I agree with you that we must show support for you here. Collegiality. The classroom cannot become a pasture for perceived wolves. Perception matters as much as truth and some parents could be upset. I expect Mrs. Blagdon and I would agree with you on that. Sandra?"

"Certainly."

"Therefore my proposal today is this: that the Disciplinary Committee commend you, Ms. Johnson on your work. That we recommend that Mr. Grant and Miss Grandy henceforth be separated as partners in labs. Also that they do not sit in close proximity in class. That otherwise this whole matter is dropped here and now and I don't want to hear of it again. Keep it in your classroom. Ms. Johnson, does that now satisfy you?"

"It helps, yes. Keeping those two apart would certainly make my job easier."

"Good then. Consider it done, the motion passed. Ms. Johnson, Janet, please, you deliver the news to your class but do so in a friendly and non-censorious manner. These are young adults we respect. Agreed?"

"Mostly so, yes, Mrs. Henderson."

"Who shall we now partner Mr. Grant with?"

"Miss Hallett, I think, that would be best. Then Miss Grandy would be with Miss Hall."

Mrs. Henderson leafed through the class list.

"That's Abigail Hallett then?"

"Yes."

"She's also on our list of special admissions."

"Oh."

"I'm not sure that's appropriate, that the only two of our students admitted under special access be paired."

"I would never have guessed."

"No parents either. Raised by the nuns. Borderline marks for entrance, basically the same story."

"Knowing her, she won't mind, Mrs. Henderson, she's very compliant. She works hard."

"Then it's done."

"I appreciate the show of support this time, I thank you both."

"No Ms. Johnson, we thank you. Sandra? Meeting over? Minutes recorded?"

"Done. There you go. Now I can catch up on this knitting. Babies, babies everywhere."

"Now let's make this clear," said Mrs. Henderson, "this is it for this year. No more Discipline Committee meetings. Janet, please, if you have any more problems with your students, resolve them in the classroom."

To which statement there was a murmur of agreement, and the committee disbanded, somewhat satisfied with their Solomon-like decision. And Ms. Johnson, with relief, imagined Stanley Grant with Abigail Hallett, who was a pretty girl herself but in a dark, understated way, totally unlike Miss Grandy's overt brilliance. Abigail was serious, not given to frivolity, certainly not one to welcome open insolence, or cater to it.

HE FLEW to Montreal to see what he could do, to tie up the loose ends, to see how he would fare by himself. Also, no better test for undercover than coming here like this, and so much closer than Calgary.

Doctor, he could say, playing the role of a university student or a businessman, Doctor, I have this problem at home, can this be done? We have heard...

He took a room at the Queen Elizabeth Hotel and dropped his one small bag, his carry-on, onto the tightly-made bed. It bounced, a trampoline effect, and was still quivering four seconds later when he left the room. Outside, crowds whirled by. Every street was six-deep with pedestrians going in all directions, and he fell in with them. Destination unknown. He looked up at Place Ville Marie, he looked up at statues of men on horseback, he jay-walked, he crossed against red lights because everybody else was doing the same. He had coffee at a stand-up counter by a window. He looked at those around him, their apparent confidence, their comfort within themselves, how they laughed, how carefree they were, and he was acutely aware of his youth, his naivety, how circumscribed his life had been so far. How simple his life was with Tryphena. The conversations he heard around him were in French more than in English, and either way they burbled past him like water in a brook.

Undercover would be like this, everybody a stranger, these office girls lipsticked, dark-eyed, anonymous, mysterious, jabbing their cigarettes into ashtrays and jumping up from their coffees and hurrying out the door. Amorous too, no doubt, girls the world over.

He opened the crumpled piece of paper with the address. He'd find it, but there was no rush. He could put it off. So he walked for three hours in the cool sunshine, as he might have done back home, on a sweet day like this.

He folded his windbreaker over his arm and went up the side of the mountain and came to a hospital, one that looked like a medieval castle. A couple came his way holding a baby. Surely this was an omen: *this is what it can be for you*, they might as well be saying to him. They'd stop him and slap him on the face in a friendly way and say *hey! wake up!* Stunned and uncertain they looked, but to be frank they also looked happy—he had to admit it—they weren't holding back on love or fascination, they were bent over their pink bundle and walking slowly. They could have stumbled on the smallest crack in the sidewalk.

Right now she'd be phoning his answering machine and leaving messages. Jack? Jack? It's me, call me back, I've called twice already. Jack? He pictured himself back home, standing over the machine and erasing them one by one. Losing her voice in his head.

He circled the side of the mountain, walking across parkland that bordered a busy road. Up a long and winding road through trees. The city fell away then, much as St. John's did from Signal Hill. He came to a lookout high over the city, and instead of seeing the ocean, blank as slate or dazzling blue, here he saw the urban conglomerate laid out below, the river with its bridges of green-metal, the smokestacks of industry, the skyscrapers of downtown. Cyclists were stopped beside him, pausing for breath.

He walked further and stood under a cross, a huge illuminated cross which must send its message nightly downhill across the city, a caution for the girls of Quebec. In St. John's, the Basilica did the same. Probably with the same checkered results. Here, French-Canadian girls sat cross-legged on the grass, tucked into micro-skirts, leaning towards each other then lying back, adjusting their sunglasses, chirping like sparrows and smoking and now and then one or two of them looked his way.

Tryphie could care less about crosses. There was no religious purpose to her life, nor to his, so in that way they were a good fit. It saved them time on Sunday mornings, time for those jaunts.

Early afternoon now. He'd left it long enough. He took a long breath of summer air, thick with humidity, wafting up the face of the mountain, unfamiliar, and he felt briefly exhilarated, briefly forlorn.

He hailed a cab. There were dozens of them like yellow-black-red ladybugs scattered in the parking lot. He leaned over the seat to show the driver the address and sat back. Up went the flag on the meter. He didn't care how much it cost, he never took another look. They drove down the mountain-side the same way he'd come up, turning left and right, left and right some more, and then they were in the tumult of the city again, one small street after another, wrought-iron stairways angling up from the sidewalks. Uniform gray the stone walls, no colours here like on Garrison Hill.

Dépanneurs—those must be grocery stores—fruits and vegetables stacked outside. Students, businessmen, working women, a neighbourhood of men in long black coats and beards, hats from another century, policemen on the corners far more casual than back home, these looking tougher too, short-sleeves, batons and guns, expecting more trouble today, it looked like, than he'd see in a year.

He could live here, he could leave home for a place like this. Even for something less than this.

The cab stopped, he paid, and he stood on a sidewalk. A street of bungalows. Neat sidewalks, small lawns. It must have been a dry summer so far because the grass was scorched brown and the flowers were drooping. Low fences to mark off the properties, only eight to ten inches off the ground, made of wrought iron instead of wood. You'd need a crowbar to rip these up.

Now, think about the plan. There is no plan. It's a reconnaissance mission and that's a French word. See what they say.

He walked up the driveway. *Ring and enter* the sign said in English. He touched a button and heard a soft chime somewhere far away. He tried the door. It opened to a coat-rack, a small tight vestibule. He had to turn sideways to get through it, then a waiting-room—a sofa, a chair, a reading lamp, an expansive window to the street, half-curtained—but at the far end was a glass partition blocking off the rest of the house.

No music, not a sound. There were magazines fanned out on a coffee table.

Then there were quiet footsteps. A uniformed nurse stood behind the glass partition, leaning down to talk to him through the cut opening, a small circle.

Whatever she said, he couldn't understand.

"I'm sorry," he said, coming closer, "I don't speak French."

"What do you want?"

She'd switched to English but he was taken back by her severity, her directness. She looked tired.

"I'd like to make an appointment to see the doctor."

"That's not possible. You are a man, sir, evidently, and this is an office for women. We do not give appointments to men."

"It's not for me, it's for my girlfriend."

"She is a patient here?"

"No, not yet."

"Your girlfriend must call herself, it's as simple as that. It's a rule of ours. So."

She stood up from behind the glass, finished with him.

"Wait," he said, "please. We live far away, she needs help. We were given this name, this address."

He offered her, through the glass, Marion Chipman's worn piece of paper.

"So she is pregnant. That's what you're telling me."

"Yes."

"The condition of pregnancy, Monsieur, is a female condition, not a male condition. Biology has deemed it to be a female condition entirely for centuries. Please, I've already said, she must call."

He stood without moving.

"Not only that, obviously you are a policeman and policemen should leave us alone. Take that message to your superiors."

Awkwardly he laughed. He couldn't believe it, what she'd said.

"I'm not on duty. I don't live here, I don't live in Quebec. I'm not a policeman here."

"It doesn't matter, tell them anyway, wherever you come from. We're tired of policemen. It's political, we're not backing down."

"That's what I understand."

"Write her name down on this. Despite your dishonesty, I will take your request seriously. When she telephones, I will know her."

She slipped the same piece of paper and a pen back through

the opening in the glass and he wrote the two words, the name he knew so well, TRYPHENA GRANDY, like that, in capital letters, watching his hand print the letters as a schoolchild would, slowly and carefully, knowing that she would never call here, that this was a charade, that he was even more ridiculous now and his undercover life was a farce, his face apparently an open book of deceit, out of his depth. Better he was not here at all.

"Your name too, so we know."

JACK MAHER, he wrote.

"And your profession."

POLICEMAN, he wrote in the same script, and he watched as the nurse tucked the paper into her pocket, folding him away with Tryphena Grandy and the name of the doctor he'd never meet. The three of them together on paper, only on paper this once, never to be so again.

After that he stepped back out onto the street, to the sunburnt lawns. No one else walked or sauntered or strolled. A suburban cemetery, that's what this was, a mausoleum disguised as houses, empty as when he arrived. A few cars were parked on the far side but they could have been there for years.

He started to walk in the direction of downtown and, at the nearest phone booth, he pulled out some quarters. The phones felt different here, something about the plastic. He dialed and spoke to the operator and felt the electrons running into the earth, down the St. Lawrence River, east under the ocean, through the fog and seagulls in Port aux Basques, then along the course of TransCanada, looping across the island, past Butter Pot, over rock, water, muskeg and dead whales, and there, the phone rang in St. John's.

"Chief? You're working late?"

"Six o'clock, I'd hardly call that late. What's up?"

"The undercover we talked about, I'm afraid it's not going to work."

"What do you mean?"

"I'm in Montreal, Chief, I'm pushing quarters into slots for this call. You have a minute?"

"Sure I do."

"I went into a place here and pretended to be someone else and they spotted me as a policeman in one second."

"What kind of place?"

"French, in the east end."

"A bar? Why in God's name did you do that?"

"It's complicated. I might not have been totally frank with you, Sir, about my situation at home. It looks like I'm going to be a father now."

"Christ, that's fast work, Jack."

"Which means I couldn't go to Calgary."

"Not sure I see the connection."

"Responsibilities at home. I can't leave."

"Not everybody cares about that."

"I care. That's the problem."

"You know you're lucky you didn't get killed in the bar. Bikers?"

"No, it wasn't like that. It wasn't dangerous."

"Okay then, it's your call, you're off the assignment."

"Simple as that?"

"Simple as that. You failed the test, you said so yourself. My first wife was from Calgary."

"Yes sir, I know."

"She didn't like it in St. John's."

"No, Sir. Windsor Lake."

The Chief laughed.

"Right, I told you, I remember now. Well, fuck Calgary, they can get someone else. I'll tell them we value you too highly to let you go. That's not true, Jack, but sometimes you have to lie. The way this has worked out, I tell you, I feel a bit jerked around. Prescott Street too, you didn't exactly distinguish yourself there. The investigation. The Sergeant though, he likes you so there's hope for you, that's what I'm saying."

"Thank you, Sir."

"Apropos of Prescott, I've been thinking. This psychiatrist, this Dr. Poole. We have a minute, right? You mention her in your notes. Guess what?"

"I cannot guess, Sir."

"She's from Bell Harbour too, the same place. I checked her out."

"Yes, Sir."

"You already knew that?"

"Yes, Sir."

"You think that's a coincidence? I don't."

"No, I agree. Once I found that out, I had her under brief surveillance."

"Open surveillance?"

"Parked the cruiser across from the office several times. Just stayed there. Turning the screw, I think I've heard you call it."

"Good."

"But she spent the whole evening with a friend. She has the proverbial cast-iron alibi. And she was on the duty roster for the hospital, I saw that with my own eyes and there's no faking that."

If he got discharged from the police, what chance would he have getting on with the Coast Guard? None. The Highways? None. Maybe the grocery store, Belbin's, stacking shelves.

"Come home then, Jack, we'll talk about it."

"Yes, Sir, sorry about the undercover."

"You shouldn't have practiced. It's not the same in real life. You could have done it. Fuck Calgary though, like I say, see you tomorrow. Not the end of the world."

Then Jack called Tryphena and the phone call he'd planned, the phone call in which he blindsided her and said, Tryphena, it's me, I'm not coming home, I'll send you money for the baby, I'm working undercover in another city and no, I'm not able to say where, and no, I don't feel good about this and please stop crying, that phone call was forgotten.

Instead he said, "Tryphie?"

"Jack! Where've you been?"

She'd been asleep, her voice told him, blonde hair hanging loose, every which way.

"Montreal. That's where I am. Remember I said I'd check it out?"

A wariness in her voice.

"I guess I do, yes."

"You just wake up?"

"A nap. I'm whacked out."

"Well, Montreal, Tryphena, I have found, is not for us."

"What are you saying?"

"It's you and me now, Tryphie, if you will."

"Say that again."

"It's you and me now, Tryphie."

"The whole cavalcade, you mean?"

"Yes."

"I'd love that, Jack, you know I'd love that."

"I hope so. I'm the fool. I apologize."

"I left you messages."

"Tryphie. I'm flying home in five hours."

"Listen to the messages."

"I will."

"Actually, wait. One of those messages says I love you. I know why I said it and I'll tell you now. Apart from you and me, that's enough, but it was actually Prescott Street, what you did there."

"The Chief thinks I'm a loser for that."

"He's wrong. You did the right thing. You're doing the right thing."

"Tryphie. Listen. I love you too."

"I'm awake now. Don't come in the morning though, we have exams. I'll see you in the afternoon."

So that's how his life changed. By not saying what he'd planned to say on the phone, by saying something different, something he didn't plan at all.

He was in Dorval two hours early. He looked at the other passengers as they drifted in. The older ones, they'd have done something like he did, once or twice when they were his age, and they looked okay. And, as far as the job was concerned, he hadn't actually lied to the Chief, had he? He replayed the conversation. All he'd have to do is talk to the psychiatrist one more time, ask her point-blank what she was doing that night. Say to her, weren't you with that old friend of yours? The one from Bell Harbour? What do you call her, the principal's wife? And she would have to say yes, yes because he already knew the answer was yes. I was with the principal's wife, she'd say, and that was it, a cast-iron alibi they could make up any way they wanted.

He couldn't stack shelves at Belbin's, not with a baby on the way.

Tryphie, hey, the guy with one arm. From the woods. Remember? Could he stack shelves for a living?

Jack! she'd say.

More than one life saved by the night ambulance. The other one was his.

"OKAY, HYGIENISTS-TO-BE, this is, as you know, the final exam. Take your places. I wish you the best."

Ms. Johnson was standing in the door to the classroom, the students waiting in the hall. Then she stepped aside and they poured in. Very little chatter today. They sorted themselves out and sat down as she picked up the sheaf of exam questions. Then she put the papers down.

"As you know, I am your invigilator. An invigilator watches and I'll be watching you. That's a warning. Now, moving on, read each question carefully. Consider your answers before you put pen to paper. Stick to the thrust of the question. If you wander from the topic, marks will be deducted. In other words, if a question concerns a molar, speak not of incisors. Once I have placed the exam papers on your desk, you may begin. We have two hours. I will need your name on every page, at the top. Any questions?"

There were no questions.

"But first, an administrative decision that I wish to share with you. After the incident in our practicum the other day, which I need not remind you of, and a preceding incident, which I also need not remind you of, the Disciplinary Committee of this school has met, and, despite the eleventh hour—this is after all the final exam—in the best interest of the school, and in the best interest of our own sensibilities, we ask now that Mr. Grant move from his position beside Miss Grandy to the seat occupied by Miss Hall. And that you, Miss Hall, sit in the vacated seat, by Miss Grandy. Please move now, the two of you."

But Stanley Grant did not move, nor did Miss Hall. They looked confused, looked at each other, and then back at the teacher.

"Ms. Johnson," said Stan, "could you explain?"

"I'd be happy to explain it to you, Mr. Grant, because repeated impropriety on your part is the reason. Repeated. And don't act surprised. I don't blame Miss Grandy in any way for the transgressions we've witnessed. Her support for you is puzzling though, to say the least. Anyway, the Disciplinary Committee has ordered that as of now you are no longer partners. For the practical part of this exam, later today, you, Mr. Grant, will be partnered with Miss Hallett, and Miss Grandy will be with Miss Hall."

"There was no impropriety, ever," he said.

"Mr. Grant, please, the decision has been made. Miss Hall, please move."

The girl stood with her pens and erasers and walked back to Stan's desk.

"Okay," he said, "but I write this exam under protest. To single me out like this cannot help but affect my performance."

"Mr. Grant, please, we know more or less what your performance will be."

"Nevertheless, register my protest please."

"Done. Now, move."

Stan picked up his materials and walked slowly up the aisle to Miss Hall's vacated seat. He looked at his new partner, Abigail Hallett. He hadn't seen her since Velma's, when she'd come outside with him, watching his mother drive away. She smiled at Stan and raised her thumb in support, a welcoming.

"Ms. Johnson?" Abigail then said, standing up quickly, "please also register my protest as well. It seems unfair, springing this on Stanley at the last moment. Also, I saw no impropriety either."

"Sit down Miss Hallett. You surprise me. But we're already late starting. No, Miss Grandy, put down your hand, you don't have to speak, I shall register your protest as well as those others who now are waving their hands. It's too late, the decision is made. What you have to realize is that the interests of the school are paramount. We are parts of a machine. I shall now deliver the exam papers and I wish you the best of luck, including you, Mr. Grant, that you will not have to repeat my class next year."

"Thank you, Abigail," Stan said.

Then the exam paper was slapped down quickly on his desk, and pens and pencils throughout the room were racing away and Ms. Johnson walked up and down the aisles slowly, slowly, watching, invigilating, and without Tryphena nearby Stan felt dislocated, but now and then Abigail looked at him and raised her eyebrows as the teacher walked away, and he was able, after all, to concentrate, now and then seeking the hieroglyphics on his sleeve, the marks from the Rosetta Stone. His centering device, originally a joke but no longer one. He'd fallen for the symbols, the intersecting lines which were as meaningless as his own life yet ultimately, to someone, might turn out to mean something.

He made quite a good drawing of a molar, he thought, the arterial supply, the veinous drainage, coloured in red and blue respectively, and the course of the nerve in yellow, the root in white, the crown, the pulp, everything as it should be.

Then he named, under the line drawings provided, ten common dental instruments.

Next, the more difficult written portion, an essay in which he was to describe the effects of various sugars (glucose, fructose, sucrose) on saliva, including a description of the acids and bases within the oral cavity and the causes of formation and deposition of plaque. Comment as well on the role of bacteria in oral health and disease. These too he answered reasonably well, lucky there because these were topics he'd discussed with Tryphena just a few days ago, and Abigail Hallett was writing quickly just three feet away so maybe she was doing okay too, and then Ms. Johnson was standing at the front and saying "Time, time, put down your pens. Put down your pens! I will collect the papers."

At the break for lunch he sat with Tryphena. They were on the steps outside the school.

"The Disciplinary Committee? How ridiculous is that," she said.

"I know. How'd you do?"

"Fine so far. And you?"

"Surprisingly well, under the circumstances."

"Two more hours and this is over."

"Don't tell me, I'm not looking forward to it."

"No one to throw up on you then."

"Even that."

"Stan, can I tell you something? A secret?"

"Sure, Tryphie."

"I'm pregnant. You're the first to know. Well, the second."

"I was wondering, Tryphie, to tell the truth."

"The vomiting?"

"It wasn't the mirror. My technique was flawless."

"Yes it was."

"The policeman, Tryphie, he's okay with this? I assume it was him."

"He's okay with it. And I'm more than okay with it."

Abigail Hallett came over.

"Am I interrupting anything?"

"No, no."

They slid over to give her room.

"Stan," she said, "you know why they put us together?"

"Your unlucky day, Abigail, that's all."

"No. They're out to get you, Stan. It's because we're special students. The only two here. We got in on what's called special access so when the time came to mess you up, they chose me. I can mess you up even more, they probably figured."

"Special access? What do you mean?"

"Disadvantaged, that's the other word. No parents."

"You're kidding."

"No, I'm not."

"Wait, wait. How do you know this?" asked Tryphena.

"I keep my eyes open. I've learned."

"You have no parents, Abigail?" he asked.

"I had a mother once, just like you did, obviously. But her I've never met, not even at Velma's. If you call that a meeting."

"How long have you been working there, in the restaurant?"

"Two years. You want to know what I was told? That my mother was a bird, a stork, and I was too heavy to carry. That's what the nuns told me but I was born five pounds so that's bullshit for more than one reason."

It was different with her than with Tryphena, in the practicum that afternoon. Her teeth weren't quite as good. Slightly misaligned. Probably more like his, with more cavities that had needed fillings over the years.

"You use floss well, I can tell that," he said.

"Yes," she said, mumbling through the instruments.

He was concentrating, trying to do a good job.

"What's that on your shirt-sleeve, Mr. Grant?"

Ms. Johnson, stopped beside them, pointing to his wrist.

"I know what you think it is, but it isn't," he said, not stopping his examination.

Abigail pushed the mirror out of her mouth.

"It's Egyptian hieroglyphics, Ms. Johnson, that's all it is. He told me, it's not cheating."

"I'm going to let it go," said Ms. Johnson, "It's so unbelievable it may actually be true. I'm no tyrant."

"Close to it," said Abigail.

"Watch your lip now, Miss Hallett."

The teacher moved on and never came back.

"Thanks, Abigail," he said.

She waited for him to add Honey, or Bunny, but he didn't.

"I'm used to people like that, Stan. There's a limit."

Afterwards, when Tryphena Grandy went off with her boyfriend in the small car he had, Stan turned and offered her a ride.

"Me?"

"Yes you, Abigail."

"In the Camaro?"

To her, he seemed shy, for God's sake. As though he really wasn't sure what she'd say.

"Yes, the Camaro."

ROWENA'S FATHER said, "Let's spend the day together, doing a few things. The boys are gone to English Harbour with your mother."

"Sure."

They went first to the store. He said that while she was away in town he got to thinking, they could rearrange things a bit, make it easier for customers to grab the things they need.

"Like move the potato chips closer to the counter."

Together they lifted the rack and carried it to a spot directly across from the cash. But that left a hole where the chips used to be and they decided they could fill that hole with fishing rods, for now, and in the winter it could be mitts and scarves.

That left a hole where the fishing rods were. They filled that with a selection of rubber boots down low and fly swatters up high. And with every move they created a hole, and filled that hole and moved on until two hours had passed.

"How's it look now, Row?"

"Different. And the same."

"You're right. I'm so glad you're better by the way, that was one hell of a time you had."

"I guess I scared a few people."

"You certainly did."

"Dad, I remember there was a store in town, they had the lottery tickets under a loose sheet of Plexiglas, right on the counter."

"For the impulse purchaser?"

"Probably, that's what I figured."

"You think that's a good idea?"

"Not really, not here."

"You're right, nobody ever wins more than ten dollars. They say it's a tax on fools."

"I've heard that."

"Row, your mother was so frightened when she heard you were in the hospital."

"I know, she told me."

"I wish I could have gone in with her, but with the boys and all…"

"Oh, I know, don't worry."

"What a time! Oh, and one more thing, I was thinking, maybe we can clear a space in the back for canned goods, we'll need room for those in the fall, berries and all. Then how about this, how about a walk up Iron Skull?"

"Iron Skull? The two of us?"

"Sure. We can close the store. Just you and I, like in the old days. The boys don't even have to know. Maybe you're too tired?"

But she wasn't tired, she was feeling strong. She'd taken her iron pills twice a day, and mostly she'd spent her time reading, kicked-back on the front porch in one of the wooden chairs she'd brought out from the kitchen. There she could lean up against the siding, or rest her legs on the railing, look out to the waves on the Reach and then, higher up, there it was, Iron Skull, just asking to be climbed, for the view.

"You want a walking stick? We have these here, carved by Mr. Buffett."

"I can steal one?"

"You can borrow it, I'll look the other way."

So they struck out together from the store about two o'clock in the afternoon, Iron Skull impassive as always, dark-faced despite the sun up high. They passed the string of houses up along the shore, theirs the last—the dog joined them—and a half-mile after that they were at the fringes of the dump. Plastic bags flew in the air and wrapped themselves on the low bushes, there to be storm-blown all the way to Chapel Island. Fat ravens and gulls were picking through the refuse, thriving.

In half an hour they reached the barasway, where she'd gone swimming, where she'd washed her clothes, where the eagle had flown over and said hello.

They sat on the side of the ocean there and threw stones into the sea.

"You've always been the finest of daughters, Row, you never caused us even a moment's concern," her father said.

Then the path upwards, which was at first wide enough for two, then it narrowed. In places they had to scramble for footing but by four o'clock they made it to the top. Bell Harbour was far away at their feet, over there. The blue of Fortune Bay fell away to the south, to the vanishing point.

"Thrum Cap, Lord and Lady Island, I've never set foot on those two, they're so small," she said.

"Which one is Thrum Cap?"

"You know which one is Thrum Cap."

"Show me anyway."

"Look down my arm," she said, and she pointed, and to look he had to nearly put his head on her shoulder.

"The tiny one there, right there, it has only five or six trees. It's the first one you'd hit in a fog, coming in. You told me that."

They had a drink of water from the same thermos. They smacked their lips with the pleasure of it.

"Of course, I worried about you too when we got the news, the hospital, but I didn't let on. I figured, at least you were in the right place for what happened. I told your mother, I said Row'll be fine. And you were."

"Dad, we should head back."

"Okay."

She bent down to re-tie her shoes and stood up, stretching. They walked steadily and more easily down the side of Iron Skull, no longer talking. Past the barasway, past the dump.

At home, as he opened the gate for her he said, "Row, one more thing, just to let you know. Your mother told me everything, it's okay what you did, it could have happened to anyone."

She sat down hard on the grass and he held her and it might have been five minutes before she was able to speak.

"I just wanted it to go away," she said.

"I know."

But he didn't really know, he just said he knew. And the dog was confused as well, watching the two of them huddled on the ground. He put his paw on her knee and then took it off. He walked in circles around them, arthritically. Then he just flopped down beside them and waited.

"THIS IS the car from Velma's, right? Now it's yours?"

"It's mine. I never asked for it, but it's mine. Watch out for the mess."

He opened the passenger door and gathered up some wrappers and flyers and newspapers and chucked them into the back.

"There you go. Bucket seats."

Abigail climbed in. She put on the seatbelt. She shimmied around in the seat in exactly the same way Tryphena had.

"Feels good," she said, "are they leather?"

"I'm not sure. I'm no judge of that."

"I think it is, Stan. It doesn't feel cheap, or look it either."

He walked around the car and climbed into the driver's seat. He turned on the ignition.

"Middle Cove?"

"I've only been there once."

"Really? Ten minutes away?"

"No car, no way to get there. If I go out of town I go to Cape Spear. I hitchhike."

"After that I'll take you home."

"That's Empire Avenue," she said.

He accelerated away from the curb, not too fast but fast enough that she felt her weight shift back to her spine.

"It's got some power," he said.

Then he put on the radio to some music and they drove without talking as far as the stoplight at Elizabeth Avenue, which was red.

"I shall demonstrate the windows," he said.

With a touch of his finger, the side windows lowered together and fresh air blew across her face. Then they rose again soundlessly, settling back into place with a quiet little *thunk*.

She laughed.

"Cool," she said.

"Abigail, we did well in the practicum, I think."

"I think so. No worse than anyone else."

"You actually think they put us together because of who we are?"

"Not who we are, Stan, because of what we are."

The light changed. He pulled away slowly and several cars passed them on the left.

"What we are," he said, "meaning…"

"Second-class citizens. Special access, bend over backwards, let them in because there's a quota. That's who we are. We're the best of the worst, in dental hygiene. And that's the real laugher. Dental hygiene."

"Why did you say back there that they put us together so you could mess me up even more?"

"Did I say that?"

"Yes. With Tryphena, at lunch, on the steps."

"Good. I'm trying to speak up, it's new for me, say what I'm thinking, not being such a pushover. I could mess you up by mere proximity, I've done it to others. It's my attitude, it might rub off. Or make you run for the hills. Speaking of which, since you only have eyes for her, what am I doing here?"

"Tryphena?"

Traffic was stopped at another light and when the car in front failed to move on the green, he honked the horn.

"There, I have now demonstrated the horn."

"Yes, Stan, of course Tryphena, everybody knows you're in thrall to her."

"I'm in thrall to her? Please use the past tense. I have received a lot of advice to break those chains and I am doing so as we speak. She has a strong relationship elsewhere and that relationship is not going away. But she's a friend, really, Abigail, you can see what she's like, she befriended me when I needed it. Thrown together by our names, you know that. So I became infatuated. No crime there."

"It's over then."

"It never started."

"She's kind, she does seem kind."

"That she is."

"Doesn't put on airs."

"No."

"She probably not once in her life has felt like saying, fuck this, fuck all of this."

"No, Abigail, she would not say that."

"That's the way I've felt a thousand times."

"Relax, we're on a drive, a simple outing."

"I am relaxed. Just telling you the way it is. Fuck all of this, that's what I feel half the time."

"Abigail, okay, if we're into this, forget the simple outing. I'll tell you something and it's not your attitude rubbing off. I have imagined, I confess, my own death. By my own hand. And once I acted upon it, without success."

Something he had never admitted openly to anyone else. Not even to Dr. Poole.

"Obviously without success, Stanley Grant! So let me tell you this, a thousand times for me, I've thought of it too," she said.

"Hold that thought. Look, we're here, the famous beach at Middle Cove."

"Okay. No more gloom and doom. It does look pretty here."

There was no one else at the small rocky beach. High cliffs on either side, this one small opening to the sea. Sunshine, very little breeze when they stood up from the car. A small stream from the hills to step over.

"Regardless of my inner feelings, it's nice to be able to drive here," he said, "all I need to do is pay for the gas, oil, insurance, Turtle Wax, tires, parking, and I can do that, I have enough money for that. In the winter the storms here, the waves are bigger, it's even better then. In my opinion."

They kicked around on the beach for ten minutes. He threw fist-sized stones into small waves.

"I'm pretty happy here with you," he said, "for what it's worth."

"Me too. See if you can skip any of these flat ones."

She demonstrated herself, with a modicum of success. Her stone skipped two or three times before sinking.

"I can't challenge that," he said.

Then he threw one so flat and hard that it skipped twenty times and then slid along the surface before it disappeared.

"Luck," he said.

They sat at the high-water mark. A few flies with no evil intent buzzed around their heads. They piled up some stones and torn kelp in the shape of a pyramid and he showed her again the letters from the Rosetta Stone, on his sleeve.

"They've been translated now after being a mystery for centuries," he said.

"No wonder she thought you were cheating."

"Thanks for speaking out on my behalf."

"Like I said, it's my new thing," she said, "you're welcome. The tide or a summer storm will soon take out this pyramid and it will be no more."

"Nothing lasts forever."

"How did you try to kill yourself?"

He laughed and lay on his side so he could see her better, her dark hair and her brown eyes very serious, looking at him.

"I was stupid. I jumped up and down on predictably thin ice and went through. I was rescued by a dog and I got my picture in the paper. End of story."

"Take me to Cape Spear, Stan, right now" she said, "I want to show you something, something like that for me."

He shrugged, happy enough to do what she wanted.

The Camaro pulled away quietly and turned up the steep hill.

"The seats are Naugahyde, not leather, I think," he said.

"Fake, genuine, hard to tell the difference these days."

How far could they fly through the air? All he had to do now was turn the wheel hard left and it would be three hundred feet straight down to the sea, to the rocks. They'd go through the gun-metal-gray railing like it was cellophane, and after that they'd have three or four seconds together, floating painlessly in his mother's red Camaro, her cast-off car.

Instead he took his foot off the gas and they coasted over the crest of the hill.

"This car likes you, Abigail, I can tell."

"Cape Spear," she said, looking at her watch, "we have time before dark, I think, if we motor."

They went through town hitting most of the lights on green and up the switchback toward the Goulds. There she felt the pull in her spine again, the power of acceleration.

"Pretty fast, pretty fast, but there is a speed limit," Stan said.

"We can't afford a ticket," said Abigail.

"We?"

"You."

Eventually the road fell seaward, the ocean came into view and then a few houses in a small cove.

"Blackhead," he said out loud, acknowledging it.

Breakers formed forty yards out, streaming through one or two jumbled ledges offshore. There'd been a storm, now finished, but the waves on the open Atlantic had their own momentum. They were high, unlike the ones back in the bay.

"So what's at Cape Spear?" he asked.

"My thin sheet of ice," Abigail said, "different than yours but ultimately the same."

"If it's yours, I don't want to interfere, maybe not even see it. If it's personal."

"I want you to see it."

"You said you hitchhike out here?"

"It's easy. Tourists."

The road retreated back into the woods before it was by the sea again and he pulled into the parking lot, cut into the side of the hill. Above them was the Cape Spear lighthouse, high on the headland.

There were only two other cars there. He parked the Camaro randomly, it didn't matter where.

They sat for a while even though she again looked at her watch.

"It's going to be a bit of a walk," she said.

Looking north through the front window of the car, there

was nothing but cliffs and headlands. The Narrows were invisible, the city invisible too, hidden in its pocket of rock. Signal Hill was gauzed over by the distance. A glittering, a flickering of late sunshine passed over the intervening sea. One fishing boat was heading home, trailing gulls.

They stepped out of the car and he offered her his windbreaker from the back seat.

"No, I don't need that," she said, "but give me the car keys please."

He flipped them over the roof to her and she caught them and then tossed them to the floormat on her side.

"If I had a car, this is what I'd do. I'd leave the keys so someone knew it was not an accident."

"I'm not sure I understand."

"Stan, think about it. If you're coming back to your car, ever, then you need the keys in your pocket. If you're not coming back to the car, ever, then you don't."

"You mean we're not coming back? Is that what you're saying?"

"It's thoughtful, if you leave the keys. Someone has to drive the car away."

"You're messing me up, Abigail."

"I told you I would."

"Sure you're not cold?"

"Actually, I am."

"So take the windbreaker."

She put it on, feeling his clothing on her body, something new and something she liked.

"Nice. Thank you. Is that a flashlight, Stan? Bring that too."

"Okay. Adios, Camaro mio," he said.

He patted it on the front bumper and they walked away, up a long field of grass. They passed the lighthouse and the light blinked at them and circled away. Three people were walking slowly down the wooden steps to the parking lot, leaving. One of them looked and waved to them so they waved back.

"They could steal our car now," he said.

"They will not steal our car. Your car."

"We can hitchhike home."

"If it comes to that."

They stood together on the highest of the cliffs, ten feet from the edge. The lighthouse was right behind them, like a wall. From there they could see south as well as north, more headlands falling away and the rhythmic roll and cresting of waves, like sheet-iron collapsing, cutting white shreds into the base of the vanishing cliffs.

"Let's go, the time's getting short for daylight."

She headed south on the well-worn path and he followed, his windbreaker way too big for her. Heather, juniper, sporadic upheavals of bedrock. Then there was a wide wetland with grass-fringed ponds and the sun was dropping faster now as it always did at dusk. Colours reflected off the ponds, yellow, pink, orange, red. Then yellow again. A run of tiny trees they had to cut through in single file. Darker in there. The path narrowed the farther they went and secondary paths branched off, barely visible.

"For berry-pickers, these," she said.

Egyptian-sized rocks the size of wrecked cars thrown haphazardly.

"The Sphinx, relocated," he said.

A large pond ringed with grass. Three ducks, swimming, turned and looked at them impassively and then they took off low and away, slapping the water with their wingtips, laughing.

"Sorry to disturb you, my little ducks," he said.

He bent to his knees and felt the cold water. It dripped from his fingers with a rustiness to it like whisky or tannin and now the sun was half-behind the dark tips of the forest to the west.

"Come on, we should hurry," she said.

How she could mess him up, more than he already was? Was she saying she was going to do something, like jump? In fact, now he felt alive. Was this happiness? She was turning to beckon him along and she'd done up the top button of his windbreaker. Now she was fully tucked into it, enveloped. Why would she do that, if she didn't care for herself, even a bit?

The path was closer now to the edge of the cliff. Wave after wave peeled in below with thousands of miles behind them, so it was no surprise they hit so hard. The *crump* sound, like a train accident non-stop, one after the other, and the rock-strewn pocket beaches were rolling and tumbling over themselves, the rocks ringing against each other, then smothering.

There it was finally, the sign she was looking for. But it was too dark to read it without the flashlight.

"Look," she said.

Empty Basket Cove, painted on a rough piece of wood.

"This is why I like it," she said, "the emptiness. The empty cove."

"Because that's how you felt?"

"You might say that, yes. A thousand times you could say that. Yes. This is my sheet of ice. Say hello to Stan."

"How far down is it?"

"Two hundred feet? Far enough."

He turned off the flashlight and the sky was filled with a billion stars. Like they'd been shot-gunned up there by some madman.

"Christ it's beautiful here," he said.

"I'm not trying to mess you up," she said, "I hitchhike, I come out here and I look over the edge but I never do anything."

"Honey," he said, "I'm awfully glad you didn't."

"Did you call me Honey?"

"I did. I'm sorry. I know it's kind of fast."

"No it's not. Stan, I'm saying what I want now too. I'm not holding back. I promised myself."

"Go ahead. What do you want to say?"

Somehow he'd come to within three inches of her face.

"Stan, I'd like you to take this windbreaker off me and put it on the ground and make love to me. Wait a minute, I want to say that more directly. Stan, I want you to fuck me here, on top of this windbreaker of yours."

He threw his head back, shocked and thrilled. He laughed with joy.

"Honey, Bunny, I have no experience."

"I'll show you. It's easy. It's way better than jumping off the edge."

"I would never do that with you, jump."

"I agree. That's something you do alone. Something I've never done and you have. You're one up on me there."

She took off his windbreaker and laid it down and turned the flashlight off and they lay together on the ground above Empty Basket Cove, the soft give of the low bushes springing back at them and the stars shaking like they were. He started to unbutton her jeans.

"Abigail, I am really, truly messed up now. I have no clue."

"We won't be second-class citizens at this, Stanley," she said, "guaranteed."

DR. POOLE was beginning to think she was coming out of this okay. Not that she would ever do it again. You can only stand up for principle when you have the skills to carry through with it. She had made a big, big mistake by not delving far enough into family history. A cringing, horrible mistake. On the other hand, she'd heard from the principal's wife that Row Savoury was doing fine. She was working in the store, going on hikes, taking her iron pills, taking her other pills, and she was applying for university. So the near-fatal mistake had corrected itself, no thanks to anything she personally had done. Thanks to good fortune.

Well, more thanks to the policeman, actually. He'd surprised her yesterday with a visit. Parked the cruiser across the road but, instead of just sitting there, he'd come to the door and knocked and out of near-terror she'd let him right in. No patients at the time. Hello, he said, I need to talk to you, for the sake of the girl. She steeled herself for the worse. He said I know you spent the evening and the night in question here at your home and I know you spent it in the company of the woman we have referred to as the principal's wife. I'm not even asking you about Miss Savoury, please note, a deliberate exclusion, but if I could have your statement to that effect, that you were in the company of the principal's wife, throughout the evening, it would go a long long way to settling this case in the eyes of my superiors. Not in your eyes? she'd asked. Mine are unimportant, the policeman had said, still standing in the waiting room with his hat in his hand. She did not ask him to expand on that, she wanted to get this over. Obviously he knew what had happened here, or strongly suspected it, he'd made that clear in the hospital. But he was more aggressive then, challenging. Now he was calm, settled. Friendly even, smiling but at the same time determined. Well, she said, I'll certainly sign a note to that effect if it puts this matter to rest, to help Miss Savoury. Please tell me the name of the principal's wife, he said, we'll need her name for corroboration. Alma Fiander, she said, and they went inside and the policeman used her desk to write out a formal statement. She signed it and he left. All over now, he said, I'd like to tell you that this case has meant a lot to me, personally. Go away, she thought, just go away, and she ushered him to the door and watched the cruiser leave.

Then this letter which she'd just read. Not posted, it was put through the slot early this morning, before seven. By an early bird.

Dear Dr. Poole,

I'd like to thank you for everything. I enjoyed coming to see you, as I'm sure you know. I liked your clock, the way it chimes, I liked the street outside, I came to like the path down the side of the house, the way your attention was entirely on me. You

*asked me if I wanted to continue seeing you and I said yes, but
since then, things have come around for me. I'm over Tryphena.
I think she's getting married. That helps. You were right, you
told me to disengage but she was so nice to me, it was hard
until now. I guess I needed more help than I thought. I was at
my lowest when I went through the ice (you know that) but I'm
nowhere near that anymore. In fact, miracle of miracles, I
actually have a girlfriend, a real one, not imaginary or beyond
the rainbow and unattainable (quite the opposite!). She's
living and breathing and that's what we're going to do
together. Not Egyptian, you'll be glad to know, she's from here.
Thanks again for the caring and the time and if I see you again
it will just be on the street or up the hill by the pond, looking at
ducks, without as many cares in the world, and I hope it's the
same for you, thanks again,*

Your patient of two years,
Stanley Grant

P.S. Cancel that next appointment!...S.G.

So maybe, as a doctor, she wasn't a total disaster after all.

The clock chimed four times. The sound he said he liked.
Well, she liked it too. It stirred up the dust motes on quiet
afternoons. Reinvigorated her.

She picked up her appointment book and crossed his name
out and never wrote it again.

"I THINK I figured it out, partly," Jack said.

She leaned over and kissed him. They were sitting on the
curb on Fitzpatrick Avenue and Kiziah was skipping five feet
away.

"The trouble is, when you're a policeman, Tryphie, you
start to think the worst of everybody. Concepts such as
constancy, forgiveness, love, they are irrelevant to the job."

She laughed.

"Same thing for cleaning teeth, actually."

"Let me finish. I'm serious. In my daily work I use, in ascending order, common sense first, then a helpfulness which is more an act than reality, then covert threats, then the reading of rights which is an overt threat, then arrest. Short and sweet. Keeping all of that out of your own life isn't easy, Tryphie. It leaks into everything, like water damage."

"Water damage! How about like tooth decay? Surely they warned you about this in school."

"You don't really know till you're out. Anyway, as time goes by, you get to think you have the answers. And the answers aren't complex. When push comes to shove, no one else's opinion counts. You become a dictator in your own life."

"You've never been like that. And lots of people who are not policemen are like that. For example, Ms. Johnson, at school."

"I should never have gone to Montreal, I'm saying. It was stupid beyond belief. I should never have tried to influence you."

"It did make me sad, the way you talked. I worried."

"I apologize again."

"Jack, we don't have to think about this anymore. Let's consider this instead: I kind of like names with a Z in them, for babies."

"Z? Like Ezekiel?"

"No, no, but I do like Kiziah, if it's a girl. What do you think of Kiziah?"

"I'm not sure of that. She, her, that girl, as you know she drives me crazy sometimes. Two of them would be too much."

He was whispering, but the snap of the rope would have drowned him out anyway. And she was singing, Kiziah was, some kind of chant that fit the beat. He couldn't make out the words.

"How about Zebra instead, Tryphie? Would you like to call the baby Zebra?"

"No, that's too much. Too new-age. I like Kiziah here though, so I like her name. And remember, don't forget, she was actually there for some of our deliberations, in the car."

"Deliberations? That's putting a nice cast on it. I hope you didn't tell your mother what I did."

"No. I thought that would be our secret."

"She probably knows anyway. Her spies."

"So. Kiziah then, if it's a girl?"

"Are there no Portuguese names? Celebrate your heritage?"

"We could look it up I guess. For a boy."

"Who was the girl with Stan, yesterday, by the way? And now he has a car?"

"Abigail. Abigail Hallett. I don't know much about her."

"But she's in your class."

"She certainly is. Stan was banished from my side to hers by Ms. Johnson."

"Banished? Why?"

"I told you before. He came into the girls' washroom and handed me my clothes. They consider that a serious boundary violation. Which it wasn't. So, anyway, get away from Tryphena Grandy, they decided. She made him move, literally change desks right before the exam. The car's a Camaro, from his real mother. That's all he got, she took off again."

"I'm sure she works at Velma's, that girl, I've seen her there. Your school is kind of old-fashioned, if they bring the hammer down for that."

"It would be nice if they hit it off."

"Who?"

"Stan and Abigail."

"Zarathustra, Tryphie, there's another Z! Can you imagine that? Thus spake Zarathustra, we'd be saying that all the time. She'd have a complex."

"Serious speech delay."

"Right. So forget that one."

"Tryphie, skip with me!"

"Kiziah! Okay!"

"I'll watch," he said.

Dusk turned to dark, punctuated by the sounds of the street. Jack Maher sat nearly at peace with himself on the curb and Tryphena and the maybe-two Kiziahs skipped until they were breathless. A sliver of moon tipped up over Fitzpatrick Avenue. Kiziah's mother called her in and she went without a murmur.

"Tryphie, hey, sit down, take a break," he said.

She was breathing hard. Her hair on the back of her neck was dark with sweat.

"I'll never forget the ambulance," he said.

"Oh, you're thinking of that again?"

"How can I help it? It didn't just save the girl, it saved us. And here we are."

"That's true, indirectly. Everybody should have one of those."

"An ambulance? Too deep for me, Tryphie, too deep."

"I think the lucky ones have it, though, on call."

"Like us?"

"Right."

They could talk like that all night, now that he was home for the whole cavalcade.

THE SAME sliver of moon that shone on Fitzpatrick Avenue slightly weakened the shocking brilliance of the stars. Underneath them was juniper and blueberry and crowberry bent and crushed, pushed out to the side.

"We'll have to wash this windbreaker."

"You think? I can do it. After all, it's mine."

"You have the experience now, Stan. No denying that."

"Thank you, Honey. I sure do."

"Roll off then. Where's the flashlight, where's my shirt?"

"Wait. We're not finished."

"No?"

"I don't think so. Ms. Johnson says do it once, you see how it's done. Do it twice, you learn."

"She's some bitch if I may speak my mind of her, even now, here. This place of ours."

"Ours, you're right. Go ahead, I like what you say. Say what you like."

"Stan, that feels good. I think actually you're a bit of a tiger."

"Sabretooth," he said.

AS FOR Row Savoury, tonight she was listening to the foghorn from the St. Jacques light. Once a minute, once a minute. The wind, what little there was, brought it in from the south. A low sound, penetrating, probably bouncing off the half-fixed wharf. The last time she'd heard such a warning was in St. John's, the night of the termination. With the principal's wife, when they were walking together on Quidi Vidi Road.

Quidi Vidi, the foghorn, the harbour. Cracks now in her amnesia. She'd been forgetting on purpose for so long now, ever since Dr. Poole suggested it, that it was getting harder to remember any details at all.

She sat up in bed.

There's the foghorn again, low and steady.

Rowena, her aunt had said to her, Oh the racket the ambulance made, it was enough to wake the dead! It howled in the streets! It was like a banshee!

If so she never heard it.

She lay back down and stretched. Arms over her head, hands to the backboard. Feet out too, all the way now nearly to the end of the mattress.

Sixteen years old, just starting out.

ACKNOWLEDGEMENTS

I would like to thank Cheryl Ruddock, Nora Ruddock, Jessica Ruddock, Martha Webb, James Langer, and Gitta Tafler for their advice and editorial guidance.

Nicholas Ruddock's award-winning poetry and fiction have been widely published in Canada and abroad. His novel, *The Parabolist* (Doubleday 2010), was shortlisted for the Toronto Book Award. In 2014, Breakwater published his short-story collection *How Loveta Got Her Baby*, and in 2016, he was a finalist for the prestigious *Sunday Times* EFG Short Story Prize (UK). Ruddock lives in Guelph, Ontario.